Nathan Woolford is a newspaper journalist, sub-editor and author.

Born and raised in Swindon, Wiltshire, his journalism career began while he was still at school with a weekend job at BBC Wiltshire Sound. He also wrote articles and features for various local papers and magazines.

Nathan graduated from University College Falmouth with an honours degree in journalism and has worked as a writer and copy editor for more than 20 years.

He is the author of the *Klondike's Circus* novels, which began in 2022 with *Trail Dust*.

Nathan Woolford

PIECE OF THE ACTION

A Klondike's Circus Novel

AUSTIN MACAULEY PUBLISHERS™

LONDON • CAMBRIDGE • NEW YORK • SHARJAH

A CIP catalogue record for this title is available from the British Library.

ISBN 9781528990134 (Paperback)
ISBN 9781528990141 (ePub e-book)

www.austinmacauley.com

First Published 2023
Austin Macauley Publishers Ltd®
1 Canada Square
Canary Wharf
London
E14 5AA

Table of Contents

Preface

Hell's Kitchen, New York
1936

"You've got a lot of talent."

The girl was leaning up in bed, surveying her surroundings with a sheepish, dreary-eyed gaze. She sat up, pulled a pillow up against the bedrail and pushed herself lazily into it.

The small attic room had a musty, acrid smell, the light emanating from the small side window giving the place an eerie, hazy feel.

Beside the bed, there was an enormous desk to one side, a dresser, various boxes and bags scattered about, and a door leading to a closet bathroom. That was it.

"Yeah? How would you know?"

He snarled as he strutted across the floor, glaring down at her.

He reached the dresser, lit a cigarette and placed both hands against the curtain rail so he could hover over the window. Looking out at the murky side streets below, his eyes flared.

Hell's Kitchen. It was all back alleys, washing lines, doorsteps and street gangs. He should know. He had spent his whole life immersed in it. Was there any way to escape? Maybe for him there was. That was his project.

Her voice brought him back to the room. "You know, you're a pretty lousy date."

He ignored her, dragging on the smoke and surveying the grim streets below.

"You pick me up at McGinty's," she continued, "a few drinks, smokes, then up to this armpit of a place. Jesus!" She looked over her new surroundings, unimpressed. "So, you going to take me out for breakfast or something?"

He blew smoke at the grimy window. "Or something…"

"How about one of them smokes?"

He threw her the packet, and she fished one out and lit it with matches from the bedside table. She studied him.

He was tall, well over six feet, lean, with craggy features and wavy black hair with sideburns. Dressed in slacks and an old white vest, he could have passed for a real-life Tyrone Power movie character right then.

"Y'know, you're a real piece of work," she blurted out. "I mean, what gives with you? You were all over me last night. Then…then this? Nuthin."

He stood there brooding, seemingly ignoring her.

"We've both grown up in this neighbourhood. We know each other's turf. I just want to know what makes you tick, Terry."

He spun around. "I told you. Please. Don't call me that."

"Woh, I'm sorry. What shall I call you?"

"Call me Kal. Kal Klondike."

"So that's what you call yourself now?"

He glared at her. "That's what everyone will call me. One day." He stubbed out his cigarette and moved towards the tiny stove in the room's opposite corner.

"You want a cup of coffee?"

"You bet." She sat up in bed, puffing away, and glanced at the desk nearby. It was covered in papers, mostly scribbled notes, but there were several sheets of typed copy lying scattered around a modern-looking typewriter, that somehow seemed out of place in the dingy room. Leaning forward, she saw what looked like a booklet from a circus show, some kind of programme. There was an illustration of a cowboy on the front and several smaller pictures.

"So, you wanna be a cowboy, huh?"

"That's right," he said, disinterested.

"I looked over some of that stuff last night. On your desk. Sounds like you've got big plans, cowboy." She laughed. "A cowboy. Here, in Hell's Kitchen!"

He looked her over with disdain. "Right."

"You've got a whole racket going on right here, haven't you? Notebooks, typewriter, those boxes of paper, those magazines…what have you got going down?"

He poured the coffee from a battered old jug. "Y'know, you ask a lot of questions, sweetheart."

She made a face. "Listen, if you don't even want to talk to me, why did you even make the effort last night? What is this?"

He handed her a mug of steaming black liquid before returning to the window. "I don't know. I really don't."

"You've got a lot on your mind, Terry. I, er, mean Kal. I don't blame you." She glanced around the barren confines. "Do you really live here?"

"Yup."

"What about your parents?"

He scowled at her.

"Oh god, I'm sorry, I forgot." She stubbed out her smoke, and went down on her stomach on the sheets. Her gaze drifted from his tall frame to the dresser. There were just two pictures. One was of him, Terry Calder, possibly three or four years earlier. The other showed an older man with thick dark hair and wearing a sheepskin coat. "Who is that?" she whispered, pointing.

He didn't look. "Eric Ribbeck."

"He is special, huh?"

"He's the greatest."

"How's that?"

He turned to face her, finally lightening up. "Old Eric is one of the greatest men in the world." He paused, suddenly mesmerised. "Every summer I go to see his show, Ribbeck's American Circus, at Coney Island. Someday…someday real soon, I'm going to join the circus. His circus. And that will be the greatest day of my life."

She eyed him curiously. "A circus? Are you crazy?"

He dismissed her with a wave of his hand. "I wouldn't expect you to understand."

She tried to sound enthusiastic. "Well, he sounds like a good role model."

"The best. He's a legend of world circus. He discovered all the greats. Marco DiGeorgio. Hans Lufstrom. Roscoe the Clown. He made them all."

Her eyes bulged as she listened, still lying among the sheets as he lectured. "Wow. And, er, where is he now?"

He laughed slightly. "Why, now, during the off-season, he is very close. He has a boathouse out on the Hudson. Still walks down Riverside Way. Every day. Before suppertime." His eyes had taken on a vacant, faraway look as he talked.

She stared at him, mesmerised. Then, with a sigh, she stood, covering her body with the sheets. Staring at him curiously, she paced around him. "Y'know, you're a weird guy, Terry."

He made to complain, but instead just waved a hand at her and walked over to his desk. He changed the subject.

"Do you know Catherine Hart?"

"Sure. Well, we went to high school together. Don't see much of her these days. She still works at the Shaker Maker."

"Yes. I know."

At this, she tilted her head. "We all knew about you boys, you know that? Right back to high school. You Hell's Kitchen boys. All of us Brooklyn girls."

"What did you hear?"

She smiled. "You were...y'know, a gang. Street kids. You were wild. Wild, crazy kids. And, us girls, we, well, we kinda..."

"You wanted some of the action." He finished for her. She giggled, fiddling with the sheets. "Sure."

He studied her and, for the first time, really appreciated her. Her spangly reddish brown hair was thick and flowing, her freckled face giving her a look of youthful innocence, while her tiny frame made her look like a child.

"Well," he snarled, "you got it."

He pushed her harshly but playfully back onto the bed, before whipping his vest off.

She took in his taut torso and whispered, "Jesus, you're a strange guy, Terry."

"Yeah," he murmured, clambering onto the bed. "That's...that's what everybody says." They kissed.

"You're a strange broad, Lucy."

She gasped. "Actually, it's Wendy."

"Actually, it doesn't matter. You can be whoever you want in this world."

Later, as the girl slept soundlessly beside him, Terry pulled away the sheets and slowly clambered out of bed.

Lumbering across the carpet in his old attic apartment, he halted in front of an old dartboard that rested on a nail hammered into the closet door.

Idly, he grabbed at a leather satchel resting near the washbasin and removed a long, but battered, James Bowie hunting knife. Standing erect 10 yards from the dartboard, he suddenly bent into an attacking poise and hurled the knife. It hit the board dead centre with a dull thud.

He smiled faintly and blew at his fingers. Wandering over to remove the embedded instrument, he paused as his eyes fell upon a tatty old photograph pinned on the closet door next to the dartboard.

The image showed a group of six youngsters, all sitting or standing around a large homemade poster that said 'Let's Go, Cobras' in giant, painted letters. At the bottom of the print, he had written: 'Hell's Kitchen. 1933'.

He looked intently. The youths were all dressed in black leather jackets, jeans and work shirts, the kind worn by longshoremen.

He saw his younger self pictured in the middle of the group. His hair was slicked back, his acne-ridden face hard and set. It was the face of an angry young man, wild and untamed.

To his left stood Heavy Brown, standing head and shoulders above them all like a man among boys. Even then, he was taller and wider than most adults.

Grasping the picture lightly in his hand, Terry thought about all the people in his life. Of Heavy. Of Wendy. Then, he thought of Catherine Hart.

He made a decision.

"So, c'mon, how about it?"

"I told you, I don't think it's a good idea."

"I'll be a real gentleman, Catherine, I promise."

He was sitting at the counter of the Shaker Maker, without doubt his favourite hangout. The downtown joint, situated at the corner of Dewey Hill and Main Street at the heart of Hell's Kitchen, was part milkshake bar, part diner, part comic book store, with the best record player in town. More important, it sold all the top ice creams.

He was nursing a chocolate fudge sundae with double coconut, and it was the most beautiful taste he had ever known. He could not get enough.

As he sat at the counter, his gaze remained locked on the giant green opaline eyes of Catherine Hart, the waitress who seemed to practically live alongside the soda pops, ice creams and liquorice, such was her working life.

She had long, thick amber hair, tanned, freckly skin and a tall slender figure. Her warm and friendly features were complimented by her soft, girlish voice.

He had been fascinated by her since the first time he had ever wandered into the joint.

"C'mon," he drawled. "It's only, like, a date. The movies and a slice of pie. It'll be fun."

She busied herself behind the counter, wiping the surfaces with a cloth. "Listen, Terry, I don't mean to be rude or nuthin." She looked him over, a look of sympathy in her beautiful eyes. "You're a nice boy. I just ain't got time is all. I spend all my day here, serving the guys. Then, I have to head back to Uncle Rocco to look after him. I'm so busy…"

"Listen," he said calmly, lighting a cigarette, while still devouring the sundae. The Shaker Maker was already filled with a low-hanging blanket of smoke. "You need to get out, Cath. You can't spend all day cooped up in this sweet store. You got to live. It'll do you good to come out."

She nervously surveyed the room around her. It was full of teenage boys. Juvenile delinquents mostly. They sat around, drinking their shakes, reading their comics, and waiting for trouble. To a man, they all wore black leather jackets, their hair draped in grease. She shuddered.

"No thank you, Terry."

He shook his head and blew smoke into the air.

At that moment, the Shaker Maker's proprietor, Enrico 'Doctore' Mancuso, ambled over, entering from an adjoining kitchen.

He winked at Terry, who smiled back. An elderly Italian with thick greying hair and a heavy limp, he was a popular figure around the neighbourhood.

"Why you not go out with this nice boy, huh Cath?" He exclaimed loudly.

She hovered awkwardly, trying to look busy.

"He right," Doctore continued. "It will do you good to get out. All day you spend your time here with me, or home with Uncle. That's no life for a beautiful rose."

She scowled at him. "It's up to me, isn't it?" She hurried across to the tables with her cloth.

Terry watched her go sadly. Then, he smiled ruefully at Doctore. "She is right for you," said the older man. "She just don't know it yet. She waits…for man who teaches college, drive fast car, lives uptown. She forget. This is the Kitchen. She needs tough guy. One day she will see."

Terry stared at the girl as she went about her rounds, wiping down the tables like a machine. He was strangely transfixed. She wore a grimy apron over white slacks and a work shirt. Yet still he was transfixed, as if she was decked out in a ballroom gown.

"Yeah," he drawled, almost to himself. "One day she'll see." Suddenly, the relative afternoon peace of the Shaker Maker was shattered by a loud bellowing that came from the entrance.

"Let's go Cobras!"

Everybody turned. It was Hawker, the gang's de-facto communications manager, leaning into the joint.

"Let's go!" he shouted in a slightly high-pitched tone. "Come on. Terry! Heavy! Turk! Eric the Swede! Axe! Paulo! Newman! Let's go, let's go, let's go!"

As if in a trance, a plethora of the figures lurking within the joint stood and walked towards the doorway, as one. The leather jacket clad group followed Hawker into the street.

Terry reluctantly left the delicious sundae behind, and followed the others outside. As if by magic, Heavy appeared from nowhere and fell into step beside him, carrying his jacket and wearing a tight tank top with his Levi's.

Henry 'Heavy' Brown, the giant of the gang. His best friend and great protector.

"This is it, champ," the big kid said huskily as they walked across the grimy, trash-covered streets. "The Barracudas are at the bottom of 29th. They brought muscle. It's been brewing. Now Paulie says we's gunna hit em."

Terry nodded, disinterested. "Well, let's see what they got, daddio." They walked with the others until they reached the next block, where a tall, fearsome-looking youngster clad in the standard jacket and Levi's and with slicked-back black hair was standing beside a beat-up old Ford, carrying a piece of lead piping and surveying the assembled group with relish.

Paul Agostino. Leader of the Cobras. He was older, somehow more man-like than the others. When he addressed them, they listened as if hypnotised, caught up in their leader's words. Many focused their attention on the giant reddened scar that flowed down his left cheek. It began at his eyelid and ended by his mouth.

"Cobras!" He snarled. "Get ready…cos this is it." He looked at the group, going from face to face, and tilted his head in a look of pride. The various passers-by—shop workers and street dwellers and such—simply ignored them as they stood like some kind of ragtag army in the garbage-laden backstreets.

Agostino continued, preaching to the youths. "I look around and I see a lot of anger. I see a lot of hatred. And…I see a lot of Barracuda-hating, wild living sons of bitches!"

The gang cheered at this, and Agostino cooled them with a raised hand. "It all ends now, Cobras. We end this. Right here and now. And then…and then the Barracudas, the Harvey Street Boys, the Angel Gang and everyone else will know that the Cobras rule Hell's Kitchen. FOREVER!"

They all cheered together. Then, like an army that had received prior training, they marched down the street and did not stop until they had travelled three blocks, to the bottom of 29th Street.

Turning the street corner, they came face to face with a crew of 10 youngsters, who were all of Hispanic origin. This group wore blue/green bowling shirts and slacks, with bowling shoes beneath. They were laying around steps that led to a deserted old hotel, several engaged in a game of marbles.

One of the boys, a wiry youngster with thick curly hair and a large nose, stood and gestured at the newcomers.

"Looky here," he cried, as Agostino and his followers stood before them, in a semi-circle formation. "We got us a bunch of Coney Island clowns! Did anyone call for some greasers?" He looked at his comrades. "One of you boys out of grease?" The others laughed, their eyes narrowed, all glaring at the newcomers.

"Well," the lead boy continued, "then why we got us a bunch of grease-soaked candy asses coming down on our turf?"

Agostino glared at him, standing tall. "This is our turf, you short-grown son of a bitch. We've warned you. Now it's time for action." Agostino surveyed the group. He could see baseball bats and a few clubs scattered among the gathering. One of them even had a policeman's truncheon.

The boy walked slowly towards Agostino, until they stood a few feet apart. They looked each other in the eye.

"Well, Agostino," he breathed, "I hope you brought the right tools. Cos we deal in pain, compadre."

"Yeah," Agostino snarled. "Well, so do we."

With that, he swung the lead piping towards the other's head, like a baseball slugger going for a home run. His rival moved with lightning fast reflexes, ducking under the powerful blow and producing a flick knife from nowhere, which he dug into Agostino's swinging arm before pushing him to the ground.

The fallen man gasped in shocked pain, before the other rammed his booted foot into his jaw.

The bell had rung. All hell broke loose. The bottom of 29th, a deserted backstreet off Dewey Hill, became a battleground once again, as the black leather jackets and the colourful bowling shirts threw themselves at each other like two packs of rabid dogs.

Knives, bats, clubs, bricks and pieces of wood and guttering were all thrown into the mix as the battle raged.

Terry did not even think about it. He charged at the first boy he locked eyes on, as two of his comrades raced to Agostino's aid. He football tackled the boy and they sprawled to the dusty asphalt, rolling over and over as both pummelled each other with kicks and punches. Terry ended up on his back, with the other boy sitting on top of him. The snarling Latino threw two straight jabs into his jaw, drawing blood on his lips and nose.

Terry tried to shield his face, but his adversary then changed his position and rammed a knee into his groin. Terry let out a scream of pure agony, and tried to roll away. Then, inexplicably, the other boy had somehow floated into the air, before being propelled across the street like a piece of garbage caught in a strong breeze.

Terry looked up. There stood Heavy, strong and silent, like a giant gladiator slaying a gang of slaves in days of old. Throwing the youngster 10 feet had been no exertion at all to him.

Heavy dropped to his friend's side and hauled him up to his feet. They both stood, Terry reeling on his feet, and surveyed the violence. As impish squeals and gasps of shock and pain filled the backstreet, the scene of utter terror played out before them. The Cobras had all but flattened the rival gang. It would last barely two minutes, the whole thing.

As one of the Latino boys was sent crashing into a barrage of trash cans, Heavy stepped forward and powerfully punched another in the kidneys from behind, incapacitating one of their rivals.

Those from the Latino gang who were not sprawled on the ground, unconscious or immobilised, took flight and quickly disappeared among the garbage cans and back alleys.

Terry and Heavy looked on at the carnage. The men in the leather jackets were soon on their feet and all stood around their leader, grunting with exhaustion and fury.

Paul Agostino had a look in his wild eyes that could only be described as euphoric. His black jacket was covered in street dust. He stumbled dumbly to one of the fallen fighters, rolling him over. It was the rival gang's leader. He moaned, hugging at his ribs, tears running down his bloodied face.

Agostino spat on him. "Big shot, huh?" he screamed. "Think you're a tough guy! Look at you! Crying like a little girl. Well, little mamacita, eat this!"

With a murderous grin, he nodded to Hawker, who calmly grabbed each of the fallen boy's wrists, spreading his arms apart and holding them aloft.

"No! Please!" the boy screamed.

Agostino laughed maliciously before taking a two-step run-up and firing his boot into the boy's face.

The insane, hideous scream that filled the neighbourhood air would stay with them all for some time. It was a primal, non-human sounding eruption, and marked the end of the confrontation.

Terry and Heavy looked on grimly. While the big man remained impassive, Terry suddenly felt sick.

Sick all over.

Several hours later, Terry sat on a swing in a deserted playground overlooking Westley Bank, on the south side of the Hudson River. This area was dominated by fancy apartment blocks and uptown bars and gentlemen's joints.

He rocked back and forth lightly on the swing, the later afternoon sun causing him to squint. His eyes were on a walkway that led down from a plaza of fancy apartments out to a riverside path.

He smiled. There he was. Same time as always. Just like clockwork.

He stopped rocking and stared, as a figure ambled slowly down the walkway and onto the riverside path, taking in the grandness of the river and the pleasant surroundings.

The man was tall, well built, with deep tanned features and a magnificent head of wavy dark hair. He wore his trademark sheepskin jacket, which kept the elder man warm as he paced along through the riverside breeze.

Eric Ribbeck.

Somehow, he looked like an inspirational figure. Even by simply taking in his afternoon walk.

Terry watched him often when he came this way. It had all started when he had recognised his great idol on the walkway last summer, dumbfounded at seeing someone whose face he had only ever known in magazine pictures and newspapers, suddenly before him, not far from his own neighbourhood.

He watched as Ribbeck ambled over to his favourite bench, right by the water, and settled softly, sitting back and taking in his surroundings.

He was from Texas originally. Terry knew that. The son of a cattle baron. He had sunk his inheritance into building up Ribbeck's American Circus. Now, he split his time between his apartment here in New York and a mansion in Atlantic City, where the circus headquarters was based.

Terry smiled as he watched the older man. Today would be different.

He skipped off the swing, left the playground and made his way slowly down to the riverside path. The sky was clouding over as the late afternoon sun began to fade.

He approached the seated figure cautiously, somehow afraid. He had played this scene through his mind a hundred times. Now, suddenly, it was upon him. Excitement, fear, desire and apprehension flooded his conscience. They were all similar emotions, he thought idly, as he walked in mini-steps down the path. A cool wind blew in from the Hudson, and he suddenly felt icy all over. The setting was beautiful for this once in a lifetime moment, as he finally turned to the old man on the bench.

He took a deep breath. "Mr Ribbeck?"

The older man did not turn immediately. Instead, he threw a cracker towards a waiting seagull, before turning and glancing at the newcomer. He studied Terry for several moments, seemingly amused by his leather jacket and jeans. Then, he studied the newcomer's eyes and took on a more sombre look. He smiled a beautiful smile, showing off a sublime set of white teeth that, together with his opaline green eyes and thick bushy hair, made him look somewhat like a Western film star.

"What can I do for you, young man?"

And that was how it had all started.

Chapter One

West Coast, California

1960

Out of a clear azure sky, a bright yellow helicopter dropped its altitude and swept over the city skyline.

A magnificent sight welcomed the occupants.

San Francisco. Its enormous skyscrapers seemed to reach up into the heavens, embracing the clouds.

The copter traversed across the coastal route, offering an awesome view of the Marina district and Golden Gate Bridge. Then, it was directly over the city heights, slowly descending among the giant towers and endless rows of apartment blocks. The helicopter slowly locked its path onto one single, monolithic building that loomed ahead like a portal into another world.

This skyscraper was bigger than almost all others, and stood tall and powerful at the far end of the great Bay, looking down upon Fisherman's Wharf and the mighty Pacific.

In the co-pilot's seat, Kal Klondike smiled majestically, almost laughing.

He glanced at the pilot, nodded, and continued to gape at the huge building as the copter began to slow and hover over it.

Like the helicopter, the giant building had bright yellow decor at its summit, with the words Addison Incorporated printed on a huge aluminium sign.

The machine lowered slowly until it touched down on a landing pad on the roof of the great behemoth.

Klondike shook hands with the pilot and leapt out onto the concrete surface, almost losing his balance as the rotors continued whirling above, causing a mighty backdraft.

He ducked as he paced across the roof, the fierce wind tugging at his suit as he walked, high above the busy city streets far below.

He headed towards a glass booth at the far end of the roof. It felt like walking across heaven this high up, he always thought.

Klondike was a tall, well-built man in his 40s, with thick, black hair and sideburns. He had bronzed, craggy features and was dressed in a tanned suit and fedora, carrying a silver-topped cane.

As he reached the clear glass booth, Daryl Addison opened a door and welcomed him. He was an older fellow, thin, wiry, with cropped grey hair and a pencil moustache. He smiled as his visitor reached the booth.

The two men shook hands warmly and got out of the blowy rooftop air, exchanging pleasantries as they moved indoors.

"Welcome back to Utopia, Kal," Addison said, placing a hand on the younger man's back.

Klondike nodded as they walked down a plush corridor towards an elevator. He could not help smiling.

"Every time I come here, I still can't believe it," he said. He turned and looked back at the glass booth at the end of the corridor. "I tell you what, that is the way to travel. The chopper got me here in no time. And what a view!"

Addison pressed the down button as they reached the elevator doors. "You can see our building from the other side of the bridge."

Klondike nodded happily. "I could see your alligator grin from up there, too! No, really, Daryl, this place is a real piece of work."

Addison nodded proudly. "So, how are the preparations going, Kal?"

Klondike kept looking around the grand surroundings. "Ah, the usual. A few loose ends to tie up. But we're good to go. Like always."

They both laughed. The elevator doors rolled open and they entered. The walls of the booth were a gaudy gold. Addison pressed the button for the 11th floor, far below.

"This is incredible, Daryl," Klondike mused. "This whole building. You're like a tycoon out here now."

"And a lot of that is thanks to you, Kal."

The elevator stopped. The two men exited, and walked down a yellow-carpeted corridor until they came to a giant double door. Addison held it open for his guest, and both waded in.

The boardroom was a long, cavernous affair dominated by a huge rectangular table that seemed to bleed right the way to the far wall. Eye opening floor to ceiling windows offered a panoramic view of San Francisco Bay, which seemed to envelope the room due to the immense glass walls.

Addison rushed ahead to a drinks cabinet in the far corner. "What can I get ya?"

"Blackjack and water."

The older man fixed two drinks and brought them over. He held his own aloft for a toast.

"Here's to another year of success for Klondike's Circus."

Klondike grinned. "Onwards and upwards, old friend."

As he tasted the dry, cool liquid, Klondike surveyed Daryl Addison. A banker, Addison had helped bankroll his circus for eight years with loans, in return for a share of the profits. That had been the way it was for a long time.

Then, after the circus's breakthrough year in 1958, everything had taken off. Klondike's Circus had made huge profits off the back of television specials, shows in Las Vegas and huge sponsorship and advertising deals. Every aspect of the business had grown enormously.

Now, the circus was a big budget show, performing in 16 cities across the USA and enjoying regular dates at the Golden Dune casino in Vegas. There were regular TV specials and all kinds of offers from entertainment companies and the media.

Addison had used his share of the profits to buy out his old bank and build up a financial services company that quickly mushroomed into a money-making juggernaut. He invested in Hollywood movies, Broadway shows, television and record producing.

Klondike had made him a partner in the circus last year, under the title of financial consultant.

Now, as they took their seats at the top of the huge mahogany table, Klondike studied his long-time associate and money man. Despite Addison's tremendous business success, the years had not been kind on him. He looked as though he'd aged 10 in just the two. His greying hair and wrinkled, haggard complexion gave him the look of a tired grandfather, which he most certainly was not.

Addison seemed to read his mind. "If only we'd known," he said with a sly grin.

"Known what?" Klondike replied, settling into a leather-bound seat.

"That the circus would take off like it did. Why, look at us, Kal. Sitting around this giant boardroom table like Wall Street aces. It was only two years ago we were covered in dust, discussing the 1958 season in that old tent of yours."

Klondike winked at him. "It was never in doubt, Daryl."

Addison chuckled. "What's definitely not in doubt is that your circus is turning into a licence to print money. Richie Plum sent me the estimates for this season. Merchandising, advertising, the midway take…it is all off the scale."

"I know, Daryl, I know," Klondike said understandingly, "I can't believe it too. It's like a wild rollercoaster ride. I'm just hoping it doesn't stop."

"Well, we can sit around talking about how stunned we are by our own success. Or…we can get down to it. Like we used to."

Klondike took a long pull at his drink. "I always prefer talking business."

"Good. Now, I read all your preview material yesterday. The press releases. The programme copy. And last night I got my map out and fingered out your route. Then I casually read that brochure you mailed me about the fancy new train you bought."

"Whatya think?" Klondike drained the glass and waded stiffly back to the drinks cabinet. He poured himself half a glass of scotch.

Then, his eyes never leaving the banker, he removed a cigar from a breast pocket and lit up, temporarily disappearing in a cloud of purple smoke.

"Well, I like it all, of course," Addison was murmuring. "But I want to know about the show. The actual show. You're up there all the time in Rio Cristo at your headquarters. I want to know what you think."

Klondike leant against the cabinet. "Well, we are going to build on last season. The principal stars once again will be Gino and Roddy. As you know, the animal acts have been phased out ever since the train crash. That is, except for the Range Riders, who operate a team of 10 horses. Corky and his clowns do their usual act. We have the Showcase Revue—"

"The freak show!"

"Right. And then we have our newcomers. The Daredevils—they're the motorcycle stunt team. The Rocking Robins, that showgirl troupe from Reno. We have the Flying Batistas, they're a family of acrobats. And, of course, the whole show is sung out by Suzi Dando."

"And what of these new acts? The Daredevils?"

Klondike studied his cigar. "Well, these motorcycle guys are out of this world. Came over from Norway in '56. Their grand climax is called the Globe of Death. Has all six of them going round and round inside a caged metal sphere. Somehow, they avoid hitting each other. It really is something."

Addison sat back. "Showgirls. Motorbikes. Singers. We really have branched out."

"Changing with the times, Daryl."

The banker took on a pained look. "And what of our beloved heroes, Gino and Roddy?"

Klondike thought for a moment, picturing in his mind the two unquestionable stars of his circus. Gino Shapiro, now acknowledged as the world's greatest trapeze artist, who had been the headline star of Klondike's Circus since day one. His 'devil drop' act of death defiance in that magical 1958 season had been labelled the most audacious circus moment of all time by the US media.

Roddy Olsen had also been a big part of that season. A handsome, young and ultra-confident ventriloquist, he had appeared out of nowhere at the start of the '58 tour and had gone on to become the breakout star, to the surprise and joy of everyone at the circus. His extraordinary voice manipulation skills and ever more mind-blowing singing and comedy routines had become a major draw.

"They are the lion and the leopard in my jungle," Klondike replied with a queer grin. "They are rivals. They are superstars. Beloved by thousands. And both have but one thing in common—an unbreakable respect for the industry."

"Are they getting along any better?"

"Hah! Well, y'know, my role is like that of a referee. But I keep them happy. Roddy is still a kid, dammit. He's still humble and grateful for everything…like he can't believe all this has happened to him. With Gino, I still massage his ego. His name still goes at the top of the bill. He remains our highest paid performer. But Roddy shares the poster with him. As an equal."

"So he is no longer the host?"

"No. We keep changing our format. But audiences seem to prefer him doing a regular gig now. He has a 20-minute slot with his puppets. It works better, I think. Heavy is the ringmaster again."

"I get that," Addison said slowly. "Keep him up there for maximum effect."

"We put Roddy on third right now. After the girls and the Range Riders, who are going to open this year?"

Addison sipped delicately at his drink. He held the glass firmly against his chest as he sat at the head of the table.

"Y'know, representatives of Eric Ribbeck have contacted me. About Gino and Roddy."

Klondike rolled his eyes. The duel never ended.

Eric Ribbeck. His former boss, mentor and childhood idol. Ribbeck's World Circus, as it was now called, was the biggest circus company in America. For years, it had been untouchable. Klondike had been a performer for Ribbeck, a knife thrower and cowboy shooter. Then, he had become a booker and talent scout. After he found that the old Texan was shaving money off the take to pay off a string of mistresses, reporters and government officials, Klondike had walked. He had formed his own troupe, and was now Ribbeck's biggest competitor. The battle to be America's biggest circus was now an annual fight.

"I've had calls. Telegrams…" Addison brought him back to the boardroom. "Ribbeck's lawyers. He wants Gino and Roddy. He said to name our price."

"There is no damn price!" Klondike snarled. "He had Gino once. And even Gino thought he stunk. He came with me and hasn't regretted one minute of it."

Addison held up a hand. "OK, Kal. Take it easy." He thought for a moment. "We are big time players now. All this talk—contracts, offers, deals…it's all part of the terrain. Let me handle it."

Klondike clamped the cigar into the corner of his mouth. "Like we said, changing times."

"Even you've changed, Kal."

"What? How so?"

"Well, look at you. You look more of a showman now. What with that fancy, silver-topped cane."

Klondike glanced down at the cane, resting on the table, and had to smile. "Hell, that was Lacey's idea. She said it made me look like circus entrepreneurs of old. Like Barnum and Bailey. Yet another publicity idea."

Addison laughed too. "Dear old Lacey. How is she doing?"

Klondike stared out the giant, floor to ceiling window at the mesmerising view of the bay. He could see everything up here. "Lacey…" he said breathlessly.

Lacey Tanner was the circus publicist and his de-facto assistant and administrator. In many ways, much of the success of Klondike's Circus was down to her. Her publicity campaigns, electrifying press releases and general management had taken the travelling show to new heights. And it was all thanks to Addison, who had seconded her to Klondike two years earlier.

"She has that effect on everyone," Addison said as he studied Klondike's wide-eyed trance. "A beautiful, fascinating woman with her finger on the pulse of popular culture."

"One in a million," Klondike added. "Sometimes, I think she has a crystal ball and can see what is about to happen next. Somehow, she is always one step ahead of the game."

"She chose you. Your circus. She could have gone to Hollywood. Broadway. The world was hers. But the wonder and adventure of that 1958 tour did something to her. Opened her eyes to a whole new world…a world of magic and wonder."

Klondike nodded thoughtfully. "We are so lucky to have her. Hell, that's another one I owe you, partner."

He took the older man's glass and refilled it. They both drank. "What are your plans now, Kal?"

"Well," Klondike rumbled. "I'm heading back to camp at Rio Cristo. If that flying lounge of yours can get me there! Then, I have a meeting with our old friend Claude Hershey at the Golden Dune in Vegas. Some kind of proposition he has."

"I love it already!"

"Yeah. Well, the circus train rolls in 10 days. Right here, of course, for our first show in Frisco. I'll join up in Los Angeles. Lacey and Heavy will take charge for the opener."

At that moment, there was a knock at the door and a pretty woman in a white blouse crept in. "Excuse me, Mr Addison. You are due downstairs at the art department in five minutes."

Addison rose. "Of course. Thank you, Susan." He smiled at Klondike. "The art department. Have you seen the posters they have done for you yet?"

"No. They are waiting for me at Cristo."

"You'll love em."

"I sure hope so."

Addison held out his hands. "I'm sorry, Kal. I enjoy our chats so much. But, alas, there is just never enough time."

Klondike put a hand on his shoulder. "Thank you, Daryl. As always. For everything."

"Of course."

Klondike smiled, picked up his cane and began walking down the long boardroom.

"You never gave me an answer," Addison called out to him.

He turned. "For what?"

"Ribbeck's offer."

Klondike grimaced. "Tell him what we always tell him. To go to hell." He walked out of the boardroom.

Rio Cristo was a sprawling enclosure that sat deep in the Brownlow hills above Napa Valley.

A giant white-stoned building sat at the head of the encampment, which served as living quarters for the majority of the circus staff and held rooms for guests and VIPs to stay in. A row of offices and store rooms bled off to one side of the main headquarters.

The pavilion structure overlooked a vast sea of trailers, cabins and giant containers that stretched across a gravelled surface. In the centre sat a miniature version of the circus big top, a large red and blue tent with the Klondike's Circus logo emblazoned all over it.

Klondike and his troupe had moved their headquarters to this secluded location after the success of the 1958 season. It was larger, more spacious and far more luxurious than their previous camp at Santa Cruz.

An unmistakeable whirring noise had made everyone at the camp glance skywards.

Heavy Brown was in his office going through some papers when the buzzing sound grew louder. With a grin, he tossed the papers aside and hopped away from his desk and out the door onto the gravel pathway that ran alongside the office block.

He looked up and spotted the bright yellow helicopter descending from the clouds. He headed for the camp's own landing pad, on the right side by a large hedgerow that served as a boundary.

"Arriving in style. I like it!"

Heavy turned at the voice behind him and smiled as Lacey Tanner strode elegantly towards him. She was dressed, as was her way, in a frilly purple dress, more suited to a Manhattan cocktail lounge than a circus. With her long, flaming red hair and giant violet eyes, she was quite a sight, especially out here.

"Coming to welcome home our boy?" said Heavy.

"Of course," she gushed. She joined him and linked her arm though his. They walked around a row of trailers. In the background, the roar of motorbikes racing around their circuit grid filled the air as the stunt riders practised.

"Y'know," Heavy was saying. "There was a time Kal would return from his meetings with Addison and we would all be worried sick. The big question would be—did he get the loan or not? We all depended on the old man's money. Just for the show to survive."

Lacey laughed quietly. "And now look. We're bringing in more green than Daryl ever could have imagined."

Heavy grunted. He was a giant of a man, 6ft 4in, a mass of brawn, half fat and half muscle. He towered over Lacey and looked down at her happily. "We make a good team, you and me. When Kal is away. Look how we been running this joint."

She smiled up at him. "Like Fred and Ginger."

"More like beauty and the beast."

She giggled as they reached the pad and conversation became impossible as the copter descended, its beautiful yellow paintwork shining in the midday sun.

Heavy and Lacey stared in rapt fascination as the machine slowly touched down on the giant rubber landing area, its rotors whipping the air and creating a mighty dust cloud.

The passenger door popped open and Klondike leapt out, carrying his cane and briefcase. Struggling to walk under the mighty roar of the blades, he swaggered over to his friends.

Lacey yelled at Heavy next to her. "Are you going to tell him or shall I?"

Heavy baulked. "You tell him, Lacey. And show him that newspaper."

Klondike joined them, shaking Heavy's hand and giving Lacey a big hug.

They began walking to the headquarters building. Behind them, the helicopter rose slowly and then, just like that, was gliding into the clouds, the whir of its motor dying in the wind.

Klondike put an arm around Heavy. "Good to be back, old buddy. As always."

"We missed you, Kal. Something about seeing a man wandering around camp in a Stetson, carrying a cane...like an army missing a brigadier."

"It was worth it to see that entrance, Kal," Lacey purred.

"Addison pulls out all the stops these days. God damn it, you should see his office building. He's living like a damn pharaoh."

"Oh, I've seen it," Lacey mused. "Old Daryl is the king of Frisco, methinks."

"It's certainly another world out there."

"And you, tiger?" Lacey breathed. "You still prefer all this?" She threw a hand theatrically towards the sea of trailers they were moving past.

"Of course," Klondike drawled. "I miss my circus even when I'm away for a few hours. Hell, I miss the smell of the place."

Heavy frowned. "Horse manure?"

Klondike squinted across the camp towards where the stable block sat. He could make out a few of the Range Rider cowboys out on their mounts.

"What can I tell ya? The sweet smell of success!"

They all laughed as they approached Klondike's office, the first one on the block next to the pavilion.

The office was large, decorated in loud red paint and featuring a lounging area with a couch and roundtable as well as a big mahogany desk at the far end. Old circus posters from seasons gone by adorned the walls.

Klondike wearily threw his cane and briefcase onto a small filing cabinet and whipped his blazer and necktie off, loosening several buttons of his shirt.

Then, as if in a trance, he waded across to a drinks cabinet in the corner and filled three glasses with scotch. Still locked in his usual routine, he fumbled for a cigar in an old box on the desk and lit up. Lacey watched the whole procedure with muted delight. She smiled. "You really do resemble a pre-programmed machine when you get back, Kal."

He wedged the cigar in the corner of his mouth and handed out the drinks. Lacey politely placed hers on a coffee table.

She joined Heavy on the couch as Klondike paced the room, sipping his drink.

"Well," he boomed, "we're in the clear as far as Daryl is concerned. He green lit everything. Felt like he has bigger fish to fry, you ask me. He's as in love with the show as ever."

He cackled aimlessly as he idly studied a stack of mail on his desk. Then, he turned and looked at the other two. The cigar drooped. "What?"

Lacey looked at him earnestly. "We got trouble, Kal."

"What! Trouble! What trouble?"

"It's probably best you read this first." She paced across to the desk and produced a newspaper clipping from a folder.

She handed it to him. "This was in this morning's California Herald." Klondike frowned at her as he took the clipping. Then, his face dropped.

The banner headline read:

JUNIOR SENSATION READY TO RULE THE CIRCUS WORLD

He began to read aloud: "The Herald has seen the future of circus showmanship. And his name is Lee Vesnick. The gorgeous star, who is just 21, has made a big name for himself with his jaw-dropping knife-throwing act, and now he is ready for stardom. Vesnick has signed with the renowned Klondike's Circus, out of Rio Cristo, upstate. And the young daredevil insists he is ready to be the star of the show and elevate the organisation to new heights."

"The knife thrower said: "It's no secret. I am the next big thing in the American circus. Kal Klondike recognised my potential and talent last year, and now, with a blockbuster contract, I am ready to show the whole country what I can do. When it comes to blades, no one can touch me. Now, I am ready. Ready to lead Klondike's Circus into the 1960s. Ready to cement my legacy as a big top star. And ready to top the bill. This is going to be my season, I can promise you that. And I simply cannot wait to…"

His voice trailed off as he held the clipping limply before him.

He looked up at the others. His eyes flared and he looked ready to explode.

"That son of a bitch!" he rasped. He screwed the paper up and hurled it onto the floor. "What the hell is he trying to pull? He was on thin ice as it is. He must be outta his god damn mind!"

"I think he is a bit, er, confused," Lacey said diplomatically.

"He's deluded," Klondike snarled. He took a long pull at his drink then prodded the air with his cigar. "It's high time I blackballed him outta here. That little punk just signed his own rejection notice." He glared angrily at Heavy. "Who the hell does he think he is?"

Heavy was equally abhorrent. "Shall I have McCabe and his boys throw him out?"

Klondike finished his drink. "The hell with that. I'm kicking him out myself. Is he in the tent?"

"He sure is."

Klondike made for the door. "Kal?" Lacey called in alarm.

"It's alright," Klondike cried back as he left the office and stormed off. "I got this."

Lee Vesnick grinned like a playful hyena as he hurled knives at a giant spinning wheel.

He was dressed in his full performance attire of black cowboy shirt with white frills and black leather slacks, with tousles lining the outer legs. His hefty scarlet belt was stacked with large silver Quiller knives, which he drew and threw at a rapid pace towards the wheel 12 yards before him.

He was virtually alone in the practice tent as he threw the knives with ease. A few roustabouts were moving equipment around the sawdust floor behind him, but that was about it.

Vesnick was a dedicated trainer. He practised his act for a minimum of five hours every day. And it showed. As he hurled his final knife at the great wooden wheel, he surveyed his results. Every knife had hit the inch-wide red circle that spanned the wheel's outer edge, where balloons would normally sit in a performance.

With a laugh, he jogged to the wheel, put the lock in place, and eagerly gathered up the eight blades.

He was a youthful, swarthy looking man, with a cocky grin, reddish brown skin and a mass of slick brown hair combed in a quiff.

As he gripped the knives, he closed his eyes and held them all before him, four in each hand.

"What the hell gives you the right to blab to the press like that?" The angry roar from behind startled him, and he turned nervously. Klondike was marching towards him, a maddening glare causing Vesnick to take a step back. He placed the haul of knives on a wooden table by the wheel.

"Kal!" he called jovially. "Welcome back. Great to see you. How was Frisco?"

"Never mind that!" Klondike raged. He stopped just in front of the youngster and loomed over him. The cigar was stuck to the inside of his cheek, it seemed. "What the hell is that interview in the Herald all about?"

Vesnick looked up at him innocently. "What? Oh that." He laughed softly. "Hell, that was nothing, Kal. Just a little promo, is all. Get the people interested. Get em curious. Ain't that what it's all about, eh old buddy?"

"I'm not your buddy, you snotty little maggot!"

Vesnick's expression changed to confrontational. "What's that?"

"Your story in the Herald? Star of the show. Top of the bill. God damn leading the circus into the 1960s. What in the wide world were you thinking?"

The youngster matched Klondike's angry stare. "Like I said, it's a promo."

"Who allowed you to say that?"

"Who said I needed permission?"

"You want to tell a pack of lies, a bunch of nonsense, to a top daily…hell, mister, you need my permission. And I tell you to go to hell!" Klondike ran a hand through his thick black hair. "What in heaven were you thinking?"

Vesnick smiled again, the cockiness returning. "Hell, it's all true, Kal. Let me prove you wrong."

"You're not going to prove a damn thing, Vesnick. You're through here!"

"Woh, woh, woh!" Vesnick snapped, holding up his hands. "Now, come on. Let's not make any rash decisions. Now, you said yourself I'm the best thrower you've seen in years. Hell, Kal, you were a thrower. One of the greats. You know how it is. A confidence game, man. You've gotta own the big top to succeed. You gotta be full of yourself to make it, man. People are going to want to see me after reading that story. Think about it…who is this crazy kid thinks he's the next big thing? It's hot, Kal."

"It's garbage, kid, and so are you!" Klondike snarled. "I warned you about shooting your mouth off around here. You're on trial with us. You're not under contract yet. The idea is you do enough to impress us, then you get the 'blockbuster contract' you dreamed up. You gotta earn it, dammit."

"I thought I did. You were hot for my knife throwing."

"Yeah, but not for that god damn black mouth of yours. You're a troublemaker, Vesnick. And I ain't got no place for a rotten apple in my circus. That damn interview is the final straw. You had your chance, and you blew it. Now get the hell out of here."

The two men stared at each other. Vesnick thought it over for a moment. Then he snarled slightly. "Ain't no one talks to me like that!"

With that, he lurched unexpectedly towards Klondike and threw a punch. Klondike expertly dodged him and grabbed the swinging arm as it flew past him. He grabbed the younger man's wrist and twisted his arm fully behind his back. Vesnick shrieked wildly.

Klondike maintained the hold, exerting a little pressure and placing his other arm around his attacker's neck.

He looked up at the sound of rapid footsteps and saw Jim McCabe, his circus foreman, and one of his roustabouts racing across the sawdust towards them. They joined the melee, grabbing at Vesnick as the youngster raged wildly.

"Get him outta here, Jim," Klondike gasped as he released his hold and the two men grappled with Vesnick and held him between them. "Everything. Give him ten minutes to get his belongings together and put him in a cab. A cab heading outta town."

"You bet, Kal," McCabe blurted as he held the youngster with his man. The two circus workers began hauling Vesnick towards the entrance flap.

The knife thrower turned and faced Klondike one last time. "You're making a big mistake, Klondike. I'm not going to forget this!"

"Really?" Klondike spat out. "Well, I have already. Now beat it!"

Vesnick was unceremoniously bundled out of the tent. As he disappeared out of sight, one last cry reverberated around the big top. "I'll get you for this!"

Then, suddenly, it was all quiet again.

Klondike looked at the exit flap angrily, then back at the knife throwing wheel. He wandered over to it and placed a hand at the top of the circular frame.

Then, with a loud curse, he span the great wheel with all his might, letting it spin rapidly as he stood there lost in his thoughts.

Chapter Two

Gino Shapiro happily exchanged well wishes and waved at various staff members as he wandered idly through the camp.

Dressed in a bright orange tracksuit with his name emblazoned on the back in large silver letters, he left no one in any doubt that he was a superstar.

With a toned, athletic physique and dark, tanned skin with slicked back, jet black hair, Shapiro had the look of a matinee idol. Of Mexican/Italian heritage, he had a striking appearance and was outrageously handsome. And he backed it up with a lively charisma and gallant attitude.

However, his showmanship, confidence and almost never-ending womanising had made him an unpopular figure with some among the circus. But no one doubted his incredible talent.

He walked past the Rocking Robins's training stage, a wooden stand erected before a small gathering of bleachers, and watched the girls in their leotards doing their exercises before dance practice began.

One of them, Belinda, came running over to the perimeter fence where he stood.

"Gino! Come to watch us go through our paces?"

He laughed softly. "Not now, Belinda darling. It is my practice time too."

She looked sad. "Maybe a drink at the bar later?"

"Sure, sweetheart. Now get back to practice."

She skipped happily back to the stage. The other Robins all seemed to gather around her excitedly.

With a chuckle, Shapiro continued along the gravel path towards the tent, gripping a white towel that hung around his neck.

As he reached the entrance flap, Klondike was just walking out. "Ah, chairman," he said happily. "You are back. How was Frisco?"

Klondike looked angry about something, but nodded at his trapeze star. "All good, Gino. All good. How is your training coming along?"

"Just fine. Me and my girl are putting the finishing touches on some remarkable routines. A few surprises! You'll love it."

Klondike looked at his bright tracksuit. He finally smiled. "You're going up now?"

Shapiro nodded. "Sure. You know me. The consummate professional. The regime never ends."

Klondike nodded inside the tent. "It looks like your 'girl' had the same idea."

Shapiro frowned. He walked onto the sawdust arena floor in wonder and his eyes enlarged as he gazed up at the trapeze arrangement high above. There, swinging back and forth on the centre ring, was the dazzling figure of Penny Fortune, his new assistant.

"Enjoy yourselves," Klondike drawled as he wandered back to his office.

"You bet…" Shapiro whispered, though his mind was elsewhere. He looked up in awe as Penny let go of the ring and performed a double somersault before landing expertly on the platform adjoined to a pillar in the corner of the tent.

He wandered over, past the safety net suspended on the ground, until he was underneath, clapping cheerfully.

"Gino!" she wailed down at him. "What kept you?"

He looked up at her in wonder. She was tall, with straight blonde hair and pale skin. Her arms and legs were toned and her shoulders sharp. An almost perfect build for a flyer.

For many years, Shapiro had been assisted by his brother Nicky, who had since retired. Then, he had built a successful partnership with Jenny Cross, a former lover of Klondike.

But that pairing had ended in disaster. Under extreme duress, Jenny had tried to kill him in a fateful night in Las Vegas two years earlier. The deranged move, an attempt in her mind at revenge over Klondike for leaving her, had been a dark moment for all at the circus and had quietly been phased out. Jenny was now a patient in a mental hospital in Seattle.

After working with a number of temporary partners last year, Shapiro had invited Penny to join him several weeks ago after spotting her at a small-town circus in Salinas. Now, she was signed on for the season.

"Penny, Penny, Penny," he said softly as he whipped off his tracksuit top and bottoms. Now, he was decked out in his famous flaming orange singlet. He began climbing the rope that led to the platform high above. He chatted casually, the exertion of the climb a minor irritant.

"You just never cease to amaze me. Now, you start practice early too. You are a great professional. My compliments."

Penny watched him climb, leaning against the platform rail. "Why thank you. I enjoy it. Being up here. It's like you said to me when we first met…it's a calling."

"This is very true," he stammered as he hauled himself up the rope. He finally lifted his wiry frame onto the oak platform, resting just 10 yards from the roof of the tent. This was his domain, up here, high above the sawdust.

"Same routine today, champ?" Penny said teasingly.

Shapiro smiled. He liked her wit, her way. She had the confidence and charisma necessary of a circus flyer. "Of course," he said grandly, whipping his arms around and massaging his right shoulder. He moved close to her, lightly caressing the rail. His dark eyes gleamed. "And maybe some more, eh?"

She folded her arms, looking unimpressed. "And what is that supposed to mean?"

He placed an arm around her as they stood looking down at the practice arena. "Ah, well, maybe tonight, I be your host, eh? Maybe a little wine. I cook for you. Tex Mex. A beautiful evening. And we develop our partnership. Our chemistry. It would be good for the act."

Penny eyed him slyly. "Good for your ego, more like!"

"Penny!" he rasped. "Please, don't be upset. We are partners now. I just want to entertain you."

She released herself delicately from his grip. "Listen, Gino," she said quietly. "I sure appreciate you taking me on and all. Truly, it is an honour. I can't thank you enough. But…" she eyed him shrewdly, then grinned. "I am here to be your team-mate. Not your bedmate. Or anything else."

"Penny, please! You misunderstand me, angel." He chuckled half-heartedly. "I am here to look after you. It is my way." He grabbed her hand and kissed it smoothly. "I am here for you. Always, mamacita. Your Gino takes care of you."

She stared at him blankly. "Right." An awkward silence filled the platform. "How about I take care of you now…as your catcher?"

He laughed. "A triple roll?"

"Sure."

Penny grabbed the ring from the support stick and pushed herself into thin air. From there, she threw herself onto the centre ring, expertly turning and sitting in the rubber seat before allowing herself to fall so that she hung upside down. She stretched her arms out wide as she swung gently.

Shapiro grinned like a cat and hurled himself onto the first ring. Swooping wildly back and forth high in the air, he built up momentum before releasing his grip and performing three rapid fire somersaults, his arms shielded over his folded-up legs. As he completed the third spin, he held out his arms and grabbed at Penny's hands as she swung out to him.

Penny swinged back and forth twice and Gino built up their speed with his legs, before releasing himself for a smooth landing on the platform at the far side of the trapeze rig.

Rubbing at his shoulder again, he looked down at the swinging Penny and nodded approvingly.

"Dynamite!" he said to himself.

"Ladies and gentlemen, my next guest is known as the man who can make anything talk. We've had him on before and he never fails to make my jaw drop. He is now joining us ahead of a nationwide circus tour. Please put your hands together for the Puppetmaster, Roddy Olsen!"

The studio crowd cheered loudly as Steve Irving made the introduction onstage in his auditorium at the ATV lot in Hollywood. Olsen was the fourth and final guest on The Steve Irving Show, a comedy and variety talk programme known for its star guests.

Audience members in the enclosed studio theatre cheered and whistled and Olsen emerged from the back, carrying his main puppet Rusty Fox and waving to the crowd jovially.

He looked barely out of his teens, with thick, shining blond hair, sky blue eyes and a California tan. He was dressed in his trademark silver waistcoat.

Irving shook hands with Olsen and Rusty. Sitting on the guests' couch next to the presenter, who was positioned behind a desk, Olsen smiled beautifully at the audience.

"Wow, it's great to be back, Steve," he said.

Rusty, a fox puppet with a quiff hairstyle and black leather jacket, came to life through Olsen's ventriloquism skills.

"Yeah, ATV is doing just great. Like my own studio—20th Century Fox!"

The audience laughed. Irving smiled down at the little fox character on Olsen's lap.

"Great to see you, Rusty. How've you been?"

"Just swell, Mr Irving. It's good to be around my kind of people again."

The presenter frowned. "How do you mean?"

"Well," the little fox appeared to say, "Hollywood is full of dummies!" Irving laughed behind his hosting desk. His wild, red hair and giant, comedic glasses made him look every inch the madcap comic. He had helped produce several TV specials for the circus, and was an old friend of Klondike's from way back in Coney Island.

"Thank you for joining us, Roddy," he was saying. "Especially at this busy time. I understand you are just about to go on tour with Klondike's Circus again."

"Yes, that's right Steve," said Olsen. "We depart in just over a week. It's a big nationwide tour, covering all the major cities."

"It must be fantastic for you, as a young entertainer. Just two years ago, you were working in holiday camps and caravan parks. Isn't that right?"

"I was, Steve. Some tough crowds."

"And some smelly ones," Rusty added with a frown.

Irving chuckled. "And now, look at you. Headlining a circus. TV interviews. A fan club. People screaming your name."

"They're screaming my name, Steve!" Rusty blurted.

"Alright, Rusty," Olsen murmured. "Yes, Steve. I have been very blessed. And I owe it all to you people…" He ran a hand through the air, pointing at the studio audience. "Thanks to all you guys, the public, the fans, for coming out and seeing our show."

Irving clapped, inviting mild applause. "Now, Roddy, what about the new season. What can we look forward to from you this year? Are your other friends, Napoleon and Tony Tan, back for the ride?"

A few cheers rang out at the mention of Olsen's other two puppets. Napoleon, an ageing, white-haired soldier and regular foil of Rusty, was a popular character. As was Tony Tan, a Dean Martin-like, tuxedo-clad Las Vegas lounge lizard and cabaret singer.

Rusty spoke next. "I'm sorry, Steve. I had them both fired!"

Olsen shook his head. "Actually, Napoleon and Tony will be with us. We have some new material, new songs and such, and hope it all goes down alright."

Irving leant forward. "I understand you have a new routine you're going to share with us now, Roddy?"

"That's right," the young ventriloquist said. A stage hand approached and handed him a tall glass of water. "This is called the amazing water watch."

Rusty frowned on his arm. "What is it, man?"

"Well, Rusty, you are going to sing Amazing Grace. And I am going to drink this big glass of water. And all the people are going to…watch!"

With that, Olsen started Rusty singing the classic hymn. Then, to the astonishment of everyone in the building, Olsen held aloft the glass and started downing the contents—while his puppet kept singing!

Olsen continued glugging until the water was finally all gone, as Rusty reached the second verse. He removed the glass from his lips as the puppet kept singing, without missing a single note.

The audience erupted with applause, all lost in wonder at how the youngster had pulled it off. Rusty bowed elegantly on his lap.

Irving was on his feet, clapping enthusiastically. "Roddy Olsen!" he cried, holding his arm out at his guest. "Have you ever seen anything like that, folks?"

The loud applause continued, reverberating around the studio auditorium.

Olsen smiled humbly at the crowd before him.

The novelty of enraptured applause had never worn off.

After the show had wrapped, Olsen had a few words with Irving and the producers on the set. Mostly well wishes and polite conversation. He said a farewell to the other guests, who were still seated in the green room behind the stage, and then shook hands with a few stage hands he had gotten to know over the years. One of them took Rusty from him and placed the puppet in a large, velvet suitcase ready for transportation.

Then, with a last wave to Irving, he began walking back to his allocated dressing room. The audience had slowly disappeared, the auditorium's leather seats now empty and deserted.

As he walked down a marble corridor connected to the studio, he felt a figure fall into step beside him.

"Congratulations, Roddy. You were out of sight, man. That show will be seen by millions tonight. They will remember your name."

Olsen did not need to look. "What do you want, Norm?"

The man chuckled slightly. "A discussion at least, son. You know what I'm all about. After what you pulled out there—another show-stopping performance, another! Jesus, kid, you're red hot right now. I, er, just want to make sure it lasts forever."

Olsen did not break his stride. "What makes you think it won't?"

"Cos you're riding around in a damn circus!"

With that, Olsen stopped and faced the man.

Norman Pierce. An agent to comedians, singers and other star performers. He reputedly had half the stage names in Las Vegas on his books. He had been trying to coerce Olsen into becoming a client for months, often turning up just like this in and around Los Angeles. He was a fat, unhealthy looking man with a clean shaven head and steel-rimmed glasses. Despite his reputation as a ruthless high-roller, he had a strange, friendly demeanour.

"Listen," Olsen said, his customary coolness fading, "we've been through this. Repeatedly. I sure appreciate you taking an interest in me, Norm. It's an honour, really. And thank you for the dinner you bought and the support. But...I'm happy as I am. I'm contracted with Klondike's Circus, and I'm not looking beyond that."

Pierce smiled slyly as he took a step forward. "But you will."

"What's that?"

"Listen, Roddy. You belong in the big leagues now. You belong with me. You just smashed the Steve Irving Show tonight. Tomorrow...who knows what's next. Ed Sullivan. The Tonight Show. Maybe The Roddy Olsen Show. You can scale those heights, man. And I can get you there."

Olsen shook his head. "Kal got me that ATV special, Circus of the Stars. He had me host the Las Vegas show. And none of this would ever have been possible without him. I owe the world and more to Kal Klondike. Without him, I'm nothing."

Pierce hovered over him. "But my dear Roddy, you can be so much more. My god! Klondike knows it. You have to think about yourself. Take care of yourself. Financially and artistically. Now, come on man."

They stood there in the dimly lit corridor. It was all unusually quiet now, despite the film crew packing up behind them.

Olsen was an affable, polite youngster, but he had largely grown up in California boarding houses and had fought to survive. He didn't like being pushed.

"What the hell kind of agent are you, anyway?" he snapped at Pierce.

The larger man took on a knowing look. "One that makes money." He lit a cigarette and looked around idly. "Lots of it. For lots of people. One day soon, Roddy, you're gunna realise that." He thought for a moment. "Listen, kid, I'm your friend. I can help you. Remember that." Puffing on the cigarette, he turned and made to walk away, back to the studio. "You call me now. I'll be waiting. Just remember what I told you."

Olsen stood there, watching him waddle away. He shook his head and continued down the corridor to his dressing room. He had just reached the door and was grasping the handle when another voice startled him.

"Roddy!"

He turned and smiled as Suzi Dando ran down the corridor towards him, coming from the opposite direction.

The circus's songstress and youngest member, she looked almost childlike with her angelic features and brown bob hairstyle.

She skipped over and hugged him warmly. The two youngsters had been tight ever since Olsen had first wandered into the circus camp two years earlier.

"Way to go, champ," she gushed, smiling widely, eyes shining. "They loved you. They all loved you. What a reaction."

"Thanks, Suzi. Great crowd. You alright?"

"Just fine, Roddy. I was in the third row. I'm so glad I came up. That water trick…it was just incredible. How on earth do you do it?"

He laughed softly as he opened the dressing room door. They both entered. The room was large, white and seemed to gleam under the bright lights. As always in such domains, a giant mirror dominated the main wall.

"One day, maybe I'll tell," he teased.

"I don't think I'll ever get it," she mused, wandering to the dresser and looking at a selection of greeting cards. "But that's the magic."

"Cartoon time come to life. That's what Kal calls it."

Suzi looked up at him, starry eyed. "I could watch you perform all day."

He smiled as he stood over the washbasin. "I could never have done all this without you, Suzi."

She shook her head as she watched him remove his beloved silver waistcoat. Then, he washed his hands and splashed cold water onto his face. She said: "There were…there were young people out there. Teenyboppers. Screaming your name…"

He laughed as he washed. "Crazy, huh? Like Ricky Nelson, with puppets!"

She brought a towel over to him. He took it and dried his face. Then, he looked at her. She stood there, as if awaiting instruction. "I'm glad you came, Suzi." He thought for a moment. "Y'know, one day soon, we're both going to be on The Steve Irving Show. Singing a duet…with a little help from my friends."

"It's alright, Roddy," she whispered, eyeing him intently. "I don't mind. I'm happy with the way things are. I…I just want you to know, I'm here for you."

He smiled down at her and tweaked her chin. "Thank you, angel. I'll never forget it."

Suzi checked her watch. "The studio car will be here soon to take us back to Rio Cristo."

"And then, after that, nothing but the circus trail."

"I can't wait. I really can't."

Olsen smiled happily as he walked back across the room. "No doubt a whole new series of escapades and dramas lie ahead."

He had no way of knowing how prophetic those words would turn out to be.

Chapter Three

Klondike sipped at the strong black coffee as he sat sprawled at his desk, going over planning grants for the forthcoming season's venues. Every detail had to be checked, or else the whole show could be turned away at any one town.

His office was eerily quiet. Lacey sat on the couch, reading and rereading her press releases. A pile of various California-based newspapers and magazines sat on the coffee table before her.

And in the corner of the office, Heavy sat comfortably in a leather desk chair, reading a brochure on the circus's new Barrowman Express train.

"I just can't help wondering…" Klondike mused softly, studying the papers, "if we ain't gunna have that season of two halves we always talk about. With Ribbeck starting out in Atlantic City and, as always, heading west, there's a point when we'll start running up the Eastern territories he's already picked through. I just don't know…"

Lacey lit a cigarette and spoke in a calm, soothing tone. "Kal, baby, we've been through this. Don't worry. America loves the circus. Especially right now. The paying public can't get enough. Just because they've seen Ribbeck's World Circus doesn't mean they aren't going to come out again to see us."

Heavy smiled knowingly, hands across his chest. "It's them Eastern cities, Lacey. We were a West Coast operation for years. Going nationwide last year was a big step for us all. New territories." He winked at Klondike. "New worlds to conquer."

Lacey laughed haughtily. "Well, you haven't done too bad in this brave new world. I saw the books. The take in Chicago last year was the biggest of the whole run."

"Chicago is a good, old-fashioned circus town," Klondike blurted as he sipped his coffee. He watched his two confederates, steely eyes looming over the top of his mug. "No, what I'm worried about is having second claim on those territories. Anyone who don't like it ain't gunna come back and see another, different show. Tight purses might not get tickets for two shows. Sure, we did alright last year but, ever since that TV special in LA, every nickel and dime promoter in America is putting a circus together."

"Kal, would you relax," Lacey purred, as if admonishing an overzealous child. "The circus world is red-hot since our TV special. People can't get enough of it. And we're at the top of the tree."

Heavy chuckled again. "A shootout with Ribbeck to be number one. Who would've thought it?"

At that moment, the office door opened and a short, overweight man with a balding head and glasses rushed in. As was often the case, his face was red and his cheeks puffed.

Klondike smiled at Richie Plum, the circus's finance manager. Plum had joined up at the same time as Lacey, again as part of a deal engineered by Addison. Despite being initially adverse to circus life, the small, insignificant-looking man had become a pillar of strength for Klondike and his staff, helping out across the board and developing a smooth understanding of the business.

"Good morning folks," he had uttered, before pacing across to the coffee pot and grabbing a mug.

"Well, let's have it Richie," Klondike rasped.

Plum poured himself a full cup of black steaming liquid. "I've been through everything. And it's good news all round."

Klondike laughed. "That's how we like it."

Plum stood before them proudly. "Even accounting for the massive outlay on the new train, I can forecast healthy profits." He took a seat on the couch next to Lacey. "According to my calculations, we only need to hit 80 per cent of our targets in each town to still hit the black. And that's just to push through the breaking even line. If we smash it, and exceed my projections, which are based on last year's revenues, well…I, er, I guess you could say the sky is the limit."

"Well done, Richie," said Lacey reassuringly.

Klondike had pulled a cigar out of the old box on his desk. He smelt it curiously. "So your projections are based entirely on last year's take?"

Plum nodded. "That's right, Kal. So, with all the alterations and improvements we have introduced this season, and accounting for the growing re-emergence in popularity of the circus across the nation… I say my projections are the tip of the iceberg. The potential profits for this year are immense." He wiped excitedly at his brow. "And think about it. We have more merchandise to sell this year. The T-shirts, posters, signed pictures, costumes and badges…all that stuff. More for the fans to engage in. Then, we have all these requests for personal appearances before each show. The firms are offering to pay upfront."

Klondike glanced at Lacey and nodded happily. Yet again, that venture had been her idea. In the run-up to a show in each town, Klondike and any number of his performers would appear at corporate events, fairs, public rallies, luncheons, anywhere that a company wanted to impress its people with a surprise guest. The firm would pay a fee, and get a collection of free show tickets as part of the deal. The ploy had worked well last season, although it tended to involve spending a week or so in each town.

"That's great Richie," Klondike said across the office. "Thank you for the report."

Plum leant forward in the couch. "If the year-on-year figures are anything like the 1958-59 leap, I predict we could comfortably be up a third. But, like I say, the opportunities are endless, especially in the East, where we are newcomers to the market. I've calculated a mean average take, encompassing a year-on-year collective of just two per cent, and even that came out at a startling high."

They all stared at the small man with the reddish face. Then, Heavy cackled knowingly. "I tell ya, Richie, one of these days we will all understand what the hell you're talking about! All we know is, it sure sounds swell. I like em apples. And you make em sound all the sweeter, my friend."

Plum smiled awkwardly. "I…I'm glad."

"Well," Klondike sighed, finally standing. He still held the unlit cigar. "That's a good bit of news to send us all packing. Roll-out is the day after tomorrow. There's a helluva lot to cram onto the train. The new midway stalls are all laid out in the stable block. We've got an army of roustabouts coming along to man it all. Should be a beautiful sight."

"Leaving on the train won't be the same without you, Kal," Lacey said quietly.

"Hell, I'll be there in LA," he rasped. "Meantime, I'm going to try and cut a few deals to get us even more green. Claude Hershey wants us for something special, I'm sure. And then I'm going to try to coerce Steve Irving into another TV outing. Or whatever he can do for us. While I'm there, I'm going to look over a few acts he has recommended. Performers with movie contracts who are looking for extra work. There's some kind of wild west show he wants me to see."

Heavy cocked his head. "Are you taking that damn helicopter to Vegas?"

Klondike laughed. "Why, sure. Addison said it's on standby to take me anywhere and everywhere."

"Unbelievable," his old friend uttered.

Lacey stubbed her cigarette out in a seashell ashtray and rose, elegantly placing a pink cardigan over her shoulders. "Well boys, I'll leave you to your card game and cigars. The next batch of press releases are being sent to the midwest territories tomorrow. I've okayed them." She waltzed over to the door and then turned theatrically. "I'll keep my usual watch on all the papers. Prepare to be dazzled by all the coverage."

The three stared at her, entranced.

Klondike finally spoke. "That's why you're the best, Lacey."

She smiled beautifully and left.

"Y'know," Heavy smirked, "she'll be running things while you're gone." He shook his head. "It's the damnedest thing. I actually like taking orders from her. Only time in my life I've had a broad tell me what to do. Hell, it feels nice. With her."

Klondike was gazing at the spot Lacey had just vacated. "That woman has had an incredible effect on all of us." His stare then fell upon Plum on the couch. "Thank god you and her came here."

Plum grinned. "There's been no looking back."

Klondike turned again to the doorway. "There sure hasn't."

The barroom in the circus pavilion was a small, neat affair, all mahogany panels and polished, oak tables. It was located directly behind the staff canteen, where a team of student caterers had a winter job feeding the staff and performers and managing the facilities.

Most evenings, the bar was busy with a mix of roustabouts and talent, who all mingled easily in the relaxed confines.

Corky, the beloved Klondike's Circus clown, was surprised to see he was one of the first patrons of the evening as he wandered in after dinner. Wearing a comedic, polka dotted yellow and black suit, he still looked every inch the clown, though he had rinsed off his white face paint.

Born John Lone, he was a wiry, agile 50-year-old who had also followed Klondike from Ribbeck's World Circus years earlier.

Now, he took a seat at the bar and ordered a beer. He looked around the room casually. Two roustabouts and three of the Range Rider cowboys were beginning a poker match at a corner table. And that was about it.

Marlon, the elderly camp bartender, brought him his drink. "You here to see the show?" he asked the clown.

Corky turned on the stool to face him. "Show? What are you talking about?"

Marlon cackled. "Two days before roll-out. Now, everyone is at the camp. All together. And they all come face to face in here, in my bar. All those crazy personalities. Hence…the show."

Corky pondered that. "I never thought of it like that."

"Come off it. I see everything back here. All those beautiful showgirls. The cowboys. That troupe of damn Norwegians. And Caesar himself, our dear Gino. It's like an opera."

Corky chuckled. "Must be very entertaining."

The bartender gave him a nod. "I like being entertained."

With that, the veteran clown put the palm of his hand directly before Marlon's face and then clicked his fingers, magically producing a dollar bill to the old man's delight. "Keep the change."

They both laughed, then turned as six men in smart red and black tracksuits entered the bar. As if on cue, the Daredevils boys had arrived. The motorcycle stunt riders were a rough, tough-looking bunch who were known for sticking together at all times. They had brought their act over from Norway in 1956 and had toured independently before signing with the circus last year.

Tip Enqvist, their leader and promoter, walked stiffly to the bar and motioned to Marlon. "Six beers and a bottle."

Enqvist was a tall, painfully thin man with whitish blond hair and black stubble. He leant against the bar and eyed Corky. "Where's the rest of your boys?" he blurted, referring to the other clowns who made up Corky's team.

Corky raised his glass. "Being good. Early nights and all. Alas, I'm the naughty one."

Enqvist stared at him, disinterested, and lit a cigarette. His fellow riders hovered around the bar.

"Hell," the Norwegian muttered, "if it wasn't for this place, we'd all go mad."

Marlon bought the drinks across, and the Daredevils swarmed over. One of them picked up the whiskey bottle and took a long pull.

Enqvist looked about idly. "Where are the girls?"

One of his riders nodded at the doors and spoke excitedly. "They're coming. Now we're here."

The glass porch doors swung open and a flock of the Rocking Robins dancers burst in, all chattering at once in an excited ensemble. They were dressed in flowery blouses and black dresses and congregated around the bar's central tables.

Enqvist turned to Marlon. "Hey, old-timer. Get some wine over there. Or whatever they want." Then, he grabbed his beer, wedged his cigarette into the corner of his mouth and led his team over towards the Robins, as if drawn by some magnetic force.

Corky shook his head as he watched them go. He then frowned as he noticed many of the dancers ignore the approaching men and stare back in the opposite direction, towards a side door that led to the canteen. Corky followed the gazes. He couldn't help but chuckle.

There he was. Who else but Gino Shapiro. He waltzed in, waving to no one in particular, arm in arm with a smartly dressed woman in a trouser suit. One of the Robins, a friendly youngster Corky knew as Belinda, raced from the table across to him. He bowed elegantly, and led both women towards the bar.

Shapiro, dressed in a flamboyant black leather jumpsuit, approached Corky. "Good evening, clown," he said loudly. "Look at you, all alone."

"Something you've probably never known, Gino," came the curt reply.

Shapiro laughed out loud. "How right you are, my dear clown. Please allow me to introduce Carol Baxter, from the Los Angeles Tribune. She is doing a feature on me for her paper. Exclusive. All access."

"Actually," the sharply dressed woman said, "the feature is on the circus."

"I am the circus!" he cried, before laughing over-enthusiastically. His arm was clamped around her back. He looked at Belinda, who hovered awkwardly to his side. "You remember dear Belinda, of course."

Corky nodded at the youngster, who was trying to catch the trapeze artist's attention.

"Marlon!" Shapiro cried. "Champagne all round. I have the honour of being in the company of two beautiful women. Nothing but champagne will do at such a momentous time."

"I'll have a soda water," Carol said dryly. She moved away from him and began looking around the bar studiously.

"Gino," Belinda was saying, as the flyer gazed after the newspaper woman. "Can we talk? About the movie people? You remember…you said you could put me in touch with someone at Asensia Studios."

Shapiro turned to watch Marlon pour four flutes of champagne. "I did? Dear angel, I know lots of people in Hollywood. You come out with me after the season, when I go to work in the movies. Then, we will figure it out." He took two glasses and handed her one. The youngster stared at it as if in a trance. She took it and had a small sip. Shapiro kept laughing. "A beautiful girl like you, who can sing and dance, you have no trouble picking up work. They love the musicals out there at the moment."

He nonchalantly clicked glasses with her and took a long pull on his champagne. As if in a panic, he looked around the bar, trying to find Carol Baxter. When he saw her talking to one of the cowboys, his face seemed to drop.

"I can't wait to go to Hollywood with you, Gino," Belinda was saying. Shapiro placed an arm around her tiny frame. "Me too, darling girl."

Suddenly, a steady murmuring built up across the bar floor. Heads turned once again, this time to the main glass doors.

"Hey look!" someone cried. "It's Roddy!"

Everyone seemed to say something at once as several people stood up in the now crowded barroom.

Olsen had walked through the main doors, with Suzy beside him. As he entered the room, several of the Robins rushed over to hug him, while the roustabouts, the Range Riders and even one of the catering staff all approached to offer well wishes.

"You were just terrific on Steve Irving, kid. Way to go!"

"Welcome back, Roddy. We saw the show. You were great!"

"That glass of water trick was really something…"

Olsen shook hands with everyone as he made his way to the bar. "Thank you, thank you," he said jovially. Suzy smiled grandly and whispered excitedly to the others as she followed him.

Finally, Olsen made it to the bar and came face to face with Shapiro, who had watched the whole episode with a wry smile.

The two stood straight and studied one another, like two gunslingers in the old west waiting for the other to draw first.

The crowd quietened down, fascinated as ever by the rivalry between the two stars. Everyone stared at the showdown. Even Tip Enqvist and his Daredevils watched with interest.

Finally, Shapiro spoke. "Welcome back, dollmaker," he said dryly. "A commendable performance on the television last night. My compliments."

Olsen stared at him blankly. "Thank you, Gino. It was a pleasure to be involved."

Shapiro seemed to laugh slightly at some unknown joke. "You make the people in TV land laugh. But can you do it again…on the road? In our show?"

Suzy moved from behind Olsen and pouted angrily. "You know damn well he can! Roddy's record speaks for itself. Why, I was in the audience last night. People were screaming his name!"

Yet again Shapiro laughed softly. "I don't doubt it, child. I just hope our doll master can do it again. In the big cities. Because this season is the biggest yet." His dark eyes shifted to Olsen. "The chairman tells me you are going on third this time. I suppose that is a good slot. For you."

Olsen's steely gaze never left Shapiro. The humour and customary coolness had vanished. "I'm happy with it."

"Si, this is good. The audience…they need warming up. Before the main event, y'know."

At the bar, Corky rolled his eyes. But Suzy had heard enough. "Gino, you talk garbage!" she cried in her high-pitched voice. "Roddy is a bigger star than you will ever be! The Klondike's Circus Fan Club has exceeded a thousand members, all because of Roddy and his puppets. And you can't handle it. You've been on top for so long, you've forgotten how it feels to be anywhere else!"

Shapiro shook his head and waved a hand through the air. "You speak highly of your hero, child. Maybe you want something more from him, eh? You think we can't all see it?"

Olsen took a step forward. "Alright, Gino. Now that is enough. Back off."

"Or what, Olsen?" Shapiro seemed to puff himself up as he stood there. "You want trouble with me, huh?"

"Jesus Christ!" one of the Range Riders called over to them as the whole group of patrons huddled around the pair. "Can't you two knock it off? You're on the same side, god damn it. The same team. Why can't you work together? To help us be number one?"

Olsen squinted at Shapiro as they stood toe to toe. "He's right," he murmured. "It's always the same story. Why the hell can't you offer encouragement? Be supportive."

Suzy had remained beside him. "Because he's scared of you."

Again Shapiro laughed wildly. "Scared? Why the hell would I be scared of a boy playing with dolls?" He ran a hand through his swarthy black hair. Then he looked up sullenly. "No, Olsen. I respect you…what you do, amigo. I know your talent. But, dammit, this is the big top, baby. We are battling to be number one! Not just in America…in the world! I need you to be at your very best. For the whole tour. Remember, you are still a newcomer here. You need to keep, how do you say, setting the bar higher. To be the best."

Olsen nodded faintly. His mind flashed back to a private meeting with Shapiro in his dressing room immediately after the TV special Circus of the Stars two years earlier. That night, Gino had suggested that if the circus ever closed, the two of them should perform together in a new show. There was a strange, surreal respect buried somewhere in the man's conscience.

"That," Olsen said quietly, "is my mantra. To get better. Every show. To be the best. The very best."

Shapiro watched him and gave a nod. "We have that in common, amigo. But, you remember, that is my name at the top of the bill. I take all the risks here. Every performer is judged through me. That's what I have to live with. That is real pressure."

The two men stared at each other for a few more seconds. Then, as the patrons watched eagerly, Shapiro finally broke into a smile. He grasped his champagne, put an arm lazily around Belinda and began to lead her away from the commotion he had created. "Come, sweetness, let's get away from all this craziness. We have much to discuss."

"If you say so," the girl mumbled, as her fellow Robins glared at her from the centre tables.

Olsen and Suzy finally stood at the bar, next to a bemused Corky. "I almost stepped in," the clown mused as he supped his beer.

Olsen shrugged. "Don't you ever get tired of being a referee, Corky?"

"Hell, sometimes, I guess. I used to be the one feuding with Gino. Now, he is more concerned with you, kid."

"I had noticed."

The veteran clown looked at the young ventriloquist and smiled. "I'm looking forward to seeing you in action again, Rod."

Olsen tapped him on the back as Suzy collected two sodas from the bar. "Right back at ya, legend."

With that, Olsen and Suzy wandered off to a corner table.

Corky watched them, and was joined by Marlon behind the bar.

The atmosphere became more relaxed as everyone settled down at their tables again.

"What I tell ya?" Marlon rasped. "It's all a show."

Chapter Four

To anyone gracing the prairies and foothills surrounding Napa Valley and Marin County, it was a most glorious sight.

Cruising gently along the railroad that ran through the quaint countryside, the red and blue painted Barrowman Express train mowed across the land like a fire cracker through a clear sky.

Compared to the usual traffic found on the Pacific Railroad—Amtrak passenger trains and freight haulers—it was a wild and exotic new proposition.

Thirty-two carriages long in total, the steel carts were painted in patterns resembling the big top, with traditional wooden signs advertising the many attractions.

Included within the realms of the railroad behemoth were staterooms for all the talent and staff, a bunkhouse and quarters for the roustabouts, a dining cart, lounge and communal carriage, boxes and travelling stables for all the show's horses, and 18 equipment storage crates.

The circus train left the main line at Napa, slowing almost to a halt, and picked up a branch line that led the few short miles to the railroad siding at Rio Cristo.

As the great Express slowly crawled towards the circus camp, workers and performers ran from their trailers and cabins to greet her. Many cheered and waved enthusiastically as the train finally slowed to a complete stop at the head of the siding, which nosed into a small, pinewood building, known as the station house, at the top of the encampment. From there, it would travel in reverse back to the main line.

A sea of activity greeted the train driver as he jumped down from his cab.

An assortment of vehicles were now being driven towards the train, ready to be placed aboard in the storage carriages. Tractors, jeeps and several small vans bounded across the gravel. The Daredevils followed behind on their red and black motorbikes, which would be stored in a special garage block onboard.

And all around, various figures walked rapidly, excitedly towards the train—their home for the next five months.

Klondike watched the whole escapade from a porch outside the station house. He puffed soberly on a cigar and eyed his ensemble with pleasure as everyone headed for the train.

As was customary, many approached to offer him a greeting.

Tip Enqvist was the first, breaking away from his team and riding his bike over.

"Good to see you, Kal," he called out as he pulled up, engine running.

"Is everything ok, Tip?"

"Just fine. The bikes are in top condition. And so are the men. Ready to be stars. Ha!"

Klondike grinned. "That's the spirit. Just do what you've been doing up to now. Everyone will be amazed."

Enqvist patted his bike. "To hear that wonderful applause in your big cities, I would've walked from Oslo."

Klondike changed the subject. "What do you think of the new train?"

The stunt rider grunted as he looked up at the great locomotive. "As long as it gets us to the people. That's all that matters."

Klondike winced inwardly. Would anyone be impressed by his new train, he wondered. "Look after your boys," he muttered as Enqvist revved the engine and waved, before motoring over towards the centre of the train.

Next to approach were another group of newcomers, The Flying Batistas. Raul Batista, his wife Maria and their young sons Tony and Rodrigo. Raul bowed as the family walked by and stopped, as if paying homage to the boss.

"On behalf of my family," Raul said in a heavy Mexican accent, "thank you again, so much, for having us in your show. We will not let you down, Señor Klondike."

"It is I who must thank you all," Klondike rasped. "You chose me! We are delighted to have you aboard. A family of acrobats…you are all incredible."

The foursome all bowed again. Maria blew a kiss. "When we come to America," she said, stammering, "we dream of being in circus show. Big top show. Now, we have dream. Now, dream is reality. You are in our hearts, Mr Kal."

Klondike smiled widely. "Bless you all," he said, trying to sound equally humble and eloquent.

The family moved on.

Klondike could not help but grin when he saw the participants of the circus's renowned Showcase Revue wander towards the railroad siding.

The bizarre group looked like a surreal representation of human extremities. There was Gargantua, the human blob, who weighed more than 400lbs but could somehow perform cartwheels, handstands and various acrobatics. Goliath, a 7ft 6in hillbilly farmer, had become the circus's giant. A sad-looking, heavily bearded man, he had no talent as such and merely paraded around, causing shock and awe to just about everyone who glimpsed him. That was his life, and he accepted it.

Following the two giants were six midgets dressed in dinner jackets. Percy Pringle and his Dancing Dwarves were a well-established vaudeville act on the West Coast circuit, who joined Klondike's Circus each summer as part of their schedule. The team performed somersaults and vaulting, and incorporated Goliath into their act, with the big man catching and holding the entire team in his midst as they jumped onto his frame.

And then there was Rumpy Stiltskin, a talented stilt walker who could complete all sorts of actions while standing on six-foot tall wooden stilts. Even now, he wandered towards the train on his tall planks.

"Well, well, well," Klondike muttered as he greeted the unusual ensemble. "How the paying public have missed you guys over the winter. Everyone alright?"

Of all people, Percy Pringle had established himself as the Revue's spokesman. "Everyone is just fine, Kal, thank you," he said in his high-pitched Southern accent. "Happy to be moving out…at last."

Klondike could not helping staring, transfixed, at the performers. They were quite a sight. "You've been happy at the camp?"

Pringle nodded. "Extremely. You've done a helluva job with this place, Kal. And this train! She looks a beauty."

Klondike smiled widely, relieved. "Wait till you see inside, boys."

Gargantua spoke up, in his usual snarling voice. "You got enough food on there, Mistuh Klondike?"

"You bet. All you want. The kitchen is well stacked." That seemed to appease the behemoth.

Klondike glanced up at Goliath, the perpetually sad old farmer. He was still wearing his denim dungarees, the same one he'd worn when they had first met.

"And you, Gol? Happy to be back?"

Goliath sighed. "I guess." He thought for a moment. "It will be nice to see all the big cities again."

Klondike patted his back as he waded past, like a grizzly bear seeking shelter.

Rumpy Stiltskin waltzed by on his stilts, and asked his usual question: "The bar all stocked?"

"Of course," Klondike rasped, irritated. "Just take it easy on that stuff, huh?"

Rumpy laughed and dismounted from the stilts, before walking slowly along with them placed over his shoulder.

As everyone slowly made their way across the camp, Klondike was joined at the station house by Heavy, Lacey and Richie Plum, who had all walked across from the offices.

They all watched in muted fascination at the scene of endless commotion before them. The circus was a well-drilled unit, of that there was little doubt. The roustabouts worked in small teams to transport the equipment and supplies into the train carriages.

Jim McCabe, the circus foreman, directed all operations, barking out orders and overseeing everything, a clipboard in his grip.

"Y'know," Heavy began, mesmerised, "one day I'm going to commission an artist to paint this scene. Then, when I retire, I'll hang the picture over my fireplace. It sure is a beautiful sight."

Lacey laughed gaily, tucking her arm inside his. "The beginning of an adventure. The open road. Cross country. What's not to love, boys?"

"I got to hand it you, Kal," Plum was saying, wandering idly before them as he surveyed the scene all around. "That train is a real piece of work. An expensive outlay, yes, but she's a beauty."

Klondike nodded happily. "You said it, Richie. Hell, it was overdue."

They all watched as Roddy Olsen, Suzi Dando and Corky the Clown walked towards the train together. They waved happily as they approached the station house.

"Roll on the midway!" Corky cried in his usual enthusiastic manner. They all exchanged pleasantries.

Olsen gazed at Lacey. She nodded back at him. Everyone in the circus knew that it was Lacey who had originally persuaded Klondike to take the ventriloquist on after he had appeared out of nowhere one day, seeking an audition. The rest was history. The publicity expert had advised him extensively, and had even chosen his stage attire.

"Ah Roddy," she gushed, "you were fantastic on Steve Irving the other night."

Olsen smiled like a child. "Thank you, Lacey. So glad you caught it."

"Are you kidding? I wouldn't have missed it for the world. Our boy…the kid from nowhere…on The Steve Irving Show! It's so completely fantastic."

"Yeah," Olsen said, "well, I owe it all to you guys."

Klondike nodded at the large suitcase Olsen was carrying. "Are the guys all ready for the new season?" he said, referring to Olsen's puppets, locked away inside the big trunk.

"You bet. They're all arguing about who the true star is. Wait till you see it."

"I can hardly wait for that," Klondike mused. He never ceased to be amazed by Olsen's voice skills.

Lacey took a few steps towards Olsen and Suzi. "You young ones take care, now. We've got some major cities on the horizon."

"Oh, don't worry, Miss Tanner," Suzi said, linking her arm through Olsen's. "We're practically circus veterans now."

With that, the two of them breezed away towards the accommodation carts, Corky following behind.

Heavy was laughing as they watched the trio walk away. "I love it!" he rasped. He turned to Klondike. "I'll be damned if this isn't the best line-up we ever had, Kal."

Klondike rolled his cigar in his mouth. "Hard to argue with that, old buddy."

"And look who's coming next!" Plum cried excitedly.

They all looked back towards the camp to see Gino Shapiro and Penny Fortune ambling across the gravel.

The flyers were dressed in their orange show tracksuits, and simply looked like stars.

Shapiro moved across to the station house, and addressed the gathering in his usual grandiose manner. "Mr Chairman," he roared, as if giving a speech to hundreds, "Madame Publicist. Mr Announcer. And my dear Richie. My compliments on a first-rate winter camp. Penny and I have been delighted with the facilities. And congratulations, Chairman, on this beautiful, new train. It is our delight to travel on board." He cleared his throat. "This experience has been truly beautiful. So, my executive team, I salute you."

He turned to Penny, who stood staring at him in dismay. "And the most beautiful part of this winter has been the emergence of dear Penny, who I have no hesitation in proclaiming as the next big superstar of the circus."

He bowed, as if ushering his partner on to a stage. Penny stood there awkwardly, then waved at the assembled gathering. "Well, what can I say? Thank you all for having me. I'm thrilled."

Klondike nodded. "Happy to have you, Penny. Just keep our superstar here in check, huh?"

"Bravo, chairman," Shapiro cried. He placed an arm around Penny. "Come, mamacita. I take you now to your stateroom."

The orange-clad pair slid away.

Again, Heavy burst out laughing as he watched them go.

The train was now slowly filling up—with people and equipment. Klondike turned to his three lieutenants. "Well, folks, you better get your bags and hop aboard. This train's gunna be blowing some trail dust pretty soon."

Heavy jumped off the porch. He shook hands with Klondike. "Good luck in Vegas, Kal."

"Thanks, old buddy. Don't worry, I'll smack it outta the ballpark."

"No doubt."

Lacey clasped Klondike's hand in both of her own. Her skin felt like silk to him. "Take care, tiger. We'll see you in LA."

"You bet."

Plum shook hands with the boss, then joined the other two in heading across the camp.

Klondike picked up his cane and jostled it in his hands as he looked on. He drawled casually to himself.

"All aboard."

A half hour later, the air-piercing wail of the train's horn told anyone within a one-mile radius that the express was finally ready to roll.

A few more toots followed and a mighty chugging sound seemed to make the earth move as the great steel wheels finally began to move.

Then, like an awoken giant, the mighty train finally began to move, a few inches at first and then slowly gliding along the track, the noise from its engines and pistons carrying in the wind.

Klondike was still stood solitary at the station house, smoking his cigar. He watched forlornly as the new train rolled away, waving absent-mindedly at the machine. Idly, he wondered if anyone was watching onboard.

The great clouds of dust that had misted up the landscape slowly drained away, and the bright red and blue express disappeared into the rolling countryside beyond the camp.

Klondike turned from the railroad siding and stared at the now empty camp all around.

The helicopter would be back tomorrow to take him to Las Vegas. Until then, he had one more night in his beloved headquarters, and then it was the open road again.

Lost in his thoughts, he paced slowly across the gravel towards the pavilion.

"Gets mighty quiet once they're all gone, don't it?"

He looked up. It was Marlon, the old bartender. He was carrying a box of glasses across from a store room. The old-timer acted as the camp caretaker during the summer months.

Klondike chuckled. "I'll bet you enjoy the peace, Marlon."

The barman walked in step with him as they approached the main building. "Can't deny that, boss man. Hell, I get the bar to myself."

"Well," Klondike drawled, "maybe tonight we'll share it, huh?" He eyed the old-timer as they walked. "You still know how to hold a straight flush?"

Marlon cackled. "Been a while, but I can still play a mean game of stud."

"Perfect. I'll be over at 8."

An old pick-up truck rumbled steadily down the main Midwest California freeway, heading south.

It was the dead of the night, and the highway was eerily quiet and deserted, the truck's headlights piercing the deep darkness and finding no other traffic.

The old motor slowed as a sign advertised O'Bannion's, one of many roadhouse cafes scattered along the freeway, sitting like liners in a vast ocean.

The truck pulled up into a side lane as it neared the roadhouse, and eventually slowed to a stop beside the parking lot.

A lean figure dressed all in black carrying a large tote bag and smaller leather case bundled out of the passenger seat onto the asphalt. As the truck pulled away again, he waved absently at the driver.

Then, he wandered across to a call box outside the roadhouse. Once inside the booth, he pulled a scrap of paper out of his pocket, deposited a handful of nickels and dialled a number written on the sheet.

"Who is this?" a deep voice blared after the third ring.

"It's me. Vesnick. You told me to call once I reached LA."

There was a pause. "Oh. Oh yeah. Right. Where are you now?"

"Pasadena."

Another pause. "Good. That's real good. OK. Get yourself set up someplace. Then, on Friday, get yourself to the Health Club. On Flanders Street. Downtown. Come for lunchtime. You got all that?"

"The Health Club? What the hell is that?"

"Just you get yourself there, sonny boy. You'll see."

"Listen, I was wondering, you said before that—"

The line went dead.

Vesnick pulled the phone away from his ear and stared at it dumbly. Then, with a shrug, he picked up his bags and left the call box, eyeing the roadhouse with curious eyes.

Chapter Five

Klondike could not help feeling deeply sentimental and nostalgic as he strode through the gaming floor of the Golden Dune casino in Las Vegas.

Two years earlier, the circus had delivered one of its most memorable shows ever in a specially constructed big top in the casino's parking lot. The blockbuster special had been beamed live on national television and had become a renowned landmark in circus folklore.

Now, the casino was doing better than ever.

As Klondike walked across the gaudy gold carpeting on the gaming floor, he smiled happily at the mass of gamblers gathered around the card tables, crap pits and slots. It was barely 10 in the morning, and the place was heaving. The endless ringing of the one-armed bandits and varied cheers of joy and cries of frustration permeated the atmosphere.

Everywhere he looked, cocktail waitresses in jazzy gold dresses waltzed by serving drinks, while patrons wandered from game to game, a pile of chips invariably in their grasp.

He had arrived the previous night in Addison's helicopter and had spent the night in one of the hotel's penthouse suites.

Having spent the morning looking around and enjoying a leisurely breakfast, he was now on the way to his meeting with Claude Hershey.

He finally moved off the gaming floor and headed for a lift bank, manoeuvring himself to a large, gold-plated elevator that had a sign saying VIP STATION above it.

A giant, musclebound man in a suit was seemingly guarding the doors.

Klondike smiled up at him. "I'm Kal Klondike. Mr Hershey is expecting me."

The giant did not say a word, merely pressing a button to open the elevator doors before motioning for Klondike to get in. He then followed suit and selected the top floor.

Up they went.

"Klondike, you old dog!"

Claude Hershey roared with laughter as he offered his guest a cigar from a silver box.

His plush executive office was on the top floor of the casino complex, and its huge windows offered a panoramic view of the Nevada desert beyond.

Hershey seemed full of delight. "I never stopped reading about you, these past two years. Ever since our big show that time." He cackled again. "Look at you…what a couple years you've had. America's great circus man, eh? You've had great success. And I congratulate you with all my heart."

"Thank you," Klondike replied, slightly off-balance. He took a cigar and smelt it with relish. "You haven't done so bad yourself, old partner. Hell, you can hardly move down there on the gaming floor. It's like market day on Bastian Wharf down there. You must be making some serious dough, Claude."

Hershey swatted a hand through the air. He produced a gold-plated lighter and they both lit up.

Klondike looked at him. He was a huge bull of a man with receding grey hair that was slicked back, above a reddened, rubbery face with fierce brown eyes.

They had known each other for years, since the early 1950s when Hershey owned a small gaming joint called The Roxy and Klondike had put on one of his first independent circuses at a ballpark that was part of The Roxy's grounds. He had been an ardent supporter of Klondike's Circus down the years and had helped generate interest from Nevada's moneymen.

"We've gone from strength to strength," Hershey was saying. "But, then again, all of Vegas has. We've got a new joint opening up every few weeks right now. The Strip is filling up. Downtown too. Seems like every little rich boy schmuck in the West thinks it would be fun to run a casino. And then there's the names coming out here. Sinatra. Martin. Garland. There's even talk of Elvis coming. Can you imagine?"

Klondike puffed thoughtfully, savouring the taste. "That newsreader was right when he called it a boom town. It's only going to get bigger, Claude."

"Damn right. Way I see it, before long there's gunna be more money here in the desert than in most other states combined. We's all gunna be in competition. Thinking of more and more crazy ways to make money."

"Everything's a competition, Claude. Look at me with the circus. It's an annual fight to be number one."

Hershey nodded. "Ever since our show, Kal. Since then, there are more casinos cropping up. And more and more circuses."

"Sure. We're in direct competition with four or five other big tops nationwide to be the main draw in America. A lot of money hasbeen pumped into our industry lately."

Hershey placed his cigar in his mouth and smiled devilishly. "Which brings me to the reason I asked you out here."

Klondike smiled. "I had wondered."

Hershey cackled again. "Yeah. Well, ever since our show in '58 I've been thinking about trying to put another circus show on. But, like I say, everyone is thinking big these days. And, well Kal, I'm thinking big too. Real big."

"I'm listening."

Hershey nodded firmly. "OK. I have a proposition for you, my man. Here is my idea." He sat back, holding his cigar and stabbing the air with it as he spoke. "A circus supershow. For the first time ever, three different big tops all combine and join together for a one-off, once in a lifetime extravaganza. Talent from different shows, all together in one tent. It will be like one of these rock 'n' roll music festivals. Star names from across the board, all performing in one show. The biggest acts. Three circuses. One show."

Klondike nodded thoughtfully, impressed. The idea was hot. It was typical of Hershey, the grand showman. "And my circus is one of the big three, eh?"

"You better believe it," Hershey said. "Klondike's Circus, out of California. Chico's Circus, out of Chicago. And Wurley's, out of New York of course. Three of the best."

Klondike smiled thinly. "You've left out Ribbeck…"

Hershey grunted. "Like that old snake would ever go for it!"

"That's true." Klondike thought for a moment. "Alright, I like it. Is there more?"

Hershey stood suddenly, pacing the room. "Three of the biggest circuses in America will unite for the ultimate showpiece of entertainment and patriotism. It will be called Superstars and Stripes. On July 4, at the Washington Polo Grounds." He eyed his guest keenly. "How do you like em apples, hot shot?"

Klondike grinned. "Very much." He inhaled deeply on the cigar and exhaled slowly. "Superstars and Stripes. That's excellent, Claude. Hell of an idea." He squinted up at his host. "Have you sounded out Chico and Zack Wurley yet?"

Hershey answered instantly. "My representatives are on the case right now. The word is they are keen. But..." he smiled knowingly. "Only if Kal Klondike comes on board."

"I might have known."

"Yeah, you're all rivals, I know that. This is a one-off. A spectacle. I'll pay you all the same fee. My angle is that the whole thing is a Golden Dune production. I run all the circuit advertising and everything in the programme."

"That makes sense." Klondike's mind was suddenly alive. "Who do you want from my troupe?"

Hershey looked down at him. "Well, Gino and Roddy for sure. Corky, I guess. And we definitely want those bikers doing that Globe of Death act. That scares the hell outta folks. I love it!"

"OK, OK," Klondike mused. "We can make this work." He thought rapidly. "I have terms as well. And maybe a bonus for you, Claude."

Hershey stared at him, transfixed. "Keep talking, man."

"Gino and Roddy should get top billing. They are TV stars. Gino has been in movies. Chico and Wurley can't match that kind of exposure. And Gino will demand he goes on last."

Hershey waved a hand through the air again. "Done, Kal. What's this bonus?"

Klondike's eyes seemed to glow. "My man at ATV, Steve Irving, may well be interested in buying broadcast rights to this...this Superstars and Stripes. It's right up his street. He has helped produce several TV specials before, so why not with this? A historic night for the circus industry?"

Hershey was grinning like a hyena. "I love it. Get him onboard and we're made. Made! I never even thought about getting this gig on TV."

"Well, it's like you said. We're all thinking bigger these days."

"Do you think he'll go for it?"

Klondike smiled, warming to the plans. "I reckon he just might. The ATV lawyers will draw up a contract. We can split the rights fee between us, Claude. That would make me executive producer."

Hershey, as was his way, burst out laughing yet again. He meandered back to his chair and fell into the smooth leather. "That's beautiful, Kal. Just beautiful. You're one step ahead of all of us on this already."

"Well, we need to draw up a stage plan. Then there's rehearsals, scripting, logistics. You, me, Chico and Wurley all need to get together for sure…"

Hershey was shaking his hands excitedly. "Leave all that to me, Kal. You get your man Irving on board and just make it to Washington for July 4."

Klondike nodded. "That should be fine. We play in Washington on June 21 before Philadelphia and then New York on July 2. Getting the express back down to Washington shouldn't be a problem." He thought for a moment. "Then, after that, we head back West. This could all fall into place just fine, Claude."

The casino owner could not stop smiling. "I studied your routes. All three circuses. I knew you'd be close by."

Klondike nodded in admiration. "Looks like you thought of everything, old partner."

"Well, it's like everything out here in Vegas. You've got to play your cards right. Hedge your bets."

"And up the ante," Klondike added, laughing.

"So…" Hershey said, extending a hand. "Do we have a deal?"

Klondike leant across the desk. "You bet we do!"

The two men shook hands warmly. The sunlight streaming in through the large floor to ceiling windows seemed to illuminate them both. They stared at each other.

"Now," Hershey muttered, rustling through some papers on his giant desk. "Just leave things to me for now. Enough business talk." He eyed his guest like a Boardwalk confidence hustler eyeing a mark. "How's your poker game these days?"

Klondike chuckled. "Good. Still on a bit of a hot streak. I guess overall this year I'm up."

Hershey nodded, eyes alive. "You want in on tonight's Executive Game?"

The Executive Game. Hershey's almost nightly poker match. Always featuring the biggest whales in his joint. It was played in a private grotto behind the gaming floor. Klondike had been invited to the big table several times down the years. The competitors were always a mix of high-rollers and rich businessmen. And Hershey himself always took a chair.

Klondike smiled proudly. "What time is the first cut?" They both laughed again.

A curious mix of scantily-clad showgirls, tuxedo-wearing players and out-of-town tourists dressed in shorts and T-shirts all wandered casually by as Klondike stood in the main corridor of the casino floor.

He was simply watching the enthralling spectacle before him, as people piled into the joint from the Strip and almost literally threw their money at the tables and slots.

It was difficult to comprehend, the sheer money-making prowess that sat all around him. A true dollar-collecting enterprise.

Shaking his head, he noticed the 'Sahara Bar' to his right and slowly wandered over, clutching a morning newspaper. His only plan right now was to read the Yankees match report while enjoying a cool beer. The Executive Game wasn't for another seven hours, so he could certainly relax.

As he strolled casually along the gaudy gold and green carpeting, he failed to notice a figure move in-step behind him.

"Let's go Cobras!"

Klondike froze all over. He went stiff as a rake, his mind racing as he wondered if he was hearing things. Had he caught sun stroke out here in the desert? He stood perfectly still. He recognised the voice. From way back. But refused to believe it could possibly be true.

Slowly, as if in a trance, he turned to face the speaker.

There in the corridor, not six feet away, stood a tall man dressed in a dark suit. His black hair was slicked back tight to his scalp. But his most defining feature, one that nobody would ever forget, was the hideous, flaming scar that ran down the right side of his face. It started at his eyelid and ended at the corner of his mouth. It was an ugly face, and had been a useful tool in a lifetime of intimidation.

Klondike glared at him in shock. "Agostino!"

The stranger smiled. "Well, well, well. You never know who's you going to bump into out here in Sin City." His Brooklyn accent was unmistakeable, a deep, throaty drawl.

Klondike was incredulous. "It's really you!"

"You bet it is," he spat out. He surveyed the circus boss shrewdly. "Terry Calder. Oh, I'm sorry, they don't call you that no more. Ain't that right, Mr Kal Klondike? Huh? The big time circus man, now."

"What..." Klondike was still struggling to believe what he was seeing. "What in god's name are you doing here? How...how did you know I was in town?"

Agostino's cold, dark eyes seemed to twinkle under the neon lights all around. "I got business out here. A stake in a casino downtown. But I was here at the Dune looking to get a little of Claude Hershey's action. Then, whatya know, I heard my old buddy Terry was here. In this very building! I didn't want to miss this chance to see an old friend. An old team-mate."

"Jesus," Klondike breathed. He found himself looking around the casino floor. His nerves were suddenly on edge. Something felt wrong. "I don't know what to say, Paul. It's been, what, 25 years? I, hell, I never thought I'd see YOU again. After all that, back then."

Agostino glared at him. He was truly a frightening-looking individual. "Yeah. Yeah, I figured that, Terry. All that stuff was a long time ago, ain't that right?" He smirked. "Look at you now, eh? You made it out. Outta Hell's Kitchen. You's one of the lucky ones. Hell, I know all about it. Your time in the Army. The war. Italy and the fall of Berlin. You's a god damn hero, man. And then the circus. Your circus. I saw your crew on TV. You's getting bigger and bigger. I'm proud of you, Terry."

Klondike nodded slightly. He was unnerved. This felt like some kind of trap. "Nobody's called me Terry in a long time now."

"That's what I hear. You've gone up in the world now. Forgotten all about your old friends in the Kitchen."

"That's not exactly true."

Agostino rolled back his head. "Oh, that's right. That big tub of guts is still watching your back. Like before. Keeping you safe."

Klondike was beginning to turn. This supposedly chance meeting was starting to feel like a shakedown. Despite his concerns, he was ready to stand up to Paul Agostino.

Vividly, like a long-forgotten nightmare, he remembered some of the old street fights he had been involved in with the Cobras all those years ago. In the back alleys, when he was a kid. He recalled Agostino's actions. That big fight with the Barracudas. The gang leader had been a vicious, near-psychotic brawler, excited by the violence.

But what now?

He motioned at Agostino's shiny suit. "You look like you're doing alright now, Paul."

Agostino smiled thinly. "You don't know the half of it. You remember the Kitchen? Brooklyn? Five Points?"

"Of course."

"Now, I own it. It belongs to me."

"What?"

"The action, man. It's all mine. Gambling, hookers, protection. I control our old districts. A Capo. One of the big five. I report only to Scalini in Manhattan." He took a step forwards and gave a sinister scowl. "I'm at the top. The top. You understand me?"

Klondike eyed him steadily, but felt uneasy all over. It wasn't hard to understand what had happened. Agostino had bossed a street gang. Their raids and actions must have eventually got noticed by the Mob. From there, he must have been initiated and somehow climbed the ranks of power within the syndicate.

"My god," Klondike breathed, "the Mob, huh? Hell, Paul, and you say I've come a long way. It sounds like you've tasted the real power."

"You've got no idea." Agostino slowly lit a cigarette. He was surveying Klondike in a peculiar fashion, like an alligator eyeing its next meal. "It's like the old days, really. We don't make trouble. We just end it."

Klondike nodded warily. He thought over his next move carefully. "Well, old friend, it has been a big surprise seeing you again after all these years. Incredible really, Paul. A real pleasure. But, ah, I'm sorry. I have so much to do. I'm sure you can imagine. Now, if you'll excuse me I—"

"You haven't given me a figure."

Klondike frowned. "A figure? What figure? What are you talking about?"

Agostino laughed humourlessly. "You don't get it, huh?"

"Get what?" He was losing patience, gangster or no gangster.

"Why do you think I cornered you down here by the crap tables? I don't waste time on reunions no more, Terry. I only talk business. Now..." he ran a hand through his wet, oily hair. "It ain't no secret. I want a piece of your circus. I done the research. Klondike's Circus is a huge earner. You're making more green than any big top in the country. You…my old compadre Terry Calder. Who would've thought? Well, now I want in." He moved even closer, staring at Klondike intently. "So. 250 Gs. For a 50 per cent piece of your action. You like? Or you gunna give me a figure of you's own?"

Klondike kept frowning. The conversation had taken the turn he had been fearing. "Paul…" he began quietly. "I don't know what you've heard, or what you think we do out here. But…there is no stake to be had. I run the circus. I own the company, with help from a few fellow investors who are close confidants." He held up his hands. "I'm sorry, but it doesn't work like that. I thank you for your interest. But you've got the wrong idea."

Agostino's eyes narrowed. "The hell I have. You know what I am. What I represent. You don't say no to that. I want in, man."

Klondike quickly looked up and down the corridor. The confrontation was on. "Listen," he said tersely, "we were friends once, Agostino. Team-mates, yeah. But that was a long time ago. You're not the boss of me anymore, for Chrissakes. We're not kids now. This is serious."

"You're god damn right it is!"

"You've got the wrong idea. You think I'm gunna give you part of my circus…you must be outta your mind."

Agostino gave him a look that could only be described as murderous. "Nobody talks to me like that."

Klondike glared back. "This conversation is over, pal. Good luck in the Mob."

"You have a debt, Calder!"

Klondike had been about to push off. "Debt? What debt?"

Agostino smiled thinly. "You forget, eh? You forget it was me who got you started in the circus business. All those years ago."

Klondike eyed him, his mind racing. He had actually forgotten.

Agostino continued. "I got you that gig as a trick shot artist on Coney Island. You remember now, hot shot? Out there by the clowns and the dancing girls. You used to gun down those pins in your fancy cowboy outfit. You forget, eh? Well, I remember. I remember, Kal Klondike. That was your stage name back then, even. Now you're trying to turn that name into a legend. And it's all thanks to me."

Klondike nodded vaguely. Coney Island. Before the war. He looked Agostino in the eye again. "I remember, Paul. And I was grateful at the time. I told you that. But…" he took a deep breath. "As grateful as I am for the help back then…" he paused again. "It doesn't earn you a piece of my circus now. This is something entirely different. This is my business."

Agostino snarled. "You're still not cutting me in?"

"You're god damn right I'm not!"

"You rotten son of a bitch!" Agostino spat the words out, his face twisting with rage. The giant scar seemed inflamed as his anger rose. "You're making a big mistake, boy! You don't cut me in, you're gunna pay the price. A different price. I'll run you outta business. I can make that happen. Then…then you have nothing!"

Klondike tensed all over, made a fist, then thought better of it. Instead, he simply turned on the spot and strode away. He didn't look back, and quickened his pace slightly.

But Agostino's next words brought him to a standstill again. He sounded mellower this time as he called after the departing figure.

"Too bad about Catherine Hart."

Again, Klondike froze all over. It was like a flashlight was probing into his past. Memories, names, places…he hadn't thought of all this in years.

With a huff, he turned. "What about her?"

"Oh, you hadn't heard?" Agostino said conversationally. He raised his eyebrows in mock surprise. Now, he was enjoying the exchange. "Well, after the war, she hit hard times. Old Doctore closed down the Shaker Maker. She couldn't hold down a job nowhere. She came to work for me."

Now, he smiled sadistically. "At one of my strip joints. Doing tricks for bills. Poor girl, she hated it. But men love a pretty lady like that. So innocent. Childlike. I tried to help her get through it all. Gave her pills. To keep her going. But, well, she got hooked. Popping pills every day. Just to keep performing at the club. Then came the drink. She was a mess. Then, one day, she didn't turn up for her shift."

He eyed Klondike intently now, talking slowly. "They found her in a gutter. Among the garbage cans. The coroner said her heart had packed up. Just slowly rotted away…"

Klondike stared at him in disgust, his chest heaving. Then, with a wild snarl, he cried: "You son of a bitch!"

He raced towards Agostino, across the corridor, his nostrils flaring and eyes bulging.

Suddenly, as if in a pre-planned action, four men in suits identical to Agostino's appeared out of nowhere, surrounding him. All were significantly taller and brawnier than him, which became apparent as they rapidly encircled him.

Klondike stopped his movement, slowing to a halt two yards before the men in the dark suits. He stiffened again as the four newcomers all reached into their jackets, showing him their revolvers. They were like a well-trained military unit, their actions identical.

"You want a piece of me, Klondike? Come on!" Agostino wore a merciless sneer as he addressed him from within the mass of bodies. "The boys'll cut you down in no time. They won't shoot you. They'll beat you to death."

Klondike looked at the group with regret. "Still hiding behind the muscle, Paul?"

Agostino smiled smugly. "These men have all killed plenty. But they ain't killed as many as me. You remember that, cowboy."

"I'm not gunna remember any of this, cos it's all garbage."

Agostino nodded. He cocked his head. "When you want to talk about our business, you can reach me at the Beaumont Club, Manhattan. That's my base." He eyed him shrewdly. "Unless, that is, you want to talk now. Maybe you've thought over the alternative, eh?"

Klondike shook his head. "I have nothing to discuss with you." Yet again, he turned to leave.

"You're making a big mistake, Klondike."

This time, Klondike walked away for good. There was no backward glances. No regrets. He just wanted to get out of there.

Chapter Six

"Ladies and gentlemen…"

Heavy Brown's booming voice thundered over the PA system as he brought the microphone to his lips.

The thousands packed onto the wooden bleachers in the huge red and blue circus tent all stopped chatting excitedly and paid attention.

The large man in the scarlet red jacket and black top hat stood at the far end of the arena floor, near the entranceway flap. Before him lay a sea of sawdust, making up the circus floor.

Heavy continued. "Welcome to the greatest stage spectacular of them all. Welcome to Klondike's Circus! And now, to open our show, the wonders of the wild west, the kings among cowboys, please put your hands together for the fast-riding, hard-driving…Range Riders!"

Applause erupted around the big top as Heavy held his hat aloft and the team of 10 cowboys burst onto the floor on their immaculate-looking palomino horses.

The riders performed their usual tricks as the horses rode around the floor repeatedly. There were leapfrogs, mount jumps and all manner of stunts as the cowboys leapt from horse to horse, switching mounts as they raced around in a circle. And the crowd lapped it up.

Klondike's Circus had arrived in San Francisco two days earlier and everything had gone to plan so far with military-like precision. The tent was erected in Golden Gate Park, and its immensity seemed to dominate the skyline at sunset and sunrise.

Now, Heavy joined Lacey and Plum at the flap as the Range Riders showed off their full repertoire of tricks to hearty applause.

Next up were the Rocking Robins, who performed chorus line-style dances to old Broadway tunes played over the tannoy. Dressed immaculately in bright red skirts and leotard tops, their routine was a shot of traditional carnival entertainment.

They concluded their act with a showgirl-style dancehall piece, all linking arms together to form a long line and kicking their legs high in tandem. Every ankle almost hit its owner's head as the dancers showed off their sublime athleticism.

When their number was over and they bowed, the applause was hearty and justified.

Heavy nodded as he watched the patrons all around him in the bleachers, endlessly clapping and cheering. From down here at the flap, the seats seemed to rise up forever, into the summit of the tent high above.

"Kal was right about these dancers," he muttered to Lacey beside him. "People like traditional circus routines. Old school entertainment."

Lacey purred as she watched the Robins wave to the audience as they skipped off the sawdust floor. "These girls are top-level performers. Many of them have studied ballet and modern dance for years."

She waved as the dancers waltzed by towards the flap and exited the arena. Heavy nodded at Lacey as he picked up the mic again from its stand. "Your boy's on next."

Then, he addressed the crowd all around him. "And now, ladies and gentlemen, behold at the talents of the modern sensation of the circus…the wizard of ventriloquism…the Puppetmaster, Roddy Olsen!"

A roaring ovation broke out as Olsen wandered casually onto the floor, Rusty Fox on his arm. He approached a fresh mic stand in the arena's centre, and sat Rusty on an accompanying stool.

His current routine was an intriguing blend of old and new material. He chatted with his beloved fox puppet first, then he broke into the new "amazing water watch" skit.

Olsen followed that up with his best-known routine, as Rusty began singing the classic folk song Rock Island Line, only to be interrupted by a new voice emanating from an old suitcase lying by the stool. This was when Olsen introduced Napoleon, his old Army veteran character, into the act.

Once Napoleon was attached to Olsen, and he had a puppet on each arm, the three of them—two dummies and one master—all sang the song together. As always, the routine drew hearty applause.

After that, Rusty and Napoleon bickered back and forth for a while, before Olsen had enough and banished them both from the stage and back into the suitcase.

This prompted the introduction of Tony Tan, Olsen's Las Vegas crooner puppet. A long line of jokes about Tan's drinking problem then followed, before Olsen and the third puppet broke out into their rendition of the Frank Sinatra classic High Hopes.

As a thunderous applause broke out at the climax of the song, Olsen brought out Rusty and Napoleon and held all three puppets in his arms, bowing and waving their arms.

The youngster then placed all three figures into the case and carried it with him while he trotted to the flap, as a steward cleared away the stool.

Heavy shook hands with Olsen as he made his way back onto the sawdust.

Lacey gave the ventriloquist a big hug at the flap. "God, Roddy, I forgot how much I missed seeing you perform. Live! With all these wonderful fans."

Olsen nodded happily, glancing up at the packed seats that rose high above. "They are the greatest." His large green eyes fell upon the publicist next to him. "And so are you, Lacey."

"Why, thank you," she said awkwardly, hovering on the spot. They both smiled at each other, then Olsen turned and carried his puppets away, exiting the tent.

Next on stage was Corky and his fellow clowns.

The circus's current clown routine had Corky performing a few solo stunts—his unicycle juggling piece and the daring human cannonball act, which saw him 'fired' from a pretend plastic cannon into a giant net.

Then all the clowns performed a classic circus staple, the firesticks sketch.

This featured several clowns setting fire sticks alight and juggling them across the arena floor, while a separate team, led by Corky, played the role of firefighters attempting to douse the flames as the entertainers ran amok on the floor.

The sketch was particularly popular with children, who laughed happily at the wild antics.

Corky and his clowns were followed by the Flying Batistas, who performed a beguiling mixture of acrobatics and contortion acts. The family's showpiece involved Maria Batista standing on her husband Raul's shoulders. Eldest son Tony then hauled himself up onto his mother's shoulders before, incredibly, Rodrigo scrambled up the three bodies until he stood aloft Tony's shoulders.

The family held the surreal, unbelieving sight for a full 30 seconds, before the boys dismounted and the human ladder slowly fell to earth again.

The performance drew more hearty applause.

The Flying Batistas left the arena floor, to be replaced by fellow circus newcomers The Daredevils.

The motorcycle stunt riders raced onto the sawdust on their yellow and black motorcycles, performing a host of loops, wheelies and even a stunt where one team member ran on foot and leapfrogged over each rider as they zoomed towards him.

But everyone in the big top wanted to see one thing and one thing only. The Globe of Death.

The huge metal sphere, which resembled a circular cage, was wheeled out by a large team of roustabouts, and mounted on a mini-stage with a metal platform beneath it.

And then it began. The riders lined their bikes up in a queue. The first Daredevil mounted the ramp and drove slowly through a door into the cage. Once inside, the cage door was slammed shut and the biker began zooming round and round inside, eventually performing full 360-degree circles from top to bottom.

A second rider entered the Globe of Death, the door closed again and the man began executing his circles, the two riders storming around the cage and avoiding each other.

From there, each of the remaining four riders rode up into the cage, until all six were in there together, their motions a blur as they spun round, somehow avoiding any collision.

Tip Enqvist was the last of the Daredevils to enter the dome. As he reached the top of the ramp, poised on the edge of the sphere, he removed his helmet and whipped the crowd into even more of a frenzy by punching the air repeatedly. Then, he joined the chasm of madness.

All six riders were in the Globe of Death for about two minutes. It was a frightening, overwhelming sight. For many, it was hard to watch such was the high level of danger. The roar of the engines was also overpowering.

At the flap, Heavy found himself frowning at the proceedings. Richie Plum had a similar sour look. But Lacey smiled her usual winning smile.

"Jesus," Heavy was muttering as he surveyed the onslaught on the senses. "Every time I watch this madness, I feel sick."

"Tell me about it," Plum said, looking on wide-eyed. "These guys have got to be crazy."

Lacey laughed haughtily. "Ah, boys. These men are professionals. True sportsmen. Look at them. This is what happens when you practise like they do. Day in, day out. They are a machine."

Heavy baulked. "The only place I've seen them practising is in the bar. They drink like sailors. Out of work ones!"

The other two chuckled and all three felt a wave of relief as the riders finally slowed in the globe and wound down. The sphere door was opened and the Daredevils slowly exited the great structure, riding down the ramp and doing several celebratory laps of the circus floor, to wild, disbelieving applause.

Then, led as always by Enqvist, they raced out of the big top through the flap.

After such an adrenaline rush for the audience, it seemed both apt and very welcome that the next act was the Showcase Revue.

Gargantua, Goliath, Rumpy Stiltskin and Percy Pringle and the Dancing Dwarves all burst on to the arena floor, performing their acrobatics and comedic routines to great effect.

The closing finale, as always, saw Goliath carrying all six dwarves on his immense frame before slowly ambling off the floor, followed by a cartwheeling Gargantua and the hopping Rumpy, who performed a daring somersault on his stilts as he exited the sawdust.

Heavy then returned to the floor for his most well-known introduction.

"And now..." he roared into his mic, "ladies and gentlemen, prepare yourselves for the first wonder of the circus world...the most incredible act in America today...an extraordinary showcase of trapeze! On first ring, the queen of the skies...an angel from high above...the beautiful Penny Fortune! And, on centre ring, the world's greatest flyer. Cheer him, love him, never forget him.

Klondike's Circus is proud to present the worldwide sensation...the debonair king of the air...Gino Shapiro!"

The audience rose to its feet as one as Shapiro and Penny slowly walked out onto the floor, dressed in their bright orange costumes. Both cast aside their extravagant, fur-lined cloaks. Penny wore a fireball leotard, while Shapiro wore his customary flaming singlet. Both climbed their support ropes to the waiting rings high above.

Once at the top, they settled on the rings and rubbed chalk into their hands. Neither looked down. There was no net. Just an ocean of sawdust. And the thousands of spectators staring upwards.

What followed was a showcase of classic techniques, as Shapiro whirled around from ring to ring, throwing and thrusting his body like a human dart. Penny acted as his catcher, taking his hands and propelling him across to the next ring in line.

Shapiro performed all the customary moves—the double sault, the triple and the standing twirl. Then, Penny clasped his ankles and hurled him even higher, before they both vaulted across to a turret at the far side of the tent roof.

From there, Shapiro performed one of his specialities, the high wire. A thick plastic band ran from the turret post to another on the far side of the tent.

With a theatrical flourish, Shapiro effortlessly walked across the entire length, as the spectators looked up in shock and awe.

As he neared the end of the wire walk, Shapiro produced a stunning cartwheel to push him onto the end turret.

Again, everyone in the crowd was on their feet, applauding wildly. Shapiro blew kisses to the audience, bowing endlessly at his station high above. Then, he grabbed at a nearby support rope and slowly scurried downwards to the floor. Penny followed suit at the opposite side.

On the ground again, Shapiro lifted his assistant with a mighty hug, before both bowed again, waved and jogged lightly to the exit.

Heavy triumphantly motored back out. "And there you have it, ladies and gentleman, boys and girls. The most incredible act in American circus."

He paused as the applause settled. "We hope you've enjoyed Klondike's Circus, friends. Here to sing us out is our resident songstress, the enchanting Suzi Dando."

Suzi smiled beautifully as she slowly crept onto the sawdust, taking the mic from Heavy as the music began blaring out over the tannoy. She wore a dazzling white and gold dress, and left no one in any doubt as to the power of her voice as she began belting out the circus's trademark anthem, Can You Feel The Magic Tonight?

It had been written years earlier by Heavy himself, and had been the circus's closing, grand finale number since day one.

Heavy and Klondike had liked the idea of a big song at the end of the show, during which all of the performers could come out for the final ovation.

Suzi was the third resident songstress to have performed the number, but everyone agreed she was the most sublime.

She stood singing in the very centre of the floor. Then, a succession of beautiful red Cadillac convertibles drove into the arena and completed a lap of the big top.

In the back of each car was each respective act, coming out one by one until all the performers were being chauffeured around in a beautiful automobile, waving at the adoring audience as they paraded slowly around the floor.

The Range Riders took it in turns to sit in their car, jumping on and off their horses as they went around on their mounts.

The Rocking Robins all stood in the back of their ride, blowing kisses and waving.

Roddy Olsen sat with Rusty Fox, Tony Tan and Napoleon all huddled up in the back seat. The puppets all waved.

The Flying Batistas, the Showcase Revue and Corky and his clowns all stood in the back of their respective Cadillacs.

Only Tip Enqvist of the Daredevils was actually seated in their allotted car, with the rest of the team riding alongside on their bikes, engines revving.

The last Cadillac in the line held Shapiro and Penny, who stood tall, wearing their fancy capes again, and waving enthusiastically as the audience screamed their names.

The procession of cars carrying the performers was another breath-taking sight.

The troupe had originally been carried around on flat-bed trucks at the end of each show, but had been upgraded to the Cadillacs for Klondike's first television special in Los Angeles two years earlier. Ever since that glorious night, they had become a staple.

Suzi reached the operatic climax of the song, and the cars slowly headed on the last leg of their lap of honour towards the exit from whence they had come.

Suzi finished singing, and leapt onto the final car as it crept past, joining Shapiro and Penny, who helped her aboard.

Then Heavy returned for a final time to the arena floor.

"Ladies and gentlemen, we hope you have enjoyed the glamour, the razzmatazz and the sheer excitement of Klondike's Circus. And we hope you can feel the magic tonight. From all of us here, thank you so much for joining us and we hope to see you again further down the coast. Next show is Los Angeles, one week tomorrow. Until then, goodnight…and god bless America."

Chapter Seven

It was one of the most iconic signs in all the world. And it had never looked more majestic.

Then again, Klondike thought idly, few had probably ever glimpsed it from up here.

The famous, white-lettered HOLLYWOOD sign seemed to encompass him completely as he stared at it from a summit high up in the green Hollywood hills.

He was seated in a small white golf buggy belonging to the ATV studios, and was halfway through a tour of the production company's lot.

Next to him in the driver's seat was his old friend Steve Irving, who had insisted on giving him a guided tour. Of his empire, as he put it. They had whizzed around in the little cab, in and out of factory buildings and outdoor sets. Then, they had hit a long gravel path and rode up into the all-encompassing hills surrounding the lot.

They passed various performers—actors, extras, animal trainers, stuntmen— who were all on their way to work from their bungalows in the hills.

Irving had pulled the buggy into an enclosure at the top, which sat opposite the legendary white sign.

"Impressive view, huh?" said the comedian.

Klondike twiddled his cane. He studied the horizon. "A land of dreams."

Irving rested his hands on the spotless white steering wheel. The zany comic even looked like a country club golfer, in yellow slacks and pink polo shirt, complete with white leather gloves. He stared at his old friend. "Something wrong, Kal?"

Klondike gazed at the trees and boulders that led to the main roads far below. Since arriving in LA the day before, he had remained deeply troubled by the shock meeting with Paul Agostino.

Everything probed at his mind. Agostino. The old Cobras outfit. Catherine Hart. The Mob. How had this all come about? A former life had suddenly re-emerged. Memories he thought long buried. And he didn't like any of it. Even more troubling was Agostino's promise of trouble…and whatever that entailed.

He had considered telling Irving about the meeting, but thought better of it. No good could possibly come of that.

"I'm proud of you, Steve," he finally blurted, coming out of his reverie. "Hell, this is your empire. You put ATV on the map. Your show. It's killing it in the Nielsens."

Irving smiled smugly. "Your boy Roddy rocked the other night. Such a great guest. The people…they love him."

"Yeah. Well, we got a great roster this year. The best ever."

"A hell of a lot of important people seem to agree on that, Kal."

Klondike studied the luscious green hills, squinting into the sun. "Does that mean we're on for Superstars and Stripes?"

Irving laughed softly. "Of course. Hell, you knew we weren't gunna say no to that, man. The last TV special we did together was a smash. This…this extravaganza you've all got planned sounds like something real special. I'd be honoured to be involved."

Klondike grinned sheepishly at his old friend. There hadn't even been a negotiation. "You've helped get me out of some tight spots down the years, Steve. I'm obliged. Really, I am."

Irving ran his hands over the smooth steering wheel. "Your specials have been given the go-ahead on my word. Their success has helped me no end. The feeling is mutual, daddio."

Klondike exhaled rapidly. He eyed the comedian on the seat next to him. "Now, why don't you tell me about what you've got lined up for us these next few nights?"

"Now, you're talking." Irving fired up the buggy's ignition again and performed a 360-degree turn in the enclosure before bombing back down the hill towards the ATV lot. "Tonight, we've got Snakeskin Joe's Wild West Show. Over at the LA Playing Fields. You're gunna love it!"

Klondike looked at him as they sped down the pathway. He wanted to tell Irving he had seen that show last fall. But he just didn't have the heart.

"Terrific," he blurted.

The buggy rattled on in the blinding LA sun.

The Health Club looked like the type of place one would avoid.

With blacked-out windows, tacky neon-lit signs outside and a huge, steel door at its entrance, it looked like the kind of joint where a secret password was required for entry.

Lee Vesnick stood at the corner of Chinese Boulevard staring at the bar. It was a seedy, cheap and run-down watering hole in LA's Pacific Bay district. And he didn't like it.

With a deep breath, he crossed the street and entered, heaving the steel door open to get inside.

Within, the bar room was gloomy, dark and filled with smoke. Two men in suits sat at a corner table playing cards. Another two, dressed in a remarkably similar fashion, stood by a pool table in the centre. Both groups, as well as a bartender, all stared at him as he crept inside.

Vesnick was 21 years old and had seen a lot in his tender years. But he was still scared, not knowing what he was getting himself into.

"You Vesnick?" the bartender called, polishing a glass. "Right."

The man cocked his head. "The boss is waiting out back. Go through the brown door."

Vesnick squinted through the smoke, saw the door, and bolted across the room, feeling and sensing five sets of eyeballs following his progress.

He knocked once on the door and entered hastily.

The room looked like a lounge in a suburban household. Two couches and a large round table in the centre, where a man sat counting poker chips. He was a frightening looking figure, with slicked back, jet black hair and a giant scar running down one side of his face. He wore an immaculate grey suit.

"Come in, Vesnick," he said quietly. Vesnick nodded and approached the table. "Sit."

He did as he was told. The other stood, wandered across to a drinks cabinet, and spoke again. "What can I get ya? Scotch?"

"Sure. Please."

The man returned to the table with two almost full tumblers. He pushed one in front of his visitor. Then he looked Vesnick in the eye, smiling at the youngster's fear.

"Don't be afraid, boy. We's gunna be friends."

Vesnick sipped at his drink, coughing slightly. "Who…who are you?"

The man sat down again, hands on the surface. "Allow me to introduce myself. Paul Agostino. Captain of the East Side, New York."

Vesnick shuddered. "You mean…the syndicate?"

Agostino chuckled. "Now you're getting it, kid." He raised his glass. "Thanks for coming out here. I have a business proposition I think you's be interested in."

"What…" Vesnick gasped, looking around the room wildly as if expecting an ambush. "What kind of business?"

"Relax. If you's in trouble, you'd be dead already. This is business." He took a long slurp at his Scotch. His cold, dead eyes locked onto the young man. "It seems you and I have a common enemy. Kal Klondike."

Vesnick's eyes widened. "Klondike?"

"That's right. He just blackballed you outta that circus of his, right?"

"Well, yeah. Hell, yes, that's right."

"So, my question to you is…you wanna get him back?" Vesnick thought of the scene in the tent a few days earlier. The humiliation he had suffered. His dreams dashed for the season.

"Sure. That…that son of a bitch has ruined everything. Left me to rot. I was supposed to be a star."

Agostino smiled an evil, calculating smile. "Perfect."

Vesnick glared at him, his anxiety lifted. "Perfect? What's perfect?"

"Easy, kid," Agostino muttered. He lit a cigarette, not offering his guest one. "I'm giving you a chance to get one over Klondike."

"What? How do you know him?"

Agostino looked across the table, his face strangely illuminated by the lit match he held absently before him. "Me and Klondike go back a long way, kid. He owes me a debt. But…he won't pay up. Won't even acknowledge it. Now, I want a piece of his circus. A piece of his action. That circus of his is a moneymaking machine. I want a cut." He leaned across the table. "And, god is my witness, I'm going to get it. If he refuses…I'm going to ruin him. For good."

Vesnick squirmed uncomfortably at the table. He had not been expecting all this. "What…what happened with you and him?"

Agostino shook his head as he inhaled on his smoke. "That doesn't concern you, kid. All I wanna know is…are you in?"

"What do you have in mind?" Vesnick said, trying to be brave.

Agostino nodded in understanding. "You wanna know your cut. Smart kid. You'll go far." He stood up suddenly and began rummaging through a drawer at the liquor cabinet. "I'll give you a one-off fee. One thousand dollars. All you gotta do is help me. Give advice. You've been a part of that circus set-up all winter, till last week. You know the schedules, the patterns, the people. Think of yourself as a kind of inside man. I want to know everything you got. Particularly when it comes to security. Who Klondike's got on board for that."

Vesnick tried to smile. "That will be easy, Mr Agostino."

"Good. Then it's easy money for you, Vesnick."

The youngster looked up, his mind suddenly alive and racing. "You mean…you mean, we're gunna bring Klondike down? You and me?"

Agostino laughed. A long, sinister sound. "Well," he drawled. "We's gunna get a little more help. From my second guest. A man I believe you will recognise."

He pulled open a side door beside the liquor cabinet that Vesnick hadn't even realised existed. A gloomy, smoke-filled corridor lay beyond. There was someone out there. A figure slowly emerging towards them, out of the shadows.

Vesnick squinted into the gloom, feeling cold all over.

Finally, the newcomer crept in. And the first thing Vesnick noticed was a giant, alligator-like grin.

He was an older man, with immaculately groomed snow white hair, a tanned, grizzled face and large Seagram blue eyes. He wore an expensive-looking turquoise overcoat, with gold pinstripes.

Vesnick could not believe his eyes. "Eric Ribbeck!"

"The one and only," the newcomer said in a loud Texas drawl. He turned to Agostino and the pair shook hands, laughing slightly. "Well done, Paul," he said cheerfully. "Now we have a fresh confederate. Whose insight is most welcome."

Vesnick was visibly stunned. "What…what is this?" he gasped.

"It's alright, boy," Ribbeck cried, pacing to the table and standing over Vesnick. It was as if he had just taken over the joint.

Vesnick stared up at him. He had seen that face a hundred times in newspapers and circus programmes.

"Calm yourself," Ribbeck was saying, "this is all just one grand business venture. Come, drink." He produced the Scotch bottle and poured them both a large shot. Then, he finally seated himself.

Agostino returned to his chair at the head of the table. Vesnick could not help staring at Ribbeck as their host began talking again. "I am out to get Klondike. Make no mistake. Eric here has plenty of reasons to want him to fail. I knew that.

So we formed us a partnership, of sorts. Our goal…to control his circus. Or kill it off. For good."

Ribbeck pulled a fancy-looking cheroot from an old leather case and lit up. The smoke smelt of forest campfires. The older man looked into the deep grey cloud, as if with regret. "Klondike was my golden boy," he said quietly. "I gave him the keys to the kingdom. Everything! And he left me. Thought he could do better on his own. Then, as if to bite the hand that fed him, that reared him…that damn yahoo thought he could rival me. Thought he could better me. Me!" He blew deep, dark smoke across the table, his face twisted in anger. "Everything he is in this world, he is because of me. And now he wants to rival me. He wants to be number one. Using everything I taught him."

"Mr Ribbeck," Vesnick stammered. "My, it is an honour to meet you, sir. It really is. I, er, I—"

"Spit it out, god dam it!" Ribbeck roared.

"Well, it's like this. I don't really understand what is going on here!"

"It's simple," Agostino said calmly across the table. "We are all now partners. If Klondike won't cut us in, we destroy him."

Vesnick stared at Ribbeck in shock. "You want to destroy Klondike's Circus?"

Ribbeck glowered at him, fiddling with the cheroot. "I want his talent. Gino, Roddy, hell all those yahoos. I want them under my big top. I want the greatest show on earth, kid. I've been on top for 25 years. That ain't gunna change none." Again, he lost himself for a moment as he stared into nothingness. "Two years ago, I tried to cripple him. To get him to sign his star performers over to me. That damn joker wouldn't budge. Well, now I'm grabbing the bull by the longhorn, dammit. I tired of reading all about Kal Klondike and his damn TV specials."

Agostino nodded as the older man finished. He turned to Vesnick. "So you see, kid, we all have a vested interest here."

Vesnick finished his drink. He couldn't think straight. But he no longer felt afraid. "So how do we hit Klondike?" he said, beginning to smile.

Ribbeck growled. "There are plenty of ways. First, we pinch. Sting him. A few men, heavies…we put some heat on. Smash up his gear, intimidate his people. Hell, smack em around some, the damn huckleberries. That's where Mr Agostino is our man. He has an army of tough guys at his disposal."

Agostino nodded. "You better believe it."

"As for me," Ribbeck continued, "I have other services to call upon. Industry people. Newspaper people." His large blue eyes surveyed Vesnick. "That's where you come in, boy."

Vesnick shifted in his seat. "What? How?"

"Hey, hey, wait a minute," Agostino mumbled, holding up a hand. "You haven't said if you're in yet, kid."

Vesnick licked his lips. He looked from Ribbeck to Agostino, then back again. He felt strangely excited, alive.

"I don't even have to think about it. I'm in. What do you need?"

Chapter Eight

A small brass band and several suited dignitaries, surrounded by the usual crowd of excited townsfolk, all welcomed the circus train as it rolled to a stop at the branch station at Ocean Drive, east LA. The band began playing For He's A Jolly Good Fellow and there was a hearty round of applause as the circus folk all began disembarking from the great express special.

The normal protocol followed by the circus involved setting up trailers and booths for the performers and support staff at the venue grounds. Most employees still slept and based themselves within their quarters onboard the train.

The trailers, along with the actual big top tent and midway stalls, were all transported to the venue, usually a short distance away. This meant an armada of trucks and support vehicles had to exit the train and load all the equipment ready for transportation.

The entire endeavour typically took a whole day to complete.

The gathered crowds at Ocean Drive continued to watch in awe as a sea of people and construction apparatus bled from the carriages. Many onlookers hoped to catch of glimpse of one of the circus's star names, even one of the giants, Goliath or Gargantua.

As the endless unloading continued on into the afternoon, a yellow taxi pulled up next to the branch railway line.

Kal Klondike climbed out, paid the cabbie and strode slowly towards the train. He could not help but smile at the scene before him as the roustabouts conducted their business in a thorough, professional manner, many now shirtless due to the intense afternoon sun.

He gave a brief greeting to Jim McCabe, who was wandering around barking orders to just about everyone, and climbed onboard a random carriage.

He wandered through the dining cart, kitchen, several equipment blocks, the stables and the bunkhouse.

Arriving at the accommodation carriages, he shuffled along, greeting his staff as he passed.

Then, at last, he arrived at the end of the train and knocked on the door of Heavy's stateroom.

Entering, he found his old friend sat at his desk going through some paperwork.

"Kal! Welcome back. How was Vegas? And Hollywood?"

Klondike wandered into the grand room and headed straight for a mini bar in the corner. "Just fine, Heav. Our friends had lots of good news."

"Do tell."

Klondike gave a brief summary of Claude Hershey's Superstars and Stripes proposal, along with Steve Irving's eagerness to film it for ATV.

Heavy looked ready to explode. "That's fantastic! Wow! I'll drink to that." He galloped over to the bar, where Klondike had poured them both a tall Scotch. "Well done, Kal. Just like you said…it was only ever going to be good news."

He hungrily gulped at his drink. Then, looking up, he noted Klondike's sombre look.

"What is it, Kal? Why don't you look ecstatic?"

Klondike removed his fedora hat and flung it onto the couch. "We got a problem."

Heavy put the glass down on his desk. "Problem? What problem?" Klondike shook his head and collapsed onto the couch. He looked up at Heavy. "You are not going to believe who I ran into at the Golden Dune."

Heavy looked down at him blankly. "Tell me."

"Paul Agostino."

The big man looked truly incredulous. His mouth gaped and his eyes looked ready to pop out. "Agostino! From the Cobras?"

Klondike nodded slowly. "It was him."

"After all these years? Jesus! I don't believe it. How…how did you know it was him?"

"Hell, he ain't changed none. Still looks like he just walked out of a street fight. Greased back hair. Scars all over his face. Trying to intimidate…make out he's tough. Besides, he saw me first. He knew I was there."

Heavy's mind was racing. He paced the stateroom idly. "Agostino…" he mumbled. "What has he been up to all this time?"

Klondike frowned. "He's in the syndicate now."

"The Mob!"

"Right. A captain, or something like that. Said he controls Hell's Kitchen. Reports to the big boss."

"Oh my God," Heavy breathed. He gulped down the last of his drink and poured another. He was about to get started on the second helping when he paused, eyeing Klondike with concern.

"Wait a minute. What in hell did he want?"

"You're not going to believe it," Klondike said weakly. "He wants in on the circus. A share of us. Plans to buy in, like in a game of stud. Says he can help us out, for a piece of the action."

"Jesus. What did you tell him?"

"Ha! I told him to go to hell."

"And?"

Klondike sat back, rubbing at his eyes. It was all too much. "He promised trouble. Said he would make us reconsider. He wants in. I guess he plans to make trouble until we let him join us."

"And if we don't cave in?"

Klondike held his hands high. "God only knows, Heav."

Heavy continued pacing the stateroom, frowning mightily. "Jesus Christ!" he blurted. "You don't need me to tell you, this is bad, Kal. Real bad. A Mob boss! Promising trouble. That could mean anything."

"I know, I know," Klondike muttered. He stood up and paced slowly to the window. Heavy joined him. They watched as the roustabouts loaded a cotton candy machine onto a flatbed truck. To the side of it, one of the clowns was juggling pins in front of several delighted children. Another was busy selling balloons to onlookers.

"Agostino has the capability, the power, to ruin everything," Klondike said grimly.

"But will he?" Heavy whispered. "If he wants us to be a part of his empire?"

Klondike nodded slowly, holding his glass as he surveyed the operations outside.

The questions whirled through his conscience, gnawing at him and putting his emotions through hell.

At that moment, there was a knock at the door and Lacey and Plum burst in. Lacey was holding a newspaper before her, while Plum carried a document wallet.

The duo exchanged pleasantries with Klondike, enquiring about his endeavours. The four all sat down around the coffee table for the debriefing.

Klondike told them everything. Superstars and Stripes. Irving. Agostino.

Spirits had been high. Until he got to the last part.

When he had finished talking, the others all stared at him. "I still can't believe it," Heavy gurgled.

Lacey put her hand to her mouth as she often did when deep in thought. She rose and began pacing the room.

"This is quite the development, boys," she muttered. She walked across to the coffee pot in the room's far corner and poured herself a cup, before lighting a cigarette. She was lost in thought. The three men stared at her, hoping for a solution.

"Stop me at any time," she said finally. "So, this Agostino figures that you owe him, Kalvin, having set you up as a trick shot artist when you were kids. He remembers you and Heavy from this gang of yours. You all went your separate ways long ago. You two joined the Army, had the war, then joined the circus. But he stuck with gang life. He rose up through the ranks of a criminal organisation. Now, he has power and influence. He sees you boys are now a success with the circus. And now he wants to be a co-owner…just like that? And if we say no…he gets nasty."

She looked down at Klondike, probing at him with her beautiful, giant violet eyes. The effect was overwhelming.

"Er, well, yeah," Klondike stammered, feeling like he was sat under a police spotlight. "That's about the whole of it, Lacey."

Plum had been shaking his head throughout. "As if we don't have enough to worry about."

Lacey nodded. "The price of success, some might say. Everyone wants to have a piece of the pie."

"But, come on," Plum snapped, suddenly angry. "There are laws, aren't there? This guy is, what, a gangster? What about the cops? The FBI?"

Klondike shook his head. "And what would we tell them? A nasty man has threatened us? We are worried about a possible attack?" He waved a hand through the air. "Besides, the syndicate is different. It's a business. A conglomerate. Run by suits…men like Addison. The difference is they use underhand tactics. They play dirty. Hell, many of their guys run cities and towns out East."

Plum stared at him. "The Mob are killers! Criminals!"

Heavy took a long pull on his Scotch. "With police, governors, congressmen in their pockets."

Klondike nodded. "They do what they want, Richie. They're bad news." He looked down, lost in time. "Agostino was a nasty son of a bitch."

Plum spread his hands. "So what do we do?"

Klondike looked at each of his comrades. "I don't know. Wait and see what he pulls. If anything."

Lacey hovered over the group, concern clouding her features. "I think that's a good point, Kal. Nothing has happened here. And, until something does, I think it should be business as usual. We have a big show at the weekend. That should be our focus."

They all seemed to agree on that, nodding in understanding. Except Klondike, who sat there lost in his thoughts.

Lacey stooped over him. "Was there anything else, Kal?"

He was struggling to shed an image from his mind. A face. Catherine Hart. He could still see her now. Innocent. Beautiful. Alone. Afraid.

"No," he said firmly, shaking his head, clearing his thoughts. "We've got to get to work." He eyed Lacey and Plum. "What have we got?"

With a sigh, Lacey moved to the desk to retrieve her newspaper. "An exciting preview in the California Times. Double-page spread."

"Fantastic," Klondike muttered, taking the paper as she handed it over.

Plum grasped his document wallet. "And I have the final figures for our stock take in Atlanta, where we get the fresh supplies. It all looks manageable."

Klondike nodded as he took the papers.

"Y'know," Plum said, his mind racing, "with this Superstars and Stripes deal now agreed, and the TV business we are now committed to…all my figures are gunna be way off. We have an extra show for one thing. The money coming in is going to be far greater. There's a whole extra revenue stream to be accounted for. I…I better make some alterations of the sheets."

Lacey nodded. "This July 4th idea is great, Kal. We can fit it in easily, and it's all extra green."

"Don't forget the profits will be split three ways," Heavy put in.

Lacey was looking down at Klondike, still sat on the couch looking somewhat lost. "This is what we should really be focusing on, Kal. The new show. The new TV special. Regardless of what the hell is going on out there, things we can't control. We have exciting times to look forward to, tiger."

She studied him with maternal concern. He barely budged. She caressed her skirt and sat down next to him on the couch, linking her arm through his. "I guess your trip brought good news and bad," she said, laughing gaily. "Can you just believe me when I say you've done great. Real great, Kalvin."

He finally smiled. Heavy and Plum looked at him reassuringly. He turned to the woman beside him.

"Well, Lacey, I guess that's all I needed to hear."

They all laughed.

It all started the following morning.

Klondike was shaving in his stateroom, dressed in a white vest as he hovered over the ornate basin in his washroom.

The main door burst open and Lacey strode in, holding a copy of the Los Angeles Tribune under her arm.

"We got trouble, Kal," she cried, slamming the paper onto the large round table in the centre of the room.

"Jesus Christ!" Klondike cursed, washing off the shaving foam and throwing a hand towel around his shoulders. He surged into the room and looked at Lacey, then the paper.

"Page six," she said calmly, lighting a cigarette.

He grunted. "When is it all going to end?"

Lacey tried to smile. "I think it's about to start, tiger."

Klondike spread the paper out on the table, turned to page six and immediately saw the problem.

With a mighty huff, he began to read…

CIRCUS OF HORRORS SHAMES LOS ANGELES

The renowned Klondike's Circus is due to play Los Angeles this weekend, performing in front of a sell-out crowd at Ocean Drive Recreation Grounds.

But the travelling show has been branded a 'corrupt outfit full of deceitful rogues' by a former performer, who is warning spectators to stay away.

Lee Vesnick, 21, spent the winter months training with the circus as a knife thrower and had expected to become a star name this year with the troupe.

However, the youngster was fired from the circus last week after threatening to go public with what he called 'shocking revelations about the running of Klondike's Circus'.

Vesnick has now lifted the lid on the terrible truth after he was thrown out for 'failing to conform'.

Firstly, he claims that the circus is soaked in corruption. The young man said: "Everyone knows that Klondike's Circus is a money-maker. Big bucks being made. But not everyone knows that Kal Klondike skims money off the top for himself. He doesn't let anyone, not any of his staff, know the true figures. That's because he keeps the lion's share for himself. If I was an auditor, I'd be investigating the finances, that's for sure."

Vesnick also detailed the 'despicable' characters that make up the travelling entertainment troupe.

He had particularly unpleasant revelations about the star of the show, trapeze king Gino Shapiro.

He said: "Everyone knows Shapiro is a notorious womaniser. Yeah, a lot of chicks really dig him. But did you know he is a sexual bully? He uses women all the time. Look at the amount of female partners he has gone through over the years. If they don't allow him to do as he pleases with them, they are out. Yeah sure, you get the job being his trapeze partner, but you got to sleep with him first. That's your audition."

And Vesnick had revelations about other star performers too.

He added: "Corky the Clown is mentally unhinged. His head ain't right. One of these days he's going to lose it in front of everyone. Those Daredevils? They are going to kill someone in the audience. I promise you. Maybe in Los Angeles. You want to risk your life? Go ahead, go to Klondike's Circus. And don't even get me started on—"

Klondike screwed the page up with a roar and hurled it onto the floor.

"Son of a bitch!" he raged. "I oughta have ripped his god damn tongue out when I blackballed him out of my outfit. What the hell is his problem?"

His chest heaved as he stood there in his vest, clasping and unclasping his hands.

Lacey puffed on her cigarette, looking up at him earnestly. "I suppose this is his idea of revenge. But there seems to be more to this…"

Klondike rubbed a hand through his wet hair. "More? Hasn't that little punk caused enough trouble?"

"Don't you see?" Lacey said softly, standing again and pacing around him. "The warning from Agostino in Vegas. Now this. Days later. That can't be a coincidence."

"What the hell has Vesnick got to do with Agostino?"

She sighed, putting the newspaper back together again. "Maybe nothing. But...like I say, this all seems a bit, er, collective."

They both stood there in stunned silence. Klondike slowly waded over to the window, and quietly studied the scene before him. The big top and the midway were assembled out on the recreation grounds. The great red and blue tent dominated the skyline, stretching into the heavens. On the ground, teams of roustabouts inspected the equipment.

"There's always someone out there." He said the words absently, as if in a trance. "Someone out to get me."

Lacey joined him at the window. She rubbed his arm. "Like I said yesterday, it's the price of success, tiger. Everyone wants a piece." There was a knock at the door and Heavy wandered in. He had a copy of the Tribune in his hands and a look of anger all over him.

He stopped when he saw Klondike and Lacey stood solemnly at the window. His face dropped.

"You heard, huh?"

It was Lacey who answered. "We heard, Henry."

Heavy tongued the inside of his cheek. "What do you make of it?" Klondike turned to face him. He had a look of finality on his grizzled, rugged features.

"It has begun."

Chapter Nine

The Los Angeles show was another sell-out, with a frenzied, red-hot atmosphere. Unfortunately, for all the performers concerned, it was the warmest evening of spring, with the temperature engulfing the big top far beyond comfortable.

The paying patrons sat in the bleachers fanned themselves endlessly as the circus tent turned into a sauna-like cauldron of sweat and humidity.

Klondike wore shorts and a T-shirt at the flap, and felt for Heavy in his full ringmaster's attire. The big man sweated profusely under the mighty top hat. Lacey also wore shorts and a loose top.

Fortunately, such was the professionalism of the troupe, not one of the performers let the uncomfortable conditions affect them.

While the Range Riders and the Rocking Robins all looked completely exhausted when they came off stage, the rest of the team seemed to make it through the show without any problems. Gino Shapiro and Penny Fortune both glistened in sweat as they performed their trapeze magic high above the sawdust, but every move was executed with the usual finesse.

By the time of Suzi's song and the grand finale, the audience seemed fit to drop, the applause a pleasant, if slightly weary, vacuum of noise.

When the Cadillacs finally completed the lap of honour, everyone in the big top seemed to struggle across to the nearest exit.

At the flap, Klondike turned to Lacey and rolled his eyes. "Oh lord," he groaned. "Let's get a drink."

Gino Shapiro sat sprawled on a couch in his private lounge on the stationary train, a huge ice pack tied to his shoulder.

He was naked save for a pair of running shorts, and looked like he would struggle to move for some time.

With a groan he pushed at the ice pack, massaging around his ever-troublesome shoulder blades. He had dislocated his right shoulder three times in his life. It had given him pain after every show for two years now. Holding the pack in place, he closed his eyes and leant his head back.

"You want to say something about this, Gino?"

He opened his eyes. Penny was standing over him, wearing a bathrobe and thrusting a copy of the Los Angeles Tribune towards his frame.

Shapiro sneered in disgust. "That good for nothing kid," he grumbled, wincing as he adjusted his position. "To think I tried to help him. Then he says something like that to the press. God damn him to hell, I spit at his picture." He looked up at Penny. Her pretty face looked angry, alarmed. "Do not believe a word of this nonsense, mamacita. That dumb kid…he just look for attention, is all."

Penny flung the paper onto the couch and put her hands on her hips. "I wouldn't believe a word of it…if it wasn't all true!"

Shapiro frowned, struggling to concentrate. "What's that you say?"

"Have you forgotten all those little chats we had? When I first joined Klondike?" She rolled her eyes at him. "Come, Penny, come to my pad. We'll have a little wine. Get to know each other a little better. Why, it sounds like you've had that chat over and over again, Gino! What am I? The latest in a long line of trapeze girls you get to have your way with? What happens if I refuse your charms? I'll be back on the road?"

Shapiro sat up and held up a hand. "Santamaria! Calm down, Penny! What the hell are you so uptight about? I told you, this kid has made it all up. He's trying to get back at the chairman for kicking him out. That is all. None of that stuff ever happened." Penny was impassive. "How do I know that?"

"Ok, ok," Shapiro said softly. He made it gingerly to his feet and stood next to her in the small lounge. "You go find one of my former flying partners, and you see if they have a bad word to say about me. All those girls. I treated them like family. I made them stars. And it is the same with you, Penny." He ran his hand through the air. "Hell, the wine, the dinners…that is just who am I. Yes, I love women. But, also, I respect women. Massively. A woman has been the lifeblood of my act since day one."

Penny cocked her head. "What about Jenny Cross? She tried to kill you."

"In the name of San Hill! She was insane. She resides in a mental hospital now, for Chrissakes!"

They both stared at each other. An uneasy silence followed. Shapiro went to put an arm around her. She shrugged him off. "Listen, angel," he said calmly.

"You believe what you want to believe. Me? I want to help you. If you stick with me…now, in future, it will help your career. I chose you because of your skill…your skill up there. Now, that is all."

Penny exhaled sharply several times. She puffed out her chest, and let it fall again. Running a hand through her long, wet hair she crossed the room. "I just don't know what to think, Gino."

He looked at her pleadingly. "Have I ever mistreated you? In any way?"

She looked downwards. "No."

"And nor will I, angel."

She finally looked him in the eye and nodded slightly. "I really want to believe that."

They looked at each other for several moments. Then, Penny mumbled a very brief apology and crept out of the lounge.

Shapiro stumbled across to the crumpled up newspaper. He picked it up, looked over the dastardly article, then angrily hurled the paper to the floor again.

The action made his shoulder sting and he winced in pain. With a huff, he flopped back onto the couch again.

The following morning, the entire enclosure around the stationary train and the recreation fields was a hive of activity as the roustabouts began loading up the express again.

Suzi Dando was combing her hair at the dresser in her room on the train when there was knock at the door.

Looking in the giant mirror, she saw the door open and Roddy Olsen stick his head through the gap.

"Looking marvellous, dear girl," he called, smiling.

"Roddy!" she squealed. "What a nice surprise. But, as you can see, I'm not, er, presentable just yet."

He smiled at her majestically. "You were born presentable, Suzi."

She giggled impishly. "Roddy, please! I have to do my hair."

"Ok, ok. I just wondering if you wanted to come for a walk with me? Down to the water. It's beautiful out there, not so hot now. We don't move out till tonight. Whatya say?"

Suzi shifted on her stool excitedly. "Sure thing. Give me 10 minutes, ok?"

He bowed theatrically and left the room. Moving down the corridor, he reached the interchange door between carriages and opened the outer door, leaping to the soft grass below.

The sun was up but was largely covered by clouds. It was warm, but there was plenty of breeze to quell the heat.

Olsen walked slowly alongside the train, watching the roustabouts dismantle the midway equipment in the field adjacent to the rail track.

Wandering along absently, he headed towards an old abandoned shed sat beside the tracks. He liked to get away from the hubbub of the work crews sometimes. It gave him time to think.

Hands deep in the pockets of his green anorak, he walked past the shed, studying a pathway that led towards the coastal road.

"Oh Roddy…"

He turned in alarm at the husky voice behind him. That was as far as he got. A fist that felt like a sledgehammer slammed into his jaw and knocked him clean off his feet. He flew backwards and rolled several feet in the grass, his jawline screaming.

There were three of them. They were dressed like roustabouts in windbreakers and jeans. But he hadn't seen them before, none of them. They were big men, full of brawn and menace.

Olsen struggled to his feet, but they were on him. One of them hauled him up like a child and pulled his arms behind his back, pinning them in place.

The two others stood before him. The first one punched him viciously in the solar plexus. Olsen had stiffened his muscles in anticipation of the blow, but it still overwhelmed him. The second man flung a wild left hook into the side of his cheek. Olsen cried out in pain.

The three men then all grabbed at him and seemed to pull him along behind the shed.

Olsen had grown up in boarding houses and spent much of his youth struggling to get by. He had been in many a street fight, but the surprise of this attack had overpowered him.

"What—" he started to say as the gang dragged him roughly. Another fist slammed into his stomach and he doubled over. He was then thrown unceremoniously to the floor.

"It's him alright," one of the men said. "This is the one whose voice box needs to be crushed. Lou, hold his arms. Jake, take the legs." Olsen found himself pinned to the ground, arms and legs held firmly in place. To his horror, he was at the mercy of the third man, now towering over him with a hand raised ominously.

"Try doing your fancy voices after this, rosebud."

He steadied himself, about to smash the side of his hand into Olsen's throat, when a hoarse, thunderous cry stopped him. "Hey, you there!"

The attacker looked up in alarm.

Jim McCabe and three of his roustabouts were racing across the field towards the melee. The man hesitated, still holding his hand in the air ready to strike.

Then, McCabe dropped to one knee and hurled something—a tyre iron—straight at the man. It struck his arm with a mighty twang.

The attacker cried out in agony, before nodding at his companions. Suddenly, the mysterious trio abandoned Olsen and began sprinting towards the road, away from the approaching rescuers.

Within seconds, they had piled into an old black Sedan and were pulling away. Gone.

McCabe pulled up next to Olsen as his men raced towards the fleeing car.

"You alright, Roddy?"

Olsen rubbed at his jawline, a green bruise forming on his cheek. He sat up and looked around in a daze. "I am. Thanks to you, Jim." He smiled at McCabe, who hauled him on to his feet, holding him steady. "What the hell was that all about? Who were those guys?"

McCabe watched as his roustabouts trooped back towards them. "Beats me. They were dressed like crew members. Probably why no one paid them any attention." He eyed Olsen, who was holding his stomach. "You sure you're ok, pal? They hit you with a coupla suckers."

"Yeah," Olsen blurted. He walked gingerly towards the train, holding his ribs. "Looks like you and your boys saved me from a hospital trip. Thanks Jim."

The roustabouts re-joined McCabe and Olsen as they walked back to the carriages.

Then, everyone seemed to pour out at once. Klondike, Lacey, Heavy, Plum and a horrified Suzi all jumped off the train and surrounded Olsen.

"What the hell happened?"

"Are you sure you're alright, Roddy?"

"Who was it? Can you describe them?"

"Call the cops, somebody call the cops! Now!"

Suzi ran into his arms and hugged him, keeping her arms around his frame as they stood there in the frenzied scrummage.

"Oh, Roddy! How could this have happened?"

"It's alright. I'm alright," he kept saying.

Klondike placed a consoling hand on his shoulder. "You're sure you're not hurt, kid?"

Olsen grinned. "Nothing a walk by the ocean and a few sodas can't cure."

Klondike shook hands with McCabe behind them. "Nice work, Jim." McCabe was frowning. "Strange place for a mugging. But I can see their game. They was dressed like my boys, like the crew. So they blended in. Then they struck upon the first guy to stray from the group. Unfortunately, Roddy, that was you."

Heavy chimed in. "They take your wallet, kid?"

Olsen was shaking his head. "This was no mugging, guys. They meant to harm my voice. The one fella said I wouldn't be able to do my fancy voice tricks anymore. He was going to karate chop me in the throat."

Klondike froze all over. He looked Olsen in the eye. "What?" he whispered.

"No doubt about it at all, Mr Klondike. They targeted me. It…well, it looks like they were trying to put me out of business." He studied Klondike shrewdly, as if sensing something. "Now, why would anyone try and do a thing like that?"

Klondike glared at him in shock, then looked at Lacey and Heavy in turn. Lacey was trying to relay a message in her eyes.

Everyone who had gathered around seemed to stare at Olsen in bewilderment. Suzi held him tighter, shuddering slightly.

"I'm sorry, Rod," Klondike said weakly. He patted the youngster's arm. "It's my fault. The reason you got hurt. You see…"

Again, he looked around aimlessly. A sea of confused faces surrounded him. Lacey seemed to be imploring him not to say anymore, shaking her head and glaring wildly.

"There are people out there who want us to fail." He finally got it out. "I can't say much more right now. But someone is out to get us. To nail us."

McCabe squinted at him. "Does this have anything to do with that newspaper article in the Tribune with Lee Vesnick?"

Klondike shrugged. "I don't know. Hell, I don't know what the hell is going on. All I know is…one of us has been attacked." He looked sadly at Olsen again. "I'm truly sorry, kid."

Olsen looked around dazedly. "Hell, it's not your fault, boss. Who could have predicted any of this?" He rubbed at his jaw, smiled down at Suzi and tried to think.

McCabe folded his arms. "You wanna tell us the whole story, Kal?"

Suzi looked on the verge of tears. "What's going on here?"

"Alright," Klondike said, holding up his hands. "We're gunna have us a council meeting. Up in the big top. Why not? I'll...I'll tell you what I know."

And that's exactly what he did.

Chapter Ten

Under a cloud of uncertainty and apprehension, Klondike's Circus rolled on across the Western States.

The big top entertained sell-out crowds in San Diego, Phoenix, Santa Fe and El Paso, before moving on to Dallas.

The shows themselves were a spectacular success, despite the oppressive heat of a truly sweltering summer.

Lacey's press releases, the rising popularity of the brand and a clamour to see the top stars in action ensured that every seat in the giant circus tent was taken. Another town, another sell-out.

Every programme printed was sold, and there were massive sales of posters, signed photographs and children's replica outfits.

Gino Shapiro merchandise was the biggest seller, closely followed by anything featuring Roddy Olsen. But the circus management was quick to appreciate that photographs and posters featuring The Daredevils were also selling well, with more and more sold at each stop.

The whole thing amounted to a marvellous dilemma for Klondike and his staff. After a telephone conference with Daryl Addison, the old man suggested Klondike invest in more different factions of merchandise.

As was often the case with such ventures, Lacey was put in charge of new ideas. To the initial humour but overall enthusiasm of Klondike and Heavy, Lacey suggested they should start selling radical new items at the midway stalls. Lunchboxes, colouring books, stickers, even Klondike's Circus-branded stationary.

Lacey put through tentative initial orders with manufacturers back in Frisco.

They were moving into uncharted new territory, that was for sure. "Whoever heard of a circus selling lunchboxes?" was how Klondike dryly put it.

The merchandise all featured pictures of the circus stars as well as the official Klondike's Circus logo, which was plastered all over just about everything.

By the time the circus train rolled into Dallas, the replica costumes were evidently selling well. When the train pulled in, the performers and staff were greeted by a sea of young fans dressed in mini versions of Shapiro's orange outfit, Olsen's silver waistcoat and Corky's clown suit, and a group of teens wearing black and yellow Daredevils jumpsuits.

Klondike could not remember ever being greeted by a warmer sight at any town—at any time.

Ballyho's was a downtown saloon off Confederate Square in Dallas, barely 500 yards from the Sidewinder Fairground, where the glorious red and blue Klondike's Circus big top sat tall and proud.

Tip Enqvist sat at the bar with three of his riders—Bo, Gunner and Justin. They had come over for a few drinks after a long day's practice, two nights before the Dallas show.

Dressed in shirts and jeans, they had attracted little attention in the crowded barroom and had enjoyed several beers while watching a ball game on the bar TV.

Enqvist downed the contents of his tall glass and slammed it down onto the mahogany bar. "Come on boys, let's get out of here."

The Daredevils had a strange, uncanny way of following and obeying their leader. Many put it down to the age difference, with the grizzled veteran Tip managing and taking care of his younger, fresh-faced charges.

The trio beside him all finished their drinks as Enqvist threw several bills on to the bar top.

The bartender waded over excitedly. "I'll see you boys on Saturday night!"

Enqvist eyed him. "You're coming to the circus?"

"You bet I am! I can't wait! Taking the missus and the kids."

"Fantastic," Enqvist slurred with little enthusiasm. He made to leave, then turned back, as if trying to remember something. "Oh, tell your little ones they can now buy Daredevils costumes at the midway.

They look great."

The bartender nodded happily. "I'll be sure to do just that!" Enqvist nodded as he walked away. "You're the man."

The riders all left the bar together, the warm night air making them a little dazed as they hit the street. They headed for a back alley that led down to the fairground site.

As if remotely controlled by some unseen force, they all stopped as one to light cigarettes.

Bo was laughing. "Y'know, this really is something else. We are like celebrities here, no?"

Gunner joined the laughter. "That must be the one hundredth time we have been stopped."

"It's crazy," Justin chimed in. "The whole town must be coming to the show. Everybody knows us. Wants to see us."

Bo whooped. "I know. And I love it."

The youngsters all laughed as they hopped down the alley. Enqvist watched them, a half-smile on his face.

"Enjoy it, boys," he murmured, following them.

"Hey, looks like more fans coming now," Bo called out, pointing behind Enqvist.

The older man turned, and saw six youths dressed in varsity college sweaters approaching from the main square.

"Hey!" one of them called out excitedly, "you're the Daredevils, right? Wow! I can't believe it's you!"

Enqvist smiled as the speaker, dressed in a University of Dallas top and baseball cap, raced towards him.

"Right," he wheezed, "that's right. You, er, got your tickets for Saturday kid? You better—"

He was stopped in mid-sentence as the man's fist exploded into his face, dislodging several teeth and almost breaking his nose.

Enqvist flew backwards, clattering into a line of dirty garbage cans that littered the alley.

Suddenly, the group were upon them.

Bo, Gunner and Justin all found themselves being manhandled by the gang of marauding youths.

Bo was smacked around the head by a garbage can lid. Gunner was held by one man and punched several times in the ribs by another.

But Justin had the worst of it. He was the biggest of the riders, and was pounced upon by three of the gang, who pummelled him with fists and elbows before throwing him against the brick wall and kicking him into the mass of overturned rubbish that now filled the alleyway.

Enqvist struggled to his feet, holding his nose. He rose just as Bo was dealt a second blow by the man with the aluminium lid. It sent him flat on the asphalt, all but unconscious. The man went to deal a third strike, but Enqvist found an old bicycle chain among the trash and hurled it around the attacker's neck, tightening it and choking him.

Gunner had somehow managed to outfight his attackers, savagely kicking the puncher in the jaw, stunning him, before pushing the man who held him into the far wall, where his back crashed into a fire ladder.

"Hey! Get the hell out of here!"

Every single man fighting in the gutter looked up at the booming hillbilly accent that thundered across the alleyway. The brawling stopped as a terrifying sight greeted the melee.

A giant apparition was moving towards the fray—slow, menacing, like Frankenstein's monster. The beast emerged from the shadows and revealed himself to be Goliath, the circus giant. Dressed as always in his denim dungarees, he presented a bizarre, but uncompromising, sight as he waded through the trash.

The attackers all stared at each other and, as one, turned and tried to run. The man being strangled with the bicycle chain took advantage of Enqvist loosening his grip in shock at the sight of the newcomer, and shuffled free before joining his companions.

Enqvist, still in agony, collapsed to the floor. Gunner gave chase to the fleeing gang. Bo and Justin were sat up, clearly the worse for wear.

Goliath surveyed the damage, then knelt down next to Enqvist. A giant hand was placed on the fallen man's shoulder.

"Hey, Tip. You ok, boy?"

Enqvist looked up at the giant. "Goliath," he stammered. "You beautiful, overgrown son of a bitch." He laughed spontaneously, rubbing at his jaw. "You must be the best weapon to have in a fight there has ever been. You want to come out drinking with us? From now on?"

Goliath smiled down at him, showing off a quarry of grimy, yellow teeth. "As long as the drink is root beer."

Enqvist nodded. "So that's what they fed ya to make ya that big." Goliath hauled him to his feet and they both tended to their fallen comrades.

Gunner returned breathlessly to the alley, insisting the attackers had got away downtown.

Bo got to his feet as Enqvist dusted him off. "Who the hell were those guys?" he gasped.

"You remember what the chief said a few weeks back in LA?" said Enqvist. "After Olsen got hit down by the train? Well, I think this was the second act."

Justin stared at him. "But that would mean Syndicate men. Those guys? They looked like a Freshmen choir."

"Yeah," Bo snarled, "but they sure as hell didn't hit like them."

Enqvist simply stared down the alleyway, to where the gang had fled. His eyes took on a distant, faraway look.

"There's no doubt now. They are out to get us."

The following morning, Klondike and Heavy listened with dread as Enqvist and Goliath explained what had happened the night before. The group were stood near the entrance of the newly erected tent, where Klondike had been surveying the installation of the trapeze rigging.

High above at the far end of the big top, a team of roustabouts on a giant scaffolding were joining ropes and wires to support units and the all-important performance turrets.

Below that, other workers were putting together the grandstands, with the arena slowly forming before everyone's eyes.

Enqvist, who wore a large plaster over his nose, finished his summary, with Goliath grunting in agreement.

Klondike thought as he watched another roustabout wheel in a section of five bleachers that were headed towards the upper tiers. "Dammit!" he spat out. Yet again, he took on a mournful look as he surveyed the bruised Enqvist. "Listen, Tip. I sure am sorry you got knocked around. Like I said in LA, this—whatever this is—is my affair. It concerns me. It's my responsibility. We'll take care of your boys."

The rider laughed ruefully. "Forget about it, Kal. We're all in this together. Your circus has given us this big chance to be stars. I'm...well, I'm just worried about what else is coming our way." Then, his eyes narrowed coldly. "This could be a disaster. My Daredevils don't need this."

Heavy was shaking his head. "What the hell is Agostino up to, anyway? He trying to beat us into submission or what?"

Klondike nodded. "Exactly that, Heav. I reckon he's gunna keep up with these attacks until we agree to let him have a piece of the circus."

103

Goliath grunted. "I'd like to get this Agostino's head in my hands." Klondike laughed. "We'd all like that, Gol."

The group slowly disassembled, with Klondike and Heavy crossing the arena floor to the scaffolding. They watched the riggers working above.

Then, Jim McCabe entered the tent. Pausing at the flap, he located Klondike and headed in his direction.

"Kal," he barked. "There's something I think you should look at."

Klondike glanced at Heavy and rolled his eyes. "Tell me, McCabe, please tell me it's not bad news."

McCabe looked on glumly. "I'm sorry. Come with me."

The foreman led them out of the tent, back across the fairground field to the train on the siding.

He walked hurriedly to one of the central carriages, past scores of roustabouts and local helpers who were unloading equipment of all shapes and sizes. Then, he stopped by a flatbed truck that held a giant red tractor-like machine with a fat wooden javelin at its head. The ground-hole puncher. It was a machine used to hammer huge holes into the ground for the tentpoles.

Klondike looked up at the mighty machine. "Something wrong with old punchy?"

"You could say that," McCabe said. "We drove it back here to load it up again last night after all the holes were made. One of the boys noticed something wrong with the engine and controls. I just got a local mechanic to pop her open. He found this."

With that, McCabe hopped onto the truck's bed and made for the front of the puncher. He delicately raised the machine's hood, which was located on its side in front of the nose and javelin. Then he held his hand out, pointing at the machine's guts.

Klondike and Heavy jumped up and joined him by the small hood. What was inside barely resembled the auto parts of any mechanical construction they knew of. Wires had been cut and the machinery looked twisted and dented. Worst of all, the battery had been crushed.

"Jesus!" Heavy exclaimed. "The whole thing looks like it's been hit with a sledgehammer."

Klondike stared at the engine in stunned silence. "Sabotage."

"You bet it is," McCabe put in.

"What the hell happened here?"

McCabe shrugged. "It had been making awful noises during the put-up yesterday and the day before. I say someone's been tinkering with it."

Klondike nodded in a kind of understanding. "Can we get her fixed up?"

"You know how rare and unusual these things are, Kal. It's done, man. It's out for the season, I say. I can get this grease man to take it back to his yard, but I doubt he'll be able to do much. Besides, we need it before departure on Monday."

Klondike thought about it for several moments, struggling to take his eyes off the mess of auto parts.

Heavy leaned close. "Now, you can't call all of this coincidental."

"I know," Klondike breathed. He shook his head and looked around, over at the big top hovering grandly above everything, and then back to the puncher, sat on the flatbed.

"OK, McCabe. Let the mechanic see what he can do with old punchy. He's got himself four days. Tell him I'll pay double—no, treble—his usual fee if he can just get the damn thing working again."

"You got it, Kal."

McCabe leapt down from the flatbed truck and hurried off towards the other end of the train. Klondike watched him go, glanced back at the puncher, then got down and wandered idly along the gravel next to the rail line.

"Listen," he said to Heavy behind him. "I need to think. Maybe take a hot shower. Shave. I'm heading to my room. I'll see you for dinner in the chow line, Heav."

Then, he headed towards the accommodation carriages at the front of the express.

Heavy watched after him, then called out: "Don't worry, Kal. Everything will be just fine."

But Klondike just kept on walking.

Thirty minutes later, Klondike was sat sprawled on a leather armchair in his stateroom.

He was wearing a white pullover and light slacks having just got out of the shower. His head had cleared, and he held a large whiskey mac in one hand as he sat there with his eyes closed.

If it hadn't been for the incessant noise outside of the assembly teams, he may have fallen into a deep sleep. However, the rest did him good.

Suddenly, there was a light rap on the door.

He sprang to attention, downing the contents of his glass, rubbing at his face and standing. Curiously, he noted he was barefooted. "Who is it?"

His response was the door opening slowly, and a handsome, dapper-looking man in a silver suit shuffling in.

Klondike glared at him incredulously. The newcomer had slicked-back ebony hair and tanned features. "What—"

"Kal Klondike!" the man boomed. "Finally we meet. It is an honour, my man. The name's Tommy Farron."

He offered no hand, but instead crept around the room, his beady eyes taking in everything as he looked his host's quarters up and down. The wide smile never dropped.

Klondike watched him in bemusement. "What can I do for you, Mr Farron?"

The man stopped moving and looked up at him. "This room is magnificent, Kal. It's like a Waldorf suite. On a train!" He laughed insincerely.

Klondike frowned. "Is there something I can do for you?"

Farron smiled majestically. "Oh yes. Most certainly."

Finally, Klondike cracked. "All right, quit the act. Who the hell are you?"

The smile remained. "A big fan, Kal. A huge fan of the circus." He waltzed over to the main window on the edge of the room and leant against the glass. "You're having quite the season so far. Right? Every show a sell-out. Merchandise sales soaring. Another TV special coming up in Washington. Business is booming."

"You're well informed," Klondike rasped. "But you haven't answered my question."

Farron laughed softly, the beady eyes dancing as they looked around. "But you've had misfortunate too, my dear Kal. Incidents. Foul-ups. Disaster could be imminent."

Klondike stiffened all over. He glared at the intruder and snarled at him, stepping towards the window with menace.

"So, Agostino sent you, huh?"

Farron raised his hands. They were five feet apart now. "Don't be mad at me, Kal. I am the peacemaker here. Not the bad guy. I can help you, man. You've just got to let me help you."

"What are you talking about, god damn it!"

Farron still retained the graceful air of a door-to-door salesman. "Have you reconsidered Mr Agostino's offer?"

"Listen, dammit!" Klondike roared, and he grabbed at Farron's jacket lapels with an outstretched hand.

"Have you? Will you accept Mr Agostino's proposal?"

Now, Klondike had him pinned against the window. With surprising strength, Farron pushed him back, causing him to lose his grip. "Listen to me, Klondike," the intruder gasped, moving away. "This is just the beginning, man. If you don't let us have a stake of your circus, things are going to get worse. Much worse. And you can take that to the bank, my man."

Klondike glared at him, before charging at him again, pushing him towards the door. "You tell Agostino to keep his nose outta my business."

Farron was impassive, seemingly enjoying the exchange. "Come on, man. You're making a big mistake. Give me the answer I want."

"You made the mistake, pal. Coming here in the first place."

He pushed Farron wildly again. Then, the door burst open and Heavy made to enter.

"I heard shouting and…" he blurted, before seeing Farron being bundled out of the room. He moved out of the way, stunned. "What the…"

Klondike was pushing Farron down the corridor to the platform door. "Help me get him outta here, Heav!"

Without further query, Heavy joined Klondike and the two men rushed Farron to the platform door. Heavy threw it open and together they bundled Farron out onto the gravel below. Incredibly, the man was still babbling about his proposed deal as he was ejected. He flew out of the train, miraculously landing on his feet outside.

He finally stopped shrieking as he hit the dirt, dusting off his immaculate silver blazer. Then, he looked up scornfully at Heavy and Klondike on the train ledge above him.

"There's still time, Klondike," he muttered, the bravado finally gone. "You can still cut a deal with us. Cut a deal…while you still have an empire to your name."

Klondike looked down at him in pure disgust. "You take your sorry ass back to Agostino. Tell him no deal. And don't you ever even think about setting foot on my train again, you sorry-looking, sorry-dressed son of a bitch!"

He rammed the platform door shut. Then he and Heavy watched out the side window as the fancy-dressed man skulked off, walking slowly across the fairground field.

"Where in hell did that guy come from?" Heavy asked.

"I dunno, he just walked into my room," Klondike muttered.

"Just like that, eh?" Heavy shook his head. "Too easy."

Klondike nodded slowly. He looked at his old friend with concern.

"Kal," Heavy said quietly. "What are we going to do about all this?"

"Hell," Klondike said with fierce determination. "We fight back."

Chapter Eleven

Eric Ribbeck sat in the study of his penthouse suite at the Murrayfield Hotel in Chicago, going through a mound of paperwork. The Murrayfield was a huge construction in the city's centre, soaring above most other skyscrapers and looking down on the streets with an intimidating superiority. And the penthouse sat at the very top of the behemoth.

Dressed in a burgundy smoking jacket and slacks, Ribbeck sat back at the large pine desk and glanced out the floor-to-ceiling window at the magnificent view of the Windy City beyond.

His circus had arrived in Chicago three days earlier, and had just begun a run of five back-to-back sell-out shows at the Elysium Fields downtown. He had booked the penthouse for a few nights to take care of various items of personal business, leaving his executive assistant to run the circus.

A hard-looking young man breezed into the study from the lounge beyond. Luca Marconi, Ribbeck's personal bodyguard.

"Your guests are here, boss," he murmured as he hovered by the door.

Ribbeck clapped his hands together with delight. "Thank you, Luca." He rose, ran a hand through his thick snow white hair, and crossed the study, moving into the giant, luxurious lounging room.

Paul Agostino and Lee Vesnick were seated on a couch and rose as he entered. Agostino was dressed in his usual sharp suit.

Vesnick wore a flower shirt and white pants, looking more like a summer camp leader than anything else.

"Good to see y'all," Ribbeck called as he made his way to an armchair opposite the couch. "Whatya think of this place? Paradise, eh?"

"Looks good, Eric," Agostino mumbled as he sat down again.

Vesnick's eyes were alive and wild as he glanced around the suite. "This place is something else, Mr Ribbeck. Hell, I never thought I'd ever enter a penthouse at the Murrayfield."

"Play your cards right, son, and you may get used to it," Ribbeck muttered. "Luca! Get us three scotches."

Marconi crossed the room to a large bar and poured the drinks, dutifully handing them out before standing directly behind his boss in the armchair.

"Can we get straight down to business?" Agostino said.

"You bet," Ribbeck spat out. He sipped his drink and then unexpectedly scowled at Agostino. "You've got some explaining to do, Paul."

"Excuse me!"

"Damn straight. What the hell were you thinking setting your boys on Olsen like that? You could have ruined his career."

Agostino was not used to being spoken to in such a manner. His skin reddened slightly, the hideous scar that dominated his face seemingly ablaze. "What the hell? I thought the idea was to push Klondike until he agreed to play ball. Hit him where it hurts. Go after his most prized possessions. That punk Olsen is quite the superstar down there. Take him out of the team and Klondike has a problem. Without Olsen, his circus ain't the same box office draw. That will make him reconsider my offer."

Ribbeck shook his head angrily. "No, no, no, god damn it! That's not what we're doing here, boy. Remember what I told you. I want Olsen and Shapiro under my big top. Signed up. Performing for Ribbeck's World Circus. With those two under contract...hell, I'll have the biggest show the world has ever seen." He leant forward and pointed at Agostino. "But not if Olsen can't ever do his tricks again. Your goons almost crushed his voice box, so I hear. That boy is gunna be one of the biggest stars in the country in a few years. Dammit all, you nearly destroyed him."

Agostino chewed it over. It had been a long time since he had been talked down to like that. He didn't like it. And he wasn't about to cave in. Not to anybody. "That's how I run my outfit. Just what we got going here, Eric?"

Ribbeck sat still, contemplating it all. He produced a silver case from his jacket and pulled out a thin cheroot, which Marconi lit for him. Then, he blew out a seemingly never-ending cloud of grey smoke.

"The deal is still the same, Paul. You will take over the circus. Your people will have control. You will sell the services of Shapiro and Olsen on to me, for an enormous fee that your people will drool over. Then, you'll set up new management for the circus and it will continue to tour at a tidy profit. I've got a manager in mind to run it for you. And, of course, I will have my all-star line-up. At last!"

Vesnick, who had watched the proceedings with a wild-eyed look, finally spoke up. "And I'll be part of that line-up, right Mr Ribbeck?"

The old man chuckled mirthlessly. "Sure, kid." But his cold blue eyes were locked on his other guest. "So that's still our deal, right?"

Agostino had some of his drink. "Right."

"So," Ribbeck continued, toying with the cheroot, "where exactly do we stand with Klondike right now? Your boys haven't broken him, huh?"

"Not yet," Agostino replied. "Along with hitting Olsen, we slapped around those stunt riders, The Daredevils. One of my top men has fixed that damn ditch-making machine—"

"The groundhole puncher…" Ribbeck put in.

"Right. We've roughed up some of his roustabouts, tried to break into the train. Along with all the negative newspaper publicity you engineered, Eric, that's quite a campaign. But my boy Tommy called on Klondike yesterday and asked him if he had changed his mind."

"What happened?"

Agostino sneered in disgust. "They threw him out. Didn't even rough him up. Just told him to leave."

Ribbeck shook his head angrily, jabbing the air with the cheroot. "God damn it! This is sticks and stones stuff, Paul. Pushing people around. Busting an engine. Hell, roustabouts have been roughed up all their lives, the dirty sons a bitches! That's not gunna work. No, we need to up the ante, boys. We need to teach Klondike a lesson. Show him our collective power."

Agostino's eyes narrowed. "What we discussed before?"

Ribbeck nodded grimly. "The big one."

"Woh, woh, woh!" Vesnick cried in alarm. He eyed the other two in panic. "Now, I agreed to be a part of this, guys. But that…that is a different level altogether. Think about it…you'd be risking everything."

The other two seemingly ignored him. An uncomfortable silence followed. Agostino and Ribbeck stared hard at one another. Vesnick started to say something, then thought better of it.

Then, a suited man, one of Ribbeck's flunkies, quietly entered the lounge, approached his boss and whispered something into his ear. The old man smiled wickedly in delight. Then he whispered something to his employee.

Turning back to the others, he cackled slightly. "Ah," he breathed, "it may not come to that, boys."

Agostino glared at him. "What you talking about?"

Ribbeck smiled as he stood up and paced towards the main door. "A little surprise, Paul. I have taken the liberty of recruiting a fresh confederate. A fourth man."

"Fourth man!" Agostino exploded. "I didn't agree to no fourth man! What is this?"

"Easy," Ribbeck held up a calming hand. "You will agree to his suitability when you realise just who he is. And what he brings to the card table. For us, he may be a wild card, if you will." He was still cackling to himself.

"Who is it?" Vesnick cried, on the edge of his seat.

"Oh, a man who hates Kal Klondike more than anyone."

Suddenly, the door swung open and a figure waded in—powerful, yet uncaring, almost as if he was lost.

The newcomer was a truly frightening-looking man. He was dressed in what looked like a safari outfit, a beige shirt and matching pants with a brown neckerchief. He had blazing red hair and a pointed beard, with deeply tanned skin. But it was the face that made the strongest impression. The man had scarred, calloused skin and looked as if he had been sick recently. The brown eyes were wild and large, almost demonic, making him look unhinged.

He stood next to Ribbeck and quietly surveyed his new surroundings.

"Gentlemen," Ribbeck announced grandly, "allow me to introduce Emile Rance."

Vesnick stood to attention, his mouth gaping. "Oh my god!" he called. "We…I, er, I thought you were dead!"

Rance looked at him with contempt. "The whole world thinks I'm dead," he snarled in a thick South African accent.

Ribbeck put a hand on Rance's shoulder and introduced the others. There were no handshakes. Vesnick and Agostino stayed back. "Come, Emile," said Ribbeck, and he led Rance to the seating area, where the newcomer merely stood while the others all sat.

Ribbeck smiled at the strange aura Rance seemed to create. "We are honoured to have you, my friend. Please, relax. A drink perhaps?"

Rance huffed. "No drink."

He stood there, rooted to the spot, as the others seemed to examine this strange and mysterious newcomer.

"Alright," Agostino said at last. "Let's have it. What's your story, mac?"

Rance glared at him, the eyes hitting him like a thunderbolt. "You people are all out to nail Klondike, right?"

Agostino folded his arms. "What of it, Tarzan?"

The South African stared into nothingness, his nostrils flaring. It was almost like he was under some form of hypnosis. "Because of Klondike, my family is dead."

"What?" Vesnick cried in alarm. "Your family? What the hell?"

"That's right," Rance continued. "Apollo, my beautiful South African lion king. And Zeus, my queen. The smartest white tiger that ever lived. Only Cassius…brave, humble Cassius survived. Klondike and his people are responsible for this. He abandoned us! After we gave him our blood. Our sweat. Our lives!"

Agostino and Vesnick stared at each other in disbelief. Then both looked at Ribbeck, who was smiling like a stage director watching his play come to life.

"Er, Eric, what the hell is happening?" Agostino whispered, eyes flicking back to Rance.

"We have got ourselves another hand, one who really believes in our cause," Ribbeck purred.

"Jesus Christ!" Agostino blurted. "He's insane, for Chrissakes!"

Rance took a step forward. "You want to say something, smart man? Say it to my face!"

Agostino stood up and put a hand in his jacket pocket. "I'll finish you if I want to, Tarzan!"

Then, Marconi flew into the middle and stood between the two, with Ribbeck appealing for calm and placing a hand on Rance's arm. "It's ok, it's ok, boys. Hell, we are all friends here. Come on! Emile, please sit down now."

Rance reluctantly sat on an easy chair, as Agostino cooled and flopped back on to the couch.

Ribbeck remained standing and lectured the gathering. "Now, listen good Paul. Our friend Emile here was the star animal trainer at Klondike's Circus. Third highest name on the bill at one stage. Then, it all fell apart after the train crash two years ago. You all know about that. Well, Emile's lions and silver tiger both escaped from the wreckage on that fateful night and disappeared into the desert plains. Of course, Emile followed. They were, as he said, his family. He tracked them. For weeks. Finally, he found the bodies in the Sierra Navarro desert. Cassius was alive, but barely. The whole troupe—man and beasts—had been left to die by Klondike and his crew."

An uncomfortable silence followed. Agostino was shaking his head, not sure what exactly was transpiring.

It was Vesnick who spoke. "How is any of that Klondike's fault?"

"It is all his fault!" Rance raged. "His train was old, faulty. It crashed like that and was torn apart. Someone had tampered with the lion cages before, making them vulnerable. And…and after it was all over, there was nothing! No mention of Emile Rance and his lions. It was as if we had never existed."

Vesnick made to reply, thought better of it, and instead finished his drink. He studied Rance with frightened eyes. "What have you been doing all this time?" he whispered.

Rance looked downwards. "I was nursing my boy Cassius. An animal reserve in Fresno took us in. I have been building up his strength again, tending to him." He looked up at Vesnick and smiled—a cold, calculating, murderous grin. "And I taught him a few new tricks."

Vesnick visibly shuddered.

With another chuckle, Ribbeck paced around the lounge and held his hands high. "OK, boys. Now we all know what's what. Emile here knows more about Klondike's Circus than any of us. He was a performer there for four years. Now, I say he is a perfect recruit."

Agostino lit a cigarette and sat back, a little more relaxed now. "That's all very well, Eric. But what I want to know is…what do we do next?"

Ribbeck paced across to the bar. The other three all stared at him, waiting. The old man ran a hand through his hair and seemed strangely pained and ill at ease. He grabbed at the whiskey bottle and, in an uncharacteristic gesture, took a pull from it. He stared at a fixed spot the others could not determine.

"Like I said, it's time to up the ante."

Later, in the early evening, Ribbeck stood on the penthouse balcony, leaning against the railings as he looked down at the sprawling metropolis far below, yet all around.

Marconi crept out from the room and brought him a cup of coffee. "Thank you, Luca," he whispered, taking a sip as he studied the clouds hovering above the peaks of the skyscrapers.

"You alright, boss?"

"Ha! Couldn't be better, my boy. I feel like a king up here." Marconi hovered nervously around him, looking about the large, marble-plated balcony.

Ribbeck turned. "What is it?"

Marconi shook his head, then looked at Ribbeck with concern. "Hell, boss, I just worry is all." He waved a hand through the air. "All this…the plans, the schemes. That guy from New York. The lion man. All of it. I just wonder…is it all really worth it?"

Ribbeck was quiet, then nodded thoughtfully. Marconi had been by his side for three years now. He had witnessed much drama in that time. His views were worthy of consideration. "My dear Luca," he drawled in his Texas accent. "It is a good point. But, you forget my mission. My lifetime mission. What all this is about. I want the greatest show on earth. Like Barnum before me. I want the greatest show there has ever been. Nothing less. It is my dream. In many ways, my destiny. I want it so bad, dammit!" He sipped at the coffee, holding the cup into his chest as he leant against the railing.

"But there is this one problem," he continued. "As long as Klondike's Circus is out there…it can't happen. Shapiro and Olsen are now probably the two biggest stars in the business. Both Klondike and I know that, I feel. So, you see, the only way to get Ribbeck's World Circus into a stratosphere all of its own is to have those two under my big top. Or rid Klondike's outfit for good. A mortal wound, if you will."

Marconi listened dutifully. He smiled up at his employer. "It's quite a dream, boss."

"Dreams…" Ribbeck said wistfully. Then, he smiled his charismatic old smile at Marconi, seemingly finding himself again. "Let me tell you, Luca. I've said it before, and dammit I'll say it again. Some people make memories. Some people make money."

He laughed out loud. "But me? I make history. History!"

Chapter Twelve

"Y'know, Roddy, I oughta go into politics."

"And why is that, Rust?"

"Cos Washington is full of dummies. I'd fit right in!"

Laughter floated down from the audience as they watched with delight as Roddy Olsen began his set with Rusty Fox on his right arm.

Olsen was dressed in his usual silver waistcoat and purple pants, with the little fox puppet wearing his trademark leather jacket and jeans. Every eye in the big top was focused on the unusual duo on the stool in front of the microphone in the centre of the floor.

"OK!" Rusty cried, "it's time for a song. What do you say everyone?" A loud cheer reverberated across the grandstands.

Roddy spoke, "Well the people want to hear you sing, Rust. What have you got in mind?"

"A fast song!" the squeaky voice replied.

Olsen gave a look of mock nervousness. "Now, Rusty, we talked about fast songs..."

"Yeah, you don't like em! You can't make me talk that fast without your lips moving!"

"Now come on, old buddy, let's pick a nice song for these good people."

"Alright. How about..." he let the sentence linger, then cried: "Rock Island Line!"

The audience let out a mighty cheer at the commencement of one of the star's most beloved routines.

"No!" Olsen cried at his puppet. "Not the Rock. Anything but that. I can't..." but the music had already begun on the tannoy.

Rusty Fox began singing with Olsen joining in with the odd line of the chorus. Then, as was their trademark, the music and the lyrics got faster and faster as Rusty began belting it out.

Suddenly, a new voice emanated from the old trunk on the floor. "Hold it, hold it!"

The music and the singing ceased. Olsen and Rusty stared at each other in shock. "Who is that?" said Rusty.

"I think I have an idea," Olsen murmured.

"Get me outta here! And that's an order!" the new, hoarse voice bellowed.

"It's coming from the trunk," Olsen said, before he left the stool, carried Rusty over to the giant case and opened it. He bent down into the confines.

"Whoa!" the harsh new voice cried.

When Olsen emerged again, he had Rusty on one arm and Napoleon, his Army veteran puppet, on the other. Napoleon was dressed in his usual GI outfit with cap.

"Holy West Point!" the old figure cried. "How many times have I got to tell you, Olsen. No singing. Not unless it's a hymn or an old Army song." Olsen made Napoleon and Rusty face each other.

"And we definitely don't allow this slimy maggot to sing any of his rock n droll nonsense!"

"I'm not a maggot! I'm a fox."

"You're a menace to society, ratboy! As soon as this fancy fair is over, I'm gunna march you to the nearest GI recruitment post and we're signing you up with Uncle Sam."

"But you can't march, old-timer. You can't even stand or sit up, or even speak, without assistance!"

Olsen laughed aloud as the crowd cheered the scene. "Ok, ok, folks. Say, I have an idea. Why don't you join in Napoleon?"

"What! Me! Are you crazy?"

Rusty laughed too and addressed the audience. "What you folks like to see me, Roddy and Napoleon all sing together?"

As the audience roared their approval, the music started up again and the trio—one man and two puppets—all took it in turns to sing one line each of Rock Island Line. Once again, the song got faster and faster. Olsen's set of three voices became mechanical as they passed each other over and over again.

No matter how many times you saw it, the ingenious display of voice manipulation defied belief. The speed, accuracy and showmanship was hard to fathom to many watching.

When Olsen concluded the song, the audience rose as one to applaud.

Twenty minutes later, Olsen was in his trailer behind the big top, sprawled on a fold-up chair in front of the dresser. He had just soaked a flannel in a washbasin of cold water and now held it to his forehead, sitting back in the chair and breathing softly.

The temperature had seemed impossibly high in the great tent, with its capacity crowd. Now, he had removed his waistcoat and shirt and put on a vest. He felt himself cooling rapidly.

The trailer door burst open and he looked up in surprise. "Congratulations!"

Lacey hopped excitedly into the small room, carrying a large bottle of champagne.

He looked at her, then at the bottle. "Miss Lacey! What's all this?" She eyed him teasingly. "You don't know what today is, do you?" Olsen looked dazed. "I'm sorry, no."

"Well, Roddy, I do know. Because it's a real landmark." She held the bottle aloft and began working the cork out with her slender hands. "You have just completed your 50th show for Klondike's Circus! It's your golden anniversary, Roddy!"

With that, the cork exploded out of the bottle and champagne gushed out onto the floor. Lacey quickly produced two flutes she had placed behind her and filled them expertly.

She handed a glass to Olsen and held her own one triumphantly before her.

"Like I said, congratulations! Here's to 50 sell-out performances! And many more."

"Thank you, Lacey."

They clinked glasses and both took a long, pleasurable sip of the champagne.

Then, Lacey waltzed to the dresser and perched on the end. Olsen, slumped in the wooden chair, looked at her. She had the air and appearance of a star herself. Dressed in a country and western style white dancehall dress, she looked like she had just wandered in from a Broadway musical.

"Wow," he whispered, "50 shows. Incredible. I never thought it possible. After all I went through. All we went through."

She smiled with pride as she sipped her drink. "Seems like yesterday, doesn't it? When you turned up at the holding camp. Asking for an audition. Oh my, what a day that was."

"Yeah, I'll never, ever forget it. I owe you and Mr Klondike everything. For all of this. All the success. Everything that has happened to me."

Lacey gazed at him with her giant violet eyes. "Roddy, my god. The day you came into our camp…into our lives…changed Klondike's Circus forever. Maybe it was all fate. The way it all happened. It's like a movie. All I know is…thank god you came. You came to us."

Olsen nodded thoughtfully. He looked up at her dreamily. "You know, Lacey, without you none of this would have happened. I know I've said it many times, but you were my champion. You argued my case back then. And many times since. It was you, Lacey…you made all this happen. We both know it."

Lacey glanced at his famous trunk, propped up against the washroom door in the far corner. "I'd never seen anyone like you. All the shows I've worked for, all the acts I dealt with. No one ever just took my breath away like that." The beautiful eyes were locked onto him now. "You're an artist, Roddy. A spectacular artist."

He rose slowly from the chair, putting his glass on the dresser and standing in front of her. Her eyes followed him.

"Well," he said quietly, "if that is true, Lacey, you must be my muse." She rose from the dresser and put her arms quickly around him, embracing him in a mighty hug. He held her tight.

Then, after a good 30 seconds, she pushed herself away and hastily made for the door. Looking back, she smiled awkwardly at him.

"Congratulations, Roddy. We're all so proud of you." Then, she opened the door and jumped out of the trailer.

Suzi Dando watched her from behind the wooden costumes hut, barely 20 yards away. She was wearing her white dress ahead of her upcoming performance, but had a cloak around her shoulders, which she now pulled closer to her.

She watched in the light of a full moon as Lacey wandered slowly away from the trailers, following a path that led back to the flap of the great circus tent that towered over everything.

Suzi's eyes followed her. Lacey Tanner was a beautiful, unusual woman, she thought. Her poise, her confidence, her whole manner. The way she spoke. Suzi had never quite got over it.

Peeking around the corner of the portable wooden hut, she looked at Olsen's trailer again. She could just about see him stood in front of the dresser.

Then, she looked up at the moon. Now, there were tears in her eyes.

119

Inside the big top, the Showcase Revue players were just coming to the end of their act. The performers were all waving to the grandstands as they trotted off the sawdust.

Lacey re-entered the tent through the flap and re-joined Klondike, Heavy and Plum in their customary position just inside the entrance tunnel. She immediately stuck herself next to Klondike, their arms almost touching, as everyone applauded the Showcase stars.

Klondike turned and smiled happily at Lacey. She smiled back. Then they all offered their congratulations as Gargantua, Goliath, Percy and the dwarves and Rumpy Stiltskin all jogged past them to the exit. Klondike watched them go and then nodded as Gino Shapiro and Penny Fortune emerged into the backstage area, resplendent in their fur-collared capes.

Heavy paraded out to the arena floor to deliver the big introduction as the show reached its spectacular climax.

"Everything ok, Gino?" Klondike asked, standing to the side of the great flyer.

Shapiro stared up into the heavens as he answered. "Si, chairman. Everything is fine. Except, that is, for these damn newspaper articles." The eyes did not budge, even as his voice grew agitated. "You ask me, we should hire a bounty hunter to find this runt Vesnick. Before he shoots his mouth off with any more lies."

Klondike nodded. "Hell, it's not a bad idea. Listen, don't read it you two. He is a desperate man. Crazy!"

"He upset Penny deeply, chairman."

Klondike looked across to Shapiro's blonde assistant, but she too was focused on the trapeze rigs dangling from the tent ceiling.

As Heavy made the grand introduction, the crowd slowly began chanting as one. "Gino! Gino! Gino!"

Shapiro allowed himself a smile as he stared upwards, still not looking at Klondike. "You hear that, chairman? The people love us. They need us. And now…" He closed his eyes, as if in prayer. "We are here."

The duo strode forward with zest, and emerged onto the arena floor as Heavy's voice thundered: "The debonair king of the air…Gino Shapiro!"

The standard massive ovation followed as Shapiro and Penny waved at the cheering patrons that enveloped their stage. Tossing their capes aside, they made for the tall ropes.

Klondike put his arms around Lacey and Plum as Heavy paced back towards them.

"Y'know, folks," he mused. "No wonder people want to take all this away from us. Hell, it's the most beautiful feeling in the world."

That Dallas show would become one of the most revered of the season. Many newspaper reviewers said afterwards that the unique connection between the performers and the audience set it apart, with many in the crowd so familiar with the stars and their acts that they were cheering before anything had happened.

Names of the performers were chanted and sang out loud by many seated in the grandstands, and the whole experience had been a warm, surreal evening.

While the following morning's reviews and write-ups were glowing, the continued uncertainty surrounding the circus and the threat of Agostino and his people was still ever-present.

That morning, everything was packed up onto the train as usual and the staff and performers quietly went about their business.

Jim McCabe was overseeing the steady deconstruction of the circus tent when someone called his name and pointed to the entrance to the fairground field.

Squinting into the sun, he saw a small truck pulling in, towing a large trailer, upon which sat the huge red ground-puncher.

"I'll be damned," he muttered.

He jogged across to where the truck pulled up, close to the rail siding where the train sat.

The local mechanic hopped out of the driver's seat and saw McCabe bounding over.

"You fixed it?" the foreman called in amazement.

The mechanic shook his head. "Fixed? No," he said in a Texas drawl. "But I got that hole puncher pole working alright. The engine ticks over just about. So you'll be able to punch em big old holes in the mud. I gathered that was the most important thing here, boss."

McCabe stared up at the big red behemoth. "Damn right."

"You'll just have to wheel it over to where you want a hole putting, with the motor on low. Now, in terms of fixing the engine for good, it needs a whole new set of guts. I have no idea where in hell you'll get the new parts for that. Hell, I never seen nuthin like this baby before."

McCabe shook his head. "That's ok. We can make it work." He turned to the young mechanic. "Mister, I can't thank you enough. Finally, some good news."

The youngster smiled. "I'm looking forward to mah fee, buddy."

McCabe chuckled. He put an arm around the mechanic and called out to one of his roustabouts.

"OK, mac, let's get things moving. Let's go, let's go, let's go."

Chapter Thirteen

The circus train rolled on to Houston the following morning.

The venue this time was the Cattlemen's Club, a huge tourist attraction on the edge of the city centre that featured rollercoaster rides and animal pens. Children could ride horses and watch rodeo displays, while patrons were free to browse the many cowboy-themed displays and museums.

The big top and midway would be pitched up in a sprawling field behind the complex that was often used for rodeos and horse riding events.

The only issue with this venue was that the nearest railway siding was a half mile away, so transportation was a major issue. Because of this, Klondike always allowed four days of preparation for the Houston show.

On the plus side, the circus team had access to the Cattlemen's Club's many outdoor trailers and practice facilities, which lay on the riding park alongside rows of temporary grandstands.

As the train pulled to a stop at the end of the branch line, the slow decampment process began.

A sea of bodies moved up and down the edge of the railway. The trucks and flatbeds were pulled down out of the carriages and put in position for loading. Roustabouts began hauling down machinery and stalls. The horses were calmly led down the ramps by the Range Riders.

Kal Klondike stood near the back of the train watching everything, an unlit cigar wedged in the corner of his mouth.

He felt like a nightclub bouncer, looking out for any signs of trouble. Ready to pounce at any moment. What was he looking for? Even he did not know. But he felt ready.

Lacey emerged from the interchange door, wearing a fashionable trouser suit. She joined him on the tarmac and watched the unloading operation.

"You look ready to strike, tiger," she murmured playfully.

"You better believe it, Lacey. I've told all the boys to be extra vigilant. At all times. My circus is on a roll. You saw those reviews yesterday. We are flying right now. Nothing is gunna change that."

She nodded vaguely. "Well, let's hope the worst is over now." She lit a cigarette and studied him teasingly.

"What is it?" he said irritably.

With that, she placed her arm through his and tried to turn him. "Come on, Kalvin."

"Come on what? Where do you think we're going? I've got an operation to watch over. We're a half mile from the venue out here!"

She didn't budge. "Kalvin, baby. You're going to go out of your mind with worry. Watching every pillar and post being taken down. Waiting to save the circus from…well, whatever. Come! Let's walk."

He tried to shake her off. "Hey, whoa there! Dammit, Lacey, this is serious!"

She wouldn't hear of it. "Jim McCabe and everyone else is well on top of it. They don't need you watching over them like a holy protector."

He looked down at her. She glanced up, with those beguiling violet eyes pleading with him. "This really isn't a good time for a walk, Lacey."

"Pah!" she said. She wrapped her other arm around his and tugged him along. "Now, I know a lovely little place. Go there every time I'm in Houston. Which isn't often, admittedly. But, hey, it's beautiful. Come on, boss man. You need a break."

Arm in arm, they walked slowly away from the train and the hive of incessant activity, down a path that ran behind an ancient-looking station house, alongside an old factory.

They did not know, could never have known, that they were being watched. Their every move. At that exact moment.

On the other side of the railroad track, in a virtually deserted old parking lot, a man sat behind the wheel of a large van. Watching. As he recognised Klondike and Lacey, his large brown eyes took on a look that could only be described as venomous.

He snarled slightly to himself. Then, he turned in his seat and made his way into the rear of the van.

"You were right, Lacey. This sure is a beautiful spot."

Klondike smiled quaintly as he wandered absently along the shore of a huge, placid reservoir. The water seemed to stretch for miles, and lapped gently at the sandy gravel that made up its perimeter. Tall reeds and hedgerows made up a boundary of sorts, hiding the beauty spot from the sprawling city heights beyond.

"What I tell you?" Lacey purred. "See? You feel better already." They walked side by side now. Klondike had his hands deep in his pockets.

"What do they call it again?"

"Lake Eerie."

He frowned. "Seems anything but eerie to me. So much peace so close to the city. Hell, this must be the last plot of land in Houston not drilled to hell by those oilmen."

She skipped along happily beside him. "Houston must be your kind of place, eh Kal."

He grunted, looking down at her. "What makes you say that?"

"Oh," she said, smiling, as if building up a joke, "you fancy yourself as a cowboy. Your old knife thrower days…that was the gimmick, right? Cowboys are everywhere down here. Oilmen. Cattlemen. Rodeo riders." She tweaked his fedora. "Men in hats."

He chucked softly. "Yeah. I always fancied myself as a cowboy. It's funny. Growing up in Hell's Kitchen. About as far from the wild west as you can get. Never even saw a horse, much less a wide open space or prairie. Apart from at the picture shows." He looked out across the wide expanse of still water. "I guess that's what the circus is all about—finding yourself. Fulfilling your dream. Finding that character, that way of life, that you always wanted. Only then can you truly be free."

"It's a calling," she whispered. Standing alongside him, they both stopped and studied the lake. Its surface was a curious oily turquoise colour.

Klondike thought for a moment. It was funny, when he had first met Lacey he had often felt deeply uncomfortable around her. She carried herself like a celebrity, a star. Her aura and quick thinking had somehow made him feel inferior. The whole experience had been irksome for him. But he had found himself following her ideas, helpless but to be at her bidding. It was strange, he thought now.

He didn't feel that way anymore.

"Y'know, Lacey," he drawled. "We're getting kinda close, ain't we?" She turned and smiled at him. "I think we passed that point in my first season, tiger."

"Er, yeah. Well, I…what I mean is. Hell!" He screwed his face up. Then he looked at her solemnly. "You're the greatest, Lacey. That's what I'm trying to say."

She rolled her head back. "Why, Kalvin?" she gushed in a high-pitched voice. "Such chivalry and grace. Oh my…" she rubbed his arm playfully. Then she looked at him seriously. "Thank you, baby. It means a lot. You're pretty great yourself, tough guy."

They continued walking along the edge of the lake, enjoying the peace. The only sound was the soft lapping of the water by their feet.

"I am so blessed," Lacey said. "Being able to travel America with you and your troupe. I love it. I love it so much. The relationships I've built up. With everyone. It's such an incredible feeling. I am so attached to everybody."

Klondike looked away from her. "Like Roddy?"

She eyed him suspiciously. An awkward silence followed. "Well, yes," she said quickly. "And all the others."

"But the kid is special, ain't he?"

She shook her head. "Of course. I…I guess I feel a certain sense of attachment and sentimentality towards Roddy. Sure I do. It all goes back to that day he wandered into the camp at Santa Cruz. You remember, of course? How I talked you into hiring him? How I pleaded his case?"

He laughed out loud. "How could I forget? That day proved to me…everything you do, everything you say, is pure gold. You're dynamite, Lacey, absolute dynamite."

She waved a hand through the air. "And you are just too sweet, Kalvin."

Unconsciously, he felt his emotions swell up deep within him. "It's true…" he whispered. "It's all true. It's, er, I just…"

Lacey looked up, moving closer to his frame. "Kal, are you…"

Then, in an instant, he took her in his arms, his tight grip shocking her as he held her before him, her feet almost going into the water. "You're everything to me, Lacey," he cried. "Hell, you know it yourself."

She closed her eyes and whimpered. "Oh, Roddy!"

He glared at her as he held her before him. "What!"

Suddenly, the peace of the lake was shattered by a shocking, ear-splitting, otherworldly roar. Birds fled from the trees as one and the bushes seemed to sway. Klondike and Lacey almost lost their footing and plunged into the water.

They steadied themselves, Klondike putting a hand on the ground as he pulled them onto the bank. He looked up in shock.

There, not 30 yards away, was an unbelievable sight, thrilling and terrifying in equal measure.

A lion was prowling along the lakeside. Suddenly spotting the duo by the water, it had stood alert, tilting its head back and roaring aloud.

Klondike and Lacey stared at the beast in pure and utter shock. They were rooted to the spot with fear and stunned disbelief.

Klondike studied the animal absently as he tried to think. Its fur was matted and blackened in parts. It looked malnourished and wild.

The lion growled in a low tone as it stood watching them with a kind of muted fury.

Lacey grabbed at Klondike wildly, moving behind him, her arms around his chest. "Kal," she whispered in fright, "what in the world…"

"I know," he muttered, studying the beast before them, "I can't believe it." He looked about them in desperation, his eyes falling on an old wooden gate barely 20 yards down the path from where they stood. It appeared to lead to a field beyond.

"Listen," he hissed, "we need to get to that gate over there. If we can just…"

He didn't finish as the lion roared again and, in a horrifying moment, put its head down and charged towards the bewildered couple.

"Run, Lacey, run!" he cried. He grabbed her hand and sprinted for the gate, in the opposite direction to where the lion was charging.

He practically dragged her through the dirt as he hurtled across the ground. They could hear the great beast snarling and breathing heavily as it closed the distance. Neither looked back.

They crested a slight hump in the earth before crashing their bodies into the old oak gate, which appeared in a gap between the reeds and hedge growth.

Klondike grabbed Lacey desperately by the waist and threw her over the top, unceremoniously dumping her in the field beyond. Then he dived at the top plank and threw himself over headfirst, landing on his back.

One second later, after Klondike flew over the top, the wild lion crashed into the gate like a juggernaut. The impact was devastating. The beast surged straight threw the wooden structure, smashing it into pieces, tearing into the field and crying out as if in fright.

Klondike rolled Lacey into the relative cover of the bushes, then grabbed at a large fencepost that had been shattered in two. He dumbly picked up one of the broken planks.

Looking up, he saw the lion turn around slowly and lock eyes with him.

Then, in an instant, it raced straight at him, snarling out loud. The noise sounded like the scream of a deranged primate.

Klondike had no time to move, barely to think. He instinctively moved the wooden post horizontally in front of him.

The lion dived for him, its jaws wide open as it flew through the air. Lacey screamed in terror.

Klondike saw two terrifying lines of razor sharp teeth as the beast flew into him. The jaws locked on to the plank, the impact sending Klondike flying over backwards. The gatepost landed next to him, the lion having instantly spat it out.

Now, sprawled on his back, helpless, he looked up in pure horror as the monster from another world slowly padded over to him. It looked down at him triumphantly.

Then, with a sickening roar of anger, the lion rose on to its hind legs and made to land directly on top of Klondike, trapping him completely where it could feast on his flesh.

Acting again on instinct, Klondike grabbed for the wooden post. He held it up vertically, noting the shattered, broken end had a nasty sharp point to it. He held it steady as the lion came crashing down.

A terrible, sickening puncture-like sound emanated from the collision as the great lion threw itself inadvertently straight on to the sharp edge of the gatepost, which thrust through its torso as the monster came crashing down.

Klondike rolled out of the way, watching in rapt bewilderment as the lion embedded itself grotesquely onto the smashed plank, toppling over to its side with the huge oak pillar stuck in its abdomen.

The beast landed and led there prone, unmoving.

Lacey screamed in anguish at the surreal sight, rushing out from the hedge line and diving for Klondike.

They hugged each other relentlessly, both grips as tight as could be as they rolled over in the grass.

He held her head away from him and looked into the wide, frightened eyes. "You alright?"

"Yes. Yes. Yes." She spoke in fits. He noticed she was shaking spasmodically under him.

"It's alright," he whispered soothingly. "It's all over."

He rubbed her back as he held her close. His eyes fell to his left, at the sight of the dead lion. He frowned as he studied the corpse. In a strange way, the ugly monster looked as if it had been dead for days.

"Oh, Kal," Lacey whimpered, "what the hell is happening to us? What in the world was that? Out here. In this remote spot. How can this have happened?"

His eyes never left the lion. "I can't explain it," he whispered, calming down. His breathing had returned to normal. "All I know is we are lucky to be alive. That lion's gone rabid. It used to be a performance lion."

She stared at him. "What! How do you know that?"

He squinted at the bloody scene before them. "How? Hell, it was in my circus for four years. Unless I'm very much mistaken."

"Kal, what are you saying?"

He finally faced her, pulling himself away from the awful sight of the bloodied carcass.

"That…that lion. That lion is Cassius."

Nobody really knew what to make of the shocking attack at Lake Eerie. And certainly no one knew what to do about it.

Klondike and Lacey had immediately returned to the train and called the sheriff's office. A call was also made to a local animal welfare farm.

A district sheriff's deputy questioned Klondike extensively in his state room on the train. He made a book full of notes, but never once opened up on what the police planned to do about it all.

When Klondike mentioned somebody urgently needed to clean up the mess, the deputy claimed he would take care of it.

Over the years, Klondike had dealt with various law enforcement officials up and down the country. All of them seemed to treat him and his staff as if they were troublemakers. Not wanting to involve them in anything, withholding information and generally sidestepping around them. It was a queer practice, but Klondike had noted it time and again down the years. It was almost as if he was running a space station full of intergalactic novelties—and no one wanted any part of them.

When Klondike mentioned he believed the mystery lion was Cassius, the deputy had treated him with ridicule and contempt, so the circus boss had merely dropped it and let the officer be on his way.

Later that night, Klondike was joined in his quarters by Heavy, Lacey and Richie Plum. It would be a meeting unlike any they had ever fronted.

Heavy and Plum sat at the main table, idly flicking over the playing cards and poker chips. Klondike paced around the room, toying with the obligatory cigar. Lacey, who had been examined by a nurse earlier after suffering shock, now sat in a large leather armchair, a blanket over her frame.

"Alright," Heavy drawled, "let me get this straight, Kal. You swear that this lion—this wild lion that sprang out of nowhere—was Cassius? Emile Rance's old pal."

Klondike looked out of the window at the sea of maintenance vehicles parked by the railroad for the night. "I got a real good look at the sucker. Up close. Cassius was with us for four years. I say it was Cassius."

Heavy was incredulous. "In heaven's name, how is that even possible?"

Klondike shook his head. "I just don't know, Heav. It is so completely fantastic."

Plum was struggling to take it all in. "You two are so lucky to be alive right now. Oh my god, what a horror story."

"It sure was, Richie," Lacey said quietly. She looked at him pleadingly. "Get me a glass of something, would ya Richie baby? Anything. I think Kal has cognac up at that bar."

Plum sprang over to the small bar in a second and poured her a glass. He handed it to her and stood behind the armchair, a hand on her shoulder.

"You poor dear. I just can't believe this."

She shuddered as she sipped the deep brown liquid. Her giant eyes darted over to Klondike. "You saved my life, Kal. There is no escaping that."

Klondike nodded wearily. "Pure instinct, Lacey. Something about having a wild lion charge at you...makes you hurry."

The atmosphere within the brightly lit room remained sombre. Heavy was still troubled. "So, let's say it was Cassius. What the hell was it doing there, at that lake?"

Plum spoke up. "Cassius disappeared after the train crash two years ago. Neither Rance, his lions or tiger were ever seen or heard of again. We never heard anything at all from Rance ever again. Hell, I thought he had either died or gone back to Africa."

Klondike nodded vaguely. "I always just thought he had started a new life. A new chapter."

Lacey was staring into nothingness, clutching her cognac. "He just raced into the desert after the crash. Chasing the animals. Like a madman."

"A madman…" Plum whispered. "He was a strange one."

Klondike wandered around the room until he was stood by Lacey and Plum. "Intensely private. Brooding. Not a great mixer. More a loner. He was obsessed, fixated completely, by his lions. There wasn't anyone else like him at the circus. Never has been."

"But, dammit, you haven't answered my question!" Heavy cried.

Klondike shrugged. "Could that lion have survived in the wild all this time?"

Heavy looked insulted. "What, and stumbled upon two old friends in the middle of nowhere? Just like that?"

Plum's mind was whirling. "Could it have somehow tracked you down? Maybe it was stalking us."

"For Chrissakes!" Heavy roared. He threw a handful of cards on to the green baize of the table. "You guys are crazy. What the hell! A wild, rabid lion stalking a circus train across America. Is that what we are going with?"

Klondike shook his head, rolling the cigar in his fingers. "Maybe it found us. Lions have a sixth sense. Instinct. Memories. Recognition. A feeling…"

"Come on Kal!" Heavy cried. He was angry now. Then, he seemed to cool slightly, and his eyes took on a haunted look. "What's more likely is that Rance is somehow involved."

Lacey froze all over. "What are you saying, Henry?"

The big man wet his lips as he leaned forward. "Think about it. That man had a control over those damn lions. They obeyed him. It was weird, man. Maybe…he could have somehow…"

"Set them upon us…" Klondike whispered in shock.

The four all stared at each other in turn. Apprehension, maybe pure fear, hung in the air like a great cloud of uncertainty.

"So Rance was tracking us?" Plum asked quietly.

Lacey was quivering. "And finally got a good opportunity. He saw us out there at the lake, all alone, and somehow set that beast upon us?"

Heavy was shaking his head again. "This is way too unlikely, folks."

"The problem," Klondike mused, "is we just don't know what happened to Rance. It is a mystery. All of this is."

Heavy took a long pull on a glass of scotch he had been nursing. "So now we've got to worry about Agostino…and Rance? Not to mention that little punk Vesnick. Jesus! What is going on here?"

Klondike wandered around the stateroom in a circle. He paused at the dresser, taking in the collection of old photos and circus posters that were on the wall. A sea of memories.

He shook his head. "I just don't know, old buddy. But what I do know is…one way or another, we're going to find out. And probably very soon."

A grim silence hung over the carriage.

Finally, Heavy spoke. "What are we going to tell the guys? This affects everyone."

Klondike nodded. "Don't worry. I'm calling a meeting for tomorrow morning. Once the tent is fully operational. We'll let everyone air their grievances."

Heavy rubbed at his chin. "I don't really know what else to say. This whole issue. It's…it's unprecedented."

Plum nodded grimly at that. "Well, I don't know about you guys, but I'm going to bed. The only thing to do with a horrible day like this is to end it."

He walked across towards the door. Heavy downed the contents of his glass and stood. "I'm right behind you, Richie." He gave Lacey a quick hug, patted Klondike on the shoulder and joined Plum.

Lacey, still sat under the blanket, looked at them both, then at Klondike. Then down at her glass.

"I'll just finish this. Hell, I'm going to need it if I'm ever going to sleep again after that today."

Heavy and Plum left the room. Klondike and Lacey looked at each other. The silence grew uncomfortable.

"About the lake…" she said quietly.

He held up a hand. "It's alright, Lacey. I, er, I don't really know what happened back there. To me, as well. I lost myself." He smiled slightly. "Lost in the moment, I guess."

She finished the cognac. Then, in slow, steady moves, she removed the blanket, folded it and stood. "I lost myself too. It happens."

He grinned. "To the best of us."

She paced over to him and put a hand on the doorknob. "I don't really know what I said. Confused, I guess." She looked at him. "Thank you, Kal. For everything."

She hovered awkwardly. He leant towards her, came back, hesitated, then stepped to the door. He gave her a quick kiss on the cheek. She patted his chest.

"Thank you again," she whispered.

"Any time."

She fled into the corridor. He watched her head down the carriage to her room.

Then, quietly closing the door, he stood there, looking around idly. He felt exhausted. With a deep sigh, he padded around the great room slowly, his mind whirling. He picked up his cane, the show cane, and fiddled with it irritably in his grasp.

Outside, the night was quiet, foreboding. And black as an abyss. He found it hard to think. Pouring a cognac for himself, he took a large swallow, swishing the liquid around in his mouth.

Then, finally, he made a decision. It was time to call Addison.

It would be late out in California, but he knew the old man would be up. Probably going through some accounts sheets.

Klondike walked behind the great mahogany desk at the very end of the room and slumped into the large leather chair beyond. Wearily, he grabbed at the telephone and dialled.

The banker answered on the third ring. "Daryl? It's Kal here."

"Kal, great to hear from you!" the voice exclaimed. "You're down in Houston, right?"

"That's right. Pulled in this morning. Setting up now for Saturday."

"Excellent. It's good to hear your voice, Kal. Your reviews have been astounding. Sell-out after sell-out! You're smashing it out of the ballpark, my boy."

Klondike smiled thinly. "Yeah, well, like I always tell ya, we got the best talent. When you got a roster like mine, you just can't fail." There was a brief silence on the other end. "You don't exactly sound ecstatic."

Klondike took a deep breath. "We got a problem, Daryl."

"Oh? I don't like the sound of that."

"Well, we're managing it alright so far but…I have a strong feeling it is going to get a lot worse."

"You want to tell me about it, Kal?"

And he did just that. The whole story. Agostino, Vesnick, the attacks, newspaper stories, the groundhole puncher, the bizarre lion incident. He finally opened up to the old man.

When he was finished, Addison was silent for a while.

"Jesus, Kal," he finally blurted, "that is quite the pickle. It sounds like this Agostino fella is trying to bring your outfit down, one piece at a time."

Klondike sighed. "Death by a thousand cuts," he muttered. "He thinks I'm going to succumb if he keeps pushing us."

"Yes, that's often how his kind operate."

"Y'know, Daryl. It's so strange. There is always someone out there. In the shadows. Trying to bring us down."

"That's the nature of success, my boy. It brings out jealousy, rage, betrayal. In this guy's case, he wants to have your successes for himself."

Klondike thought for a moment, trying to piece it all together in his mind. "What are your feelings, Daryl? Any suggestions?"

"Sure." He sounded surprisingly alert. "Let me look into this Agostino. Ask around. One of my many associates may have run into him somewhere down the line. There will be something out there…somewhere…that may be able to help."

"Thanks. I sure would appreciate it."

"Forget it, Kal. I'm invested in the circus too, remember. It's my job to help."

Klondike smiled whimsically. "You're a good man, Daryl."

The older man chuckled. "In a bad world."

Then he hung up.

At that exact moment, another telephone conversation was just beginning far, far away.

Paul Agostino, back at his headquarters at the Beaumont Club—the joint he owned in Manhattan—had just put in a call to the private, exclusive number he had been given.

The number was known by barely a handful of people, and was the direct line to Eric Ribbeck's private carriage onboard the Ribbeck's World Circus express train.

The sprawling carriage looked like a penthouse from a five-star hotel, with crystal chandeliers, fur-lined carpets, Oriental rugs and gaudy, golden drapes.

Ribbeck was seated in a throne-like chair behind an antique ship captain's desk in the centre of the room. He picked up the receiver to his old-fashioned telephone on the first ring.

"Yes?"

"Eric. It's me. I'm at my club now. I've just spoken to the boys. They're on the way to Houston now."

"Excellent," Ribbeck said calmly. "What happened with the lion man?"

Ribbeck shifted in his seat. "I haven't heard back from Rance yet. No matter. There's plenty of time."

Agostino paused, shaking his head. "I don't like it. That son of a bitch looked crazy to me, Eric. You think he's gone loco?"

"The hell with it! How would I know? He wants Klondike, that's all I heard. But nothing's happened yet, I assure you. If Kal Klondike was killed, or even injured, I'd know about it."

"What exactly is Rance doing? Planning an attack? Or what?"

Ribbeck's nostrils flared angrily. "How the hell would I know? I asked him what he wanted to do. Told him our plan. He said he wants to make Klondike pay. I told him where that yahoo was, in Houston. Gave him the details. Then, next thing I knew, he was gone."

"Jesus Christ!" Agostino blared. "The guy is a psychopath, Eric. He is a threat to everything. Our whole plan."

Ribbeck shook his head. "Let him be, Paul. He's out there, trying to disrupt Klondike and his troupe. As I see it, that fits in with our operation just fine." He cleared his throat and tried to change the subject. "Now, tell me about the boys in Houston. The big one."

"Alright," Agostino muttered. "We're on for the big one. It'll happen on Saturday night. At the show."

"After the show, of course."

"The hell with that! We want maximum carnage. We'll do it at the start. This will send them a message they won't ever forget."

"Are you out of your cotton-picking gourd?" Ribbeck was incredulous. "We want a circus wreck, not a god damn massacre! That would be like the Little Big Horn, dammit! A slaughter. You don't know what you're saying, man. You'd be putting thousands of lives at risk."

Agostino rubbed his brow in frustration. He tried to remain calm. "Yet again, Eric, I think we's on different wavelengths. I thought we was out to finish Klondike."

"Yeah, but not like that! What the hell is wrong with you?"

"Listen," Agostino spat out. "I thought you said you knew about me and my people? You knew who you was dealing with? We ain't no Saturday night wrecking crew, daddio. We're the real deal. We don't wreck…we destroy!"

Ribbeck was shaking his head in utter dismay. "And I'll remind you of our deal, god damn it. This is all about you getting control of the circus, and me getting the talent. It's not a war zone out there!"

A stony silence followed. Agostino took a long sip on a Martini he was nursing. He looked idly about the small, private room he sat in. "Alright," he murmured, "so what do you say, man?"

Ribbeck had calmed down. He cast his mind back. "Do you remember…" he began, as if in a trance. "When you first came to me, Paul? You came to me, remember? You asked for advice…help, backing, guidance. You wanted to know all about the circus business? You remember, eh boy? Well, I told you I knew how to make this all work. And, damn it all to hell, this is not the way to do this. My way is the correct way."

Agostino rolled his eyes. "Alright, so we do it when? After the damn show?"

"Correct. After."

"I just don't get how that will hurt Klondike."

Ribbeck cackled. "Are you kidding, boy? What is a circus without its tent? Besides, the outcry of it all, the scandal, will be a hammer blow."

There was a brief silence. Then Agostino said: "Alright. That's what we're gunna do then."

"Make it happen, son."

"Don't you worry about that. It's done."

Ribbeck hung up and gently replaced the antique receiver on his phone. Then, he slumped in his great chair, shaking his head and cursing to himself.

When Agostino had first proposed a partnership, he had eagerly accepted, enthralled by the gangster's links to Klondike and the prospect of finally overthrowing his great rival. He had been seduced by the man's talk of the Mob—power, influence, muscle, hired hands. His desire to take over Klondike's Circus.

Now, after several weeks, he could see the union was imploding. The man was a hoodlum. Nothing else. His strongest desire, even more than wealth, was for violence. Ribbeck could see that now.

The old man thought about it all for a long time, sat alone at the desk in his private carriage.

He took one of his favoured cheroots from the silver case on the sleek surface and lit up, watching the thick grey smoke rise to the ceiling.

One thought prodded mercilessly at his conscience. It wouldn't leave him, so he said it aloud.

"Where will it all end?"

It was the dead of night. Bright headlights illuminated an old barn just off a remote highway.

A large brown van rumbled off the main road onto a dirt track that led up to the barn.

The vehicle slowly edged into a weed-ridden patch of gravel next to the abandoned old structure and the engine died.

A man pushed himself out dejectedly from the driver's side onto the dirt, almost falling. Slamming the door, he trudged towards the eerie-looking barn, pulling open the huge wooden door.

He wore beige safari-like fatigues, smeared in what looked like slime.

With a sigh, the figure lit a match and held it to an ancient-looking lantern, until the interior of the barn was fully lit.

The planked flooring contained several bales of straw that had been ripped apart with the straw assembled across the floor like some kind of carpeting. A battered old mattress sat in a far corner, next to what looked like a gas stove.

Above, on a landing, sat various pieces of long-forgotten farming apparatus.

Emile Rance walked slowly into the grimy confines.

Then, as if suddenly possessed by some unseen force, he threw himself into the sea of straw, rolling uncontrollably and crying out in rage. His hands clawed at his flaming red hair and his legs kicked out.

"No, no, no!" he cried repeatedly. Then, with a primal scream of anger, he yelped: "Failure! I failed you all!"

Rising to his knees, he shuffled over to the far wall of the barn, the straw clinging to his clothes. He knelt upright, shaking slightly.

Then, as if responding to a starter's gun, he clenched his fists and began punching the wall repeatedly. Left followed right, as he knelt there slamming his fists into the oak panelling.

Before long, blood began seeping over his hands, as his knuckles opened up and his skin was shred. The wall began to turn crimson. But Rance didn't seem to notice. He just kept punching the wood.

Over and over again. As he jabbed, he said the same line repeatedly.

"What have I done? What have I done? What have I done?"

Chapter Fourteen

"So, there you have it folks. All of this must sound crazy. Now, I'd like to know your concerns. Hell, anything!"

Klondike finished his summary of the previous day's lion attack, interjecting the report with his belief that the circus was somehow being targeted for destruction.

He had called the meeting for 10am, with all performers present in the newly erected big top, which had been set up in the old rodeo field.

Now, all of the troupe were seated in a far corner of one of the grandstands. Spaced apart over five rows of seats, they all sat huddled in their usual little social groups.

Klondike had stood on the sawdust before them to deliver his update, Heavy just behind him.

As was often the case during such gatherings, the huge empty tent made for an eerie spectacle, the towering rows of bleachers dormant and seemingly forgotten.

As Klondike finished his address, he absently paced the arena floor, looking up at the shocked faces of his team.

He waited.

Finally, someone spoke up. And it was Corky of all people. Seated in the very middle of the ensemble, he was dressed in full clown attire, including his face paint.

"This is all unbelievable. First, we had the attacks on Roddy and the Daredevils. The equipment getting trashed. But a lion attack! And the fact it may be Cassius!" The clown's face looked sad, despite the make-up. "I just don't know what to say…"

Olsen, sat as usual with Suzi in the second row, spoke next. "Are you sure you're ok, Lacey?"

Lacey, sat on the front row with Plum, turned to him and smiled. "Yes, thank you. Shaken up. Shocked. But nothing more." She smiled demurely at Klondike before them. "Thanks to super Kalvin, here."

"You could've both been killed!" This from one of the Range Riders, who were all seated at the back of the group. "A lion on the loose! I never heard of something so crazy!"

Tip Enqvist spoke next. "This is getting out of hand, man. We need some protection out here." He turned to Goliath, sat directly behind him. "I say let's get the big man patrolling the grounds at night. Ain't no one gunna mess with him."

"Can he fight a lion?" cried Suzi, who was clearly shaken up.

The giant Goliath suddenly stood, like an otherworldly apparition rising from an ocean. "Hey, I'll do whatever it takes to help. I don't like none of this one bit."

Gargantua, sat next to his stablemate, joined in. "I'm with Goliath. This is making me feel sick."

Enqvist grunted. "That was all the pies you been eating."

At the front, Klondike held up a hand. "Alright, alright. I know. This is all very unsettling. At the moment, I'm not sure what exactly to do. But, one thing is for sure. I want all of you to keep a close eye on our base camp. The train. The tent. The midway. Everything, dammit. And be on guard. Watch your step. Anyone notice anything unusual, anything out of place, you let me or Heavy know. You got that?"

There was a slow grumbling of acceptance from the assembled group.

Klondike studied the ensemble. He could almost taste the uncertainty.

Then, his eyes rose to the top of the gathering. There, two rows above anybody else, sat Gino Shapiro. The king of the mountain. Dressed in his orange tracksuit, he sat back, arms folded, legs hanging over the bleachers in front.

"You're very quiet, Gino. What say you?"

Shapiro sat there brooding, as if none of this had interested him. He shrugged.

"You talk of this misfortune, chairman. Si, it is terrible. It is bad. I know. But what I hear no one talking about is the most important thing of all." He looked angry now. "The show! We have two days before showtime. This ill talk could ruin us. I look around, I see a lot of sad, sour faces. You think the people want that? Do you? No!" He stood up, with the grace of a natural showman. "I say we focus on what really matters…the next show. And the most important people of all…the audience. Without them, we are nothing. And we must never forget that."

Klondike half-smiled. Shapiro never ceased to amaze him. Despite his womanising, showboating and love of materialistic possessions, all Gino Shapiro ever truly cared about was the circus itself. He came across as arrogant and extravagant, but his desire for perfection and wish to elevate the whole troupe, and not just himself, were an example to all of them.

"The show must go on…" Klondike said to the group. "Very true, Gino."

"We're lucky we even have a show!" cried one of the Rocking Robins, who were huddled together on the far left.

"Yeah," Goliath grunted, "this is all madness!"

"Don't you see!" Shapiro was repugnant. He waltzed along his row of seats into the main aisle. There he stood proudly, addressing the troupe. "That is all the more reason we must succeed. We are performers. Talent. People, some people, will always have it in for us. You rise above hate, animosity. That is how you achieve! How you climb to the top."

He looked down briefly at Klondike. The two of them had been together since the very beginning. Day one. When Klondike had separated from Ribbeck's World Circus to form his own troupe, enticing Gino along with him. Together they had built an empire. "Listen to the chairman," Shapiro told the team. "Watch out for these…these banditos who mean to hurt us. But, dammit, we want no drop in standards. We are the best. We demand the best."

A strange hesitancy reverberated around the grandstand. A few murmurings followed.

Penny Fortune, who had been sat on her own in a far corner, clapped her hands. "Bravo, Gino, bravo," she called.

Klondike nodded as he tried to study the sea of faces before him, gauging reactions. There seemed to be a general acceptance of Shapiro's rallying cry, with a few reservations.

Lacey stood up and joined Klondike and Heavy at the front. She addressed the group as everyone slowly stood and made to leave. "We have local dignitaries and VIPs from the Cattlemen's Club and the chamber of commerce coming out to visit today, folks," she announced. "Usual rules, please. Charm them, make them laugh, answer their questions."

The ensemble slowly dispersed, with everyone making their way to the flap, walking past Klondike, Lacey and Heavy.

Shapiro slowly wandered down the aisle, eyes locked on the circus master.

"My shipmates are restless, chairman," he said casually. "That makes me nervous. I worry the ship will capsize."

It was Lacey who answered. "Don't you worry, Gino. They are all professionals. True professionals. When they get under those bright lights, when the spotlight is on them, they won't fail. They are all like you—at the top of their game."

He laughed softly. "Pretty speech from the pretty lady." He smiled hypnotically at her. "I hope you are right, madam publicist." Another laugh. "But, of course, you are always right. My compliments, madam." He bowed gallantly, before looking back at Klondike.

"This can be a record-breaking year for us, Kal. Our biggest ever. With the super show in Washington as well. We cannot fail." Klondike smiled at the flyer. "I look to you to lead by example, Gino. In and out of the big top."

Shapiro smiled beautifully at him, then gave a nonchalant wave before turning towards the exit.

"Always, chairman, always."

That night, many of the performers and staff gathered at the Sandman, a luxurious bar and dining lounge located in the Cattlemen's Club's main enclosure.

Western and rodeo memorabilia filled the walls of the joint, with a long antique bar found at the far side which had imitation bull's horns attached to each end. An attached balcony looked out over the rodeo field, where the red and blue big top stood tall and dominant. The sea of midway stalls had also been assembled outside the tent.

Shapiro wandered into the bar a little after eight, and wasn't surprised to see many of his fellow performers seated at long tables with food and drinks.

Corky, as was often the case, was stood alone at the bar sipping a beer. Shapiro joined him, ordering a cognac from the bartender. "Gino, my dear old friend," the clown began. He was still in his comedy suit, but his face was clear now. "I must congratulate you. A beautiful speech earlier in the tent. I'm glad you said all that you did."

He held his beer aloft. Shapiro took his drink and reluctantly touched glasses.

"Good for you, clown." He took a long pull on his cognac, closing his eyes. "Sometimes, I think we are a dying breed. The traditions of the circus are lost on some of our comrades, no?"

Corky snorted. "Maybe we're just getting old."

"You speak for yourself, clown."

At that moment, Shapiro's eyes darted to the entrance as if pulled by a hidden, magnetic force. Penny Fortune was walking in, dressed in a beautiful country-style buckskin frock.

Several cowboys who had been drinking in the far corner leapt to their feet and raised their hats. She smiled casually before making her way to the bar.

"Penny…" Shapiro exclaimed. "Words cease me. You look truly beautiful."

She leant on the bar and surveyed him. "You don't look so bad yourself, superstar."

"What can I get you?"

She smiled dazzlingly. "Surprise me."

He ordered a white wine spritzer and smiled back at her.

Corky managed to butt in. "You two make a sensational couple, I must say. Y'know, up there on the rings."

Shapiro ignored him. "It's a pleasure to see you, Penny," he told her quickly. "You don't usually, er, mix with the rest of the talent, huh?"

She rolled her eyes. "Well, at times it's like travelling with a pack of wild predators, all staring at me like I'm fresh meat." She pouted at him. "And you, Gino. With your lines, your never-ending charm offensive. Half the time, I'd rather stay in our lounging carriage and read my magazines."

He lit a cigarette, offering her the pack. She refused. "So, why now Penny?"

She threw her head back. "Oh, I dunno. Some of the things you said this morning. They really resonated with me." She stood directly before him, eyeing him intensely. "You really do care about the circus, don't you? More than anything."

"Of course, mamacita," he cried. "The circus is my life. It is everything to me. I want Klondike's Circus to succeed more than anything. It is…"

He stopped abruptly as Tip Enqvist appeared next to them, listening in on their conversation. He held a bottle of beer and looked menacing, as he often did.

"The hell you say!" Enqvist drawled. He stared at Penny, his eyes slowly looking her up and down. "Your beloved circus is gunna go to hell, Shapiro. These people, whoever the hell they are, ain't gunna stop till we're through. We

143

need to strike back. And fast. Never mind the glory of the big top. This is a battle."

"Nobody was talking to you, biker," Shapiro snarled. "Why don't you take a hike?"

Enqvist sniggered, taking a long swig from the bottle. "You don't care about any of us, do ya pal? As long as the circus keeps making money, with your name up in lights."

"You're gunna be seeing lights in a minute, amigo!"

"Listen," Penny hissed, moving between the two men. She frowned at Enqvist. "You're wrong, Tip. And you have no right to talk to Gino like that. He wants the circus to succeed so that we can all benefit."

"Hell," Enqvist said, laughing, "he's telling you all this to get you to sleep with him, girl."

"Alright!" Shapiro cried, clenching his fists. "Now that is enough!"

This time, Corky stepped in and tried to move the pair apart. "Alright, take it easy you two. This isn't accomplishing anything." He glared up at Enqvist. "I wish you'd stop looking for trouble, Tip. We have enough problems out there…as you've already said. We don't need our own people fighting. Now come on!"

Enqvist kept his eyes locked on Shapiro. "I'm just telling it as it is." Shapiro stood tall, glaring back. It was Penny who spoke next: "You heard what the boss said. The show must go on."

"Yeah," Enqvist growled, "but at what price?"

With that, he skulked away from the bar and re-joined Bo and Justin at a roundtable near the balcony.

Corky watched him with regret. "What the hell is his problem?"

Shapiro shook his head. "Is great shame. He and his boys are fantastic talents. Some of the best I've ever seen. What they do is beyond our world. But…he behaves like an overgrown juvenile delinquent. His mouth is full of garbage."

They turned away. Shapiro smiled again at Penny. "So…"

Suddenly, a large cheer broke out in the far corner of the barroom. The cowboys had all started clapping.

Shapiro craned his neck and looked across. "Santamaria!" he cried. "What now, god damn it!"

Then, he threw his head back in dismay as he saw Olsen and Suzi making their way into the room.

The ventriloquist shook hands with the cowboy group, signed an autograph, then guided Suzi across the floor. He stopped when he noticed Shapiro staring at him.

"Gino," he said.

"Olsen," was the stern reply.

"Oh my," Suzi gushed, looking at Penny. "You look just wonderful, Miss Fortune."

"Thank you," she replied quietly.

Olsen eyed the room. "Looks like the whole team are out."

"Yeah," Shapiro said dryly. "We're all having a ball."

"Well, excuse us," said Olsen, and he led Suzi across to the balcony, where they sat near the railings.

Penny propped an elbow on the bar. "You still don't like him, do you?"

Shapiro grunted. "The doll man? Hell, he is a crazy kid. Our rising superstar. Everybody seems to love him. Me? I just don't really get it. Never have."

"Everyone thinks you're insanely jealous of him. You do know that?"

He laughed mirthlessly, signalling to the bartender for another cognac. "Jealous…pah! I don't believe in it. It is for the weak. No, I don't hate Olsen. In fact, he has the one thing that few people in the circus have. An important quality." He looked at her intensely. "My respect."

Penny nodded thoughtfully. Then she said: "Have you eaten?"

"No," he murmured. "Let's get a table. Somewhere out of the way."

On the balcony, a waiter delivered a bottle of wine to Olsen and Suzi, pouring them each a glass before disappearing again.

The outdoor enclosure was less busy, just a few couples seated spaciously. Several patrons were stood looking out at the vast circus tent on the field before them.

"What are we doing?" Suzi suddenly blurted at him.

Olsen looked at her quizzically. "What? What do you mean, Suzi?"

She shifted in her seat uncomfortably. "Come on, Roddy. We do everything together. Breakfast. Dinner. Drinks. All the time. It's no secret here. Why, the other day one of the roustabouts gave me some flowers. He said, 'I hope your boyfriend won't mind.' You see my point? So, what are we doing? Are we dating? Is this dating?"

Olsen nodded slowly. He sipped his wine. "Hell, Suzi, I thought we were pals. Real close pals. Heck, you're like a sister to me. You know that. Your support since day one...I couldn't have achieved anything without you. You know all this."

"So..." she whispered, her face a mask of innocence and confusion. "We're just pals? Hanging out."

"Well, er, that's what I thought."

She studied him, her light brown eyes wide and lost. "Is that all we will ever be? Is that what you want, Roddy?"

He hesitated, flapping internally. "Why, sure. I...I didn't realise you wanted more."

"Oh, I don't even know what I want." She threw her hands in the air.

"Listen," he said calmly. "What we do have, Suzi, is very special. I wouldn't want to do anything to jeopardise that. Anything to hurt you in any way. No one can replace you in my world."

Suzi still looked upset. "You have feelings for Miss Lacey, don't you..."

He baulked, shifting slightly. "Well, sure. Lacey has championed my act since day one. You were there, Suzi, you remember how it went down. Without Lacey, I wouldn't even be here. She has advised me, nurtured me, helped me with all these new ventures, like publicity and all the media stuff."

Olsen paused as he noticed Suzi shudder slightly, her face pale on the floodlit terrace. "But, listen," he continued, "she is a manager. A business associate. I am a client to her. That's how it is."

Suzi picked up one of the menus sat forgotten on their table. "I think she has feelings for you."

He shook his head. "Not those kind of feelings, Suzi."

"She is a beautiful, glamorous woman. Intelligent. Classy."

Olsen thought fast. "That is true. But it is also irrelevant."

They both stared at each other as the night grew silent around them. Crickets chirped relentlessly in the background as they stared out at the great circus tent towering all around them. It seemed to light up the night with its bright colours.

Finally, Olsen spoke. "Can't we just be friends? Aren't you happy with that?"

She tried to smile. "Of course, Roddy. You know how I feel. I am just...just in awe of your talent. Your act. Your way with people, especially me. I just don't ever want that to end."

He looked pained. "But why would it end?"

She shook her head. "Ah, come on, Roddy. We all know you're destined for bigger and better things. For lights shining brighter. You're too talented to stay here forever."

"I like it here."

"Yes, but there are so many other avenues, ventures. Hollywood. Las Vegas. Broadway. The world is yours, Roddy." She studied him sadly, the eyes wide in fear. "And I worry we won't have this anymore."

Olsen frowned. Then, he reached across and clasped her hand softly. "Listen, Suzi," he breathed. "We will always have this. No matter what roads we both take. Which paths we choose. We have been through too much together. Our bond transcends any venture or avenue. Now please don't worry about this. I am there for you. Always."

With that, she smiled beautifully, looking like a child overjoyed by delight. She laughed in fits. Then she said: "Hey! Why don't you join me in the fall for the off-season? The Christmas shows are wonderful. Then, maybe you can come and meet my folks back in New Hampshire."

He grinned, sipping his wine. "I can think of nothing I'd like to do more."

They both laughed. The atmosphere changed instantly. A waiter approached the table. "Are y'all ready to order?"

Olsen and Suzi looked at each other, then down at the barely touched menus. Then they spoke together in perfect harmony. "Hamburgers with fries."

Ribbeck's World Circus was in the middle of a four-night stay in Minneapolis, the climax of which was back-to-back shows at the Zenith Show Grounds over two nights.

Eric Ribbeck was enjoying a late supper alone at the antique desk in his private carriage. He flicked through a seemingly never-ending pile of news pages reviewing his circus shows, and those of his rivals. Every few minutes, he would chew down another bite of the roast duck in plum sauce his chef had personally thrown together.

Finishing the meal, he clutched the glass of Cabernet Sauvignon next to the plate and quietly pondered his present predicament. His thoughts were interrupted by a loud rasp at the door.

Luca Marconi then entered, pacing down the long carriage, his face a mask of concern.

"Luca!" Ribbeck snapped. "At last. What is the word?"

Marconi stood before the great ship captain's desk. "You're not gunna like it, boss?"

"You located Rance?"

"Nuh huh," Marconi mumbled. "But we got a report from the sheriff's office in Houston."

"What? What did they say?"

Marconi fidgeted with his hands. "It appears that Klondike and that fancy dandy broad he's hanging out with got attacked. By…by a lion!"

Ribbeck's eyes widened in horror. He put his glass down. "You cannot be serious!"

"I'm afraid so, boss. According to our man down there, the lion impaled itself on some kind of spike. Killed. Klondike and the broad were ok. They survived. The media are saying the lion had escaped from Houston Zoo. The biggest zoo in Texas."

Ribbeck hammered a fist down onto his desk. "God damn it!" he roared. "This is getting out of hand, Luca. I've lost control."

Marconi looked lost. "You think that lion belonged to Rance?"

Ribbeck glared at him. "You think it's all a coincidence? For Chrissakes, man. Of course it was Rance. He set his damn monster on Klondike." His ageing features took on a haunted look. "He…he means to kill him."

Marconi simply stood there, uncertain of what to say. Deep down, he was feeling very confused.

"My god," Ribbeck groaned. He ran a hand over his face, massaging his eye sockets. Then he took a heavy gulp of wine. "Agostino was right. This guy is crazy! He's out there now. A loose cannon. Waiting to fire."

"Forgive me, boss" Marconi blurted quietly. "But surely, in his own way, Rance is helping us? We want to destroy Klondike's Circus, right? With Klondike gone, you and Agostino can pick up the pieces, no?"

Ribbeck was shaking his head angrily. "Dammit all, Luca. Like I keep trying to tell you people, I don't want a massacre. I'm not a killer, dammit. I'm a businessman."

A stony silence followed. Marconi simply nodded.

Finally, Ribbeck spoke. "Well, hopefully after tomorrow night, this will all be over. Thank god. Klondike will be through, finished. Me and Agostino can go about our business. And we'll all be richer."

Marconi seemed satisfied with that. He turned to leave. "Alright, boss. I'll be in the outer carriage if you need me."

"Thank you, Luca."

Marconi left and Ribbeck finished his wine. Rubbing at his temples, he returned to the pile of news pages. He picked one from the top, a local newspaper report on their Des Moines show five days earlier.

As he read quietly, there was another knock at the door. "Dammit, what now?" Ribbeck rasped.

But the door opened slowly and the old man was surprised to see a new visitor. Lee Vesnick.

"Vesnick!" he snarled. "What the hell do you want?"

The youngster crept in slowly, eyeing the grand and opulent furnishings of the private carriage with wide, gaping eyes. He was wearing a long grey trench coat and looked like a young studio film star with his slick pompadour and matinee idol looks.

"Wow!" he exclaimed, studying the interior of the cart. "This is some office, Mr Ribbeck. How the other half live, huh?"

"What do you want?" Ribbeck spat out.

Vesnick moved over to the great desk and sat down in the leather seat opposite Ribbeck's throne.

"Well, you see, it's like this…" Vesnick muttered, avoiding eye contact. "You been good enough to let me roll with your circus for a few weeks now, Mr Ribbeck. It's all very nice. Your troupe are incredible. First rate talent. Right across the board. I'm really enjoying the—"

"Get to the point, god damn it!" Ribbeck looked ready to explode.

Vesnick held up his hands. "Alright. I was just wondering what your plans are for me, Mr Ribbeck?"

The older man was seething. "Plans? What plans?"

"Well," Vesnick said quickly. "You said if I help you and Mr Agostino bring Klondike down, you'll fix me up with a spot in your show. And, hell, I sure am ready to throw before an audience again. It's been a long while since I performed and I'm hungry to get out there."

Ribbeck glared at him, calming slightly. "Listen, kid," he snorted. "You're here as an adviser. You're helping us with this little project. Forget about joining my show for now. That is a…a long-term vision, if you like. Got it?"

Vesnick stared at him, hurt showing in his large brown eyes. "Wait a minute. That's not what you said back in Los Angeles. You said I'll be working for you. As talent. That was weeks ago. And I haven't done a damn thing yet."

"Listen to me, god damn it. I haven't got time to worry about that. You just do as you're told, knifeman. You'll get your money. You'll get your three squares a day. Thanks to me. Then, when Klondike's Circus is finished…then we will talk again. Now…" he gave Vesnick a look that could only be described as murderous. "Do me a favour, kid, and get the hell out of here."

With that, the older man returned to his papers, sipping his wine. Vesnick sat still for a moment, then slowly rose and ambled across the floor, head down.

He left the carriage. At the interchange door outside, he strode down to the ground. Marconi was stood there, centurion-like, smoking a cigarette. Vesnick nodded at him, but only received a stern stare in reply.

With a sigh, the youngster wandered away from the stationary train and down the dirt track that led to the show field. The immense purple and green circus tent rose before him, stretching to the heavens.

He closed his eyes, envisioned the roar of the crowd, the gasps of astonishment, and let the feeling float through him.

Then, he headed to the circus encampment and to his allocated trailer.

Chapter Fifteen

Young and old, rich and poor, the curious and the seasoned circus-goer all made their way across Houston to the Cattlemen's Club on Saturday night.

Cowhands from local ranches, oil field workers, even rodeo riders from the club itself were all drawn to the big top that evening—many wanting to see just what all the fuss was about.

The grandstands within the great tent were full an hour before show time. The crowd buzzed with a kind of steady excitement as the clock drew nearer to 7pm.

Unusually, and only because it was a big show in a wealthy city, Klondike took a seat in the front row, close to the flap, where he was joined by Heavy, Lacey and Plum. He looked at each of them. No one showed any sign of distress or uneasiness.

Everyone had an air of deep professionalism and calm about them, from the roustabouts helping with last minute technical issues, to the stewards showing spectators to their seats.

They all knew Houston was a money show. TV crews, radio commentators, a sea of press, all waited patiently among the masses in the bleachers.

It felt like a big show night, Klondike thought as he looked up at the rows of men in suits and Stetsons. He had never seen so many cowboy hats.

Oilmen. Ranchers. Cattle barons. They all sat there like excited children, clutching cotton candy sticks, drinks and programmes. Suddenly, the pre-recorded sound of trumpets thundered through the tent and the audience cheered, before all held their collective breath.

Heavy leapt down from his seat, ran a hand through his immaculate scarlet blazer, adjusted his top hat, and walked gracefully into the centre of the arena, where a mic stand stood ready for his introduction.

"Ladies and gentlemen…"

The sell-out crowd quietened down, every pair of eyes staring at the big man in the middle. It was showtime.

Heavy roared his words. "Welcome to the greatest stage spectacular of them all. Welcome to Klondike's Circus! And now, to open our show, the wonders of the wild west, the kings among cowboys, please put your hands together for the fast-riding, hard-driving…Range Riders!"

The sight of a team of cowboys gallivanting around the tent on horses was the perfect introduction for this show.

Many of the men in the audience cried out "Yee-hahs" and waved their hats in the air at the sight of their kind of entertainers.

As the Range Riders began their array of stunts and riding tricks, the big top quickly became a cauldron of wailing.

The applause grew louder and louder…and Klondike just knew the night would be a hit. Or so he thought.

In the end, to the immense relief of performers, roustabouts, Klondike and his management team, the show went down without a hitch.

Everything ran smoothly, as it had at the previous stops on the tour, and each performance was greeted by a jubilant reaction.

Houston simply loved them all.

The Range Riders, the Rocking Robins, Roddy Olsen, Corky and his clowns, the Flying Batistas, the Daredevils, the Showcase Revue, Gino and Penny.

All were greeted like international superstars, as the audience revelled in their dazzling exploits.

Sat in front of the patrons, Klondike could only smile at the reactions emanating from all around him.

Then, at the grand finale, as Suzi Dando began singing and the dazzling Cadillacs slowly made their way onto the circus floor, the cheers and applause ran out in one continuous wall of noise.

The performers all took their bow on their respective convertibles, waving to their fans in the grandstands. The cars slowly cruised along, completing their circuit of the arena floor.

In that moment, the circus stars were kings and queens among the Houston city folk, promoted to the highest of pedestals, adored and revered in equal measure.

On the final float, where Shapiro and Penny stood waving while soaking up the applause, it felt like the ground was moving.

As always, Shapiro played the role of king, draped in a gold cape and throwing yellow Texas roses into the crowd while blowing kisses to the smiling faces. The constant showman, he continually whipped the patrons into more of a frenzy by cajoling them with waves and signals to cheer louder.

It was a beautiful scene to end the extravaganza, as it always was. Then, as Suzi ran across to the final car and was hoisted up by Shapiro and Penny to join them, it was suddenly all over.

The Cadillacs completed their lap of the floor and headed for the exit.

Heavy returned for a final time to the arena floor.

"Ladies and gentlemen, we hope you have enjoyed the glamour, the razzmatazz and the sheer excitement of Klondike's Circus. And we hope you can feel the magic tonight. From all of us here, thank you so much for joining us and we hope to see you again further down the line. Next show is New Orleans, one week from now. Until then, goodnight...and god bless America."

Jim McCabe watched in rapt fascination as the scores of patrons fled the exits, leaving the awe and wonder of the circus behind.

It was like an avalanche of humanity, as thousands poured out into the night again. They made their way through the midway and back to the main Cattlemen's Club attraction.

McCabe was standing in the now forgotten ticketing booth, watching the crowds disperse as he toked on a cigarette.

After a show, his team took on the clean-up operation that night, before dismantling everything the next day.

He waited for the sea of people to become more sparse, once the first few waves had exited the field.

Then, with a sigh, he moved into the midway and walked slowly towards the tent. An over-excited little girl ran into him, clutching a programme and a poster. She raced off without a word. McCabe shook his head and waded on.

He spotted one of his roustabouts, Wilson, walking towards the flap with a giant brush.

"Everybody set, Wilson?"

The man nodded, putting the brush over his shoulder. "You bet, Jim. Me and the boys will start by the entranceway." He looked into the night. "Them local boys who signed on are taking the far end. Out there now."

McCabe froze. An alarm went off in his consciousness. "What local boys?" he barked. "We only have local teams for set-up and dismantling. You know that. They ain't due here tonight."

Wilson shrugged. "Maybe they didn't know. Or maybe they's just keen."

"I told them to come back on Sunday," McCabe said angrily. Then, he panicked. "Follow me!" he cried.

He took off in a sprint, circling the tent and racing around its perimeter. Wilson tried to keep up.

The two hurtled past the dying embers of the night's spectators, desperately trying to avoid barging into anyone.

Finally, they made it to the other side of the big top.

McCabe stopped running abruptly. Chest heaving, he looked around with wild eyes. This part of the field was completely empty, just the wall of the tent and the old rodeo grandstands lying deserted in the night. The solitary tent exit was bare.

"That's funny…" Wilson muttered.

Then, he saw McCabe staring at something inside the big top.

The foreman took a few steps forward in shock then let out a mighty cry. "Oh my god!"

McCabe raced towards the small entrance into the tent. He shouted out one word only, but that was enough to set off a wild panic for anyone within earshot.

"Fire!"

Inside the big top, there were a handful of people left scattered around.

Klondike, Lacey, Heavy and Plum were all stood by the flap having a discussion. Five or six roustabouts were already inside, cleaning up by the first row of seats. Several random spectators were still in the grandstands, seemingly not wanting to leave.

McCabe's wild cry had gotten everyone's attention.

Klondike and his crew all turned as one as the foreman came racing in, waving his arms in shock.

He had their attention. Then, they saw it.

At the far end of the tent, to the right of the flap, was a truly shocking sight. A terrifying wall of burning red flame was rapidly ascending the wall of the big top. Silent and deadly, it seemed to lick at the tent fabric as it ate more of it up.

Everyone stared in shock. The blaze seemed to dance as it shot up, reaching the ceiling in seconds.

McCabe was racing around like a madman. He cried up at the few spectators high up in the stands. "Get the hell outta there! The exit! To your right!" They complied, running desperately past the seats and down the aisle.

Klondike watched the flames in shock for a second more.

Then, he leapt into action. Pushing his arms out wide, he encircled Lacey, Heavy and Plum and helped move them out of the flap.

Then, he barked orders. "Richie. The control room. Call the fire department. Now! Heavy, do a perimeter of the tent. Make sure there is no one left hanging around. Lacey, get to the trailers and make sure no one tries to get back in!"

The trio dispersed instantly. Klondike looked around helplessly, eyeing everything left inside the big top. The mic stand. The trapeze rigging. The high wire platforms.

There was a mighty crack. The fire had spread from the fabric of the tent onto the grandstands. Each unit of seating was connected to the next with an interlocking mechanism. Before long, the fire would encompass the entire structure.

He looked up in desperation. The ceiling was already ablaze. A thick blanket of black smoke was growing like an infernal fog around him. McCabe was running up and down the aisles, checking for any more spectators.

"Jim!" he screamed, trying to be heard above the insane crackling. The sound of his circus burning. Dying. "Are we all out?"

McCabe ran down the aisle he was on, hopped over the safety boarding and jogged over to Klondike near the flap. "There's no one here, Kal."

Klondike could not help staring in horror at the burning bleachers. Minutes, he thought. Just minutes earlier, and thousands of people—children everywhere—would have been in mortal danger. Amidst the terror all around, the unimaginable hell he faced, a strange nagging feel tugged at the back of his mind. Something didn't add up.

"Kal!" McCabe hollered above the crackling. "Let's get the hell outta here! It's gunna burn. All of it."

The smoke was wafting across the floor in great clouds, making breathing almost impossible.

Klondike and McCabe staggered through the flap entrance, arm in arm, coughing violently.

They lurched out into the field and surged on towards the bundle of trailers located at the back of the rodeo ground. The heat was searing.

Then, reaching the perimeter of the field and the old rodeo gates, both turned and surveyed the otherworldly horror before them.

Klondike squinted into the bright inferno, 100 yards before him.

It didn't seem real. An unthinkable nightmare he had never endured. Now, it was happening. And there was nothing he could do about it. The fire roared on. He watched as it crept across the roof of the big top and down the sides.

The sight before him was a surreal apparition. He could see half the tent, the red and blue stripes a cheerful reminder of the magic of the circus. But the other half of the giant structure was a massive ball of deadly fire.

Lacey and Heavy suddenly appeared, joining them by the gates. Many of the performers also gathered, everyone looking up at the horrific sight that seemed impossible. All they could do was watch helplessly. Confused. Scared. Dead inside.

Then, just as it seemed the blaze would engulf the entire tent, a piercing sound echoed through the night that came as a relief to everyone.

It was a chorus of fire engine sirens.

Chapter Sixteen

The following morning, Klondike stood on the grounds of the rodeo field and surveyed the considerable damage.

Before him, like the carcass of a slain prehistoric behemoth, lay the remains of the big top. It was now little more than a blackened hulk of ash and debris. The mess just sat there in the field, an ugly mound of burnt-out material that stretched for much of the park's length. The air smelt of rotting fabric.

Klondike had been out there all night. He stood now, arms folded, watching teams of roustabouts sort through the wreckage. His eyes were reddened and tired, his leather jacket covered in ash and tears.

Everyone associated with the circus had kept their distance from him up to that point. He was lost in his own thoughts. The sheer magnitude of the predicament was lost on no one.

In every possible way, the morning could not be any bleaker. Heavy and Plum were stood 30 yards behind Klondike at the gateway to the rodeo ground. They were looking at him, not the debris.

"He's been standing there for hours," Plum said in despair.

Heavy was shaking his head, as he had for much of the night. "It's so hard to comprehend anything like this happening. I…I feel like I've lost a family member."

"Yeah," Plum mumbled sadly. "I know what you mean."

"Thank god it happened after the show. Oh my god."

Plum looked down. He appeared close to tears. "Can you imagine?" Heavy's stare was fixed, cold. "I don't even want to."

They looked up as Lacey marched past briskly. She was carrying a flask and was heading for Klondike. They let her go.

Klondike sensed a presence join him on the field.

Lacey, wrapped up in a trench coat and wearing a headscarf, stood next to him and slowly unfastened the lid to the flask, which doubled as a cup. She poured the coffee then handed it to him.

"I thought you could use this."

He did not move for several moments. Then, slowly, he turned and took the offered cup. "Thanks," he murmured. He squinted into the blackened mess before him as he sipped the steaming liquid.

Lacey merely stood next to him. "Like the end of the world," she whispered.

He continued staring at the remains of the tent. His voice was bitter and hoarse. "I never thought it would happen."

She watched him, feeling his pain. "Kal," she said gently. "I know what happened last night was a disaster. But…but we have a lot to be thankful for. If that fire had gone off during the show…well, god only knows what kind of tragedy would have befallen us. The children, the kids having the time of their life…"

He nodded. "And that's just it. The children. The families. I can't get that out of my mind."

"It's too terrible to think of."

Then, Klondike looked angry. "I can't believe they went this far."

Her eyes widened. "They?"

"Of course," he grunted. "They!" He looked at her, noted her surprise. "Come off it, Lacey. Of course it was them. McCabe said some of the local crewmen were on site when they shouldn't have been. This was an orchestrated, organised attack."

She put a hand to her mouth. "Oh lord. An attack! It's so completely…so…"

"Inhuman." He spat the word out and sipped his coffee. His whole body quivered. "Just look at the mess they made of my big top. God damn them all to hell!"

Lacey could not help staring at the blackened hulk before them. It was hard to fathom how a fun-filled circus had stood there just hours before.

"Listen," she whispered. "I know this might not be the best time to bring this up, Kal. But, well, there are going to be questions.

Inquiries. Concerns. People are going to demand answers after this catastrophe. How could it happen?"

Klondike frowned at her. "Well, dammit, we're going to give them answers. We will tell anyone who wants to listen that we are under attack. That saboteurs are out to nail us. This is not our doing, any of this. Criminals are targeting us…and they need to be stopped!"

Lacey took a step back. She looked around quickly. "That's quite a statement, Kalvin."

"Damn right! My mind is made up, Lacey. It's time. It's time to hit back. And, as God is my witness, that's what we're going to do. Agostino has to be stopped. The law aren't going to do anything. It's time we did."

She hesitated, hovering awkwardly beside him. "Er, Kal, I think we need to address our present predicament first. Surely. I mean…we are in a god almighty mess right now."

Klondike looked at her and finally seemed to calm himself. He downed the rest of the coffee. "You're right, Lacey. Of course. It's just like we keep on saying…the show must go on. Somehow."

She tried to smile, and grabbed at his arm. "Now, that's the spirit, tiger. But, ahem, there is a significant problem here."

"Yeah," Klondike groaned. "How do you have a circus without a tent?" He glanced back at the charred remains of their big top. He thought for a moment. "Well, five of the grandstand blocks are alright. The other five were destroyed. The trapeze rigs, the audio equipment, the safety hoardings…all gone. So, we have some bones still working. It's up to us to get the rest going again."

She tried to smile. "Yes. That's wonderful. But…but we don't have a tent."

He looked downwards. "Yeah. Let me make some calls. There must be a solution out there somewhere."

They both looked up as a young cowboy approached. He wore jeans, with a giant buckle, plaid shirt and Stetson. All the staff at the Cattlemen's Club seemed to dress like that.

"You Klondike?" he blurted.

"Right."

"Mr Bullstrode wants to see ya. Right now."

Klondike groaned internally. Horace Bullstrode was the owner and chief executive of the Cattlemen's Club. Klondike had practically begged him to host his circus last year.

"Alright. Where do I find him?"

The youngster looked at him in shock. "The executive office. Second floor. Just follow the signs."

With that, he marched off again.

Klondike looked at Lacey. "Wish me luck. How the hell am I going to explain what we've done to his rodeo park?"

She gave him a hug. "Go get em, tiger."

"Just what in hell are you trying to pull, boy? I let you use my field for a circus. And you turn it into the great fire of Houston!"

Horace Bullstrode looked exactly like the wealthy, well-living cattle baron that he was. A huge, 300lb glutton, he wore a brown waistcoat over his plaid shirt, with the obligatory giant belt buckle resting in his midriff like a commemorative plate. His large Stetson seemed to flop at the sides.

He sat behind his desk in the executive office looking as if he was stuck in the seat. The giant floor to ceiling window behind him offered a sorry view of the sea of debris caused by the fire.

"I'm real sorry about what happened out here," Klondike said slowly. "But the fire was nothing to do with me. It was arson. Caused by criminals. The fire investigators will tell you the same thing."

Bullstrode was furious, his face a deep pink. "But it all happened on your watch, dammit! Don't you understand? You could have caused a massacre out here."

Klondike was trying to remain calm. "Like I said, the fire was caused by criminals. I regret the whole incident, but it was not my fault."

"The scandal, the shame of it all," Bullstrode was whimpering, his voice turning into a curious high-pitched wail. He rubbed at his fat, leathery skin with a handkerchief. "Folks will be talking about this for years, Klondike. The Cattlemen's Club is one of the premier tourist attractions in Houston. In Texas, boy. You think people are gunna want to come here now? Do you? The scene of an inferno. A disaster!"

Klondike took a deep breath. He walked a few paces to the huge window, and surveyed the remains of the great tent from the elevated viewpoint. "The damage is colossal, Horace. My circus has suffered a mortal blow. Our tent is destroyed." He turned back to the desk. "We have a show in five days. In New Orleans. We are screwed."

Bullstrode did not flinch. "That's your problem, dammit." He angrily hurled the handkerchief down onto the desk. "Now, you listen, boy. You listen real good. I let you put up your damn tent on my rodeo field. You came to me with the proposition last year. Don't think I forgot about that, sonny. You promised me big numbers, more interest in the Club. The spotlight! Coverage in newspapers and magazines. You sold me the idea, Klondike. And now…look! Look at the mess you've left me in. Why, I oughta sue your ass."

Klondike held up a hand. "With all due respect, sir. I beg to differ." He pointed to the window. "Look out there. Now, once the boys have cleared up all that mess, all you're gunna be left with is charred ground. Black spots. All you need is gravel, soil, whatever it takes to make everything look normal again. I'll happily pay for all that, as well as the clean-up operation. The fire did not touch anything else on your property. The department arrived in fine time. Thank god."

Bullstrode was looking intently down at his field. He nodded slightly. "God damn ash pit," he murmured.

"Listen," Klondike said smoothly. "We'll make it right. I owe you—"

"You're god damn right you owe me!"

"Right. So, I'll speak to my public relations lady and my main backer. We will give the Cattlemen's Club free advertising in the programme for the whole of next season. As well as extra ads on our hoardings. Then, after the season, we will come up with some dates and I'll offer you all of my performers, for free, for a function of your choice at the Club. Anything. Now…" he strode to the desk and leant over the large man. He smiled charismatically. "How do you like them apples?"

Bullstrode stared at him. He looked shocked, but gradually began nodding, the early beginnings of a smile forming at the edge of his lips. "So this is how you work, you circus folk. Well, that's certainly a start. Hell, I like the way you talk, Klondike."

Klondike sat on the desk. "So? Whatdya say?"

Bullstrode looked up at him. "That offer…does it include the Range Riders?"

Klondike laughed wildly. "Of course!"

The big man finally grinned. "In that case, you have a deal. But, like I said, it's just a start."

Klondike shuddered visibly, the relief pouring out of him. That was one hurdle crossed. "Thank you, Horace."

They shook hands.

The comeback was on.

Klondike's Circus had suffered an almighty blow but, as the big top manager kept reminding everyone, it wasn't over yet.

It was a miracle no one had been killed, or even injured, in the fire. Now, the main focus for Klondike and his staff was salvation. Of the circus, of the season, of their future.

The devastation of the fire dominated the local news, and scores of reporters and photographers had gathered at the Cattlemen's Club to pore over the blackened carcass of the big top. Of course, many speculated about the tragedy that would have befallen Klondike's Circus if such a catastrophe had occurred during the show itself. No one seemed interested in following up the rumour that arson had been committed.

Klondike was questioned by fire specialists and yet another deputy from the sheriff's office. He explained that the fire was caused by gang members working for Paul Agostino, out of New York. His claims, predictably, were dismissed. The deputy insisted the fire was an unfortunate accident. The thought of mobsters from New York somehow being involved was a wild, distant fantasy to a young deputy yet to experience life beyond Texas.

Once again, Klondike felt like the general consensus was that everyone in town just wanted him and his people to move on. This time, he would be happy to oblige.

Klondike called an emergency staff meeting for the afternoon, with the location the Sandman barroom.

But first, he wanted to make a call to Addison. There was much to discuss.

"Kal! How are you? How is everyone? Thank god no one was hurt!"

Klondike's eyes widened. "So, you've heard?"

"Of course. Everything. I was awaiting your call." Addison sounded alert and ready.

Klondike settled into his chair behind the desk in his stateroom. He had a lit cigar in his ashtray and another cup of coffee on the go. He rubbed at his tired eyes.

"OK. Good. We're all fine. The fire started about ten minutes after the grand finale. Everyone had left. The crowd had gone. It was the strangest timing."

Addison moaned. "Oh god. I cannot imagine." He exhaled a deep breath. "Dear lord, what else are you going to hit us with?" Klondike nodded. "Feels like that right now, Daryl."

"What are you going to do? I know for a fact you have absolutely no intention of quitting. Of cancelling the season."

"Not even a consideration." Klondike sipped his scotch, then placed the cigar in the corner of his mouth. It felt good to be back in the sanctuary of his stateroom. On the train. Away from the reporters scrambling for a scoop. The cowboys all glaring at him.

"Now," he drawled into the receiver. "We got us a show in New Orleans in four days. Sure, we're gunna get a lot of bad publicity about the fire. A lot of negativity. But, when all is said and done, we got us one major problem ahead of the next show…"

"You haven't got a tent," Addison said in a queer tone.

"Right. We're a big top outfit without a damn big top."

He thought he sensed joviality in Addison's tone. "I'm one step ahead of you, Kal."

"What's that?"

"I heard this morning that the tent was gone. I made some inquiries. It's what I do."

"Oh?"

"Now, listen, Kal. I got a plan that is going to save you. Possibly, save the circus itself."

Klondike was on the edge of his seat. "I'm all ears, Daryl."

"I spoke to my people in New York. Zack Wurley's outfit always carries a spare tent in transit. It's a premier big top, same class as your one. Of course, Wurley is committed to Superstars and Stripes in Washington with you and Chico's Circus. Now, he knows that your troupe is the key to the whole production. And if your circus is in trouble, it will affect the super show. So, Wurley has agreed to let you have his spare tent until the end of the season. That's the whole of it."

Klondike was incredulous. "Daryl!" he roared down the phone. "That's fantastic. I don't believe it!"

Addison chuckled. "You better believe it. I spoke to Wurley's foreman earlier. He is sending the tent by courier. One of his own men is delivering it down to you guys in a transit truck. How about that?"

"It's too good to believe," Klondike rasped. His mind was racing. "Daryl, I don't know how to thank you. And to do all this the morning after the fire. God damn it, you're one in a million. I would never have thought of that."

The older man cleared his throat. "There is one issue, though."

"And what's that?"

163

"Wurley's outfit is in Seattle right now."

Klondike's thoughts raced. That had to be 3,000 miles away. "Jesus! He's at the other end of the country."

"Right. So, unfortunately, there's no way they'll be able to get the tent to you by the time of New Orleans. Believe me, Kal, I've thought it through. Even considered getting a private jet. But, well, there just isn't the time. It's too soon."

Klondike thought frantically. Finally, he surrendered. "You're right." He twirled the cigar between his fingers. "OK. Leave New Orleans to me, Daryl. The mere fact you've arranged for another tent is priceless. It's true what you said—you've saved the circus!"

Addison laughed softly. "It's like I always say. I'll do whatever it takes."

"We're lucky to have you watching over us, my friend."

"Well, I got you your new tent. But that's not all I've got, Kal."

"Jesus Christ! There's more?"

"You recall our last conversation? About Agostino? I said I'd do some digging around? Make some inquiries…"

Klondike sat bolt upright, staring at the window opposite. "What did you find?"

Addison sounded exasperated. "You're not going to believe this, Kal. My man in New York tells me Agostino is looking to break into showbusiness. Wants to work as a manager for stars. Already owns a piece of several singers, mostly cabaret acts. It's all a part of his so-called empire. But he really wants to own a circus. Likes the circus boom, they say."

"Yeah," Klondike drawled dryly. "I gathered as much."

Addison continued. "Apparently, he has been seen with an old friend of ours. A very old friend."

Klondike froze all over, closing his eyes. "Ribbeck," he said the name bluntly, already knowing it was true.

"Right. Eric Ribbeck. Now, I don't know what sort of union the two of them have got going on. But my man reckons they have been seen in Agostino's club in Manhattan."

"What in the world…" Klondike mused. He shook his head. It was all too much. Agostino. Vesnick. Rance. And now Ribbeck, his great nemesis. A mighty cabal, out to stop him. Destroy him.

"That's it," he finally whispered.

"What's that?" Addison replied.

"That's it. They're all in it together. I see it all now. Ribbeck wants me finished. His great rival out of the way, so he can then cherry pick my talent. Agostino wants to run my outfit, maybe join it up with Ribbeck's World Circus. Vesnick is helping as revenge for my firing him. And Rance…well, he is mad about what happened to his animals. Damn! It all makes sense. They're all in it together."

Addison was silent for a moment. "That's quite a bunch, Kal."

Klondike was adamant. "It was their doing, Daryl. All this. The attacks, the negative press. That lion. And now…now the fire. The worst move yet. They could have caused a slaughter of innocents."

"You're sure about the fire?"

"Absolutely." Klondike rubbed his eyes, downing more coffee. He felt exhausted and exhilarated in equal measure. "Listen, Daryl, we need to plan our next show. I'm meeting everyone later this afternoon. I'll update them on all this. We have to plan for New Orleans. Now!"

"Of course, Kal. I understand."

"But, believe me, Daryl, when I tell you. We have to hit back. At all of them. We need a plan. We need to strike. Or else…well, that's not even worth thinking about."

Addison did not hesitate. "Sure, Kal. Listen, call me when you can. I'll keep making enquiries. Agostino has his dirty fingers in all sorts of pies. I'll learn more about him. There will be something. Some kind of opening…where we can nail him."

Klondike hammered his fist on the desk. "That's the spirit, Daryl. I'll be in touch. Things are moving way too fast. And Daryl?"

"Yes, Kal?"

He smiled, wishing he could see the old man right now. "Thank you. You've smashed it outta the park with this. Again! Thank you from the bottom of my heart."

"Don't mention it."

They said their goodbyes.

Klondike merely sat there at his desk, his mind whirling. Thoughts ebbed and flowed at frenetic pace within his consciousness.

The fire. Horace Bullstrode. New Orleans. A new tent. The cabal out to get him. How to strike back.

He had dealt with all this in under 12 hours.

The deadly inferno had shaken him as much as anything that had ever befallen the circus. The pain and sorrow, the anxiety, had been enormous. But now, after his chat with Addison, he was feeling a wave of relief and anticipation hit him. And something else.

Absently, as if in a trance, he reached down into the lowest of the four drawers attached to his desk. From the drawer, he grabbed a small envelope and brought it up to the surface, delicately emptying its contents before him.

The pouch contained a wealth of old black and white photographs, many of them torn and battered. Squinting into the mix, he found the one he was looking for and held it up in the light.

The picture had been taken many years previously. It showed Klondike as a young man, possibly in his late 20s, shaking hands with a middle-aged man, dressed in a fur coat, who had thick black hair and bushy sideburns. Eric Ribbeck.

They had been partners. The master and his apprentice. Full of hope and expectation. All those years ago.

Klondike studied the picture, cigar in mouth. His dark eyes took on a deep understanding.

"I knew it was you, old friend," he said. "I knew it was you."

Chapter Seventeen

Paul Agostino sat upright in the giant four-poster bed in his penthouse suite at his club in Manhattan.

Nestled comfortably within the soft feathered pillows and silk sheets, he leisurely surveyed his breakfast tray as he sat there in his favourite burgundy pyjamas.

Smoked salmon, eggs benedict and buttered toast. A cafetiere of fresh coffee. New York coffee. He poured a cup and sipped at it, before greedily devouring the salmon and eggs.

As he neared the end of the meal, there was a knock at the door. "Get in here!" Agostino called out to the steward.

An elderly man in a black suit entered the room, carrying a newspaper.

"This morning's National Review," the man said. He handed the paper to Agostino before turning on his heel and fleeing.

Agostino put his knife and fork down and grabbed at the newspaper eagerly. Going through the pages with an expectant expression, he finally settled on page 10. With a deep smile, he began to read…

A NIGHT OF TERROR AT THE CIRCUS
By Hank Darlow

What started out as an evening of magic and entertainment at a circus on Saturday night turned into a show of pure horror.

Residents of Houston, Texas, had come out in force for Klondike's Circus. What they saw was a night of terror.

A deadly inferno swept the big top at the conclusion of the night's festivities, with the blaze destroying the tent—and nearly everyone inside it.

Truly, it was a miracle that nobody was killed in this atrocity. Women, children, the young and the old. All had been seated inside the arena, enjoying the show.

All would have perished if the fire had started but seconds earlier. The death toll would have been in the thousands. The aftermath unthinkable.

It was surely an act of God that kept the flames back until most people had left the tent.

But that fact should not gloss over what was an unimaginable disaster.

The blame for this catastrophe lies firmly at the feet of circus owner and manager Kal Klondike. His blatant disregard for fire safety rules and procedures and obvious use of outdated, unsafe equipment have caused this horror.

The sight of giant flames eating away at the big top, as families left after a night of fun, has led this correspondent to call for the immediate blacklisting of Mr Klondike and his cronies.

Last night was a near-miss. But how much longer until we have a slaughter on our hands?

As long as these unsafe Wild West shows are allowed to continue, all paying patrons are in danger.

Our children go to a circus to sit wide-eyed at acts of trapeze and clowning. Not to fear for their lives.

I am hereby calling for Klondike's Circus to be permanently closed down. Anyone who opposes my notion should have a close look at the pictures accompanying this article of the horror in Houston.

Agostino laughed with delight as he finished reading the editorial. Pushing his plate aside on the breakfast tray, he slurped at his coffee and lit a cigarette.

Holding the paper aloft, he looked at the author's by-line underneath the headline.

"That's some nice work, Hank," he said aloud.

He thought to himself, sinking back into the pillows. Some equally uncompromising stories from the other reporters on his payroll across the country ought to inflict maximum damage.

And there he was. Waiting in the wings. Waiting to pick up the pieces. And then cash in. Sell off the hottest talent in the country. Asset stripping is what his fancy pals in Wall Street called it. Now, he was going to get some of that action for himself.

Old man Ribbeck was right, he thought. This way of doing things was better. More enjoyable, among other facets.

With another chuckle, Agostino picked up the National Review and reread the story.

The atmosphere within the Sandman bar-room was pensive, like a stockholders' meeting at a firm facing bankruptcy.

It was like a wall of silence, with everyone staring at Klondike up front.

Hope, fear, longing…every emotion imaginable stared back at him on the long faces.

Klondike stood at the head of the room. Heavy, Lacey and Plum were seated at a round table just behind.

Then, the performers were all sat in bar seats before them. For some reason, that was still not obvious to him, Klondike had requested the troupe all sit in specific seats.

Shapiro, Penny, Olsen, Suzi and Corky all occupied the front row. Tip Enqvist and the Daredevils then sat in the next grouping, along with the Showcase Revue performers.

The Batista family, the Rocking Robins, the Range Riders and all the clowns then grouped together at the back.

Jim McCabe was standing at the side, nursing a tall glass of beer.

Klondike had been updating the team on all that had happened since the fire. His meeting with Horace Bullstrode. The telephone call with Daryl Addison. He even threw in his own thoughts, which was an unusual but welcome initiative.

"Now, I know what you're all thinking," he drawled, as the sea of faces before him looked more and more withdrawn. "That we're getting deeper and deeper into a mess we can't get out of. That with each show, things are getting more out of hand." He held up a fist. "Well, listen. We just need to get New Orleans done and dusted. Somehow. Then, once we have Zack Wurley's spare tent—god bless him—we can really get down to it. We'll be back."

The expected cacophony of alarmed exasperations erupted from the seats.

But the sound of Enqvist's booming voice drowned out the others as he stood up and faced Klondike.

"You really believe that, Kal?" he cried. "That everything will go back to normal? For Chrissakes, you fools! People are out to get us. Gangsters! The law ain't helping. This is all crazy!"

"We need to hit back," Goliath put in. The giant was sat behind the Daredevils and seemed to have become an unofficial member of the group.

"Alright," Klondike said, holding up a hand. He frowned as he spoke. "Listen, all of you. We will hit back. I promise. Daryl is on the case with that right now. Formulating a plan. Plans! But…right here, right now, our number one dilemma is New Orleans. We have three days. Two really. We're heading out tomorrow morning. It's about a seven-hour run. But, folks, showtime is 48 hours later. And…" he looked around helplessly. "Well, our big top is a burnt-out mess on that field out there."

McCabe spoke next. "When is that fire investigator's report due in?"

Klondike shrugged. "Hell, I don't know. A week. Two weeks. We'll be long gone."

"If they can prove it was arson," McCabe continued, "we can find the local crew, link them to this Agostino and nail him."

"A waste of time," Heavy bellowed from the back.

Klondike nodded. "Heavy's right. You think a top mob guy like that don't cover his tracks? Those local rednecks you took on won't even know who they were working for. Guaranteed. This is how gangs work. They have a paper trail."

"Dammit!" Enqvist said, standing up again. "There must be some way of getting to him."

It was the quiet and unassuming Suzi who spoke next, to the surprise of many. "They could have killed everyone. Families. Children. Won't somebody think of the children?" Her voice quivered as she spoke. "Somebody has got to make this stop." A deathly silence filled the bar-room. Lacey stood and joined Klondike at the front of the gathering.

"That's all we are thinking of, Suzi," she whispered. "The horror of it all."

"No one was ever going to get killed," McCabe spat out from the bar. "This was a planned attack. Whoever did it wanted to destroy the circus. The tent. The equipment. Not the people. Believe me." He looked around the faces now glaring at him. "What! You think it was all a coincidence? Everyone leaves, then the tent goes up in flames. Come on!"

"Jim's right," Klondike said steadily. "These people are out to ruin the circus. There can be no doubt. They hit the tent. The ground hole puncher. And they hit the talent. Roddy. Tip and his boys. It all fits."

Corky raised a hand like a child in a classroom. "They want us to cancel the season. A circus is nothing without its tent."

"That's right," Heavy said. He too had rose and was now pacing the bar-room. "These guys figure we'll quit. The scandal of the fire. All this negative press. The anger of the paying public." He held his arms aloft in a mock expression. "How can we go on?"

Klondike nodded. "But these punks reckoned without the will and pride we all have. Dammit all to hell, we've been through rough times before. I'm talking about the train crash. The Jenny Cross incident. And each time we've bounced back stronger. We have prevailed. And, in heaven's name, that is what we're going to do this time, people. As God is my witness."

Lacey stood strong beside him, seemingly lifted by his resolve. She continued the speech, like a relay runner accepting a baton. "We have a responsibility. To the people of New Orleans. And every town left in the schedule. A responsibility to put on the best damn show in town. To give them their money's worth. To let them see and cheer for their heroes. For you all..." she lifted her arms in a theatrical gesture, as if awaiting a thunderous ovation.

None was forthcoming. Instead, the performers studied her curiously.

"Pretty speeches," someone snarled. It was one of the Range Riders at the back. "But we all know what's going on here. That show, Superstars and Stripes, in Washington, is a big money spectacular. The profits will be enormous. You two don't want to ruin your circus's reputation before then. Anything wrecks that show and all those dollars will suddenly disappear. You're protecting the Washington show, and we all know it."

A slow murmuring of approval rippled through the group. Klondike and Lacey looked at each other nervously.

Then, from nowhere, Raul Batista stood up at the back. He was wearing gypsy clothes and looked tired and frail. Everyone turned and stared at him as he cleared his throat.

"I am frightened, Mr Kal," he said weakly. "My wife is frightened. My family is frightened. We are all frightened. Of an attack. Of more fires. This...how do you say? This is not what we had in mind when we sign with you."

Another chorus of angry murmurings broke out.

Next, one of the Rocking Robins cried out from the back. "We shouldn't have to put up with all this. Nobody should!"

Goliath suddenly stood and glared at the dancers. "You don't like it, get the hell outta here! We don't need you!"

A panicked wailing erupted from the group of women.

"Alright!" Klondike cried, holding up a hand again. It had no effect. An argument was breaking out within his troupe. He could feel a mutiny rising.

He looked out across his team. The trouble was forming towards the back. And then, suddenly, he realised the subconscious reasoning behind his seating plan. It all made sense.

His eyes went to the front. Shapiro was staring back at him silently, arms folded, ignoring the chaos. The flyer nodded. Klondike nodded back.

Then, Shapiro jumped to his feet and joined Klondike and Lacey at the front.

"Silence!" he screamed. Everybody stopped talking at once, more in alarm at the sudden cry of order than anything.

Shapiro stood there, arms raised, as if preparing to preach a sermon.

"That is enough," he cried. His beautiful face took on an ugly sneer as he surveyed his team-mates. "Shame on you, my fellow artists. Shame on you, you circus people. Just listen to yourselves. Angry at the people who are jealous. Frightened by the life on the road. You don't have the privilege of knowledge when it comes to this situation. None of you has. None of you has the responsibility, the pressure, the worry."

He paused, eyeing Klondike briefly and pacing before the group. "You are talent. You perform for the people. And that, my friends, is the most beautiful way of making a living in the world. And you all know this, no? That is why...that is why you are here now, amigos. With me. Because you are the best! The best!"

Everyone was silent, all eyes on the flamboyant Shapiro. "Now," he scoffed angrily, "I hear a lot of poor mouth. A lot of distrust. You dare to question our chairman? Our chairman...who has taken us all from a level of moderate success to the top, the very top, of the circus world. It is thanks to Kal Klondike we have fame. We have fans. And you should never forget that. Not one of you. Now, you all listen, because this is very important..."

"I had many offers when I was younger. From circuses all over the world. England, Germany, Italy, Mexico, even Japan. Places you've never even heard of. They all want Gino. But I chose to follow Kal Klondike. Why? Because he believed in me. And he was honest, caring and put his people first. And he always has. Now, you all believe me. I have been here longer than any of you. And what I say is true."

He suddenly stood tall and projected his arms wide. "So, I say to you now. Follow me. And follow Kal Klondike!"

Everyone, Klondike included, stood mesmerised by the grandiose speech.

Shapiro offered his hand to Klondike, and they shook on it. Then, Lacey hugged the great flyer and everyone started talking at once. Penny leapt up and stood by Gino, her arm around him.

Then, Olsen, Suzi and Corky stood also.

"I stand by everything our high-flying friend just said," the clown announced. "And I joined at the beginning too." He smiled at Klondike. "Always trust the boss, folks."

Olsen chipped in next. "And I second all that as well. We all need to keep going with this, guys. We can do it."

Suzi added: "We can make it. We've just got to stick together."

Somehow, the troupe had been split into two factions. Standing and sitting. A great hush descended over the bar-room.

Enqvist stood from the pack still sat down. He nodded slowly, looking back at the Range Riders and the Rocking Robins. Goliath rose also and stood menacingly behind him.

"Alright," Enqvist muttered. "Alright. I agree this is a fantastic outfit. And, well, there are gunna be a few bumps on the road. It's just a lot to take in, is all."

Klondike nodded. The relief was flooding through him like a tidal wave, yet he remained impassive. "I know. And I'm real sorry about all the trouble."

Goliath spoke again. "We still need to strike back, boss."

Heavy wandered in front of Klondike and answered for him. "Don't you all worry about that." He eyed the group with a bulldog expression. "That is a problem for management. You guys just need to go out there and do your thing every week. Shine! Like the stars you are."

"Which brings us back to our current predicament," said Percy Pringle, sat buried within the Showcase Revue group. He raised his head. "What are we going to do in New Orleans? And beyond…if this so-called reserve tent don't show up!"

A mighty hush swept across the bar-room. Yet again, everyone stared at Klondike.

The circus manager looked at Lacey next to him. She smiled awkwardly. Then he looked at Heavy. And then Shapiro.

There were a lot of blank expressions.

"OK," Klondike finally said, sounding calm. "Now, we're due to appear at Tessier Showground. Downtown, not far from Bourbon Street. French Quarter. It's where the action is down there. My proposal is we relocate to a concert venue. Maybe an assembly hall. We do the show indoors."

Everyone looked at him curiously.

"A show in an actual building?" said Suzi in a high-pitched voice. "Why not?"

Klondike was smiling now. "We did it for the ATV special and we've done smaller gigs in indoor arenas. It can work."

Lacey was looking at him quizzically. "Of course, it means less attendance, less revenue. No midway. We're restricted to whatever space is on offer. And whatever equipment is inside. And, of course, how on earth are we going to book anywhere at such short notice?" The others were astounded. She had reeled off the list of problems like a machine.

She smiled demurely at the expressions. "And, most important of all, we have thousands of fans in New Orleans waiting to get tickets in advance at our box office. People wanting to see our stars. How many of them are going to be disappointed at missing out as we can only accommodate several hundred in an indoor venue?"

Heavy nodded bullishly. "Losing the tent is the biggest blow of all. When you put it like that, Lacey, we can all see how valuable it is."

Lacey folded her arms, looking from Heavy to Klondike. "I think going into an indoor venue would turn fans against us. Besides, we will never get anywhere decent with two days of notice."

Suzi looked demoralised. "Is there no other way of getting a tent? Where can we find one?"

Klondike shook his head angrily. "Big tops aren't made en masse at factories. Daryl has worked absolute wonders to get us one. It's just the damn logistics...we can't get the sucker here in time for New Orleans."

Lacey delicately eased her silver cigarette case out of her handbag. "We just need to find a way to get everybody to see us. Hell, we're docking next to one of the most colourful and celebrated streets in the country. It's party time all day and all night down there. We just have to find a way of joining it."

She lit up and surveyed the long faces. Everyone seemed deep in thought. The performers all retook their seats. Klondike wandered across to the window and looked out at the rodeo field. Heavy joined McCabe at the bar, reaching for the coffee jug.

Suddenly, a quiet voice broke the bitter silence. "That's it!"

Of all people, it was Richie Plum. The small, bespectacled man had remained silent throughout the entire proceedings, seated behind Klondike. Now, he rose slowly, poking the air with a finger.

"That's it," he said again. "The street! We do the show in open air. Outside. In the showground. That way, everybody can see it. And more."

He looked around wildly, as if seeking endorsement. "It can work. We can set up a trapeze rig using the support poles and spare rigging. The high wire can go anywhere. The Range Riders and the Daredevils can do their thing in the open. The Globe of Death can be attached to the platform outside. And all the other acts can just perform in the open air. It…it can be done!"

Plum clasped his hands together and strode triumphantly into the collective warmth of the rest of the group.

"The branch line cut-off is at the showground. That's just a few blocks from Bourbon Street. We just need a few temporary grandstands to join the ones that survived the fire and…well, think about it, it will be like normal. The stands will form an arena, and anyone else can sit or stand in the aisles. People will flock to see us."

A stunned silence gripped the others. Klondike slowly approached Plum. He looked serious, then his face broke into a hyena-like grin. "Richie, my friend, that is ingenious."

Plum looked shocked. "Really? You…you mean you agree?"

"Sure," Klondike barked. He laughed softly. "Y'know, I never thought of it like that. We can practically do the whole show in the open air. Ha! I never even considered it."

Lacey was nodding furiously. "Why Richie, that's a fabulous idea. And just think of the novelty value. An open air circus. We can drum up some excellent publicity. People will be curious."

"That's just what I was thinking," Plum said excitedly, his face reddening. "We can turn this awful situation to our advantage."

Lacey's eyes were widening. "It will be the first show of its kind ever in America!"

"Woh, now, just a minute." It was Heavy, returning from the bar. "Now, I don't want to be the bad guy here but this is uncharted territory for us. You can't just plunge headfirst into this. We haven't even had an outdoor rehearsal. And, dammit, this all goes down in three days!"

Lacey beamed at him. "What can possibly go wrong, Henry?"

He glared at her. "Well, what if it rains?"

She waved a hand through the air. "In Louisiana at this time of year? Pah!"

Heavy still looked dubious. "I just don't know…"

Klondike clapped his hands. "Listen, we're booked into that show ground, so we're already there in theory."

He turned and looked at Shapiro and Penny, who were seated on the edge of a table, deep in thought.

"Gino," he said sternly. "You and Penny are the ones up there. This will affect you two more than anyone else. What do you think?"

Penny turned to look at Shapiro, who rubbed his shoulder and eyed Klondike. His voice was casual. "Si, it can be done. I do it once before, with my brother, back in Mexico. When we were kids. All I demand is to check that rigging before we go up."

Klondike nodded. "Of course. And you, Penny?"

The blonde simply grinned. "I'm beginning to trust our dear Gino here with my very life. If he says it's alright, then that is good enough for me."

Plum punched the air. "That's it then!"

Klondike put a hand on his shoulder. "Well, Richie, I think we need to put it before the whole group."

Incredibly, everyone seemed to be in agreement that it was a good plan. Various comments punctured the excited atmosphere.

"I would love it," said Olsen.

"It's not a problem for us, we can ride anywhere," added Enqvist.

"It sounds like fun," said one of the Rocking Robins.

"Hell, it's the only real option now," opined Corky, clapping his hands together.

Everyone started talking at once. It was striking how the mood had changed in a matter of minutes. Optimism seemed to surge through the team now.

Klondike smiled widely and looked across at Heavy. The two old friends stared at each other for several moments.

"Well," Klondike drawled. "What d'ya say, old buddy?"

Heavy chuckled deeply. "Hell, I'd say we got us an open air circus!" Everyone cheered at that. Lacey strode straight for the bar.

"Now, I'd say that calls for a drink!" Nobody argued with her.

Chapter Eighteen

The Barrowman Express train rolled elegantly through the bayous of west Louisiana.

The red and blue special made a startling sight as it sped past the reed-covered swamplands—a backwoods world bereft of modernisation and industry.

The railroad ran far through the foresty land but, at the end of the line, lay one of the most colourful cities in the country in New Orleans.

The land of Cajun culture was set to play host to America's first open air circus of modern times.

That thought alone excited the occupants of the train as it sped eastwards into Louisiana.

Klondike and Heavy were sat in the circus manager's opulent stateroom, playing poker at the roundtable. The duo were known to while away the train travel time playing cards, often discussing business as they battled for each other's chips.

Heavy had just shot a deal. He glanced out the window as several houses came into view, the first for what seemed like an eternity as they passed through the bayous.

"New Orleans, here we come," he mused. He swept up his hand of cards off the table's smooth green baize and glanced at his old friend opposite. "And yet another first for our beloved outfit."

Klondike surveyed his hand, toying with a solitary chip. "You said it, Heav. Out in the open. Like street performers of old."

"I just hope all our spare equipment works. We haven't used the old microphone in years."

Klondike chuckled. "We'll find out soon enough, old buddy. We're gunna have to roll out a rehearsal as soon as we get there. Everything needs to be checked out."

Heavy studied his cards, then seemed to lose interest, his thoughts drifting. "It's funny, you know," he whispered. "All these shows we've put on down the years, Kal. All the extravaganzas. The ATV special. The golden tent in Vegas. New York. Chicago. Los Angeles. And now this! This show in New Orleans. This could be the one they all remember."

"And to think…" Klondike said slowly. "It all originated from a disaster."

Heavy shook his head, running a hand through his receding hairline. "My god, what a state of affairs. I still can't believe it. To think…our big top is gone. Gone forever. It seems so inconceivable."

"I know, Heav, I know." Klondike stood up absently, the poker match suddenly forgotten. He leant against the window and watched the countryside fly past. He could feel the great wheels below rattle along the track.

More constructions were coming into view now. Farms. Civilisation. Soon, they would see skyscrapers once more. Smoke rising from factory chimneys.

He turned to Heavy as he watched the world slide by.

"The tent is gone," he said slowly. "Back there, behind us. But the future…the future is at the end of the line."

Heavy sat back, grinning. "And what lies ahead? In our future?"

"The same as always." Klondike returned his stare to the window, the land outside. He spoke in a grizzled whisper. "New worlds to conquer."

The following morning's New Orleans Herald carried a bombastic front page headline:

HISTORIC OPEN-AIR CIRCUS IS HERE!

The article then read:

The rumours are true! A live, open-air circus is coming to Cajun Country this weekend, the first in our city's history.

Klondike's Circus, which has thrilled New Orleans with its daring and dazzling feats for the past two summers, is pitching up for Saturday's spectacular.

But this will be a circus like no other. Indeed, this big top will be without…a big top! That's right, circus officials have confirmed the show will go ahead in the open air.

This shocking development has arisen after the Klondike tent was destroyed in a fire last week. Contrary to reports elsewhere, no patrons were ever in any danger during the blaze.

No, the only casualty was the tent itself. Unable to get a replacement in time, circus boss Kal Klondike announced last night that his show will go ahead at Tessier Showgrounds on Saturday, with the stands and the stage all out in the open.

Though he will no doubt be praying any unseasonal showers don't rain on his parade, there is essentially little change whether the show is indoors or out.

However, the act most affected by the new format is the trapeze performance, the show's celebrated climax.

The world famous Gino Shapiro and his beautiful sidekick, Penny Fortune, will be open to the elements, hovering high above the sawdust floor.

It is not hard to imagine several tweaks being punctured into their act in the name of safety. And sanity.

Nonetheless, this will be a historic night. The spectacle of an open-air circus alone is mind-blowing.

Expect a night to remember...

The townsfolk of New Orleans had never seen anything quite like it. The Tessier Showground, a giant promenade just a few blocks off Bourbon Street, looked like a giant, otherworldly carnival, dominated by the bizarre sight of a bowl of scaffolded seats that looked like an abandoned building site.

Here sat the open air circus arena. Without the great tent enveloping everything, the circle of grandstands joined together as one, resembling a skeleton of bars and pipes, all holding rows of seats in place.

In front of the great skeleton was the midway, with its colourful sea of cabins and attractions bleeding out towards the street like a glorified shanty town.

New Orleans was a town of parties and festivals. But the sight of the new-look Klondike's Circus, set up and ready for custom, was far from glamorous or exotic.

However, as Lacey Tanner had predicted, it was a prominent novelty for anyone who saw it.

The circus-goers, who had waited for the arrival of Klondike's Circus all year, were queuing at the portable ticketing booths as soon as they were erected.

And they were joined by the curious, the intrigued and those who simply had to see what was going on.

On show day, Tessier Showground was packed. It felt as if everyone was clamouring to get a glimpse at the open-air circus, many wondering just how it would all play out.

A core of press representatives had gathered outside the newly erected grandstands to compare notes. All of them—newspaper reporters, magazine journalists, TV camera crews and radio news people—were huddled together, struggling to know how to lead on a story like this. They were divided on their opinions.

"This is crazy...like the Mardi Gras gone wrong," said one. "I ain't never seen anything like it," said another.

"They will be talking about this for years," opined one of the older reporters.

They stood staring at the trailers on the far side of the assembled grandstands, where various workers were racing around, busy with last-minute preparations.

"The stars are all in those trailers," one of the TV people said. "Why don't we just go over and talk to them? Maybe get an exclusive!"

"Why do that?" the older reporter said. "We have an exclusive already. America's first open-air circus. And none of them will know what to tell us anyway. This is a first for everyone, including all of them."

Everyone in the press pool nodded in agreement.

"Come on," a youthful magazine writer said excitedly. "Let's get in our seats up there. I can't wait any longer!"

As one, they all hurried to a partition in the grandstands and showed their press passes to a steward.

As the group disappeared into the unusual-looking structure, more and more patrons left the midway and headed towards the stands. The entire showground felt alive with excitement and energy.

Lacey Tanner was walking slowly around the midway stalls with Bob Slater, the city council's head of culture and entertainment.

"I can't thank you enough Bob for letting us go ahead with this," she gushed as she led him around the various attractions.

"Are you kidding?" he exclaimed, looking around the stalls with childlike enthusiasm. "This is incredible! An outdoor circus! The publicity alone has been worth it."

They stopped to watch a teenager at the shooting gallery. The youngster fired five shots, hitting four ducks.

"The way I see it," Slater continued, "it don't make a hell of a lot of difference to us whether your show is in a tent or outside like this. But there's no doubt doing it like this has generated a load of interest. My phone hasn't stopped ringing from interested parties, wanting to advertise their firm at the showground. Wanting me to fix them up with tickets." He laughed boisterously. "Hell, somehow I'm the flavour of the month at city hall again!"

Lacey giggled sweetly. "I'm glad. Just let me know what I can do for you."

He raised an enquiring eyebrow. "Am I still on for the meet and greet with the performers afterwards?"

"Of course!" she cried. "Now, let me get you a stick of cotton candy." She led him to the confectionary booth and fished out her purse.

Slater watched the youngster behind the counter whip up the fluffy pink floss and licked his lips. "Why, I feel like a kid again."

Lacey laughed gaily. "That's the idea, Bob."

Slater began laughing too. Then, suddenly, the sound of trumpets blaring echoed across the showground. Everything stopped. Then, the midway was suddenly abandoned as the patrons surged towards the grandstands, and the entrance areas.

It was showtime.

"Ladies and gentlemen…"

Heavy Brown's booming announcement, enhanced by a hastily assembled microphone and sound system, reverberated around the showground like a clap of thunder.

A general hush descended across the thousands of excited fans crammed into the bleacher seats, stacked high and encircling the round, sawdust-covered stage area below.

Many more were packed into the spaces around the grandstands, everyone desperate to get a look at this entertainment novelty.

High above, a makeshift rigging sat suspended over them all, the trapeze equipment connected to several giant tentpoles that had been secured into the earth.

Heavy looked around at the endless sea of humanity. Every eye in the stands was fixed upon him. Holding one hand aloft, the other clasped on the microphone, he bellowed out his greeting. "Welcome to the most incredible, the most fantastic, the most mesmerising show on earth. Once seen, never forgotten. The show of the hour. The show with the power. Always great. Never faked."

The all-American jamboree. The bash that will leave you full of glee. It's here, it's live and it's ready to blow you all away!

"So, ladies and gentlemen, sit back, relax and prepare to be enchanted. My name is Heavy Brown, and I give to you…Klondike's Circus!"

The crowd broke into a rapturous applause, with screams of delight and wild cries breaking from the seats.

Then, from the specially created entrance behind Heavy, essentially a gap between two grandstand platforms that led to the trailers, a flurry of activity erupted.

Heavy continued. "And now, to open our show, the wonders of the wild west, the kings among cowboys, please put your hands together for the fast-riding, hard-driving…Range Riders!"

The team of 12 horses ridden bareback by the riders dressed as cowboys all raced into the sawdust clearing, passing either side of Heavy and descending on the circus floor, before beginning a galloping circle around the arena. Round and round the bareback riders went, performing various tricks on their mounts as they moved.

Some stood on the horses' backs, one short rider performed a headstand on his mount, before all performed vaults over various wooden jump obstacles laid in the circus's centre. One rider then held on to two horses' manes and was pulled along in-between them as they gallivanted around the floor, while another ran at the flying triumvirate, before ducking between the rider's legs.

Four of the horses then laid down, while the others took it in turns to jump over the group.

At the conclusion of the act, each of the riders made their horses stand on its hind legs and perform a bow. The stallions then trotted backstage, with the riders waving their goodbyes.

As the applause broke out, Heavy returned to the middle and grabbed his mic.

"Wonderful people of New Orleans, prepare to be dazzled by the delightful dancers of Klondike's Circus. More rock 'n' roll than even the Rockettes. Ladies and gentlemen, I give you…the Rocking Robins!"

The dancers raced out into the open circus floor in their dazzling red and silver leotards.

They immediately launched into their customary numbers as the old Broadway tunes played over the tannoy.

High kicks, somersaults and cartwheels were everywhere as the Robins whirled across the sawdust.

As always, they concluded their act with the showgirl-style dancehall piece, all linking arms together to form a long line and kicking their legs high in tandem.

The human chain slowly went around in a giant circle as the Robins, all linked together, continued their kicks to the delight of the applauding spectators.

As the music stopped, they jogged slowly off stage, waving and blowing kisses to the fans.

"The Rocking Robins!" Heavy bellowed, holding an arm aloft. He waited for the dancers to clear the floor.

"And now, ladies and gentlemen, it is my great pleasure to introduce to you the modern sensation of the circus...the wizard of ventriloquism...the Puppetmaster, Roddy Olsen!"

Olsen strutted into the open arena. He was dressed in his silver waistcoat and purple pants, and held Rusty Fox by his side. "Good evening," Olsen cried, waving to the audience. "Good evening and thank you for joining us for America's first open air circus. My name is Roddy Olsen and—"

Right on cue, Rusty interrupted: "Roddy, Roddy, Roddy. My dear boy. No one cares who you are. We all know all these people are here to see me. Rusty Fox. Teen idol. Singing sensation."

Olsen looked down at him. "Rusty, what have I told you about interrupting?"

"I don't know. I was too busy looking cool."

Olsen sighed. "Ladies and gentlemen, may I introduce my dear friend Rusty Fox. I must apologise for his bad manners."

"Hey, put a sock in it, Roddy. Without me, you're nothing. I'm the star of the show."

Olsen laughed. "Well, we'll let these good people be the judge of that. So, Rusty, you must be pretty excited. Here we are, in party central, New Orleans."

"You betcha! This is where a teen idol like me belongs. I'm the world's most famous fox...now I want to meet all the chicks!"

The audience laughed good-naturedly. "Y'know," Olsen said to the puppet, "we've got a huge show tonight. All out here under the moon and stars."

"That's just perfect."

"For what?"

"My singing, man." The fox burst out into a rendition of the ballad Blue Moon. The audience clapped as he sang.

"Ok, ok," said Olsen. "So you can sing. What else can you do?" This was one of his standard routines. "I do impersonations," said the puppet. "Look, here's my impersonation of the so-called king of comedy, Steve Irving."

The fox puppet bent low and grabbed its foot with its mouth, holding it there for comedic effect.

"Next," the puppet continued, "my impression of chat show queen Linda Schneider." He then proceeded to slowly fall over backwards. "And, finally, here is the mayor of New Orleans, Jim Brannigan." Right on cue, Rusty put his foot in his mouth and fell over backwards.

Cheers and applause broke out across the stands.

"Thank you, thank you," Rusty was saying to the audience.

"Alright," Olsen cut in, "not bad, Rusty. Now, we're going to bring out another of our friends for another song…"

"Woh," Rusty snapped. "I thought I was doing all the singing tonight?"

"Er, no, Rust. You're here to help me."

"What! They told me I was the star of the show."

"No, Rust. I'm the star and you—"

"No, I'm the star!"

The two bickered back and forth, Olsen utilising his remarkable voice throwing skills to make it sound like the two were talking over each other, at the same time. It was a phenomenal trick, with the ventriloquist going head to head with his puppet. The audience sat awestruck, many open mouthed at the magical action.

Finally, Olsen removed a wad of sticky tape from his pocket, ripped a piece off with his teeth and placed it over the mischievous fox's mouth. Then, Rusty continued to make noises, with Olsen dropping his tone to make it sound like a muffled grunting. The audience applauded his genius.

Then, incredibly, Rusty produced a piece of tape as well and slapped it over Olsen's mouth.

Somehow, the ventriloquist began talking in Rusty Fox's voice. "This is ridiculous! Wait a minute. How am I talking? Your mouth is taped shut, Roddy! What the!"

With his spare hand, Olsen ripped off both bits of tape.

"Oh lord! What madness!" he said, the audience in fits of laughter. They were still chuckling when a new, older voice emerged from out of nowhere.

"Get me outta here! And that's an order!" the new, hoarse voice bellowed.

"Aha," Olsen cried, "that sounds like our friend!"

"He ain't my friend," Rusty moaned.

"It's coming from the trunk," Olsen said, before he left the stool, carried Rusty over to the giant case next to the mic stand and opened it. He bent down into the confines.

"Whoa!" the harsh new voice cried.

When Olsen emerged again, he had Rusty on one arm and Napoleon, his Army veteran puppet, on the other. Napoleon was dressed in his usual GI outfit with cap.

"Holy West Point!" the old figure cried.

Olsen made Napoleon and Rusty face each other.

"Dammit, Roddy, I thought I told you I don't ever want to see this slimy maggot ever again!"

"I'm not a maggot! I'm a fox."

"Ladies and gentlemen," Olsen said aloud, "may I introduce my very good, very old friend. They call him…Napoleon."

The crowd cheered in recognition and delight at the appearance of the army puppet.

Napoleon shouted his greeting, "Major-general, US Army. Retired. But still in combat. With the menace of rock 'n' roll."

"Hey, old man," Rusty said, "why don't you do us all a favour and go back to bed."

"Why you little squirt!" Napoleon roared. "Once this damn show is over, I'm gunna come looking for you, ratboy. Then I'll wipe that stupid smile off your face."

"The only thing you're gunna be looking for is a Zimmer frame."

"Ok, ok," Olsen interjected, separating the warring puppets. "Listen guys, we're all here to sing a song for these good people. Not to argue aimlessly."

"Song!" Napoleon blurted. "What you got in mind, son? A hymn? A little country and western?"

"You know what we're singing, old man," said Rusty impishly.

Napoleon's face dropped. "Oh no! Not the Rock?" The crowd cheered wildly.

Olsen cried out in alarm. "No! Come on, Rust. Anything but Rock Island Line!"

But the music had already started. Rusty began singing the classic folk song, before a reluctant Olsen and Napoleon joined in.

Each took it in turns to sing a line as the song got faster. As always, Olsen's astonishing voice manipulation made the whole thing a spectacle of showmanship.

One man. Three voices. Toy puppets brought to life as if by magic. When Olsen finished performing the song, the audience rose as one to applaud. The celebrated sketch was a perennial crowd-pleaser.

Thanking the fans, Olsen placed Rusty Fox and Napoleon back into his suitcase and removed Tony Tan, to more cheers from all around. He sat on his stool and placed the new puppet on his thigh.

"OK, folks, this is another old friend of mine. Direct from The Sands, in Las Vegas, Nevada, please welcome lounge singer supreme Tony Tan."

The tuxedo-clad figure nodded and waved as Olsen controlled his movements. "Thank you. Thank you. Wonderful to be back here in New England."

"Er, Tony, we're in New Orleans," said Olsen nervously.

"Oh, right, New Orleans. Bourbon Street—my favourite street in the world!"

"So, how you been Tony?"

The puppet looked sad. "I still can't stop my drinking problem."

"Drinking problem?"

"Yeah. Once I start drinking, I can't find enough drinks!" Soft laughter reverberated across the arena.

"Well, Tony, we're going to do a trick next involving a glass of water."

Tony's eyes narrowed and he glared at Olsen. "Water? You disgust me, Roddy!"

Olsen laughed and held out his free hand as one of the stewards brought him a pint glass full of water.

"Ladies and gentlemen, this next act is called the amazing water watch."

Tony frowned on his arm. "What?"

"Well, Tony, you are going to sing Amazing Grace. And I am going to drink this big glass of water. And all the people are going to…watch!"

With that, Olsen started Tony Tan singing the hymn. He then held aloft the glass and started downing the contents as Tony kept singing.

Olsen continued drinking, the water level slowly going down. All the while, he sang via the puppet.

This new trick was truly bewildering, with many in the audience staring at the twosome, man and puppet, as the song went on. Olsen kept on glugging until the water was finally all gone, as Tony reached the second verse.

He removed the glass from his lips as the puppet kept singing, without missing a single note.

Wild applause broke out, as a general gasp of shock reverberated through the showground.

As the clapping continued heartily, Olsen and Tony took turns and finished the song together, alternating between lines. Then, Olsen held up his free hand.

"Ladies and gentlemen, you've been a fantastic audience. From me, Rusty, Napoleon and Tony, thank you very much. And see you again. You're beautiful."

Olsen picked up his case and, with Tony still on his right arm waving to the audience, bounded across the sawdust towards the stage exit.

"And now," bellowed Heavy as he strode back into the centre, "it gives me great pleasure to introduce to you all, one of Klondike's Circus's legendary performers and a hero beloved by all who see him in action. Ladies and gentlemen, please welcome the world's greatest clown, Corky!"

The beloved clown entered the open-air arena to jovial applause. The other circus clowns followed in his wake, clapping also. Corky was dressed in his favourite attire of yellow chequered suit, crooked tie and brown bowler hat.

He began by riding a six-foot tall unicycle, catching various items as the other clowns threw them up at him. An iron, stool, imitation ham and basketball were all dispatched, with Corky catching each one.

He then threw each piece back at one of the others, before hoisting himself up, twisting in mid-air, and riding the cycle with his hands while balancing himself vertically. The crowd whistled and cheered as he did a lap of the floor.

Then, as the cycle was led away by the other clowns, he was handed an opening set of six juggling pins. This was where Corky truly excelled as an entertainer. He began juggling, gaining more momentum, going faster and faster until the red pins were a blur of motion. One of the other clowns tossed another pin into the mix, then another. Corky moved them around expertly, never pausing or even blinking.

Finally, he rounded up the pins in his customary manner, catching them in the front of his pants. Bowing gamely to the applause, he handed over the pins and then began one of his famous tricks.

Holding an imitation bowling ball, that was really made of soft rubber, he juggled the black ball, a tennis ball and a marble. As he kept the items floating, the revue clowns took it in turns to throw small dough balls into his mouth, which he duly ate.

Next, he juggled four small rubber balls in the 'high juggle', sending the items up to 12 feet in the air. As he kept going, he mounted another clown's shoulders and was paraded around the floor.

His juggling finale was a stunning sight. A backstage helper set alight four pins with a gasoline feeder and a lighter. Corky again jumped up onto the unicycle. The lit pins were handed to him and, as a drumroll sounded on the public address system, he juggled the flaming pins while riding the cycle. From any kind of distance, it looked as if he was juggling fire.

The audience screamed as one as Corky finally dismounted the unicycle, with the on-fire sticks all tossed high into the air and caught by the clowns.

"And now," came Heavy's voice, as the ringmaster moved towards the star clown, "we come to the piece de resistance. Corky will now perform for you his most daring feat of all…the human cannonball!" A giant, old-fashioned cannon was wheeled out from the back into the near side of the floor. The clowns pointed it at a huge net that had been assembled on the far side of the floor.

The 'cannon' was in fact a giant catapult, with a huge spring inside that could fire a human 50 yards through the air. Corky donned a pair of airman's goggles and a pilot's cap and climbed into the cannon via a ladder.

As a drum roll sounded, a clown lit an imitation fuse at the rear of the cannon. This was done purely for effect. The coiled spring was activated by a switch underneath that the assistant clown pressed with his foot once the flame reached the end of the fuse.

With a bang, Corky shot out of the cannon's mouth and flew across the circus floor, shaping his body like a dart, arms crossed over his chest for safety. His body slammed into the tilted net, and the clown bounced several times in the lining before manoeuvring himself onto the ground.

"There he is, Corky the Clown!" Heavy roared as Corky and his assistants offered a bow, gave a wave and headed for the entrance way again.

The brawny ringmaster chuckled to himself as he looked back at the exit area again. The next set of performers were all waiting behind the massive grandstand. It was all going like clockwork. "Lovers of the circus," Heavy began in his booming voice. "Prepare to be shocked by the most alarming, most incredible sights in all the world. Prepare yourselves for…the Showcase Revue!"

Klondike was watching the proceedings from the gap between the grandstands that led from the stage to the trailers beyond.

His usual position for shows, in the flap doorway of the tent, seemed a distant memory right now. But, all things considered, this wasn't much different. It was still the same spot.

As the acts performed in front of him, he could not help but glance at the clouds, the darkening sky and the great abyss above them. A glowing moon was emerging as the evening wore on, illuminated by the circus lights.

It was a surreal sight. But the show itself had changed little.

He smiled as the Showcase Revue performers raced out into the open. Heavy's dramatic introductions reverberated across the night air.

"Ladies and gentlemen, please give a large welcome to the human blob. All 500 pounds of him. You'll never see anyone quite like…Gargantua!"

"And now…the world's tallest man. I give you…Goliath!"

"The world's smallest dance troupe. Here they are…Percy Pringle and his Dancing Dwarves!"

"And, the tallest man of medium height you will ever see. The stilt walking sensation. Rumpy Stiltskin!"

As the audience lapped up the group's eclectic repertoire of skills, Klondike shook his head in wonder.

He glanced at Lacey and Richie Plum, stood as ever beside him. "All that panic," he mused quietly. "All that worry. And for what? Look at all this. The show is just the same."

"It's just the surroundings that have changed," Plum opined softly.

"Right."

Lacey looked around, taking in the cheering fans in the stands and the sky above.

"It worked tonight," she said cautiously. "But we have got lucky to an extent. We relied on New Orleans' fine and reliable weather. But, just imagine. Rain, high winds, excessive sunlight. Even fog. It could have been a disaster."

Klondike nodded. "I guess the great man upstairs decided we'd had enough bad luck this season, and smiled down upon us this time."

"Definitely," said Plum, looking skywards. "I was worried about the wind for Gino's act. But just feel it. Nothing! Not even a slight breeze. He'll be fine up there."

Klondike leant against a metal pole amidst the grandstand scaffolding. He looked up at the trapeze rigging attached to the tent poles.

"I sure as hell hope so."

The Flying Batistas somersaulted and cartwheeled their way onto the arena floor, before launching into their customary display of acrobatics.

Unusually, the audience reaction to the family of acrobats was fairly reserved. That is, until they performed their finale.

The human pole had to be seen to be believed, as Maria and Rodrigo climbed onto the shoulders of Raul before Tony scrambled up onto his brothers' shoulders at the top and stood tall.

The surreal sight of four humans, all stood on each other's shoulders in a vertical line, caused an almighty gasp across the open show ground. The family held it stiff as a rock for fully 30 seconds, before slowly dismantling.

The crowd cheered as the Batistas jogged back off stage.

Then came an electrifying sound that reverberated around the Tessier Showground. Many had been waiting for it, longing for it, for a long time. Now, it was here.

The ear-splitting roar of the Daredevils' motorcycles.

Behind the entrance, the riders were purposefully revving their engines boisterously, whipping the already excited crowd into even more of a frenzy. The audience were cheering just at the sound, they hadn't even seen anyone yet.

Heavy wandered into the middle and raised a hand.

"You can hear them coming!" he screamed. "Ladies and gentlemen, prepare to be electrified, prepare your jaw for a dropping, and get set for one of the most scintillating sights in America today. Klondike's Circus is proud to present the greatest stunt riding crew in the world. And their incomparable Sphere of Death! Let's hear it for…the Daredevils!"

Screams and cheers poured from the seats all around as the yellow and black-clad riders on their bikes came hurtling out of the blocks. The noise was deafening, a combination of the cheers and the exhaust of the rampaging sickles.

The Daredevils performed two laps of the floor and then began their usual repertoire of tricks. Riders stood on their saddles, performed handstands on the handlebars, executed elaborate wheelies and even swapped bikes while at breakneck speeds.

Then, Bo performed his usual routine of getting off his bike and standing in the middle, performing leapfrogs over each rider in turn, launching his hands off each man's helmet.

As the audience lapped it up, their excitement went up a notch as several stewards began wheeling in the great Globe of Death.

The huge metal globe was mounted in its usual spot on a mini-stage with a detachable ramp beneath it.

The Daredevils then lined their bikes up in a queue.

As each one entered and performed endless, ever faster loops around the globe, so the cheers and cries of alarm from the spectators grew.

By the time five riders were inside, the full effect of the incredible, death-defying act could be felt.

The bikers were a blur as they spun round, somehow avoiding any collision.

Then, Tip Enqvist slowly rode his bike to the top of the ramp, poised on the edge of the sphere, a steward opening the door invitingly.

As always, Enqvist removed his helmet and began punching the air wildly, pointing inside the Globe of Death like a madman. The cheering crowd were in another world, a distant galaxy, as they watched the madness unfold.

Then, in a heartbeat, Enqvist was inside the globe, racing round and round in a straight top-to-bottom pattern, as his team maintained their circles in perfect harmony.

Once the Daredevils had all been together inside the giant metal ball for two whole minutes, they systematically slowed their engines as the door was opened up, allowing them to depart one at a time. The great roar of the engines eased, only to be replaced by the awestruck screams of the fans.

The mighty applause continued as the Daredevils slowly rode down the ramp in single file, halting at the ground and removing their helmets.

Each held their headgear high in one hand in celebration as they soaked up the acclaim, waving and bowing as they sat easily in their saddles.

They had never experienced such a reaction. The cheers could be heard beyond the showground. Even in Bourbon Street.

And, in the circus trailers just beyond the makeshift big top, the noise was equally overpowering.

Gino Shapiro was lacing up his boots.

He looked up at the window in his trailer as the applause erupted down from the stands. It was a wild, crazy sound, like a buffalo stampede or a natural disaster.

Standing, he looked out at the huge grandstands towering above. Then, he glanced idly at the other trailers scattered around at the far end of the showground. It was like a campsite. Bystanders wandered idly by the trailers, everyone staring at the great structure before them.

Shapiro grunted as the applause grew. He took one last look in his dressing mirror. The orange singlet seemed to glow. He tied his great cape around his neck, held it on the inside over his arms, and opened the trailer door, descending the three steps.

Penny was waiting, snuggled under her cape. "Ready to make history?" he asked softly.

"Oh, I was born ready, champ." She smiled a dazzling smile. There was only joy, no nerves.

Shapiro nodded and, like a machine, they strode boldly, arrogantly, towards the clearing between the stanchions that formed the entrance.

Heavy was just beginning his introduction as the Daredevils slowly angled their way out of the arena, gliding past the two trapeze stars towards their makeshift compound at the back. Each of the riders gave a wave or thumbs up as they passed.

Then, Gino and Penny were walking past the stands and into the open-air circus. Klondike, Lacey and Plum all joined the applause as the duo entered the fray.

Heavy was flourishing with his introduction. "Prepare yourselves for the first wonder of the circus world…the most incredible act in America today…an extraordinary showcase of trapeze! On first ring, the queen of the skies…an angel from high above…the beautiful Penny Fortune! And, on centre ring, the world's greatest flyer. Cheer him, love him, never forget him. Klondike's Circus is proud to present the worldwide sensation…the debonair king of the air…Gino Shapiro!"

The crowd cheered heartily again, as Shapiro and Penny strode out grandly in their trademark fireball orange attire.

After a bow, both looked up at the trapeze rigging set out above. Each walked to an opposite end of the arena to a waiting tall rope and heaved themselves up, rapidly soaring towards the night sky, and leaving the crowd beneath as they hauled on their ropes.

The tentpoles on which the ropes were attached rose about 10 feet higher than the top of the stands.

As they ascended to the summit, they pulled themselves from the ropes onto their respective rings, which hung suspended from an elaborate rigging of ropes and wires spreading across the pole tops. From there, as every eye in the arena gazed upwards, they began to swing back and forth.

The standard routine had been tweaked for this performance. Shapiro, who had been swinging wildly, hung by his hands only and propelled himself onto a side turret, which had been affixed to a tentpole.

Penny wrapped her knees over her ring and fell back, swinging upside down in the support position, arms outstretched. With a cry, Shapiro dived off the turret onto his ring, performed a textbook 360 swing over, and propelled himself towards Penny, who caught his hands and swayed him back and forth once before hurling him onto the turret at the opposite end of the trapeze set-up.

The audience cheered, their 'oohs' and 'aahs' echoing across the showground as Shapiro flew back and forth. He completed the same routine in reverse. Then, on his third pass, he executed a double somersault between his ring and Penny's, before she swung him up onto the support turret. For his return trip, he substituted a double somersault for a scrunch-sault, clasping his knees with his arms, and vaulted back across the air.

Arriving at the turret again, he held his arms aloft and soaked up the applause. With nothing but an 80-foot drop and the empty ground below, the act was, as always, an incredible sight.

Penny then performed her standard ring act, swinging herself over and over before hanging by her legs, arching her back and grabbing her ankles.

As the crowd gasped, Shapiro dived onto his ring, stretched himself, holding on with his hands, before spinning over several times with stunning velocity. Letting go of his bar suddenly, his body flew into the air like a dart. He held his arms out wide and performed a helicopter fall as he dropped the 12 feet or so back to his ring, which he somehow landed on in a sitting position.

Vaulting back to his turret, Shapiro then performed the classic double loop, swaying over to Penny, who carried him back and forth several times at great speed, before releasing him.

He spun high into the air, and turned his body around twice in mid-air, before guiding his frame to the far side, landing on the support beam with cat-like grace and agility.

The two trapeze artists waved jubilantly as cheers filled the stands. Then, Heavy's voice boomed again.

"And now…the master trapeze artist, Gino Shapiro, will perform the ultimate feat of gravity defiance and grace…the high wire."

Shapiro slipped down his support rope to get prepared for his customary finishing act. The high wire had been set up far below, with the plastic-coated lead wire stretching out 20 metres between two giant plastic platforms, raised, for this performance, 30 feet off the ground.

As Shapiro slid down to the platform nearest the audience, the customary drum roll began.

The master showman, Gino took his time, rubbing a small pot of white powder into his stockinged feet and staring silently at the wire.

Then, with a theatrical flourish, he let his arms level out wide and slowly mounted the narrowest of bridges. Looking nowhere but straight-ahead at the opposite platform, he carefully but confidently crept across the wire, his arms stiff as support beams as they extended either side of him, his steps coming in short, almost balletic movements.

As the audience held its collective breath, the entire showground silent as a crypt, Shapiro crept to the opposite end of the wire, then paused. With a sudden, alarming motion, he flung himself upside down and executed a perfect cartwheel to see himself over the threshold and across the final two yards of the wire.

With another theatrical flourish, he flipped himself onto the far platform, regained himself, and stood mightily; the eyes of everyone in the makeshift big top bulging at the sight of his acrobatics.

After a second of stunned silence, a raucous standing ovation followed, with every audience member on their feet cheering the incredible feats of the master trapeze maestro.

True to form, Shapiro stood gallantly on the platform, arms raised aloft, waving cheerfully and blowing kisses to the adoring audience. It was a stunning ovation, and lasted almost 60 seconds.

At the entrance, Klondike laughed in a curious manner, relief his overwhelming emotion.

He joined the applause as Shapiro mounted the ladder that would finally reunite him with terra firma.

As Shapiro hit the deck at last, a collection of stage hands steered the platforms and stage equipment away.

Penny was on him in an instant. They hugged, then held each other's arms aloft for the audience, followed by a long bow.

The duo jogged across the sawdust. As they headed into the exit way, Klondike embraced them.

"You did it, Gino! You did it!" he cried, shaking the flyer by the shoulders. He hugged a somewhat bemused Penny.

"Piece of cake," Shapiro panted, his chest heaving and the sweat covering his skin.

"It was incredible," Penny added.

Lacey handed them both a towel. "What was it like up there?" she gasped excitedly.

Shapiro cackled. "I could see the Mississippi River!" They all laughed.

Then, in an instant, Heavy's voice returned one more time.

"And there you have it, ladies and gentleman, boys and girls. The most incredible act in American circus."

He paused as the applause settled. "We hope you've enjoyed Klondike's Circus, friends. Here to sing us out is our resident songstress, the enchanting Suzi Dando."

Suzi smiled beautifully as she slowly crept out onto the sawdust, taking the mic from Heavy as the familiar music began blaring out over the tannoy.

She wore a dazzling white and gold dress, and left no one in any doubt as to the power of her voice as she began belting out Can You Feel The Magic Tonight?

As those beautiful, sparkling Cadillac convertibles began roaming around the floor for the circus's traditional grand finale, the most incredible thing happened.

Suzy sang the words—and a large portion of the audience inexplicably joined in.

Suddenly, a chorus of several thousand were serenading the performers in their cars as they completed their lap of honour.

It was a breath-taking sound, even catching Suzi by surprise as she lost herself for a moment, before quickly recovering.

Many in the bleachers stood and sang along as if rising for an anthem. The lyrics were belted out into the night air.

Klondike, Heavy, Lacey and Plum stood at the edge of the sawdust truly awestruck.

The circus's beloved anthem had never sounded so beautiful. And so important.

A faint smile crossed Klondike's face as he gaped at the stands, slowly turning to see the full effect of the song on the fans all around. There was singing everywhere.

"I'll be damned," he muttered.

"This is something else," Lacey whispered in awe.

Heavy was stunned. "How do they know all the words?"

The four of them just stood there staring up at the stands, lost in the moment.

High above, the moon and the stars seemed to shine.

With the voices of the singing fans filling his ears, Klondike looked from the grandstands next to him up to the sky above.

The scene was almost otherworldly, like nothing he had ever experienced before. He could not help but smile as he took it all in. "Yes. Yes, I will be damned."

Chapter Nineteen

"Why, that rotten son of a bitch!"

Eric Ribbeck slammed down the newspaper he had been reading. He glanced up at Marconi in disgust.

"For Chrissakes," the old man snarled. "We set his big top alight. Destroyed it. He goes ahead and does the show in the open. And, dammit it all to hell, it's a roaring success!" He cursed loudly, rubbing at his eyes. "What gives with Klondike? Hell, he could pull a silk purse out of a mule's ass! He always comes up trumps."

Marconi picked up the crumpled newspaper and read a few lines of the story. "It seems the people like this idea of an open-air circus, huh boss?"

Ribbeck simply grunted at him.

They were in his executive carriage in the Ribbeck circus train, which at that moment in time was pounding across the Rockies North-West railroad towards Denver. A beautiful view of the golden mountainous terrain filled the giant state windows as the sleek train passed over boulder-strewn rockways.

"He doesn't have a big top. Yet he's still doing shows," Ribbeck muttered incredulously. He rose from his great throne seat behind the antique desk and absently paced the room. He stopped at a coffee pot resting on a stove near the bathroom at the far end.

Pouring a cup, he eyed the rocky land that whirred past as the train chugged along.

"Well, Luca, we'll see how long he can keep this trick up for. You can't run an open-air circus for long, boy. There's the logistics. Not to mention the weather."

"Right boss."

Ribbeck sipped his coffee with a rueful look. The grim silence was broken by the sharp rattle of the telephone on the main desk.

Ribbeck closed his eyes. Marconi answered it, spoke a word or two, then addressed his employer.

"It's Agostino in New York."

"I know."

Ribbeck ambled back to his chair at the desk, dismissed Marconi, then spoke into the receiver.

"Good morning, Paul."

Agostino didn't bother with any pleasantries. "You've seen the news?"

Ribbeck sighed. "Just read a review. And glanced at several more."

"What gives?" Agostino hissed. "He did the show without his damn tent. And it was a success! A hit."

"I can't believe it myself. Even considering something like that. So damn brazen! I can't believe the people in New Orleans went for it."

"For Chrissakes, Eric! We're going backwards. Klondike's Circus is getting bigger each week. What the hell is happening to our plan? You said destroy the tent and we'd destroy Klondike's outfit."

Ribbeck snorted, the anger rising. "What can I tell you? He played a brave hand. And it won him the pot."

"What the hell is that?" Agostino blared. "You sound like a fan! I thought we were going to screw him over, man! And look at what's happening. He's getting stronger. Our negative press coverage is in the shade. The media loves him. Even after that damn fire. That disaster. What are we doing, for Chrissakes?"

"Alright, alright, take it easy," Ribbeck snapped back. "We need another route. Just let me think and—"

"You've played your last card, Ribbeck!" Agostino was suddenly wild with anger.

Ribbeck froze. "What did you just say?"

Agostino sounded equally steely. "I said you're out, farmboy. Your plans and schemes have done nothing. Not a god damn thing! If we'd set that fire during the show, it would have crippled him. The outcry would have ruined him. We would have been set…the circus would have been all ours to do whatever we wanted. You talked me out of it, Ribbeck! You! And all your press contacts…they aren't doing a damn thing!"

"Now, just wait a god damn minute…" Ribbeck shouted into the receiver.

"For what!" Agostino cried back. "More bad ideas? You's outta touch, man, you's not got the right head for this kinda work."

"You came to me!" Ribbeck shot back. "You came to me, boy. With this big oil well dream of getting your hands on that circus. We have a partnership, dammit!"

"Yeah? Well, not any more old man. I'm done with you and your damn Texas ways. Stick to your clowns and your horse manure, man. Leave the tough stuff to me and my boys."

Ribbeck was dumbstruck. "Are you dissolving our partnership, Paul?"

A few sharp breaths followed down the phoneline. "You're lucky I don't send an executioner down there to finish you off, old man."

"Why, you snotty little bastard!" Ribbeck roared. "You think you're bigger than me? Do you? You and your Manhattan nightclub and your fancy broads? Why, if I was with you now I'd hit you so hard you'd be wearing your ass for a hat!"

"Keep dreaming, Tex," Agostino rasped. "I've got a circus to wipe out. Maybe when I'm done with Klondike, I'll come after you."

"The only thing you'll be coming after is a surgeon if you even try to…"

He stopped, realising the line was dead.

Ribbeck's face was a crimson mask as he seethed angrily, glaring at the receiver in his hands.

What had just happened? He tried to process everything in his mind, his anger refusing to shift. It had been a long, long time since anybody, anywhere, had spoken to him like that.

"Luca!" he screamed.

Marconi was stood opposite the desk within 10 seconds. "You alright, boss?"

"No, I'm not, god damn it!" he cried. He looked up at Marconi, who seemed to shudder under the electric gaze.

"Get me that yahoo Vesnick. Get him in here. Now!"

Marconi merely stood there. He looked pained.

Ribbeck glared at him. "What?"

"It's the damnedest thing, boss," Marconi said nervously. He looked at his hands helplessly. "No one has seen him. His room on the train is empty. His belongings are all gone. I…I don't know where he is."

Ribbeck gave him a cold stare, a vein on his forehead looking ready to explode. "Are you saying that grease-haired little punk has jumped ship?"

Marconi looked down. "It would appear so, boss."

The expected explosion of rage never materialised. Ribbeck just sat there, staring into nothingness. He shook his head, then whispered angrily to himself.

"Well, if that doesn't put the bull in the hog pen."

It was barely 10 o'clock in the morning, but already the champagne was flowing in the circus trailers.

Klondike, Heavy, Lacey and Plum were all celebrating the previous night's show in the designated management trailer, which had been their headquarters for the New Orleans date.

Klondike had arranged a meeting between the four, which had quickly taken a jovial turn when Lacey had burst in with a bottle and glasses, demanding everyone have a drink.

The trailers were still scattered outside the hastily erected outdoor arena, and little of the gargantuan clean-up operation had yet begun.

The management room was like a portable office, consisting of a desk, chairs and a couch. Midway litter from the night before seemed to be everywhere.

As they all chatted excitedly, recalling memorable moments from the night, Lacey suddenly held up a hand in a grand gesture.

"Alright everyone," she cried, as if addressing a classroom. "May I have the honour of delivering a toast. Yes, a toast. A toast to the wonderful performers and management of Klondike's Circus, who defied the odds last night to put on one of the most memorable, most enchanting shows ever witnessed in America. It will live long with us all. Especially that...THAT finale. That singing. Oh my, what a wonderful experience."

She eyed Klondike mischievously. "To our wonderful Kalvin Klondike. Who put it all together. And inspired everyone to rise to the occasion."

She turned to Heavy. "And to Henry Brown. Our beloved ringmaster. Who called the action, act by act."

She next faced little Richie Plum, who was sitting on the arm of the couch. "And my dear Richie. Richie, who came up with the idea of doing the circus in the open to begin with! Well done, everyone. And..." she raised her glass aloft. "Cheers!"

They all had a sip and thanked her for the speech.

"And to you, Miss Lacey Tanner," Klondike said, holding his glass out. "For being the inspiration for, well...hell, for all of this." He looked at her solemnly.

"We all know it was your sweet talking with old Bob Slater that got this over the line. You made it happen as much as anyone, Lacey. I've said it before, I'll say it again. You are an ace card in this operation. Ain't no doubt."

She put a hand over her mouth and threw him a sultry glance. "Oh, Kal. Please. The fizz and the praise might go to my head."

Heavy was studying her. "Hell, Lacey. Sweet talking is your speciality. You could make anybody do anything for you."

Plum nodded. "It's true."

Lacey took a long gulp on her champagne. "Now, boys! Do come along. Let's not go overboard!"

"It's hard not to," Plum blurted. "I mean, Jesus! Look at what's happened. All this trouble we've had on the trail. Then the tent is destroyed in that horrible fire. We almost had a mutiny on our hands. Then that show last night. That singing!" The small man seemed fit to explode. "God almighty! We're not just surviving the crisis...we're excelling here."

Lacey nodded sagely. "I don't want to get overexcited at all. But, Richie is right. You guys haven't seen the reviews yet. Alex Armstrong of the Louisiana Express is calling last night one of the greatest circus shows of all time."

Klondike was shaking his head in dismay. He looked out the window at the towering grandstands. "Who would've thought it?"

They were all silent for a moment, lost in their own thoughts. Then, from out of nowhere, a familiar old voice broke the peace from the doorway.

"If that's champagne, I want some!"

They all turned and stared in stunned silence at the small trailer doorway.

There, resplendent in a dark blue suit, stood Daryl Addison. He looked weary and tired, but his smile seemed to promise more good news.

"Daryl!" Klondike gasped in shock. He seemed to sway slightly as he leapt up and greeted the newcomer. "You crazy son of a bitch! What in the world are you doing here?"

Addison smiled warmly as he entered the barren confines and shook hands with everyone, giving Lacey a huge hug.

"You think I'd miss out on this! This historic moment." He stared out at the makeshift, open-air circus. "I'm just sorry I missed the big show. Why, what an incredible night it must have been."

Klondike was incredulous. "You...you came? All the way down here. What? To say congratulations?"

Addison chuckled as Lacey brought him a full glass. "Wonderful to see you, Daryl."

Addison held his glass high and nodded at each of them. "I came to say congratulations all right. And more." He took a long sip. "Ah, that was worth the journey…just for that!"

Plum stared at the older man. "How did you get here, Mr Addison?"

"My executive helicopter to Phoenix," he barked. "Then, from there, I got on the overnight special to New Orleans. A cab brought me here, to the showground."

Klondike patted him on the back. "On behalf of all of us…thank you for coming, Daryl. It means a lot to see you here." He hovered beside the banker. "Any word on the tent?"

"I've heard nothing more," Addison said casually, surveying the inside of the trailer with seeming distaste. "But there shouldn't be a problem. It's on the way."

He picked up a valise he had placed onto the floor by the door and heaved it over to the table. Suddenly, he was all business again. He turned slowly to face the room.

"There is much to discuss."

They all stared at him. Klondike had a knowing look. "You've got a plan!"

Addison smiled thinly. "You bet I do."

Heavy stared from one to the other. "I'm sorry. A plan? What plan?"

Lacey shivered slightly. "Does that mean what I think it means?"

Klondike nodded. "A plan to strike back!"

Addison studied his old friend. "I told you I was going to go to work. Make some enquiries. It's taken a lot of calls, but I have a proposal Kal."

"Hey, hey, wait a minute," Plum was saying nervously, his face a mask of confusion. "What is this?"

"I asked Daryl to help us find a way to hit back at Agostino and chums." He looked at his three trusted confidantes in earnest. Then he sighed. "Listen, it's like I told you. Daryl has good reason to believe that Agostino and Ribbeck have formed a partnership. A union. With Vesnick and Rance too. Like I said back in Houston, this is serious. We have to find a way of breaking it. Ourselves." They all slowly looked back at Addison.

Lacey spoke softly. "OK, Daryl. Why don't you tell us what you have?"

"Alright." Addison stood boldly before them. "Let me start with Agostino. He is without question the most dangerous of the group. He have to tread very carefully here. I have found out all sorts of interesting bits and pieces from my people in New York."

He took a quick sip from his champagne flute. "Our man Agostino is the Mafia captain of the Upper East Side. A top man in New York. His pride and joy is the nightclub he owns in Manhattan, the Beaumont Club. But, in the last few months, he has started fancying himself as an entertainment mogul and has become a manager for cabaret singers, many of whom perform at his club. Like many businessmen, he has become enamoured with the circus industry since watching your TV special two years ago. So, Ribbeck and Agostino seem to have some kind of partnership going on, whereby they will ultimately take over Klondike's Circus—or ruin it if they can't."

Klondike looked ready to burst. "What's your idea, Daryl?"

Addison held up a hand. "Right now, Agostino is taking on lounge singers. Cabaret acts. Even doing the interviews himself, such is his obsession. Now, this no-good devil is up to his ears in rotten dealings. As you would expect. The circus plan, this horrid enterprise with Ribbeck, is the latest. And I have reason to believe it's his masterplan."

Heavy looked bewildered. "This isn't filling me with confidence, Daryl."

Addison took a step forward, his eyes wild with excitement. "Now, here is what we do. We need a woman. A beautiful woman. She will pose as a cabaret singer and meet Agostino for a so-called interview. In the evening…in his penthouse. I have been informed that is how he does it. She will enchant him, of course. Then, she'll state her ambition of singing in a circus, just like Suzi Dando, her hero. Agostino's vanity will get the better of him. He will boast about his plans to take over our operation. And maybe…just maybe, with a little prodding, he will reveal his whole scheme."

He stood very still, like an actor having just delivered a monologue in a play.

The others looked somewhat underwhelmed.

"That's all very well," Heavy said slowly, "but what good will that do anyone, Daryl? We need evidence. Who will believe this woman you speak of?"

Addison rummaged through his valise for a moment, then spun around triumphantly. "They won't need to believe her. For she will be wearing this!"

He held up what looked like a small tape recorder with a tiny microphone attached.

Klondike stared at the device. "A wire!"

The others looked at him, then back at the recorder. "Like in the cop movies," Heavy muttered in shock.

"That's exactly right, Henry," said Addison. "A police buddy of mine lent it to me. It really is state of the art. Records perfectly. I've even tried it out."

"Excellent, Daryl. A fine plan," Klondike said. "But it all depends on whether Agostino will talk. Now, tell me, have you got anyone in mind for the woman? Someone you know?"

It all went very quiet in the small trailer. Addison's eyes lifted from the recorder and settled on Lacey. She stared back at him in shock. Addison spoke softly. "There's only one person in the world I'd trust to do this."

Klondike was incredulous. "Now, woh, wait a minute! Lacey? Are you crazy! This is dangerous work, Daryl. The risks are huge."

Lacey simply stared at the device in Addison's hands.

"I know," the older man whispered. "I'm just being honest, though."

"Come off it, Daryl," Heavy snarled. "You can't expect our Lacey to do that."

"Absolutely not," Plum put in.

They all slowly turned to face Lacey, who was frozen to the spot. She was the only one who had not spoken. Her huge, beautiful violet eyes seemed to dance as she looked around at the concerned male faces surrounding her.

"It's ok," she whispered in a curious tone. "Really, it's ok. It's all ok, boys."

They all frowned at her. "What's ok?" Heavy blurted.

She nodded in some form of understanding. "You need someone you can trust. And only someone who truly cares about the circus will have the will to go through with it. Plus, I know what to say to glean the incriminating evidence out of him. How to, er, lead him on. How to set the trap." She looked up at Addison. "Why, it's perfect."

"You forgot the most important ingredient," Addison said, smiling.

Lacey looked lost. "And what's that?"

Klondike answered. "You're a beautiful woman."

She ran a hand through her red hair, flustered.

But Klondike was not convinced. "Listen, Lacey, you can't be serious. You actually want to do this?"

She stared at him coolly, her gaze impenetrable. "I believe in your circus, Kal. You know that. I'd do anything to save it. Don't you see?"

"I know that," he answered smoothly. "But this…this is another level, Lacey. This is dangerous. Agostino is a psychopath. You don't know him. What if it all goes wrong? God knows what might happen."

"That's why you and Heavy will be there with me."

"What!"

"We will take the Transatlantic Express to New York with Daryl. You and Heavy can wait outside. Any sign of trouble…well, I'll scream. And you two can swoop in and save the day."

Klondike and Heavy looked at each other in dismay. "God damn it, Lacey," Heavy cried. "Agostino will have armed guards in his place. They don't use fists. They use guns!"

"Yeah," Klondike drawled, "and you seem to be forgetting we have a circus to run. Our next show in Memphis is on Saturday. And the train, our train, is rolling tomorrow morning. And, dammit all, we still haven't got a tent."

"Richie can run things while we're gone," Lacey said casually. She was warming to the plan, and it deeply disturbed Klondike. "He has done it before. If we can get in one night this week…well, we can be back in time for Memphis."

Klondike shook his head angrily. "This is all crazy!"

Addison had watched the exchange with interest. "Well, we will have to come to a decision, one way or another. But setting up the interview shouldn't be a problem. I have the talent manager's phone number right here, on a business card." He patted the valise.

Klondike stared at him. "You and your wise guy ideas!"

Suddenly, Lacey grabbed his hands. "It can work, Kal. It can work!" She looked around wildly. "Remember what Heavy said just now? I can sweet talk anybody into doing anything."

Heavy frowned. "I wasn't talking about gangsters."

An uncomfortable silence filled the trailer. Klondike lit a cigar. Plum refilled everyone's glass with champagne. Heavy began absently shuffling a deck of cards.

Addison shifted awkwardly. "Well, it's a plan," he mumbled.

Lacey sat down on the couch, still staring curiously at the recorder on the table.

Klondike wandered over to the window and stared out. Things were moving out there. McCabe's team had begun the mammoth task of dissembling the grandstands and bleachers. The local work crew were all on site. McCabe had seen a record level of interest for roustabout jobs, such was the fanfare accompanying the circus's arrival.

"Listen," Klondike said tersely. He picked up his cane, which had been propped against the couch. "A lot depends on getting Agostino to talk. And, hell, what about Vesnick, Rance and good old Eric?"

Addison looked up at him. "Well, that's the beauty of the plan, Kal. Hopefully, Agostino will incriminate them all as he boasts of his grand masterplan."

"That's taking one hell of a big chance," Klondike muttered.

It was Plum who spoke next. "You know Agostino, Kal. You talked to him recently. In your opinion, is he the kind of guy who would talk up his empire? Who would brag like that?"

"To a pretty lady," Heavy put in.

Klondike stood there mulling it over.

Lacey spoke from the couch. "It will be up to me to get it out of him. By playing up to his vanity." She looked at them all and smiled whimsically. "By batting my eyelids…"

"Argh, for Chrissakes!" Klondike roared. "You must be delusional." He stared at Addison. "She will be all alone up there! What if something goes wrong!"

"Actually," Addison said simply, "she won't quite be all alone." He pulled a larger, more traditional tape player from his valise and held it aloft. "We can all listen in on this. The hidden recorder transmits to this. Things get ugly with Agostino, we will know."

Klondike wandered over to him and stared down at the tape player. It looked like something from a radio station. He ran his hand over its surface.

"Looks like you thought of everything, Daryl."

Addison tried to smile. "Safety has to be the most important consideration."

"She will still be all alone up there!"

Addison held his hands aloft. "Listen, it's up to you, Kal. You are the chairman. You asked for help, advice, a plan…well, I delivered. I just can't see too many ways of getting at a crime kingpin like Agostino."

Klondike nodded absently. He stared at each of them in turn. His dark eyes lingered on Lacey, sat there on the couch, innocently looking up at him, seemingly lost. He thought of his feelings for her and shook his head irritably. Then the face of Catherine Hart flashed into his consciousness again. He remembered his feelings for her too. Then, the sneering and arrogant features of Paul Agostino slowly merged in his mind. The blazing eyes. The horrific scar. The frightening encounter in Las Vegas played out in his head again.

Finally, he roared aloud. "Hell, I just don't know."

"I can do it, Kalvin," Lacey whispered.

"No, you think you can."

Heavy stood beside Klondike. "We need to do something, Kal. Next time, the fire might start during the show."

Plum shook his head. "I still say let's get the cops in New York on it."

Klondike snorted angrily. "I keep telling ya, he owns the cops."

"Say we do get incriminating evidence on tape," Heavy suddenly blurted. "Who do we give it to? Not the cops, huh?"

Addison spoke up. "Just leave that to me, Henry. I know a leading prosecutor in Manhattan. And, besides, there are others. Even Agostino's business rivals will help if we get the material." Everyone seemed to nod slowly. A bitter silence filled the small trailer.

Then, out of nowhere, there was a knock at the door.

Klondike answered, and McCabe stuck his head through the tiny doorway. "Hey, Kal. I just got a cable from the boys back at the Cattlemen's Club in Houston. Zack Wurley's foreman is there now. He has our tent!"

Klondike grabbed his arm. "You're kidding!"

The brawny McCabe chuckled. "Nope. They're right behind us now. Want to know where we want delivery."

Klondike thought for a moment. Then he barked: "Tell him to meet us at the Beale Recreation Ground in Memphis. We'll be there by tomorrow night."

McCabe nodded and turned back to the midway.

Klondike spun around. "You all hear that? The new tent is coming!" They all stood in excitement. Klondike glanced at Addison. He looked down, feeling somewhat awkward.

"Listen, Daryl," he said slowly. "I didn't mean to get angry just then. It's just…just that…"

"We're all worried about Lacey," Plum put in.

"Right," Klondike drawled. "Anyway, this business with Wurley's back-up tent. Well, you delivered big time there. We're all indebted to you, old friend."

Addison finally smiled. "It was a pleasure."

The old banker joined Klondike at the window, and they stared out at the mass clean-up operation going on all around them. Slowly, the others all joined them. They all watched as the roustabouts continued to dissemble the stands.

Lacey stood next to Klondike, absently clutching his arm. "It's alright," she whispered.

"I know," he whispered back. "I know."

Chapter Twenty

Lee Vesnick awoke with a mighty tremble, slipping out of the narrow bed and landing on his knees on the cold, hard wooden floor.

He rubbed at his unruly brown hair in shock. Another damn nightmare, he thought.

Sitting up on the floor, he moved to the grimy old window and stared out at the streets below.

Downtown Chicago. Taxi cabs lined the bustling streets and a sea of hobos mulled around, getting in each other's way.

Vesnick pulled himself up, straightening out his vest. The tiny room had been his home for three days now. A boarding house behind a liquor store. Twenty rooms. One bathroom.

Pulling on a black shirt, he studied the leather satchel holding his beloved blades. He was about to pull them out for a polish when a sharp rasp at the door startled him.

"Vesnick? You in there?"

It was Holman, the super.

With a heavy gulp, he opened the door a crack.

A huge balding man wearing a flower shirt over a dirty vest stood menacingly in the doorway.

"Good morning, Mr Holman," Vesnick said cheerfully.

"Don't give me that! Where's my money, kid? I let you skip the advance for that whole week's payment upfront. You said you'd pay on Tuesday. Well, that's today, stupid. So pay up!"

Vesnick ran a hand through his thick hair. "Well, y'see Mr Holman, I thought I was gunna get a gig set up by today. But…well, it just ain't happened."

"Gig? What are you? A singer or something?"

Vesnick looked at him. "Or something…"

"Well, it don't matter, grease-head. Either you pay what you promised, or you're outta here."

"Just let me get a gig set up and you'll have your money, sir."

Holman glared at him. "What am I? A damn charity case? Listen bum, are you going to pay me or what?"

Vesnick shrugged. "I don't have the money!"

"Right. I'll give you ten minutes to gather your things and get the hell outta here. Ten minutes. Then, I'm calling the cops. You follow?"

Vesnick thought desperately. "Ok, ok," he said quickly. "How about a bet? Huh?" He pointed down the corridor at an old movie poster stuck on the far wall some 20 yards away.

"You see that poster down there, of the couple kissing? Well, I'll bet you I can throw a knife from here, and hit the man in the forehead. Dead centre. If I hit it, we can postpone my payment till Saturday. If I miss, I'll pay you double. On the Saturday. What d'ya say, Mr Holman?"

The super looked at him in utter bewilderment. "What are you, crazy or something? That's gotta be the dumbest thing I ever heard." He made to walk off, shouting as he moved. "Nine minutes."

Vesnick watched him go then skulked back into his room.

Slowly, he picked up an old tote bag and began packing away his clothes.

Bourbon Street in downtown New Orleans was alive and bustling that night as citizens hobnobbed around the famous drag, many hoping to catch a glimpse of one of the stars of the previous night's circus.

Many wandering the street turned to look as someone called out the name of Tip Enqvist, the leader of the stunt riding team.

Enqvist was wearing a suit and walking slowly along with a blonde-haired woman on his arm, who clung to him proudly as well-wishers shouted their greetings.

Enqvist casually waved and shook hands in the busy street until he came to The Crawfish, the street's most famous restaurant.

"Here we go, Theresa," he said to the woman as they entered, "like I told you back at the bar. The finest eating house in New Orleans!"

Her eyes were wide in wonder. "Wow. I always wondered what it would be like to eat at The Crawfish." She pointed. "Just look at those tables. Beautiful."

A small, eagle-eyed waiter rushed over excitedly as they looked around in the doorway.

"Well, good evening, Mr Enqvist," he cried with delight. He stood before them. "We were hoping we might see you tonight. Usually, all the VIPs passing by stop off at The Crawfish. Why, that stunt you and your men pulled last night—that Globe of Death—it was just incredible."

Enqvist grinned and pulled the woman in for a kiss. "Y'hear that, sweetheart? VIP? You're in the big leagues now, baby."

"Now that I met you, I am," she gushed.

"Good to have you here, folks," the waiter was saying. "We've already got one of your colleagues here..."

"What!" Enqvist hissed.

"Why sure. The star of the high wire. Gino Shapiro!" The waiter pointed to the back, and Enqvist squinted through the smoke to see Shapiro and Penny sat chatting at a booth.

"You can sit opposite them," the waiter carried on excitedly. Then, without hesitation, he led them to the back of the room, where all was quieter and darker.

Shapiro had been reciting a story to his female assistant when the waiter appeared abruptly before them with the two new customers.

"Well, well, well," Shapiro mused, eyeing the stunt rider. "Look what the cat dragged in. Mr Daredevil. And friend." He half-stood and bowed at Theresa.

"Hi Tip," Penny said sweetly.

Enqvist made the introductions to his enchanted date, then they sat at the table offered by the waiter. A bottle of wine appeared almost immediately.

"What brings you here, Enqvist?" Shapiro said once everyone was settled.

"The same thing as you, man. We're celebrating." Penny spoke to Theresa. "How do you know Tip?"

The woman looked at her blankly. "Well, we just met. A few hours ago. At the Ferryman Inn."

Enqvist rolled his eyes. "Like I said, we're celebrating. That was something else out there last night. Me and the boys have never felt such...such electricity in an audience. We hit the rails tomorrow. So tonight...well, I have the company of a beautiful woman. In the brightest spot in town."

Shapiro smiled knowingly. He winked at Penny. "I too have such fortune, biker. A beautiful woman. A sublime wine. This place...nothing but the best."

He laughed to himself, then looked serious. "Did you see the people out there? On the street?"

Enqvist nodded as he drank an entire glass of wine in one swallow. "Yeah. I felt like Marlon Brando. Everyone seemed to be cheering for me."

Shapiro grinned. "They were singing my name."

Penny shook her head. "They loved us all, guys. They loved the show. The whole show."

Suddenly, there was a commotion at the front door. Someone was shouting. A woman screamed. They all turned to look.

Roddy Olsen and Suzi Dando were just entering The Crawfish. The same little waiter was dancing before them, looking ready to burst.

"For Chrissakes," Shapiro muttered as they watched the scene. He turned to Penny. "So much for privacy, mamacita."

Predictably, the waiter led Olsen and Suzi to the back area, motioning them to a table behind Enqvist's.

"Oh my!" Suzi cried as they realised their colleagues were there. "It's like a circus reunion back here. Hi everyone!"

The four seated all muttered greetings.

Olsen clapped his hands as he seated himself. "Gino. Penny. Tip. You were all fantastic last night. My compliments to you. What a night!"

"Obliged, dollman," Shapiro said weakly.

"Hey!" Theresa suddenly blurted, pointing at Olsen. "You're that puppet guy! I seen you on TV."

Enqvist glared at her, then at Olsen.

"This..." Suzi said grandly, "is the Puppetmaster. Roddy Olsen. Star of Klondike's Circus. The greatest name in big tops today!"

"Knock it off," Enqvist snarled. He looked at Suzi. "What are you? His agent?"

Suzi pouted at him. "No. I'm his friend."

Theresa looked spellbound. "Girlfriend?"

An awkward silence filled the tables. Suzi remained impassive. "No, friend."

Olsen looked at her. "Best friend." She laughed in a childlike manner.

"Well," Shapiro said in a tired voice. "This is all very sweet and beautiful, kids. Why don't you celebrate with a soda pop." He sniggered. "Now, if you all will excuse us. Me and the beautiful Penny were trying to have a quiet, private evening meal."

"Oh, it's alright," Penny said mischievously, winking at him. "A bit of company is just swell."

He baulked at her. "It is?" He cursed, and looked at the newcomers. "Who's next, dammit? The whole circus might as well pitch up here now!"

It was all silent for a few moments. The waiter returned to take everyone's order. Then a boy delivered more wine to each table. Olsen cherished the taste of the rich red wine, then stood, raising his glass.

"Alright," he said quietly. The others looked up at him in surprise. "Whatever differences we may all have…let's just put them aside for this night, huh? I declare a toast. To Gino and Penny. And to The Daredevils and Tip. After one of the greatest nights in circus history. My friends, I salute you."

They all drank. A strange, eerie atmosphere seemed to grip the tables.

Finally, Enqvist addressed Olsen. "You did good too, kid."

Suzi seemed to beam at this, rubbing her hands together with glee. "Now, isn't this nice, boys? Y'see, we can all get along. Think of how much better, stronger, the circus would be if everyone just supported each other. Just think…"

Shapiro nodded absently. "Now, all I ask, as the first star of our circus…all I ask is you all keep this level of performance up. Right the way through to Washington…and beyond! The people, they demand it."

Olsen raised his glass again. "I guess we can all drink to that, Gino."

"You bet," Enqvist blurted. "There will be many more ovations like last night. The Daredevils will ensure that!"

"We all will," Penny said quickly.

"Yeah sure," Shapiro muttered. He seemed amused. "We are all stars. Like the clown always says. When you have this many stars all together, what do you give the audience?"

He smiled beautifully at the others, who waited somewhat bewildered.

Shapiro whispered the word, "Heaven."

Two blocks away, at the top of Bourbon Street, a quiet and sincere atmosphere greeted the roof terrace bar of the Alhambra Hotel.

It was a beautiful setting, with patrons afforded a view of the whole street and, indeed, much of the city beyond.

The terrace sat on the rooftop of the sprawling hotel, with the bar itself inside a small awning and glass doors leading out to the exposed decking, where tables and high stools littered the space. The air was warm and sweet smelling at this late hour, and the terrace was full of couples on dates or enjoying a post-show beverage.

Klondike and Lacey stood in the far corner, a bottle of champagne sitting on the edge of a small wooden wall that served as the terrace perimeter.

Klondike, wearing a white shirt and brown slacks and minus his fedora, poured them each a glass.

Lacey, wearing one of her many cocktail dresses, watched him with a half-smile.

"Gonna be hard to say goodbye to this city," Klondike was saying as he poured.

She looked down at the buzzing street below, its constant carnival-like atmosphere, and had to agree. "Nowhere in this world like New Orleans."

They clinked glasses, eyeing each other as they took a first sip. "Immaculate," Lacey whispered.

He leant against the wall, elbow over the side, and took a deep breath. "This has been the first time we've really been able to talk about…about the lake. About what we said."

She threw her head back. "It's been non-stop drama ever since practically."

He fixed her with a stare. "And more to come…"

"Listen," she whispered, looking ill at ease. "We both said some things that were, ah, unexpected. Why…why can't we just agree now that we…well, we get along. We make one hell of a team. We are perfect…at running the circus. Together. And, well, we like each other. I mean, like being together. For the show."

The words fell out of her like a broken voice recorder, and she recoiled as she spoke, stammering wildly.

Klondike smiled. "I don't regret what I said, Lacey."

She glared at him. "You said I mean everything to you, Kal. Is that true?"

He shuffled awkwardly. "Ah, hell." He looked at her seriously now. "Sure it is, Lacey. What you have done for me, my circus, everything. You are just…just on the highest level for me. Above everyone else."

She raised a tentative eyebrow. "And?"

His shoulders sagged. "And I seem to remember a conversation we had two years ago. After the Golden Dune in Vegas. About how I'm not right for a relationship. With any woman. Not with the way my life is. Hell, there's no room for romance. For love! For any of that stuff. My circus is my life. You know that. Everyone knows that!"

He was looking at her in despair. She pouted slightly, running a hand through her long red hair.

An awkward silence fell over them as a soft breeze tingled the rooftop terrace. They both sipped champagne.

"Let's not forget what you said back at the lake," Klondike said quietly.

Lacey put a hand over her mouth. "I...I haven't forgotten."

He frowned, confused and eager to hear more. "Are you in love with Roddy?" he blurted.

She visibly shook. "Oh my lord! That...that just came out. I couldn't help it, Kal."

"But surely it came out for a reason."

"Oh," she took a long gulp on her drink now. "Oh, I just don't know. You have to understand. I think about Roddy an awful lot. I feel like he is my biggest discovery. It's like I'm Colonel Parker and he's Elvis. Or something! He is on my mind an awful lot. I've nurtured him and advised him. Guided him along. It's a special relationship we have..."

Klondike was uncharacteristically aggressive now. "He's a good-looking kid. A teen idol."

"No!" Lacey squealed. "That's not it, Kal. I promise. I...I can't explain it. I don't know what to say."

"Is it love? Really?"

Her face dropped. She suddenly looked very lost. Her huge, beautiful eyes looked sad and innocent.

Klondike grabbed her arm. "Hey, it's ok. I'm...I'm sorry. I shouldn't have pushed you like that." He studied her. "Hell, at the end of the day it makes no difference to me who loves who. Just as long as we're all happy."

"Is that really true?" she said softly.

He couldn't stop looking into those eyes. "It's just...it's just that you're...special. You're special, Lacey."

She wiped at her eyes. Then she looked at him seriously. "I'm not in love with Roddy. I just think he is the most incredible man. The most talented. Even he doesn't know how talented he is."

Klondike squinted. "I'm sure he likes you. Hell, along with half of the boys on my outfit!"

Another awkward, eerie silence followed. Klondike poured them both a top-up, and casually glanced down at the street far below. It was packed with night-time revellers. Even on a Sunday.

Lacey finally smiled, and tried to change the mood. "I'm looking forward to our next date, tiger!"

He glared at her. "What!"

She smiled knowingly. "Well, after that time you took me ice-skating after our first season. Then, last year at the end of the season, we went on that boat trip. So…" she eyed him teasingly. "I can only imagine what you've got planned for me this September!"

He stared for a moment, then cackled loudly. "Hell, that would be telling!"

They both laughed. Then, Klondike turned serious again. "We've got to get to the end first, Lacey."

She looked around the terrace, which seemed to be emptying. "Well, it looks like this season is going to have a lot more drama than the others, baby."

"You're still not taking this seriously!"

She looked at him with mock concern. "This trip to New York is business, Kal. It's still business. Besides, I'm a perfect fit for this. You and the boys all said it yourselves. I admit, I've never done anything remotely like this before, but…but I can do it!"

He shook his head. "The fact you want to take a risk like this…going into the lion's den. Just for the circus. I…I don't know what to say. Hell, that's why you're so special, Lacey."

She frowned, her face taking an unusual hardened look. "I want to nail this Paul Agostino. For good. How dare he threaten our people like that!" She locked eyes with him. "I want to nail him, Kal."

He nodded, somewhat bewildered. "OK." He sipped his champagne. "Well, as you know, Addison has set the whole thing up. We leave Memphis on Tuesday night on the Transcontinental Express. We're all staying at the hotel opposite this Beaumont Club in Manhattan. Then, well, it will all be up to you, Lacey."

She chuckled, tilting her head back. "The star of the show."

"This time, for sure. We'll just have to go through everything with Daryl on the way to New York. Everything has to work like clockwork. That snake Agostino cannot smell a rat. That is essential."

"Daryl seems to have thought of everything."

Klondike nodded vaguely. "I'm beginning to wonder if he wants to start work as a spy. He is surprisingly good at all this."

Lacey placed a hand on his. He shook slightly.

"And you, tiger?" she said in a sweet, soft voice. "Are you alright with all this?"

He wiped a hand through his thick, black hair. "Just worried, Lacey. Worried about you. Hell, worried sick. If anything were to ever happen to you…"

"Your circus would suffer?"

"No. I would suffer."

They both stared at each other, her hand still on his.

In the light of the full moon, they both thought independent thoughts for several moments. The noise and clatter from the ever-busy Bourbon Street drifted up and seemed to touch them.

She smiled at him, linking her arm in his once again. "Now, why don't you be a good old boy and get me a bowl of fresh gumbo from one of the stands on the street down there?"

He laughed as they made to leave. "Gumbo? The food of the streets down here, Lacey."

She sighed. "I wouldn't have it any other way."

Arm in arm, they drifted across the terrace and into the bar room at the far side.

Chapter Twenty-One

"Hey, Eric! Take a look at this."

The sprawling midway was barren and bereft of activity at this early hour. Almost like a ghost carnival. Empty stalls, no hawkers, not even a running candy floss drum. Many of the attractions still had covers over them, their operators not yet up and about.

Eric Ribbeck was walking around the stalls absently, surveying his empire at its most peaceful and vulnerable. Hands tucked deep into the pockets of his dark blue trench coat, he walked slowly, with Marconi following behind obediently.

The call had come from Veronica Hunslett, his executive assistant. She wore a similar trench coat and came galloping over, holding aloft a newspaper.

"What's this?" Ribbeck hissed as she approached.

"This morning's New Orleans Star," she proclaimed, looking stern and business-like. "Take a look at that front page."

Ribbeck held the paper before him, taking in the front page banner headline:

CIRCUS STARS LET THEIR HAIR DOWN AFTER HISTORIC NIGHT!

Beneath the head was a large picture showing several figures sat around in a restaurant, all holding glasses in a toast, smiling for the camera.

He read aloud from the page in a dry, rueful tone: "After one of the most memorable nights in New Orleans' rich circus history, the stars of the show were all on hand last night to celebrate their success in the most exclusive joint in town, The Crawfish."

"The principal players from Klondike's Circus were all there—trapeze artist Gino Shapiro, ventriloquist Roddy Olsen and stunt rider Tip Enqvist. And word soon spread, with a large crowd gathering outside the eatery, all hoping to catch a glimpse of the talent…"

Ribbeck stopped reading and simply stared at the picture. Marconi and Veronica both watched him curiously as he slowly ran a hand across the image, as if trying to bring the figures to life.

"There they are," he whispered absently. "All together."

A cold wind blew across the midway, giving the morning a bleak and unwelcome feel. All was still silent.

"Seems like the three of them are getting along a little better," said Veronica.

Ribbeck was transfixed, staring at the picture. "After that New Orleans show, those three aces are now unquestionably the biggest stars in America today. Now, there can be no doubt."

"Come on, boss," Marconi said cheerfully. "What about our guys? Dirk Tempest? Walt Reilly? Calipso the Clown?"

Ribbeck shook his head. He finally looked up. His eyes had a haunted look. "We're falling behind."

Veronica looked at him uneasily. "OK. What do you want to do, Eric?"

The older man threw the newspaper to the dirt below. He rubbed at his eyes tiredly. "Argh, the hell with it. The whole damn trail drive is up in smoke. Plans, schemes…. ain't nothing working, god damn it."

He pulled one of his cigarillos from the silver case in his breast pocket. Marconi automatically hovered next to him with a lit match. Ribbeck lit up, and puffed hurriedly, clouding them both in thick smoke.

"And still nothing on Rance? Or that damn snake Vesnick?"

"Nothing, boss. No word."

Ribbeck nodded. He glanced at Veronica. "Miss Hunslett. What is the take so far for tomorrow's show?"

"About two thousand tickets sold so far, the advance box office has seen a steady stream. Looks like the bulk of the take will be pay on the night."

Ribbeck shook his head in disgust. He looked across at a large trailer beyond the end gateway of the midway. The communications shack.

"I need to make a call, y'all," he said quietly, and ambled across to the trailer. Veronica, knowing that was a dismissal, turned and headed back towards the big top. Marconi followed his boss at a distance of ten yards.

Inside the empty trailer, Ribbeck wandered slowly across the floor, sat on an office chair and plugged in one of the portable telephone receivers. He consulted a small notebook fished from his pocket, then began dialling a long number.

Marconi walked in and waited at the doorway, lighting a cigarette. The line rang for some time. Then, a gruff voice answered.

"Who is this?"

"Norm. It's Eric Ribbeck here. Long distance."

More than one thousand miles away in LA, Norman Pierce almost choked on his morning coffee.

"Eric! What a surprise. Jesus! You always just call out of the blue like this at seven in the morning?"

"My apologies. It just suddenly hit me I hadn't checked in with you in a while."

Pierce wiped at his mouth with a napkin and smirked to himself. "I would've called you if I had any news."

Ribbeck seemed to sink in his chair. "Dammit. So no more progress with Olsen then?"

"I'm afraid not. Listen, that kid is young. Fresh. Green. He is yet to see the chaos and confusion of life in the limelight. Of stardom. Of notoriety. Booze, broads, night life, vices. None of that means anything to him. He's a damn boy scout, Eric."

"When did you last speak with him?"

"In person? In LA, back in the spring. After he did Steve Irving. I've sent a few telegrams to the circus since they hit the road. But nothing. Some of my people have dug around. But, well, there just isn't any dirt on him."

Ribbeck's face dropped even further. He seemed to age as he sat there listening. "And what about Shapiro?"

Pierce grew agitated on the other end. "Hell, Eric, I told you before. That damn ballet dancer don't talk to me no more. It's a waste of time even trying. Ever since I got that broad fired on that show he was working on. Barbara Selwyn. He never forgave me for getting her that contract with Steel Pictures, who promptly went bankrupt."

Ribbeck shuddered. "Ah, yes. That! I remember." He looked around morbidly. The trailer was dank and felt like a giant garden shed. "It looks like the only avenue left is the almighty dollar."

Pierce's voice was curiously high-pitched. "You're gunna make an offer to Klondike? A fresh one?"

The old man had tired of the conversation. "Something like that," he mumbled. "You take care now, Norm."

221

With that, he simply put the receiver down on the telephone set. Ribbeck sat quietly, looking depressed and absent.

Marconi slowly wandered across the floor towards him. "What can I do to help, boss?"

"Just…tell me," he whispered, seemingly in awe. "Tell me how…how this all turned to horse manure. Everything! It all seemed so beautiful. I had assembled so many pieces in place. Winning pieces. Winning hands." He looked up at Marconi, and his crystal-like blue/green eyes seemed to glow. "And one ace."

He looked out the window angrily and spoke almost to himself. "Where the hell is that yahoo Rance? He was supposed to be the key to all this. And look what happened."

Marconi looked downwards. "That lion man was nuts, boss. Nuts, I tells ya."

Ribbeck looked up at him and seemed to nod.

The small clearing in the dense woodland featured long, reedy grass and a pond. At one end, a large figure stripped to the waist was chopping wood with a rusty axe. As each log was chopped in two, the pieces were pushed off a small piece of decking with the axe head, and another log was put in place. The incessant sound of the chopping echoed far around.

A large brown van was parked at the edge of the secluded clearing. Two middle-aged men, dressed as country hikers, had approached the spot, having been drawn in by the sound of the chopping.

They stopped in their tracks and stared at the unusual sight before them. The red-haired, red-bearded man was wearing just a pair of dirty, beige slacks. His back and torso were covered in callouses and reddened patches of skin. He looked sick, as if he had been very unwell recently.

The man noticed he had company, but continued chopping.

"Hey, mister," one of the hikers called out. He chuckled. "That must be quite a fire you're planning there."

The other gestured at the pile of chopped logs. "Yeah. There won't be a forest left at this rate, pal."

They both laughed softly. The stranger ignored them, lining up more blocks. The forest became eerily quiet.

The two hikers looked at each other nervously. They studied the man's many wounds spread across his shoulders, chest and neck. Then they approached him further.

"Sir," the first man said. "Is there anything wrong? Can, er, can we provide you with any assistance?"

Finally, the strange man turned and glared at them. They were both startled at his fiery, almost murderous look.

"No!" Emile Rance growled. "No help." He hoisted aloft the axe. "I have everything I need, right here."

The speaker backed off. But his companion edged a little closer. "Hey," he whispered in shock. "Don't I know you from somewhere, pal? You were in that show, right? I can't remember what it was. I saw it once. It was a carnival, or a circus, or—"

"No!" the man shouted angrily. He stared at the speaker with wild, crazy eyes, towering over him as he held the axe over one shoulder. "There was no show!" Then, he seemed to calm slightly. "You are mistaken. You understand?"

The two hikers crept backwards, almost in unison. The man had an unusual foreign accent. It sounded deep and from another world.

The hikers moved faster now. "Let's get outta here," one said to the other. They made a hasty exit. Within seconds, the duo were out of sight.

Rance wasn't watching. He ran a finger along the axe head. Then, as if an alarm had gone off, he looked up quickly.

There, stuck to a tree trunk about 20 yards away, was a poster. It was THE poster. The Klondike's Circus poster. 1960 season.

Rance snarled like a wild animal. He gazed at the printout with venom in his stare. Then, with a cry of alarm, he threw his arms back, holding the axe high above his head. Taking a pace forward, he shot his arms ahead in a rapid action, releasing the axe in a perfect hurling motion.

The axe span round and round like a cartwheel, before the razor sharp head impaled itself into the poster, slamming four inches into the tree bark.

The tip of the axe head was resting midway through the word KLONDIKE'S.

Rance stared at it for several moments. Then, he threw his head back and began roaring with laughter.

The disturbing noise seemed to echo through the entire forest.

The circus train was hurtling north at top speed, swapping the swamplands and bayous of Louisiana for the vast plains and gravel pits of Mississippi.

Memphis was the next stop, and it was just a few hours away.

The train was generally quiet as it made its way upcountry. Most of the staff and talent were sleeping or relaxing after the excitement and adrenaline rush of New Orleans.

Lacey was sitting in the observation carriage, just two carts back from the very front of the great behemoth.

Funny, she was thinking, every time she came up front like this to have a moment of reflection, the carriage was always completely empty. Like now.

With its huge windows running the length of the carriage on both sides, the unusual room was the perfect place to soak up the environment outside and see the world as it raced by.

Lacey was seated on one of the high stools by the glass, cradling a coffee and smoking a cigarette. She wore a robe over her silk pyjamas.

She looked up as the inter-carriage door swung open.

There stood Roddy Olsen. He looked different, dressed in a sweater and jeans and looking unshaven and raw.

He smiled as he approached, then took a stool next to hers. "Mind if I join you?"

She looked at him with her enormous violet eyes. "I figured you'd be around."

"Oh? How's that?"

She studied him. "You want to talk me out of it." She nodded to herself as she took a drag on her smoke. "Kal has told all you guys about the plan. About New York. He didn't like the idea himself. And now…now you're here to say your piece."

Olsen gazed out at the fields whirling by outside. An endless sea of green and turquoise. "I can't believe this is happening. And that you're going through with all this, Miss Lacey."

She followed his gaze. "I know."

He turned to face her. "It's all so dangerous. These people…they are bad news, man. I should know. I saw them up close, real close, remember?"

"Oh, Roddy," she said in a wistful, faraway tone. "Please. I appreciate your concern but…well, this is happening, and that's all there is to it. I will be perfectly safe. I promise. Kal, Heavy, even Daryl, will all be there with me. Just across the street. So, please. Enough. I can't handle any more worried whispers."

Olsen looked down. "I wish I could be there with you all."

"Oh, come on!" she moaned. Then, she smiled mischievously. "Besides, you and Gino will have to help Richie. He's running the place for the next two days. He'll need your help."

His face suddenly seemed to harden. "Man, if anything happens to you up there…"

"Please, Roddy!" she almost shouted. "Enough of this! I will be fine. Alright? Please just stop now."

He seemed to fall into his shell. "It's because I care, Lacey."

She shuddered slightly. Then, she gazed into his Seagram blue eyes, and absently ran her hand though his wavy, straw-blond hair. They looked each other straight in the eye.

"I know you care, Roddy," she whispered. "And I care about you so much. It is I who worries about you, you know. And your future. All the worlds you are going to conquer. Your success. Your fame. It is all there, right there, before you. Just ahead of you on the path. It's all so completely fantastic. And it's all yours, Roddy."

Olsen smiled deeply. "There you go again," he said happily. "You always believe in me, Miss Lacey. Always. From day one."

She leant forward towards him. "I can guide you, Roddy. We both know it. Just keep doing what you're doing. Me and Kal will care for you."

"You always have." He looked around the carriage idly, as the mighty Mississippi River came into view alongside the railroad tracks outside. "Now you just keep safe up in New York, Lacey. For God's sake."

Lacey smiled up at him. "And you, Roddy Olsen, keep safe down here. We need you at your best for Washington. For Superstars and Stripes." Her tone lowered to a conspiratorial whisper. "There's a lot of money in that show, Roddy. A lot of publicity. TV, press, the works. Every circus man in the country will be watching. Having a super show like that, with three big tops joining together. It's one hell of a big deal."

Olsen laughed softly. "I can't wait."

"That's the spirit," she gushed. She studied him, smiling. "Don't forget to keep practising now."

They looked at each other. Then, a voice that sounded like a tannoy announcement sounded throughout the carriage. "Attention all passengers. Next stop on the 1960 magical circus tour is Memphis, Tennessee. All change, please. All change."

Lacey stared at him in astonishment. Olsen remained impassive. His lips had not moved.

He winked at her. "How was that?" They both laughed.

The Klondike's Circus train rolled into Memphis several hours later. The Express pulled in at Memphis Grand Station before switching lines and cruising a mile south on the branch extension that led to Beale Recreation Ground. The local work crew was already gathered together waiting for them.

As everyone disembarked and the slow process of unloading the equipment began, a large group of children ran excitedly across the recreation field to the branch line, autograph books at the ready.

As always, the whole area quickly became a cacophony of noise and commotion as the initial stages of the set-up operation began. Klondike leapt down from an interchange platform of the train, and was followed by Heavy and an excited-looking Daryl Addison. The old banker looked somewhat out of place in his expensive dark suit. Klondike smiled at him and placed an arm around his shoulders. "Well, Daryl, it was good to have you onboard the old circus train again."

"My pleasure," said Addison, running his hands down his suit. He looked at the gang of youngsters running about the train. He chuckled. "Still the same welcoming committee, I see."

Heavy smiled at the children. "Always. Every town, every city. Everywhere."

Klondike watched briefly as Jim McCabe began instructing the local work crew, who had gathered in a large circle with the roustabouts. Several workers were already unloading crates from a central carriage. Behind that, he could see the Range Riders leading the horses out of their stable boxes and onto the gravel pathway. "Alright Daryl," said Klondike dryly. "What time is our train leaving from downtown?"

"One hour." Addison looked up and down the Express. People seemed to be everywhere, getting on with their jobs. "Our cab will be here, at the recreation ground, in about 30 minutes."

Klondike nodded as he looked over the work crews. Then, he turned and saw Lacey and Richie Plum approaching, both smiling broadly. Plum wore a burgundy blazer and looked somehow more official. Lacey had a green trench coat on, a giant carpetbag over one arm.

"Well boys," she squealed as they approached, "take me to New York, New York. It's my kind of town!"

They all laughed. Addison said: "Glad to see you're keen, Lacey."

She smiled broadly. "Always, Daryl."

Klondike tapped her arm proudly, then addressed Plum. "Well, Richie," he barked. "This is it, son. You're now officially circus manager. All this…all this is yours. Until our return."

The small man beamed. "An honour, Kal."

"You got this, Richie," Heavy said, slapping his back.

"Your most important duty," Klondike rasped, still looking around at the work crews, "is to take receipt of the new tent. It'll be here any time. The roustabouts shouldn't have any trouble with it, the design is the same as ours. It may be slightly smaller, but I doubt it. Still, McCabe and his boys will make it work."

Plum looked ready to explode. "Wow! This is really something."

"You bet," Klondike said. He thought for a moment. "Look, I'm sorry this is all happening on your watch, Richie. Hell, what can I tell ya! This has been a season unlike any other. Everything that's happened to us…well, it's all got out of hand. But now…now we're getting it under control again."

Plum looked around, the pride evident on his cherubic features. "You sure are, Kal. I wish you all the best of luck in New York."

He took a hold of Lacey's hand and squeezed tight. "And good luck to you, Lacey dear. Go get that son of a bitch!"

She hugged him, then stood beside Klondike and Addison. "Don't you worry, Richie. Just keep everything ticking over here, alright."

Heavy shook hands with the little man. "Run a tight ship, boss man."

Klondike doffed his hat at him. Then he led the way across the field towards a small pavilion on the far side, where they would wait for their taxi.

Richie stood there beside the train, watching them go. He stood there for some time, lost in thought.

Then, he slowly wandered the length of the train, walking around the work crews as they unloaded vehicles, crates and all the midway equipment.

His plan was to check in on everyone and see to any needs that might arise. He wanted to talk with Shapiro, Olsen and Enqvist. For some reason, he felt compelled to make sure they were happy and comfortable. How he looked up to them, he thought idly as he walked down the gravel path.

After a few moments, McCabe appeared and fell into step with him. "Well, boss man," McCabe said dryly, "how does it feel to have the keys to the kingdom?"

Plum chuckled. "Like owning the world's greatest toy train set as a kid."

McCabe grunted as they walked. "Well, the toys are all in order, buddy. All the stocks have been checked. Nothing is in bad shape. Unloading should be done within a few hours."

"And the groundhole puncher?"

"Just fine. Thank god."

Plum nodded. He thought for a few moments as they walked down the railroad path. "Everything alright with the local crew?"

"Sure. All good boys."

"OK. Great." He made to turn. "Listen, Jim, I need to check in on all the talent and then I—"

He cut off abruptly as he noticed a large truck turn into the main recreation ground entrance behind them. It was not the vehicle that caught his attention, but the giant sign running down its side. The words said: WURLEY'S CIRCUS. NEW YORK.

"Oh my god!" Plum cried. "It's the tent! It's here!"

McCabe studied the lorry. "Perfect timing."

Then, Plum was off, racing towards the new arrival like an overexcited child. With a huff, McCabe bounded after him.

The Wurley's Circus truck pulled up on the grass next to the line, by the head of the train. The driver, a huge man in coveralls, leapt out and began to stretch.

He saw the two men approaching hurriedly. The teams of roustabouts behind them seemed to be following. In fact, as he looked, he soon realised every pair of eyes in the park were now on him.

Plum and McCabe made it to the truck. "One of you Klondike?" said the driver.

"You just missed him," said Plum breathlessly. "I'm Richie Plum. Acting manager."

"Plum?" the driver spat out in amusement.

McCabe waded in. "We'll take possession of the tent, son. I'm McCabe. Circus foreman."

Now the man grinned. "Well, buddy, we got us the same job. I'm Hank Torrance. Foreman for the Wurley outfit."

"Great. How about that…" McCabe murmured, disinterested, as he made his way to the rear. Without asking, he yanked open the back doors and stared inside.

He smiled. Just as he thought. Green and purple. The colours of Wurley's Circus. All they could see inside the interior was a sea of green and purple, the great vinyl-enhanced polyester tent laying on the deck, folded over and over again.

Plum was gaping at the sight. "Jesus. It's all very different to our red and blue."

"Yeah," McCabe said, smiling wistfully. "And it's our venue for the next eight weeks, pal."

Hank Torrance stood behind them, then looked up in astonishment as the roustabout crews all descended upon them, swarming the truck.

"Alright, boys," McCabe cried, climbing onto the rim of the truck bed. "This is it! Our new tent. Let's make our palace!"

Everyone seemed to move for the back of the truck as the great fabric was slowly lifted out, its mass distributed between the men. Torrance stood there in awe. He turned to Plum, who was watching the work crew.

"You, er, need a hand, boss?" he muttered.

Plum looked up at him. "You're a beautiful man, Hank. Anyone ever tell you that?"

With that, they both helped with the removal of the tent.

Chapter Twenty-Two

The atmosphere in the private first-class stateroom was pensive, with a strange kind of surreal excitement in the air. Part fear, part longing. It was an usual sensation.

The Transatlantic Express was now silently steaming through the mid-eastern states. Dusk had passed. It was night outside. The windows now offered a black wall, littered with rail lights that flew by outside.

Klondike, Heavy and Addison were all sat at a round table in the private room. All three were staring at Lacey, who stood entranced at the dresser in the far corner.

The public relations guru was in another world entirely, delicately examining a gaudy pink dress that looked like it had been taken from a Las Vegas stage show. It had ruffled feathers attached to its sides and shining rhinestone gems across the chest.

"My, my," she whispered in awe. "I bought this number seven years ago. Even at the time I asked myself, 'What am I doing?' Ha! I must've worn it, what, on three occasions. And who would have thought…after all that time, it has finally found a purpose. As part of a disguise! Of all the things."

The three men looked at her, but there was no humour. "Well," Addison finally said. "You certainly look the part, Lacey. But…" he smiled. "Are you sure you can actually play the part?"

Lacey looked up from her dazzling dress. She threw him the most beguiling of grins. Placing the pink number over the back of a chair, she stood before them, as if in an audition, and placed one hand on her hip.

"Gentlemen," she said in a sly, husky voice. "Allow me to introduce myself. Cherry Valance. Cabaret singer, with 15 years of experience. Hell, I've played all the stages there are to play. Vegas, Atlantic City, Broadway, Los Angeles. Even a summer tour to Paris. There ain't an audience I've sang to that didn't find Cherry sweet enough…"

They all murmured in approval.

"Dammit, Lacey," Heavy roared, "you're good at this. Too damn good."

Addison nodded. "Just like I said. A natural."

They all turned to Klondike, seated in the middle at the table. He smiled at her. "Very good, Lacey," he said softly. "Very good, indeed. Just don't get complacent playing the stage star. Our man Agostino can smell a rat. Just play him along."

"Why Kal," she said playfully, "Cherry doesn't need to play anyone along. She can make a man do anything for her!"

Addison was all business. "The tricky part will be to move the conversation along to the circus."

Lacey seemed to brush him off as she swaggered around the stateroom. "We've been through this, Daryl. I can handle it."

Heavy was transfixed as he watched her wander round. "You sure are convincing, Lacey. If I didn't know better, I'd have you down as a celebrity. All the way."

"Why, Henry, I am a celebrity," she gushed, before throwing her head back and letting out a haughty laugh.

Klondike and Addison looked at each other, somewhat befuddled. Then, the old banker looked down at some papers spread out on the table before him. "Alright. Well, everything is fixed. My man in New York has worked wonders. You've got your audience with Agostino and we are booked in at the hotel opposite. Just like that." He looked up and studied Lacey seriously. "It really is all down to you now, my dear."

She placed an arm over a hat stand in the corner. "Beautiful."

Klondike was looking down at the papers. "Listen, Daryl," he barked. "What about this policeman contact of yours? Are you 100 per cent sure he can be trusted?"

Addison did not hesitate. "He is incorruptible. That is beyond dispute."

Klondike frowned. "You mean, you think he is. Hell, Agostino's outfit has every lawman in the city in their pocket, what I've heard."

"That's the beauty of it," Addison said in wonder. "Our man is a Detroit cop. Brought in to New York to take out the gangs. It's all part of a police operation, as I understand."

Klondike nodded slowly. He idly removed a cigar from his jacket pocket and rolled it between his fingers. It was a sign he was satisfied.

"I just can't believe it," Heavy was saying. "Look at us. Off to New York. Like gunslingers off to right wrongs. How in the hell did we get involved in all this?"

Klondike sneered. "We said no to crime. To the syndicate. We refused to give a cut. To allow those animals to push us around. Hurt people."

"And now," Lacey put in from the corner, still prancing around in her role as Cherry Valance. "Now, it's a team effort to stop it all."

"Right." Klondike lit his cigar, watching as always as the deep purple smoke drifted above his head in a billowing cloud. "And to top it all off, we've left our circus behind. In the hands of our finance whizz. Just so we can ride off into Dodge, all guns blazing."

There was a sudden silence for several moments. Lacey began gently packing her bright pink dress into a dry-cleaners clothes holdall.

Heavy wandered over to a suitcase, produced a bottle of cognac, and poured them each a generous glass.

"It's incredible," he said to Klondike as he hovered over him. "Going back to New York again. After all this time. Back to the streets. Our old life."

"I just wish it was for a show," Klondike said quietly.

"Hell, we're not even taking in a Yankees game," Heavy moaned.

"Well, they're at the Reds tomorrow anyway. I got my radio." Klondike took the filled shot glass and slowly sipped the strong, revitalising liquid. He was feeling overwhelmed. Again. He rubbed at his eyes with his fingers, his mind sluggish and weary.

A vision formed in his head. There she was again. Catherine Hart.

He still had not told any of them about her. About what Agostino had told him. What had become of her. It all made him feel sick. Would Heavy even remember her, he wondered? She was his boyhood crush. Then, he had forgotten all about her. The Army, the circus…that had been his life. His world. Hers had been a different path. A dark and harrowing one.

He shook his head angrily, trying to think. The other three were all staring at him.

"Kal?" Lacey asked in a tiny voice. "Are you alright?"

"Fine. Just fine."

She wandered to the table and stood over him, eyes full of concern. "Are you sure there is nothing else? Nothing about New York you haven't mentioned?"

He shook his head again. "No! No. I'm just so god damn tired. What with this season…the tent, the trouble, the publicity, the people. And now this! Trying to nail a gangland kingpin! My god, it's all too much."

Addison sipped his drink, upright and alert as if sitting in on one of his stockholders meetings. "It sure is, Kal. And yet here we all are."

Klondike rubbed at his face. Then, he pulled a pack of cards from his satchel on the floor beside him.

"Come on, Heav," he barked. "Let's play. Man, I can't remember ever needing a game like this!"

Heavy chuckled as he pulled his chair round, then rubbed his hands together.

"Deal me in," Addison said with sudden relish. "I've always heard a lot of talk about how good you two are at poker. About time I saw for myself. I'm quite a player myself, y'know."

"Well, good luck," Heavy said humorously.

Lacey stood over them like a mother scalding her children for playing truant. "How on earth can you play five card stud at a time like this? Are you guys crazy?"

"Well, you know the drill Lacey," Klondike said, cigar in mouth. "When we're on a train, and business is concluded…then, we play. Always been that way."

"Always." Heavy put in.

Lacey, hands on hips, wandered around in a circle, eyeing the table as Klondike shot his deal.

Idly, she grabbed at Heavy's bottle and poured herself another shot. The three men all settled down around the table, studying their hands.

With a shrug, Lacey downed her cognac and paced across to the window, climbing onto an armchair and gazing out at the black wall of night-time beyond. There was nothing to see out there. Just the floodlights racing past.

She rested her head gently on the back rim of the chair. New York, she thought. The home of so many wonderful attractions.

Broadway. Greenwich Village. Central Park. Macy's. Fifth Avenue. And crime. Gangsters. The Beaumont Club. And the Mob.

She shuddered slightly. Then her eyelids began to grow heavy.

Lacey just sat there thinking to herself. Beneath her, the noise of the locomotive wheels on the track became like a pulse.

Before she knew it, she had dozed off in the chair.

They arrived in New York at lunchtime the following day. Travelling by cab from Grand Central Station to Upper Manhattan, they saw a plethora of sights as they roamed through the midday traffic.

It was colder, windier in the Big Apple, a stark contrast to the heat of the south they had experienced over the past weeks.

The circus folks felt as if they had landed in another world. The streets were littered with people, car horns punctured the air constantly and the whole asphalt jungle was filled with a deep unnatural smog.

Glancing out the taxi window, Klondike observed a group of policemen hustling a street gang into the back of a paddy wagon. "It's good to be back," he uttered dryly.

As they moved into Manhattan, the streets were slightly less dense with people. The buildings seemed even taller, the cars slightly jazzier, but the unclean air was still the same.

Then, the driver slowed outside a tall white building that had a cinema-style marquee hovering over its revolving door entrance. Bright purple letters said:

THE BEAUMONT CLUB. BEST NIGHT OUT IN TOWN. PLAYING TONIGHT—STAN STONE. THE CREOLE GIRLS. THE GREAT BARAZZO.

The yellow cab pulled in at the building opposite, a greyish flat stone monolith-like structure called Hotel Durango.

They all departed, Klondike looking around to check if their arrival had attracted any attention. With his fedora pulled low and his coat collar high around his ears, no one would ever have recognised him, not even a close friend.

As he paid the cabbie and made to join his friends at the hotel entrance, Klondike allowed himself a quick glance across the street to the Beaumont. It looked devoid of life at this early hour. His dark eyes moved upwards, scanning the windows of the rooms above.

Then, with a huff, he lifted his bag and joined the others.

Just as Addison had promised, their suite on the third floor overlooked the nightclub opposite.

The huge room was cheaply decorated and somewhat basic. One of the most expensive suites in the low-budget joint, it suited their needs perfectly.

They had enjoyed a large and leisurely lunch ordered via room service. Then, the atmosphere had taken on a business-like feel. Klondike now stood at the window in his shirt sleeves, pacing back and forth and eyeing the Beaumont Club with steely eyes.

Addison was going through what he called his 'spy equipment', which was laid out on the dining table. The wire, the recorder, a spool of black recording tape. He went about his business in a cool, efficient manner.

Heavy was reading a pamphlet about the Beaumont Club they had seen in the hotel lobby.

As for Lacey, she was the busiest of them all and had an array of jobs to attend to. And they all concerned her transformation into Cherry Valance. Right now, she was in the bathroom working on her hair. She was styling it herself, and would also be applying her own make-up, skin treatment and nail work. A Park Avenue beautician would have proud, Klondike had told her. After lunch, Lacey had run a hot bubble bath and had simply led in it for an hour, going through the night ahead in her already over-animated mind.

At about three o'clock, Klondike stopped pacing at the window and looked down at the street opposite.

A giant silver Cadillac had pulled in at the kerb next to the Beaumont Club. Two well-dressed heavies rushed from the nightclub's entrance and almost fell over themselves opening the car's rear door. They both stood back.

Klondike stiffened all over. A man wearing a grey suit, a beige trench coat draped casually over his shoulders, emerged from the car. He looked up and down the street, a long-time habit, then up at the club. He patted the men's faces with a leather-gloved hand.

"Heavy! Daryl! Come here," Klondike rasped, his nose against the window pane. "It's him! Look."

Addison and Heavy were there in seconds, and all three stared down at the sidewalk opposite.

"That's our boy?" Addison whispered.

"Damn straight," Klondike muttered. He eyed Heavy. "You recognise him, Heav?"

"Jesus…" Heavy stammered. "It's been over 20 years. All I remember is a grease-haired punk in a black jacket. This guy looks like a Wall Street businessman."

Klondike eyed the scene below ruefully. "That's the idea."

As they watched from the hotel window, Paul Agostino slowly wandered into his club, stopping to talk to another man at the door before entering.

Then, the glitzy Cadillac pulled away and the street was suddenly empty again.

At the window, the three men slowly turned away. Addison spoke first. "Strolling around like the king of the city. He really thinks he's untouchable."

Klondike grunted. "He's in for a shock."

Addison returned to the dining table and his array of equipment. He let out a deep breath. "Tonight the tables get turned. On him and his mob."

Heavy liked that. "Well said, Daryl."

Klondike collapsed into the couch, running a hand through his thick black hair. He seemed somehow in pain as he spoke.

"I just hope this all works out."

Paul Agostino sat at a huge ivory desk in his office at the rear of the Beaumont Club.

Casually sipping a martini, he was going through some papers that summarised the previous week's take at the club.

He looked up as a large, muscular man in a black suit entered. Jimmy Felco, his personal assistant.

"Hi boss. How was Atlantic City?"

"Jimmy," Agostino muttered, his eyes falling back on to the figures laid out before him. "Same as always. Booze, broads, blackjack. Hell, I loved it." He laughed softly.

"Did that song and dance man agree to come down and perform here?"

"Not at first," Agostino said icily. He smiled an evil smile. "It took some persuasion. Now, ah, he will be here next week. A month-long engagement."

"Nice work, boss."

Agostino chucked the papers on to his desk. "And here, Jimmy? What goes on?"

Felco stood straight, looking somewhat awkward. "I'm sorry, boss. Not a lot to report."

"No word from Ribbeck? Vesnick? Farron?"

"Nuthin."

"Dammit!" Agostino dabbed at his face with a cloth. He finished his martini and indicated for Felco to make him another. "How did this whole business get so god damn complicated?"

Felco returned with a full martini glass. "If I may, boss?"

"Go ahead."

"These circus people…they's a different breed. Live with a different code. They's all hillbillies. Gypsies. Westerners. They don't understand money, deals, our kinda business." Felco stood before Agostino, looking down at him. "It's not our world, boss. Maybe…" he took a deep breath. "Maybe we shouldn't have gotten involved in all this."

Agostino glared at him. His dark brown eyes seemed to become inflamed. "Listen," he barked, "that circus is a golden goose. It lays golden eggs. Comprende? And, worst of all, it is run by a sucker who owes me. Owes me for all of his success. Now, I'm gunna have that damn big top in my empire, no matter what! Klondike is a cowboy. His outfit are a bunch of flatheads and oddballs. We tried to ask nicely for a piece of the action. But…but now we're gunna take it. All of it!"

Felco seemed to wobble slightly. "What is the plan, boss? Is…is there a new plan?"

Agostino recklessly knocked back his second martini. "This time we're gunna hit em. Hit em proper. Get Klondike and his pals cornered. Then, we'll threaten to kill em. Kill em all. Unless…unless he signs the circus over to me. No more stupid attacks. I'm gunna be there myself." He looked at Felco with cold, calculating eyes. "He's gunna pay for all the trouble he's caused me."

Felco nodded and walked away from the desk slowly.

"Hey Jimmy," Agostino called after him. "What is the schedule tonight? Remind me, huh?"

Felco paused near the doorway. "You're taking that call from the chambers of commerce at 7. Then, at 8, you're meeting that cabaret singer from Vegas, remember? Miss Cherry Valance."

"Ah yes," Agostino said with a faint grin. "That should be cute. Our man Felix said she is pretty good, huh?"

Felco nodded and left the office.

Agostino sat back at his desk and lit a cigarette. Two solitary thoughts consumed him. Finding new acts for his club. And running his own circus.

It was a wonderful notion, he thought, the circus. It would be like a hobby, a little plaything for him, to mould and develop as he saw fit. He would take in the odd show from time to time. Like the chief executive of a sports team. But the running of the business would be down to a manager who would answer only to him.

What fun he would have, he thought idly, scouring the globe for talent, all kinds of bizarre acts, to appear in his show. Agostino's Circus. He saw the venture as a distraction. A little creative enterprise to help take his mind off the pressures of the Syndicate. With a deep sigh, he leant his head against the back of the chair.

He said it aloud happily. "Agostino's Circus."

The street outside had grown dark and full of shadows as night-time slowly descended. The only real source of light was the dazzling neon-lit tubing of the marquee above the Beaumont Club. This explosion of illumination lit up the whole sidewalk outside the premises.

Klondike, incredibly, was still keeping an active vigil at the hotel window. He studied the traffic, watched as well-dressed patrons entered the club. The street was busy now, alive with the night.

Heavy and Addison were standing around the dining table, both smoking heavily having brought fresh packets from a machine down the hall.

"How do I look?"

All three turned to the bedroom door at the silky voice penetrating the silent atmosphere.

The three sets of eyes all widened at once.

There she was. Lacey stood at the door, hands on hips, looking like a foreign countess from a world none of them knew existed. Her bright pink dress seemed to shine, its feathers looking fresh and glittery. She had an immaculate silver fur coat draped over her shoulders, a gold alligator-skinned handbag over one arm.

Her skin was the colour of honey and her hair looked cinnamon. Everything seemed to shine and sparkle.

And Lacey was loving her new look, smiling warmly, the confidence and grace oozing out of her.

The three men all clapped as if on cue. They simply didn't know what else to do.

"Lacey…" Klondike stammered. "My god. You look terrific!"

Addison trumped him. "Divine, my dear. Divine."

Heavy was trying not to gawk. "Yeah! A real piece of work!"

She laughed haughtily, throwing her head back and wandering around the room like a sleek meerkat.

"Oh boys," she breathed, in her Cherry Valance accent. Then, she eyed them in a business-like manner. "Alright. So I pass the first test?"

"With flying colours," Addison said happily. He went straight to her and studied her frame. "The wire go in alright? Are you comfortable?"

She patted the fabric of her dress, just below her chest. "It's attached. Can barely feel it. The mic head is about an inch below the line of the dress. Just like you said, Daryl."

The older man smiled. "Then you're all set, dear."

Klondike came over and took her hand. "The drapes in the suites above the nightclub are open. So, any trouble, you should be able to signal. I'll be watching the whole thing. And we'll be able to hear every word."

She eyed the windows behind him. "So close. And yet so far."

He nodded nervously. "Any last thoughts?"

Her giant, beautiful eyes looked into his. They were truly entrancing. "Only one," she whispered. "Let's go get this guy."

With that, she turned dramatically and headed for the door.

Chapter Twenty-Three

"Miss Cherry Valance."

She walked elegantly through the penthouse door at the loud introduction, entering a huge, sweet-smelling room that looked more like a royal suite.

As she wandered inside, Jimmy Felco silently closed the door behind her. For a moment, she was awestruck. The penthouse room was laid with thick, brown carpets and Oriental rugs, while oversized leather seats and couches, all cream-coloured, seemed to be everywhere. There were two bars, and she could just make out a conference table in another room at the far side.

"Miss Valance!"

Paul Agostino materialised from a washroom behind one of the bars.

Lacey turned suddenly, then slipped straight back into her new persona.

"Mr Agostino," she said excitedly. She held out a hand, knuckles up. "What a delight. Thank you for seeing me."

Agostino rushed over and took her hand in his, planting a lingering kiss near her wrist. Then he looked up and smiled broadly.

Lacey could not help shuddering. He was a truly evil-looking man, the hideous scar that ran from his right eyelid to the corner of his mouth looking like a crater in a dynamited rock quarry. His slicked back ebony hair and reddish skin were oily. His brown suit looked like it had been stolen from Bloomingdale's.

"A true pleasure," he was saying, smiling like an alligator. "Thank you for coming. We are honoured by your presence. My compliments. May I?"

He moved behind her and removed the fur coat, taking it to a stand in the corner. Lacey watched him. She wasn't fooled by such gallantry. All too well, she recalled the stories Klondike had shared about her host.

"May I offer you a drink?" he boomed as he returned. She held her head high. "Martini please."

"Ah, a woman of taste. Ha! You are in the right place if you appreciate Martini." He waded over to the larger of the two bars, turning and eyeing her.

As he mixed the drinks, he threw his hand around before him. "You like my place, huh?"

"Very much," she said. "This is all so beautiful."

"Please, be seated."

Lacey sat on the edge of one of the leather couches. She positioned herself opposite the windows.

Agostino came over and handed her the Martini. "Enjoy," he whispered as he leant over. She tensed. His breath smelt strongly of alcohol. Something inside her buzzed. That could only help her predicament.

"To the Beaumont!" she said in an airy tone, taking a sip.

As he sat along from her on the soft leather, she took a cigarette from a silver case in her bag and boldly held it for him to light. With a smirk, he duly obliged, then lit one for himself.

"It is wonderful to meet you, Miss Valance," he finally said, leaning back. "You come highly recommended from my talent manager, who heard about you from a contact in Vegas. Your singing is said to be entrancing. And, well..." he looked at her with predatory eyes. "Just look at you, huh."

She batted her eyelids and waved a hand through the air. "Oh, please, Mr Agostino."

He seemed to get animated, almost laughing. "You are happy to be here, no? In Manhattan?"

"Why, sure. Of course. It's all so exciting." She took a deep breath, ready to play her first brave hand. "To be here right now. At the Beaumont. To be involved with you...the Syndicate!"

His eyes seemed to twinkle. His face froze for a second. Lacey held her breath, almost afraid to look.

"So..." Agostino breathed. "You know about us, huh?"

Lacey played it cool, not even flinching for a second. "Of course. Why? Doesn't everybody?"

He sneered. "Hard to tell," he mumbled. "All depends where a person is coming from. But you, Miss Valance...you have years of experience in Vegas. The Desert Inn. The Sands. It's only natural you hear my name, no?"

She batted her eyelids again. "Why, of course, Mr Agostino." She inhaled her cigarette deeply, blowing out a long cloud of smoke. "And how I have wanted to perform here, at the Beaumont."

He sniggered. "You hear about some of the guys we get in here, eh? Sinatra. Martin. Bishop. Don Rickles."

"Of course," she gushed. "That's why I was so happy we could arrange this meeting."

"OK," he mused, leaning back. "Why don't you tell me about yourself, Miss Valance?"

She was ready for this. Throwing her head back, she started talking slowly. "Well, I was born and raised in Santa Monica, California. From high school, I was always singing. I joined a girl group after graduating. The Sugardrops. We performed at county fairs, town halls, colleges, you know the like. From there, I got noticed by a record producer. From Acosta Records. He invited me out to Los Angeles to cut some tracks."

She paused, eyeing him as she sipped her Martini. "Let's just say that didn't work out. But, I did meet a guy who offered me professional representation. Within a few months, he had got me a gig at The Belltower in Carlton City. Lounge singer. Cabaret. Two shows a night. It went well. Vegas is just 50 miles away. Word got around. Then, before I knew it, I was offered shows at all the major casinos on the Strip. That led to gigs all over the country. And even a tour of Europe." She paused and threw him a sultry, sideways glance. "Hell, there ain't a stage worth singing on that I ain't sang on."

Agostino clapped his hands. "Bravo, Miss Valance. Bravo."

Lacey rolled her eyes. "I guess you could say things kinda just snowballed."

"Like a thunderbolt," he added. "It all happened at once."

"Yes, that's right."

He was still smiling widely. "And what now, eh? New worlds to conquer?"

This was it. A perfect opening. She looked at the windows wistfully, as if lost in thought. "Well, that's a funny thing, Mr Agostino. I am now looking to reinvent myself. Go down a fresh path. You know what I mean?"

"Sure. I see it all in the time in showbusiness." He inched closer on the couch. "What do you see yourself doing now?"

Lacey looked at him, as if uncertain. "Have you ever heard of Suzi Dando?"

His eyes widened. "Sure. I, er, I know of her very well. What...what of her?"

"That's where I see myself. Singing for a circus company."

He glared at her. "You're kidding!"

She looked down sadly. "You probably think I'm crazy. Me! With my furs, my dresses and my reputation. Travelling with a damn circus! But just look at what that girl has accomplished. She is known across the country. Fans in every city. And all because she is touring. Constantly. No one fixed gig." She leant forward. "Did you hear about what happened to her in New Orleans?"

Agostino was transfixed, looking somewhat perplexed. "Er, yes. Sure, I heard what happened. The crowd, all of them, everyone, starting singing. They all joined her."

"Fantastic!" Lacey cried, growing more confident with each second. "I can only imagine what a feeling that must've been for her. People love her. She has a nationwide appeal." She gazed at the windows again. In the dark night outside, she could make out their room window at the Hotel Durango across the street.

"That…" she began, "that is what I yearn for."

In the hotel room, Klondike, Heavy and Addison were sat at the dining table, the large tape recorder in the middle, its spool whirling round and round as it recorded everything.

Addison looked up. "Perfect."

Klondike nodded slowly. "He played into her hands there."

Heavy looked elated. "She's smoking, man."

Klondike rose as they continued listening to the conversation. He walked to the window and looked out. In the haze of the penthouse's lighting, he couldn't see much through the suite window opposite.

He turned at the sound of Agostino's voice on the recorder. "This is truly remarkable, Miss Valance."

"How's that, Mr Agostino?"

She stared at him innocently, sipping her Martini.

Suddenly, he rose and paced to the dresser. He produced a white cloth and dabbed at his face absently.

"Truly remarkable," he repeated.

She waited, and he slowly wandered around the suite, as if in a daze.

"Klondike's Circus," he said in wonder.

"Yes, that's right. I believe Suzi's title is circus songstress supreme."

Agostino paused by a lampshade, twirling the cloth in his hands. He looked as if he was trying to solve some kind of puzzle. Lacey shifted slightly on the couch, trying her utmost to remain impassive. This was it, she thought desperately.

"What would you say, Miss Valance," he uttered casually, circling the couch, "if I were to tell you I was taking over Klondike's Circus?"

She had practised this moment many times. She turned in her seat, her violet eyes wide in fright, her mouth gaping. "What? Are you serious? You? The circus? I…I don't believe it. Can't believe it."

To her immense relief, Agostino chuckled slightly. Though he still looked perplexed. He stood before her now.

"Well, you better believe it. Kal Klondike and I are…old school friends. He is handing me his circus…to take it on, further, you know. He wants me to run it from now on. Everything should be in place for next season."

He smiled at her mesmerically. "Now, Miss Valance, what do you think of that, eh? Incredible coincidence, no?"

She was ready for this path also. As if acting out lines familiar through rehearsals, she made a queer, annoyed face and spoke in a sharp whisper. "Please forgive me, Mr Agostino. I mean no disrespect. But…well, I know for a fact that isn't true."

His eyes widened in horror. "What!"

"Well," she said quickly, "I read in the papers just yesterday that Kal Klondike has committed to running his circus next season. He was quoted as saying that nothing, or nobody, would ever make him give up his beloved circus. No matter what, he said. There were pictures of him with all his sponsors and investors. It was a big media call. Everyone celebrating how he will keep on touring."

Agostino's face had dropped. "I must have missed that."

Lacey spoke in a quivering, quiet tone. "It's alright, Mr Agostino. I understand. If I was a successful Syndicate man like you, I would want to own a big money-maker like that too."

He threw the cloth onto the couch. "I will own it!"

She glared up at him. "But I thought—"

"Forget what you think you know," Agostino snapped. Something had changed in him. Turned him. Gone were the charm and fine manners. In their place, the wild street thug who had killed and maimed plenty. She contained her sudden fear, performing like a Broadway stage actress. Now, she smiled seductively, as if excited by the strong words.

"Oh my," she breathed huskily. "This sounds exciting."

He smiled too. Confidence suddenly seemed to surge through him. He puffed his chest out. "You know of me, Miss Valance. So you will know that I am a man who always gets exactly what he wants."

"Oh, Mr Agostino," she whispered, "I knew you were powerful. But, well…"

"That's right," he rasped. "What I want, I take. Just like that."

"And…and you want Klondike's Circus?"

"You bet. I want that golden goose. It will be my pride and joy. The heart of my business empire. The jewel in my crown. And…" suddenly he turned and faced her, staring wildly. "And you, Miss Valance, you could be the star of the show! Now, what do you think of that, eh?"

Lacey put her hand on her chest and panted excitedly. "Oh my word," she blurted, "this is all so fabulous. I can't believe it!"

Agostino fell onto the couch beside her. He was significantly closer to her this time. He grabbed at her hand roughly, and kissed it again. "Incredible, no? Just like that, you see all your dreams, all your plans, all fall into place."

She gently withdrew her hand. "But, Mr Agostino, I still don't see how you are going to run the circus. Forgive me, but this doesn't add up."

He sneered at her. "You just leave that to me and my people, huh."

She gave him a pleading look, eyes wide and innocent. "But how? How can you do it?"

Agostino shook his head, staring at her. "You know about us, no? What we do? Me and my people?"

"You…you mean the…the mobsters?"

He laughed. "Yes."

She leant closer, showing fear and what she hoped was desire on her features. "You're going to use violence? Guns?"

"What we call a hostile takeover. We use our muscle. It always works. Klondike may resist at first, but eventually he will surrender to me. They always do."

Lacey felt elation inside, her heart pounding like a jackhammer. She remained calm. "What…what are you going to do?"

Now, Agostino was just plain enjoying himself. The power. The enchanted woman. He casually lit a cigarette, not offering her one. "That's simple. We threaten to kill him. Unless he hands us his circus. That will be the last threat."

"The last?"

"Well, the beauty of all this is…it has already begun." He laughed like a juvenile.

As disgusted as she was, Lacey remained the perfect actress. "Oh my god! What have you done?"

He looked about idly. "Knocked em around a bit. We hit a few of his guys. Busted up some machinery. Showed Klondike who he is messing with. He is one stubborn son of a bitch. That is why we are going to make this one last threat. I am tired of all this nonsense. But soon…soon the circus will be mine."

Lacey could not believe she was getting this much out of him. Time for another big hand. She flung herself forward on the couch, as if having a sudden realisation. "Oh lord! It was you, wasn't it? It was you and your mob who…who started that fire? The fire in Houston?"

He leant back, his face trying to mask his irritation. "Sure. And…and even that didn't stop them."

"But you could've killed people! Women and children. They get thousands in those big tops." Her anger was not feigned.

Gracefully, Agostino remained cool. He seemed to be tiring of the exchange. "And all the deaths would have been on his hands. If he had signed over the circus to me, none of it would've happened."

Lacey decided that was enough. He had revealed all she had hoped for. Now, it was time to cast the net wider. She acted flustered.

"My, my," she breathed. "This is all so exhilarating. May I have another Martini?"

Agostino was momentarily lost in his thoughts, sat back in the couch thinking. Lacey suddenly realised he seemed drunk. Perfect!

"Sure," he said at last. He took her glass from her, rushed to the bar, and began mixing them both a drink.

Lacey took another deep breath. "Do you have any contacts in the circus world? To help with all this?"

Agostino huffed, his smile containing little warmth. "I did. The best in the business. Eric Ribbeck."

She leant on the couch, looking across at him. "Ribbeck! Wow. He is a legend in showbusiness. What happened?"

He walked back with the two glasses full. "Let's just say he didn't deliver on a lot of his promises."

"You mean he was going to help you run Klondike's Circus?"

He handed her the Martini, before taking a long slurp on his one. "That was the idea. But he is an old man. Weak. And a southerner. A farmer. He started out throwing pitchforks of manure for a living. Can you imagine, eh? No, he didn't approve of my methods. So...I tossed him aside."

Lacey leant forward. "So, he knew of the violence? What was going on?"

She realised immediately she had made a mistake. One probe too far.

Agostino gazed at her, confusion masking his ugly features. It suddenly hit her that he was more drunk than she realised. And that this may not be a good thing.

"You ask a lot of questions, Miss Valance."

Now, she quivered all over and there was no hiding it. She tried desperately to recover. She remembered her lines.

"Oh, I'm so sorry, Mr Agostino," she said in a childlike voice. "It's just that...well, y'know, all this tough guy talk is just so...so exciting. I feel like I'm in a movie or something. I just can't get enough."

"A movie," he blurted. He smiled cruelly. "A movie where the bad guys always win."

She winked at him. "Those are the kind I like."

She had been silently praying for a miracle. Then, miraculously, one happened. She got an out. A way to escape this madhouse.

There was a knock at the door. Jimmy Felco wandered in. "Sorry to interrupt boss," he called. "There is a call for you in the club. Guy says he is the manager of a club in Queens. The Rhinestone."

That was a signal. Klondike or Addison were on the other end of the phone. They would hang up as soon as Agostino answered. They had all agreed this would be their opening attempt at getting Lacey out of there at the first hint of trouble.

Agostino looked back dumbly at Felco. "The Rhinestone? Jesus! That takes me back." He thought for a moment, eyeing Lacey in confusion. "Well, er, I..."

This was her moment to scram. She shot up, finished her drink and made to leave. "It's alright, Mr Agostino. Please, take your call. I must be on my way. I still have to meet my agent downtown."

He made to say something, but could only watch as she raced across the room, making for the coat stand.

"Thank you so much for agreeing to see me. I have had a wonderful time. Enchanting!" She made a conscious attempt to slow down. Turning, she eyed him mischievously, delicately draping the fur coat over her shoulders. "And I have never been so excited in my life. At your, er, stories." Now, she threw him a sultry glance. "I hope we can do it again. Sometime soon. Real soon."

She held out her hand for him. Agostino shot across the carpet, his suspicions and doubts suddenly forgotten. He grabbed at her hand and kissed it hungrily. He kept her hand in both of his.

"We will do it again soon, Miss Valance. And so much more, of course."

She felt complete disgust all over, gently removing her hand from his grip. "We have much to discuss, it would appear."

"So much." He walked to the door, and held his hand out to the corridor. "Please, Miss Valance. Jimmy and I will walk down with you."

Lacey internally breathed a mighty sigh of relief as she finally exited the penthouse. She remained cool all over as she led the way down the grand staircase. Agostino and Felco followed.

"You are staying in the city?" Agostino asked.

"Of course. All this month."

"Where can we reach you?" said Felco.

"The Carruthers Hotel. Uptown."

Both men seemed to murmur their approval. When they got to the bottom of the stairs, Lacey did not wait to be asked, but simply strode towards the grand revolving doors at the front of the foyer. All she wanted was to be on the outside. Safe, in the street again.

She turned at the door. Agostino and Felco were stood watching her, as if hypnotised.

She smiled beautifully. "Goodnight, boys." Then, with a theatrical flourish, she was gone.

Agostino chuckled slightly, slapped Felco on the back, then headed into a telephone booth adjacent to the nightclub's main floor.

Ten seconds later, he stormed back out.

"Jimmy!" he barked. "There was no one there. That line was dead, man. What the hell!"

Felco simply shrugged.

And that was that.

Lacey blundered into the room, emotionally and psychologically exhausted. Tears were in her eyes and she was almost gagging. Klondike and Heavy were on her in a second, holding her up and carrying her across to an armchair. Addison poured a large cognac and brought it to her.

"Lacey! You did it! You did it! God damn it, you were sensational," Klondike was exclaiming, shaking like an overexcited child.

"It worked, Lacey," Heavy put in. "You made it work. I ain't never heard anything like that."

She took the offered cognac without a word and surprised them all by downing almost the entire glass in one go. She quivered and was sobbing, the tears quickly wreaking havoc with her excessive eye-make-up.

"Are you ok?" Addison said. "You look like you're in shock."

She stared into nothingness, still quivering.

"Say something!" Klondike rasped.

"I'm alright. I'm alright." She spoke in an exhausted whisper, running a hand across her face. She was shaking badly. "I can't believe all that just happened."

"It all went as we hoped. As we planned." Heavy was kneeling beside her, smiling happily. "He played right into your hands. He gave it all away. Incriminated himself big time. Talk about a smoking gun. We got everything."

She finally smiled, patting Heavy and Klondike as she breathed in heavily. "I can't believe he said all that."

"Lacey, my dear," Addison was standing to the side, and spoke with his usual authoritative tone. "That was a true masterclass in deception and undercover operation."

"I don't know how you kept it all together," Klondike whispered, his arm wrapped around her tight. "You were just beautiful in there." He kissed her on the forehead.

She nodded at all of them, but still shifted uneasily in her seat. "What kind of man is he? To speak so easily of so many sins."

"He's not a man," Klondike said, his eyes blazing. "He's an animal. And now he is going to pay."

Lacey looked at him and nodded, still shifting as if covered in itching powder. "Can we just get out of here?"

Addison stood over them. "Our train is first thing in the morning. We will get a cab down. But not before we drop off our prize…" he indicated the tape recorder on the dining table behind him. The spool of tape had been removed and sat next to the recorder.

Addison continued. "We'll drop it at the police precinct on our way. Our man the captain will pick it up. My..." he smiled wistfully. "I wish I could see his face when he listens in."

Lacey hugged herself, pulling the fur coat over her frame. "I just want to get as far away from here as possible."

Klondike rubbed her shoulder reassuringly. "Thank you," he whispered.

Then, he rose and crossed to the window. He glared out at the Beaumont Club, taking in the dazzling, neon marquee lights and the smartly dressed patrons now entering.

His dark eyes locked onto the windows of the penthouse suite above. He whispered to himself.

"Got you, you son of a bitch."

Chapter Twenty-Four

It was a surreal sight. Yet nonetheless, an awe-inspiring one. The bright and beautiful green and purple big top sat, tall and proud, in the bright summer sunshine at Memphis's Beale Recreation Ground.

As the last rope support was hammered into the ground by a roustabout, everyone slowly gathered at the front, ahead of the tent's entrance flap.

First, the work force of roustabouts and local, signed-on crews moved to the head of the big top. Then, slowly, as if drawn by some inner impulse, the occupants of the train emptied out of their staterooms and crossed the field to join the hands.

A general muttering of appreciation seemed to pulse through the group as everyone stared up at the new tent. Many faces wore a mask of confusion, so used to the traditional red and blue colours that anything else seemed inconceivable.

Richie Plum moved to the head of the gathering, his eyes locked on the great tent before him. He moved subconsciously to the flap, and peered in like an excited child. The bleachers were all set up, even the sections of grandstand that had been spoilt by the fire, which had been repainted.

Jim McCabe joined the temporary manager by the entrance.

"Me and the boys have put up Kal's tent a hundred times," he said slowly, removing his hat and wiping his brow. "And, I tell ya, this was no different. It ain't smaller at all. The fabric is lighter. But, apart from that, it was all the same. Just those damn bright colours is changed."

Plum smiled at him as he took in the interior. "Well done, Jim. A seamless transition, you might say."

McCabe grunted. "Looks like half the town is coming out to see the big top. And it's not even showtime!"

Plum turned and stared in shock as streams of townsfolk appeared on the field, all heading towards them as if in a trance. Soon, the talent and roustabouts stood admiring the tent were joined by a huge crowd of mostly well-wishers and the curious.

Plum wandered in the direction of the train. He saw that Shapiro, Penny, Olsen, Suzi and the Daredevils had all gathered at a raised platform near the railroad siding. They had become almost overwhelmed by fans now eager to bag an autograph and meet the stars of the show, and the small stone embankment made for a neat enclosure.

A hearty atmosphere of excitement and energy buzzed through the proceedings. And Plum soaked it all up with pride. Another sell-out was surely on the cards, he thought with glee.

"Excuse me, sir," a voice barked behind him. "Where can I find Kal Klondike?"

Plum turned and came face to face with a distinguished-looking man in a black suit and bowler hat.

"Mr Klondike is out of town on business. He left me in charge. The name's Plum. Richie Plum."

The newcomer extended a hand. "Chester Martin. Mayor of Memphis. Pleased to make your acquaintance, Mr Plum."

"An honour, sir!" Plum beamed, gripping the hand firmly. "Welcome to Klondike's Circus. How may I be of service?"

Plum noticed a small entourage of associates behind the mayor, including a young woman incessantly making notes on a pad. "Thank you," said Martin. "And, might I add, welcome to Memphis." He looked around happily, nodding towards the goggles of children and teenagers trying to get close to the stars on the platform. "What a fantastic sight. We are all looking forward to the show on Saturday, Mr Plum."

"Got your tickets, sir?"

"I sure have!" he chuckled as he watched some of the youngsters going through a show programme that been handed out. "Been waiting a long time for this. Always a highlight of the summer, your circus."

"Is there anything I can do for you right now, your honour?"

The mayor giggled impishly, seemingly embarrassed. "Hell, son, I want to meet the star of the show. The guy whose face is on all the posters downtown. I…I think he is just incredible. My wife, too."

"Why, sure," Plum cried. He caught Shapiro's eye on the platform and beckoned him over. The trapeze artist said a few words to the gathered fans and vaulted over a metal bar onto the grass.

"Gino Shapiro, the debonair king of the air," Plum announced as he walked over. "Please say a big circus hello to his honour, the mayor of Memphis, Chester Martin."

Shapiro smiled widely. "Mr Mayor."

Martin grinned awkwardly. "A true pleasure, Mr Shapiro. Keep up the good work, now."

"Always, Mr Mayor. Enjoy our show."

Shapiro turned and shook hands with each of the mayor's followers. Martin crept up to Plum. "I was actually hoping to meet that ventriloquist fella," he whispered. "You know, the Puppetmaster."

Shapiro heard every word and turned, a look of bemusement on his face. Plum saw he had heard and thought for a moment. Before he could answer, Shapiro returned and spoke in an angry tone.

"Roddy Olsen," he said flatly. "Of course. The next big circus sensation."

Martin seemed unaware of any awkwardness. "Yes, yes, that's him."

Shapiro looked back to the platform. His voice was dour. "It appears our young Roddy is busy. Now, he runs. Back to the train. Trying to escape his adoring audience."

"Ah well, never mind," said the mayor. He looked at the train. "Mind if me and my people have a look around?"

"Sure. Go ahead," said Plum.

Martin shook hands with them both and then galloped away, followed by his team.

Shapiro watched them go, hands on hips. He turned to Plum, who tried to smile up at him.

"You know, little man," Shapiro said sternly. "You are good at bean counting. Numbers. Figures. Maybe you should stick to that, eh?"

With that, he wandered lazily back towards the crowd. His mood was somewhat appeased by a young woman suddenly lunging at him, asking if she could have her photo taken with him.

Plum could not help grinning. Truly, he was having the time of his life.

At that exact moment, the southbound Transcontinental Express was gathering pace as it sped out of New York state, heading for the Mid-Eastern states on its long, winding journey down to Texas.

In their private stateroom, Klondike, Heavy and Addison all watched Lacey as she sat in an armchair, knees raised up into her frame, staring at the window with relief.

Dressed in purple slacks and a pink sweater, she looked almost a different person to the one who had enchanted the New Yorkers the previous evening. But, as always, she still looked glamorous.

Klondike wandered across the room to her as he felt the wheels below them picking up speed. Outside, rows of houses and industrial sites whizzed past, soon becoming a blur.

He stood by the chair. Lacey's gaze was fixed on the world outside. He followed her stare. The mighty skyscrapers of the Big Apple were still just about visible in the mist enshrouding the horizon behind them.

"You alright?" he drawled.

"Fine, tiger," she whispered. She looked up at him and smiled. "Just watching New York disappear. I can't wait to leave that place behind. All the corruption. The filth. The crime." She visibly shook.

"There's a lot of good come outta New York too, y'know," he said. "Even me and Heavy!"

She raised her eyebrows in mock surprise. "All sorts of characters!" Then she looked back at the disappearing buildings. "Well, I'm just glad we're out of there now."

Heavy appeared next to her with a cup of coffee, made from a pot in the room's corner. "You really took one for the team last night, Lacey. None of us will ever forget it."

She ran a hand through her long, shiny hair, still styled from the previous night. Taking the coffee, she blew on it wistfully. "I will certainly never forget it, Henry. The night I became a spy."

Addison spoke from the far corner. "Truly, none of us will ever forget last night, Lacey. I am, well, in awe of what you did."

She batted a hand through the air. "Ah, come on guys."

Klondike looked back at Addison. "Well, our part of the show is over. Let's just hope your police captain does the rest, Daryl."

Addison nodded slowly. Then, Klondike looked out of the window at the skyscrapers disappearing behind them.

He said a silent prayer.

Paul Agostino was laughing to himself as he exited the Beaumont Club with Jimmy Felco and another of their goons following close behind.

A sleek black Cadillac had pulled up at the kerb and a chauffeur, dressed in a grey driver's outfit, had jumped out and was now opening the rear doors.

Agostino, in a dark suit with a beige trench coat draped over his shoulders, smiled at the chauffeur and prepared to duck into the car.

"Captain Agostino!" a stern voice called from behind him.

He hesitated, and turned slowly.

A large man with immense shoulders, a bullish neck and jaw and receding hair stood in front of the club, flanked by two equally intimidating characters in suits.

Agostino sneered. "What is this? I thought there was only two Brothers Grimm."

His two companions laughed.

The bullish man smiled thinly. "We haven't met. Allow me to introduce myself. Captain Dan Richards. NYPD." He opened up his trench coat to reveal a police badge.

Agostino glared at him, then the badge. He glanced at Felco, then shook his head.

"Something I can help you with, chief?"

Richards smiled with all the warmth of an Arctic wolf. "You could say that." He removed a piece of paper from a jacket pocket. "You're wanted down at the station for questioning. A rather interesting piece of media has come into our possession. Concerning you." He held up the paper. "This is a warrant. But I'd rather you come quietly. I'm sure you do too, Agostino. Right outside your club and all."

Agostino looked up and down the street. The confident demeanour had vanished. Now, he resembled a startled jackrabbit.

He snarled. "Listen. There must be some mistake, flatfoot. You need to speak to Captain DiGeorgio. Down at the Park Avenue Precinct. He'll set you right. We's old friends." He grinned. "It's alright, man. We all make mistakes."

He made for the car again. Richards' deep voice halted him. "You don't understand. DiGeorgio was reassigned."

Richards moved in close now, smiling devilishly. "And I'm his replacement."

Suddenly, Felco moved between them. "Hey, cop. You got it all wrong. Now get the hell out of here, less you want to lose your teeth."

Richards' two companions grabbed Felco by the shoulders, hauling him back. He shouted obscenities across the sidewalk as he struggled to free himself.

"Jimmy!" Agostino called out, quietening him. He held up a hand. Richards looked back at Felco. "Try anything like that again and I'll put you in a damn labour camp."

Agostino waved both hands in the air. "Ok, Captain. Ok. This has gone on long enough. Come on, now. I don't think you know who you're dealing with. You're new around here, so I forgive you. Let's just all forget about it and move on."

Yet again, he tried to climb into the car. This time, the policeman grabbed his shoulder, holding his arm in a vice-like grip.

"I know exactly who you are, Agostino," he whispered in a rasping tone. "Now, I don't want a scene out here in the street. But, god help me, I'll create a hornets' nest out here if I have to. Now…" he eyed Agostino with a steely stare as the gangster turned to face him. "Come with me into my car right now and down to the station. Or, I promise you, you're gunna be eating the asphalt. You follow?"

Agostino glared at him for several moments, a look of pure disgust masking his dark, scarred features. He locked eyes with Richards, then slowly nodded.

"Alright, cop. We'll do it your way. But, I tell you now, you're making a big mistake."

"That may well be," said Richards calmly. He led Agostino away from the Cadillac and pointed him in the direction of a brown Sedan at the end of the street. "We'll have to straighten it all out down at the precinct."

The other two policemen abandoned Felco and the other goon and followed behind Richards.

"Hey boss, what do I tell Palancio? And the other Capos?" Felco shouted at the departing group.

Agostino didn't answer. He merely allowed himself to be led to the Sedan. He was thinking frantically. A strange, unknown feeling was circulating through him.

And it was one of dread.

The Creole Club in downtown Memphis was filled to capacity that night. Every table of the jazzy, trendy dance joint was taken, and the bar area was jam-packed with well-dressed hepcats. Loud, swinging blues music blared out over the speakers, and the dance floor was equally busy, with bodies jiving across the vinyl flooring.

Gino Shapiro and Penny entered the club, both smiling broadly and nodding as various patrons recognised them and waved or called out.

In a ruffled white shirt and black leather pants, Shapiro looked like a matinee idol of sorts, while Penny wore a turquoise cocktail dress and looked equally eye-catching.

The duo made their way through the crowds, Shapiro trying delicately to place his arm around her, only for Penny to consistently shrug him off.

"Let's get a drink," Shapiro shouted above the blare of the music.

"That can wait," Penny said mischievously. Then, she grabbed his arm and pulled him after her. "I want to dance. This beat is out of sight."

"Sure, sweet cita."

They made their way into the pulsing mass of bodies on the overcrowded dance floor. Penny began twisting her body to the beat as Shapiro danced softly, swaying his feet happily.

As if on cue, they joined together as one, Shapiro pulling her close in a waltz-like movement. As he held her, they moved in time with the music, like professional dancers.

Then, with a flourish, Shapiro made to swing her out before him, holding her hand and propelling his arm rapidly. As she spun around as part of the move, Shapiro suddenly cried out aloud. Grimacing, he released her and grabbed at his shoulder. He bent over and rubbed at the joint, cursing to himself.

Penny stopped dancing, concern masking her face. She moved next to him and put an arm around his frame.

The patrons on the dancefloor stared in alarm at the scene for several moments. A semi-circle of bodies gathered around.

Then, Penny gently guided Shapiro out of the melee and they walked gently towards the bar.

"Let's get that drink now," she said in his ear.

"Si. And do I need it."

A bar steward brought over the icepack.

Shapiro nodded his thanks before snatching it off him, undoing several of his shirt buttons and shoving the freezing pack up against the skin of his shoulder blade. He gasped in a strange kind of pleasure as he rubbed the pack around inside the shirt.

Penny watched him gravely.

They were seated at a small table at the very far corner of the Creole Club, Penny having helped him over. Now, they were far from the music, the jiving bodies, the mayhem. They were strangely alone all of a sudden.

She sipped her cocktail, eyes riveted on Shapiro's face. He had his eyes closed and was whispering to himself in Spanish as he massaged the shoulder.

"Gino, I—"

"One moment." With his free hand, he fished into his pants pocket and pulled out a small plastic wrapper. From the wrapper, he retrieved a tiny silver pill and placed it on his tongue, before washing it down with a sip of his champagne.

"What the hell was that?" she demanded.

He held his head back, the pain very evident on every pore of his being. "A little helper," he murmured.

Within seconds, his eyes seemed to come to life again, and he held the icepack in one spot, his arm across his exposed chest to keep it in place.

"Listen, Gino," she said. "We can't ignore this anymore. This…shoulder problem is becoming more and more frequent. You told me before it snapped once a year. But this is, what, the fourth time this season?"

He knocked back more champagne. "What of it, Penny?"

"What of it?" she gasped in shock. "Jesus Christ, you're not going to have an arm left at this rate. The pain, the trauma…hell, this concerns me too don't forget. We depend on each other up there on the trapeze. How long is it before a disaster?"

Shapiro glared at her, grimacing still. "I have faced disaster before, damn it."

"And that crazy Cross woman almost killed you!"

"She was insane! How many times must I tell you!"

258

"And that almost cost you your shoulder! Surely, Gino, surely you can see it's just a matter of time before it happens!"

Shapiro shook his head insanely. "No, no, no. I am not hearing this talk, Penny."

She leant over to him, her eyes full of concern. She adopted a different approach. "Listen. I'm only telling you this because I care about you, Gino. I still care. You have the management. The talent. The fans, all the fans. But how many of them actually care about you. You! Gino Shapiro."

He gave the slightest hint of a nod. His dark eyes took in the wild, overpopulated dance floor set out before them. The blazing music made him shake.

Penny made a decision. She placed a hand on his free hand and spoke sincerely.

"Gino. I think you should retire."

He shook her hand off angrily. "I won't hear such talk, Penny. Retire! Puh!"

She inched closer. "You must retire to save yourself, Gino. Please! Think about what I'm saying."

He took several deep breaths, the hand with the icepack starting a massage pattern again. He looked at her, seemingly hurt. But his deep dark eyes had an almost hypnotic effect on her as he spoke. "You know my catchphrase? Diamonds are forever. And so is Gino Shapiro. Well, it is true. Listen to me when I tell you, Penny. I will never retire. Never! I am the star of the circus. The biggest circus in the country. Maybe in the world. And I will always be the star. My name at the top of the bill always. That is how it will always be. You know why? No? Because I need it!"

Penny backed off slightly as Shapiro's features took on a frenzied, almost animal-like look. "I need it like regular guys need oxygen. I need limelight. I need stardom. It's all I need to survive. I depend on it…cherish it. It is everything to me. You know this, I think. And it has always been this way with me. It is what makes me the greatest. The people…they love me. And I love entertaining them. Forever."

Her eyes were wide, disturbed, as she listened. "But at what cost?"

He grunted. "This…" he gestured at the shoulder and the ice pack. "This will not slow me down, signora. Oh no. I can handle it."

"What, by popping pills?"

259

He flashed an angry snarl at her. "As long as I'm the star, it does not matter. Whatever keeps me at the top, I don't care. I need…I need to stay at the top."

Penny's eyes suddenly glistened in a look of understanding. "It's him, isn't it?"

He glared at her. "Who? What is this you say?"

"Roddy Olsen. He's a threat to your crown here, isn't it? You are scared to death he will take your beloved spot at the top of the bill. Come on, Gino. It's no secret. You've admitted as much several times. With Roddy's TV appearances, his fan club, the teeny boppers…you've never been able to handle it."

Shapiro waved a hand through the air in disgust. "The dollmaker. He thinks he can take my spot? Puh!"

"But this is why you keep on going through the pain barrier, isn't it? You can't give up your top spot."

He shook his head angrily. "Alright, we all know I don't like the kid. But my need to perform goes beyond all that, Penny."

She was angry now. "That sweet boy treats you with nothing but dignity and respect. Even while you try to humiliate him. Why, oh why, can't you just get along with him? For real?"

He looked at her for a long moment. Then, he nodded in some kind of vague understanding. He closed his eyes. "Penny. I have been in the circus since I was 12 years old. In my father's Excelsior Show in Mexico. Tours to Europe. With my mother's family's circus in Italy."

"Me and my brother Nicky were flying on centre rings as teenagers. I made my big top debut at 15. You know it, the circus…the beautiful circus…it is in my blood. For life. I have forgotten more about the circus life than most people will ever know. And, hear me now, I tell you…"

He took a deep breath, looking almost sad. "Olsen is a talented performer. Of that, there can be no doubt. But his act, this dolls business…it has no place in a circus. Maybe on the midway. But under the bright lights, I tell you no. No!"

"Is that what this is all about? Tradition? Circus folklore?"

He leant back, grimacing at the pain in his shoulder. His eyes crept back to the sea of nightclubbers gathered before them.

When he spoke, his voice sounded bitter and twisted. "He is taking it all away from me." Then, he downed the rest of his champagne.

Penny looked at him, confused. "Taking what? The fans? The adulation? The attention?"

His eyes remained fixed on an unknown spot on the dancefloor. "La dolce vita…" he murmured sadly. "The sweet life. That sweet life that comes with being the star. The best of everything. The way people look at you, talk to you. Everything…"

She nodded, finally understanding. "There you go. Was that so hard?"

Still, he stared beyond her. Then, abruptly, he rose from the seat, holding the shoulder intently. "Come on. Let's get out of here!" She watched him for a moment, then jumped up and trotted after him as he lurched towards the exit.

Chapter Twenty-Five

The beautiful yellow and white circus tent was eerily quiet at dawn the following morning. Ribbeck's World Circus had pitched up in Wichita, Kansas, and the shiny great big top looked sparkling in the early morning sun as a slight breeze rippled through the canvassing.

Eric Ribbeck was seated alone on the front row of one of his wooden grandstands, surrounded by empty seats and a sea of sawdust.

He was staring dumbstruck at the front page of that morning's National Tribune.

NIGHTCLUB OWNER AGOSTINO ARRESTED! MAJOR LINKS TO ORGANISED CRIME!

Ribbeck swallowed heavily as he read the article. There didn't seem to be any explanations of evidence as yet, just a sea of allegations and rumours.

He thought frantically, trying to remember his last conversation with Agostino. How they had left things. It all seemed a blur now. With a nervous glance, he studied the pictures of Agostino on the inside pages. There were snaps of him with Sinatra and several wealthy New York socialites.

He continued reading, learning that Agostino had been the subject of some kind of sting operation.

Suddenly, there was a noisy commotion of some kind at the entrance flap to his left. Several voices shouted. He looked up irritably, tossing the paper aside.

"What the hell…" he rasped as he stood up, putting on his dark blue trench coat.

Luca Marconi came racing in, looking stunned. "Boss!" he cried. "Boss. You ain't gunna believe it! He's here! He's here!"

Ribbeck stared at him in shock. "Who's here, god damn it?"

"I am here!"

The booming voice from outside made him almost fall. But it was more the recognition of the accent that shook him than the actual pitch of the roar from outside.

Ribbeck and Marconi looked at the flap in horror as a huge man appeared in the doorframe. He was decked in his standard beige safari outfit and looked as if he had survived a forest fire, his skin covered in welts and scar tissue. The thick red hair and beard had grown, and he now resembled a figure from the realms of Viking folklore.

"Rance!" Ribbeck hissed, unable to stop staring at the newcomer, his eyes bulging at the man's shocking appearance.

Emile Rance walked slowly towards them, like a machine. Then, he stopped, just a few paces away. He said nothing, but looked at Ribbeck with wild, savage eyes.

The old circus boss could not help gaping at him, he looked so wild and ramshackle. "Rance," he said again, trying to regain some kind of composure. "What…where in hell have you been all this time?"

Rance stood like a statue, arms out wide beside him, fists clenching and unclenching. "Preparing."

Ribbeck shot a look at Marconi, then back at Rance. "Preparing? Preparing for what?"

"The attack on Klondike and his circus."

"What?" Ribbeck spat out. "What in god's name are you talking about? We had a plan. You remember that? You were supposed to wait. At the hideout. I was going to send for you when we needed you. You can't just disappear like that, damn it."

Rance shook his head. His voice was a dull monotone, devoid of emotion. "I began the plan! I went after Klondike. I am tired of waiting."

Ribbeck could not help taking small steps backwards. Something about the man was deeply unsettling. Even more than usual. Marconi was also slowly backing away.

"That damn lion attack of yours fouled everything up, Rance. You busted our plan up. You should've told me. Hell, you should've stayed in touch. Everything is a mess now."

Rance suddenly roared, sounding eerily like one of his lions. "He took Cassius away from me!"

At that moment, Ribbeck realised without any shadow of a doubt that the man was mad. He knew suddenly that there was nothing more to be said. Whatever partnership they may have had was expired. Long gone. No one could work with this.

He grabbed lightly at Marconi's arm as they took another step backwards.

"Shall I take him down?" Marconi whispered.

"Good god no! It's not us he wants."

Rance had remained still as the two men backed away. Suddenly, he threw his head back and raged at them. "I listened to you, Ribbeck! You said we would destroy Kal Klondike. You said we would cripple him. You made all those promises. And what has happened? Nothing! Why did I listen to you? Why?"

Rance threw his hands over his face in a demented gesture. He cried out aloud. "You have done nothing, Ribbeck! You only talk. That is all you know."

Ribbeck and Marconi were watching him in a kind of rapt fascination. It was like a character from a horror movie had crept into their big top. They were almost too paralysed to act.

"But me…" Rance was raging, his chest heaving as he got more and more aggressive. "I know. I know what to do. I know exactly what to do. Cassius may have failed. But I can stop him. I can stop Klondike. For good."

Then, he stood very still and looked across at Ribbeck. It was a look the older man would never forget. "And that," Rance snarled, "is a promise. And after it is over, then you can thank me." His eyes traversed across the interior of the grand circus tent. "You can all thank me. I…I am your saviour."

Then, in a flash, he was gone. Out of the flap, marching into the outside world.

Marconi made to run after him. Ribbeck grabbed his arm and pulled him to a stop.

"Let him go, Luca. Let him go."

"But, boss," Marconi rambled. "That son of a bitch is crazy. He shouldn't be out walking around like that."

"Just let the damn yahoo go. Out of here. Out of our lives. I don't want to hear of him again."

Marconi walked to the flap and stared out at the midway. "What do you think he meant?"

Ribbeck breathed slowly, his heart rate dropping again. "He wants Klondike's blood. Hell, that suits us."

"Boss, he looks like he just escaped from the loony bin. Dressed like some kinda safari hunter and all."

Ribbeck nodded, still deeply disturbed by what they had just witnessed. "A safari," he whispered. "Only this one has human prey."

Marconi grinned at that. Then he looked back outside again. "What do we do now, boss?"

Ribbeck thought for a moment, eyeing the newspaper he had discarded moments earlier.

"It would seem," he muttered quietly, "that we need to come up with a new strategy."

NIGHTCLUB OWNER AGOSTINO ARRESTED! MAJOR LINKS TO ORGANISED CRIME!

Lee Vesnick looked over the front page headline for the umpteenth time that morning.

Confused and ignorant, he had seen the news as an opportunity, not a problem.

He had arrived in New York on the red eye Greyhound. Ten of his last 12 bucks had paid for the ticket. He had planned on renegotiating some kind of deal with Agostino. Face to face.

Anything would do, he had decided. Even going to work for him as a knife man.

But now, on seeing this news, Vesnick's mind had swirled. He had formed a fresh plan, and one that should hopefully provide him with safety and comfort. Maybe accommodation and a new life. Certainly protection from the potential storm he felt brewing around him.

He was standing on the corner of 48th street in Manhattan. He carried a tote bag and his beloved knives satchel, and was dressed in his black leather jacket, jeans and a cotton shirt. And that was it. All he now had in the world.

Vesnick was cold, hungry and very alone. More alone than he had ever been in his life. The year he had originally envisaged for himself had imploded. Now, his dreams had turned into a nightmare.

Standing on the street corner, as scores of people and an endless stream of New York traffic soared past him, he looked up with a squint at the building before him.

Seventy-seventh Precinct. New York Police Department. With a final nod, he marched forwards, head down.

Vesnick pushed through a large glass door and jumped at the scene before him as a uniformed cop tried to calm down a frantic woman trying to attack an elderly man in the station foyer.

He walked purposefully to the reception desk, where a large man with a handlebar moustache looked down at him.

"Yes, young man?"

Vesnick took a deep breath. "I would like to speak to Captain Richards. I have information on the Paul Agostino case."

It was night-time when the cab pulled in at the Beale Recreation Ground in Memphis.

The whole field was lit up by tall floodlights and the neon tubing of the midway attractions.

"Well, I'll be damned."

Klondike climbed out of the taxi and stared in wonder and astonishment at the great green and purple big top that dominated the park. It looked like his old tent had been painted with fresh colours. The whole construction seemed to sparkle before him, and he felt the unusual sensation that he had stumbled into someone else's circus—despite his name being the one in lights.

He staggered out of the car and into the midway. Lacey and Heavy followed and Addison paid the driver, smiling as he gaped up at the new tent.

"Looks like old Zack Wurley came through for us," Heavy said as they all walked like brainwashed robots towards the green and purple behemoth.

"It's so beautiful…" Lacey mused as they inched closer.

Addison caught up with them, a broad grin dominating his face. "What did I tell you, Kal? Wurley meant what he said. He wants to protect the super show in Washington. Besides, he didn't need a spare tent. Now, just look at that big top."

Klondike was shaking his head in disbelief. "Incredible." For what seemed the umpteenth time, he put an arm around Addison and thanked him. "You've done it again, Daryl. How many times are you going to save us?" He eyed the tent again. "Just look at that beauty!"

Addison chuckled as they passed the midway shooting gallery. "I protect my investments. Especially the golden geese."

As they neared the tent, they saw the procession of shiny Cadillacs entering the circus through the flap. They had arrived as the finale, the grand parade, was concluding. The last convertible was just motoring in, barely moving as it rolled into the arena. They could see Shapiro and Penny dressed in their gold and orange showtime jumpsuits.

Heavy laughed. "Just in time for the final applause."

They walked briskly after the Cadillac and entered the great tent. The sight that greeted them was as breath-taking as ever.

The Cadillacs were trooping around in a circle, showcasing the performers, who waved at the cheering fans, all on their feet cheering in the stands, which seemed to stretch to the heavens above.

The applause had reached its height as Klondike and his friends walked in.

Suzi was just hitting the climax of Can You Feel The Magic Tonight? Her arms reached upwards as she belted out the last lines one more time, standing angel-like in her shiny white dress in the arena's centre.

Klondike looked up and around at the cheering fans, feeling their energy pulsing through him like electricity.

"It's good to be back," he bellowed at Lacey beside him. She nodded absently, lost in the moment. Her smile and cheery demeanour had returned, he noticed.

Then, Klondike caught sight of Richie Plum, standing coolly at the edge of the sawdust—the circus boss's spot.

Klondike moved up behind him and slapped him on the back. In an unexpected gesture, Plum hugged him, then Lacey and Heavy. Addison got a cool handshake.

"Business as usual, Richie," said Heavy happily, eyeing the enchantment around them. "Looks like you've done us proud."

"Had the time of my life," said Plum happily. "Just look at these fans. They love the circus."

Klondike nodded as he watched. The procession of Cadillacs was heading towards them for the final exit.

Then, Heavy's pre-recorded voice sounded over the tannoy system. "Ladies and gentlemen, we hope you have enjoyed the glamour, the razzmatazz and the sheer excitement of Klondike's Circus. And we hope you can feel the magic tonight. From all of us here, thank you so much for joining us and we hope to see you again further down the line. Next show is St Louis, one week tomorrow. Until then, goodnight…and god bless America."

The group at the flap watched, clapping enthusiastically as the cars drifted by, all of the performers greeting them as they left the show. Lacey unexpectedly rested her head on Klondike's shoulder. "You're right," she whispered. "It is good to be back. Back home."

Chapter Twenty-Six

Two days later, the circus train was roaring north through Tennessee and Kentucky on the way to St Louis, Missouri. It was a nine-hour journey and everyone was in good spirits.

Addison had agreed to join the crew all the way to Washington and seemed delighted to be involved in the day to day operation.

As the express raced through the Kentucky backwoods towards Olgarth, many performers had gathered in the lounging carriage to relax and enjoy the jovial atmosphere.

Klondike wandered in through the inter-carriage door and smiled as he saw everyone sat in the easy chairs chatting.

Olsen, Suzi and Corky were all telling a story, with a captive audience of Goliath, Gargantua, the Batistas, several of the Range Rider cowboys and even Penny, who, like Gino, rarely socialised with the majority. Several of the Daredevils were also on hand, standing in the corner by the coffee maker.

"Here he is!" Suzi squealed as Klondike walked in. They all clapped heartily. Klondike waved them off.

"The coolest-looking crimcfighter I ever saw," said Corky.

"Yeah, we're gunna have to start calling you Dick Tracey," said Penny.

Klondike nodded. "Yeah. Well, let's just see what happens. But, like I said, the real hero is Lacey. She pulled the whole thing off."

"Are you sure she is alright?" asked Olsen.

Klondike looked at him. "She's fine, kid. Resting. In her room."

"Well," Corky said buoyantly. "We'll all buy her a drink up in St Louis. No doubt."

A few of the others cheered loudly.

Klondike nodded. "Listen," he barked, "I'm a little behind with admin and meetings and such. Does anyone have anything they'd like to raise with me? Any problems, worries or the like?"

A room of blank faces all looked up at him as the wheels rolled on smoothly beneath them in the carriage.

He grinned. "Hell, that's how I like it. See you all in St Louis." With that, he wandered off and through the inter-carriage door.

There was silence for a moment. Then, Suzi looked around, exasperated. "So…now, where was I?"

Gargantua answered. "You was just saying about all those guys performing in Wurley's Circus. How you know em. And, er, how we'll see them in Washington."

"Oh, right…" Suzi continued telling her story for several moments. Then, a steward walked in from the outer carriage behind them. He had a piece of paper in his hand.

"I have a telegram here for Mr Klondike."

Suzi halted her story once again. With a mock roll of her eyes, she greeted the newcomer. "I'll make sure he gets it."

Klondike was sat at his desk, reading the morning papers. He had seen the National Tribune's coverage of the Agostino arrest. Now, he was desperate to accumulate as much knowledge of the case as possible. He had paid a newsboy to buy a copy of every paper in town before they'd left Memphis that morning.

Now, he sat back as he leafed through America Today, blindly groping for his coffee cup.

A separate pile held all the local papers, holding the reviews of the Memphis show.

A third pile of file paper held Plum's latest figures and a few of his 'managerial notes' from the weekend.

For once, though, all that would have to wait. Klondike only wanted to read about Agostino in New York.

His fingers found the handle of his cup and he pulled it over absently, sipping the steaming liquid.

Outside, on either side of him, the giant windows showed the luscious green Kentucky countryside rolling by as the train maintained a steady cruising speed.

Klondike put his cup down again, absorbed in a feature about Agostino and his famous nightclub. He leant back in the thick leather chair.

He did not hear the door push open.

"Finally, I find you."

Klondike almost leapt out of his chair at the unexpected voice before him. He dropped the newspaper to the desk and looked up. His surprise turned to abhorrent shock and astonishment as he took in the grizzled figure stood directly ahead, like an apparition from his worst nightmares.

"Rance!"

Klondike stared in fright and sheer amazement. His former lion tamer and animal trainer was here. In his office.

Emile Rance looked like he had been living in the wild. Klondike shook his head in horror. He had not seen the South African in two years. Not since that dreaded, horrific night in Munson, California, when his beloved train had crashed. He could still remember the eerie sight of Rance racing off into the night, chasing his escaped lions. The fear he had felt as the animals disappeared into the civilian world hit him again now.

He studied Rance now with wild, unblinking eyes. The lion man was dressed in his old circus attire of a beige safari outfit. His red hair and beard were wavy and unkept. It was a surreal, unsettling sight.

"Finally, I find you…" the intruder repeated.

"Jesus Christ!" Klondike rasped. "What in god's name are you doing here, Rance? Where have you been all this time? And how in hell did you get on my train?"

Rance stared at him with cold, dead eyes. He stood perfectly still, casting a shadow over half the room. "None of that matters. All that matters is this…this moment. This moment I have waited for…for so long."

Klondike thought rapidly, looking around his desk in desperation. "Why didn't you ever contact me, dammit?"

Rance took a step towards the desk. "You've killed all my lions now, damn you!"

Klondike squinted at him. "I knew it! You set that beast upon me in Houston! What in hell were you thinking? We could've been killed!"

There was no response, just that cold, emotionless stare behind the beard. Klondike looked into the man's eyes. "What do you want here, Emile?"

Rance snarled at him. "What I have wanted for two years." He shook his head slightly. "To watch you die!"

That did it. Klondike pushed his chair back and shot up. He made to push his way around the desk, determined to attack the madman.

In a lightning move, Rance reached behind him and pulled a handgun, holding it before him as if he was on a target range. Klondike froze in mid-step, staring at the gun in dismay. They were six feet apart.

"Your days are over, Caesar."

Klondike frowned. "What did you call me?"

"Caesar. The way you run your empire, and all within it. All hail Caesar!"

Klondike tried to think. Rance held the gun with a steady hand. He could see inside the nozzle.

"You're crazy!"

"I am right!" Rance yelled, suddenly looking sad. "I am just. And I am vengeance." Suddenly, he seemed to explode. "You took them away from me! My beauties! My life! My everything! It was you, Kal Klondike. All you. You and your circus. Damn you all the way to hell."

Klondike raised his hands, palms outwards. "OK. Listen, Emile," he said smoothly. "This isn't the way to do this. We…we can settle this. The proper way. Come on! No one needs to die."

"You're wrong, Caesar," Rance said bitterly. "You need to die. For what you did to my family."

At that moment, the door swung silently open again at the head of the room. Klondike saw Suzi enter the carriage, behind Rance. It was obvious she had heard part of the exchange and had crept in cautiously.

Klondike kept his eyes firmly on Rance, not letting on that someone was behind him. He could see Suzi was carrying something in her hand. And she was slowly creeping up behind the gunman.

"Alright," Klondike spluttered, trying to stall Rance. "Why don't you just go ahead and kill me. But, before you do, there is something you have to know."

Suzi was two yards behind him now. She looked absolutely petrified as she crept closer.

Rance was confused. The gun remained steady. "What? What must you tell me?"

Klondike tried to stay cool. Suzi was almost on him. She raised her hand. He saw now that she was carrying a megaphone. The type McCabe used to call out to his roustabouts during rollout.

"A secret," he said quietly.

"Secret? What is it?"

Klondike gulped. "Your lions. They are still alive!"

"What!"

Suzi brought her hand crashing down as hard as she could. Due to the size difference, her tiny wrist barely reached Rance's shoulders. But, crucially, she smashed the metal megaphone into the big man's cervical vertebrae.

Rance wailed like a stricken animal and plunged forward.

Klondike was ready. Quick as a cat, he stepped to his left and palmed the gun hand away from him. As Rance tumbled into him, he grabbed the arm and slammed it with all his strength into the cabinet next to them. The shiny handgun fell to the floor and rolled underneath the desk.

Klondike kept a hold of Rance, clutching his shirt. He turned to Suzi. "Get help!" he bellowed.

The girl was out of the door in a second.

Klondike leant the dazed Rance against the cabinet. He had forgotten how big the man was. He closed his fist and sent a lightning fast cross into the intruder's jaw.

Rance's head snapped back. But, when it came forward, the eyes were wide and angry. Klondike moved a pace back and sent two hard jabs into his ribs. Rance gasped and spluttered in pain. He groped wildly, still reeling from the megaphone blow.

Klondike was relentless. He slammed another blow into Rance's solar plexus, then rammed an uppercut into his face as he buckled over. It was like punching an elephant.

Klondike stepped back again, his breath coming in uneven gasps. Rance wiped at his bloodied nose. He looked stunned, and wild as hell. Klondike took up a classic boxing stance. He threw a hook.

This time, Rance put out a strong hand and caught the blow. He crushed Klondike's hand in his own, causing the circus manager to cry out in alarm. Then, in an unexpected show of velocity, Rance threw his other hand at Klondike's midsection and, suddenly, with alarming strength, he picked him up, clean off his feet.

Grabbing Klondike's belt for support with one hand and clutching his collar with the other, Rance lifted him clear above his head like a wrestler. Then, with a hideous roar, he hurled Klondike across the room like a doll.

Klondike flew through the air and crashed thunderously into his beloved desk, slamming onto its surface before barrel-rolling off it and onto the floor beyond. Papers and stationary, even his coffee, exploded into the air.

Klondike felt like he had gone through a cement mixer. He sprawled onto the red carpet, rolled slightly, then led on his back, breathing wildly. Papers covered him from head to foot.

He finally pulled at the edge of the desk and hauled himself to a crouch. Looking up, he saw Rance rushing out of the room.

Watching in stunned disbelief, he saw him head out of the window in the interchange and make for the train roof.

Shaking the cobwebs free from his head, Klondike gingerly got to his feet. He looked about for the gun, but it was nowhere to be seen among the carnage all over the floor.

He raced to the door and headed into the interchange platform. Thrusting his head out of the opened window, he was just in time to see Rance climbing smoothly onto the roof of the fast moving carriage.

Klondike did not even stop to think. Despite the insane rush of air pulling at his clothes, the trees and quarries racing by at boundless speed, he pulled himself out into the open and stood on the window ledge, before grabbing at the side of the train's outer roof beams and pulling himself clumsily upwards.

The atmosphere was giddy and the stream of air almost overpowering. He hauled himself up and, throwing his right leg up onto the beam, slowly shuffled onto the roof of the carriage.

Clinging on as the vacuum of cold air ripped at his skin, he was shocked to see no sign of the madman.

Shaking his head, he looked down. The railroad pilings hurtled along below. He rose to a crouching position, staring down the long and winding line of the carriage roofs that spread out before him like a pathway.

Suddenly, the blustering air was punctuated by a savage roar. Klondike turned, just in time to see Rance diving through the air and crashing into him. It was like being hit by a battering ram. The shock sent Klondike sprawling, and he almost fell clean off the carriage, his head and shoulders going over the side.

Then, Rance was on top of him. Pinning him down helpless with his immense weight and power, the lion tamer clamped his meaty hands around Klondike's neck. Then, he began to squeeze.

Klondike immediately felt himself blacking out. The stranglehold coupled with the relentless vacuum of air ravaging his face made it impossible to see straight.

He was hanging over the side of the speeding train as Rance led on top of him, his hands mercilessly encircling his neck and squeezing. With his remaining strength, Klondike shuffled his legs and brought his left knee up fast, thrusting it straight into his attacker's groin.

That broke the grip. Rance cried out and rolled over, to the roof's centre, clutching himself in agony.

Klondike rubbed at his neck and felt himself coming back to life. He pulled himself back, away from the edge.

He led there, breathing wildly and looking at Rance. The big man rolled away further, cursing to himself.

Then, a curious thing happened. Both men slowly rose to their feet. Rance to his full height. Klondike, dazed and struggling for breath, into a squatting stance.

Then, with a battle cry of pure terror, Rance charged at him like a rabid bull. As he hurtled across the roof, Klondike suddenly realised his plan—he would kill them both in one final death charge. He subconsciously realised they were travelling over a bridge, which sat raised above an old rock quarry with ravines that slipped far, far below. They both would die, sent tumbling off the train by the power of Rance's drive.

Like an enraged buffalo, Rance came thundering up to him on the roof of the racing train. But Klondike was ready for him.

As his attacker swept into him, he flipped onto his back, grabbing Rance's shirt collar and placing a foot into his midriff.

With immaculate timing, he dropped onto his back on the very edge of the carriage roof and hurled Rance over him, using the man's pace and power against him to send him flying over his fallen frame and straight off the roof.

Rance's eyes blazed in horror as he went over Klondike and flew through the air. He seemed to be suspended in mid-air for a moment alongside the speeding train, before dropping like a stone into the ugly quarry beneath.

Klondike managed to roll over and watch the final moment of Emile Rance's life as the South African lion tamer fell down, down, down and into a deep, gravelly ravine. His trademark beige outfit seemed to blend into the brown gravel as he was swallowed up.

Then, the train was over the bridge and away, ploughing alongside a giant swamp, the quarry behind them.

Klondike led on the roof in stunned silence. The relentless rush of air was overpowering as the train raced on.

He rolled on to his back and closed his eyes. "Oh my God," he rasped.

The next few hours represented a surreal episode for Kal Klondike. A foreign world, the normalities of which he was not accustomed.

Suzi Dando had raised the alarm, and the train duly slowed and stopped a few miles after the quarry, eventually rumbling to a standstill at a rural station stop serving a town called Ansecola. An immediate call was put in to the sheriff's office. Klondike announced an immediate emergency meeting of all staff at the station forecourt. There, he tried to explain what had happened. The whole thing was like something out of a nightmare. His own people didn't even believe him.

Afterwards, seeing as how they would need to hole up in Ansecola for a little while, everyone—all staff, roustabouts and performers—was given a free pass to do as they pleased, either in the town or back on the train.

Klondike met with the town sheriff, Luke Easton, at a small office within the railway station complex. Easton had dispatched a team of deputies, along with an ambulance crew, to the rock quarry to search for the body.

"Alright, alright," Easton drawled as they sat in the small dispatcher's office. The sheriff glanced down at his notebook, having interviewed several members of the circus team already. "So, Mr Kal Klondike. Operator and owner of Klondike's Circus. Now, y'all say you were attacked in your train car by this, er, Emile Rance. Who used to work as your lion tamer. Until he disappeared two years ago. You say he…that he came back to your circus. Looking for revenge. For the death of his lions?"

Easton looked at him with dismay written all over his features. Klondike sighed. There it was again. That look. Worn by an official of authority. Just like back in Houston, and in so many other towns. That look…seemingly reserved solely for circus folk such as Klondike. Almost mocking in nature. As if its wearer cannot believe that there is crime and malice in men and women who go from town to town entertaining, clowning, selling candyfloss.

"That's right." Klondike tried to hide his bitterness. His mind was already over-active after the fight with Rance. The fatal fight.

"He came back to kill you? To shoot you?"

"So it would appear."

"But why wait so long? After all this time?"

"Listen, sheriff. It was fairly obvious to me that Rance had lost his mind. I saw it in his eyes. He's gone crazy. Ranting and raving about his lions. He blames me for everything."

"And he suddenly just appeared…out of nowhere. In your office."

Klondike shuddered. "I couldn't believe it. I didn't know he was still alive. Or in this country."

The sheriff leaned forward, excited. "Yet you knew that it was his lion what attacked y'all in Houston? You said you killed his lion in self-defence! Now ain't that so?"

"Well, yes. But he admitted he set it upon me and Miss Tanner. He meant to kill us."

"All this talk of lions wandering around is kinda hard to believe."

Klondike glared at him. "You think this is all fiction, sheriff?"

"Alright, alright." Easton cooled slightly. "Now, you say he pulled that gun on you and then this singer gal hit him?"

"Right. Then I knocked the gun to the floor."

"This gun?" The sheriff held aloft a small cellophane bag with the shiny handgun inside.

Klondike marvelled at the weapon. "Yeah."

Sheriff Easton nodded, scribbling more notes and absently rocking back and forth in his chair. "OK," he finally said. "OK. Now, this is a tough old pickle to straighten out, Mr Klondike. We'll have the gun checked for prints. The boys are down at that rock quarry looking for the body of this here Rance fella. God help them. We've got a witness to his actions in this Suzi gal. But…" he looked up, squinting at Klondike. "Fact of the matter is, boy, you just killed a man."

Klondike stared back at the man in the Stetson. His eyes took in the gleaming tin star at his breast. "I'm very aware of that."

Easton nodded. "Good. Cause we's might have some more questions for you. Real soon."

"Am I free to go, sheriff?"

He thought for a moment. "Yes. Just stay this side of state lines."

"We have a show on Saturday in St Louis. Is that alright?"

The sheriff gazed out the window. "That's just fine. You let me have the telephone number in that office of yours though."

"Sure."

They got up together and walked out into the forecourt. An old man, who was sweeping the sidewalk, seemed to be the sole employee of the railroad stop. Everyone was either back on the train, parked behind them, or wandering through town.

"This is a small, simple town," Easton was saying quietly as they walked. "Maybe a burglary now and then. A bar fight in town. A little fraud. You get the idea." He stopped and eyed Klondike with suspicion. "We ain't never had nothing like this. Circuses. Lions. Madmen pulling guns. A fight on top of a train." He shook his head and spat onto the asphalt. "No sir. Something like this…a drama, if you like…hell, it could stir up a hornet's nest in a simple town like this."

Klondike looked at him blankly. "What are you trying to tell me?"

Sheriff Easton stared out at a fixed spot in the hills beyond. He sighed. "Get your people together and get the hell out of here, Klondike. I'll call you if and when I need you. Just don't you make me come up there to St Louis to get you, ya hear?"

Klondike nodded. "I hear you."

With that, he turned sharply and merely walked away, back to his train.

The roustabouts managed to round everyone up within an hour, and the train was soon rolling north again.

Heavy and Lacey were helping Klondike put his office back together again after the fight earlier. A strange, subdued atmosphere gripped the plush stateroom.

As Klondike poured them all a glass of Scotch, Heavy gathered together all of the many pieces of paper that covered the carpet. "I guess we'll never know…know what was going through his mind," Heavy was saying absently as he checked each paper, forming a new pile on the desk.

Klondike handed him a glass, before sipping his own drink. "His mind had gone. Of that there can be no doubt."

Lacey was visibly shaken. "Oh lord," she gasped as she dusted down the carpet. "When will it all be over? All of this madness! When will it end?"

"What the hell else can happen?" Heavy blurted.

Lacey shuddered. "My…it's like we're cursed this season."

"And yet," Klondike barked, holding his glass aloft, "on we go. Still in one piece. Sell-out show after sell-out show. All the way up to Washington."

Heavy tried to smile. "Nothing can derail us, eh Kal?"

"Come on, boys," Lacey cried. "We are a circus. Not a crack team of crimefighters. Why, oh why, is all this happening to us?"

"I said it once before," Klondike said quietly. "We are a success. People don't like success stories. You create rivals. Conspirators. Enemies. And some will stop at nothing to nail you."

Lacey was still shaking slightly. "I can still see that lion, back in Houston. How it came at us. I've never been so frightened." Her giant violet eyes locked onto Klondike. "And now this! He was here! Emile Rance was here!"

Klondike swallowed the Scotch and looked out the windows with a cold, angry snarl. When he spoke, his voice was uncharacteristically bitter. "That son of a bitch is with his lions now. Forever."

Heavy and Lacey looked at him, shocked at the grim finality of his words.

At that moment, Addison burst into the stateroom, waving a telegram in his hands.

"Hey folks. Wait till you see this!"

Lacey shook her head. "Oh Daryl, dear. We can't cope with any more shocks. What in god's name is it now?"

Addison raced across the carriage and joined the others by the desk. "You're not going to believe this," he said, somewhat breathless. "I just heard from my man in New York. Agostino has been charged. Arson and intimidation. And…conspiracy to commit murder. He's just been given a trial date."

The others stared at him in shock. "Murder?" Klondike rasped. "What the…"

"Yes, yes," Addison said quickly. "All due to the fire in Houston. Lacey here managed to get the key words from him. He admitted it, then said he had wanted to start the fire when the tent was full."

"That big top was full of children, families," Heavy said. "They are gunna nail him for this."

Klondike grabbed Lacey by the arm. "You did it, Lacey! That tape has changed everything."

"It sure has," Addison said. "Without that tape, Agostino wouldbe free as a bird. Now, the cops have plenty to pin on him. And he's already confessed to it."

"Incredible," Heavy mused, his eyes wide with wonder.

"And you haven't heard the funny part yet," Addison said, barely able to contain himself. "It has been reported that the final nail in Agostino's coffin was a key testimony…brought on by one Lee Vesnick!"

A joint gasp rattled through the carriage as everyone drew a deep breath.

"Vesnick!" Klondike snapped. "So he was in on it the whole time. Just like we said. Unbelievable."

"Looks like he decided hooking up with Agostino wasn't the way forward though," Heavy muttered.

Addison nodded. "Yes. So he turned on him and went to the police. It could be that he learned plenty about Agostino and his cronies." The three men were practically jubilant by now.

But Lacey just could not return to normal. The eyes had lost their sparkle. Ever since New York. She slowly sat down in an armchair in the corner. The room went very quiet as they watched her.

Klondike walked over with the bottle and poured her a generous top up. She gulped more of the brown liquid down. "It's all too much to take in," she whispered, awestruck. "What have I done?"

"You've helped stop a madman," Heavy said loudly. "Thank god."

Addison was nodding rapidly, still holding the telegram. "You've done your civic duty, Lacey. You've probably saved lives, truth be told. You've done us all proud, that's for sure. And what's more…" he smiled down at her beautifully. "You have saved the circus."

She nodded absently, the eyes still wide with fright.

"And now," Klondike said softly, tapping her hand gently, "I think it is safe to say…it's over. It's all over, Lacey."

She suddenly jumped up and hugged him, arms clamped around his neck. He held her, closing his eyes.

"It's all over."

They finally reached St Louis at nightfall.

The train slowly rumbled down the branch line to the Sinton Centre, a sports complex whose football field would host the big top and midway.

As it was so late, the full unloading of the equipment, stalls and tent accessories would commence the next morning.

But, as everyone piled out of the train after the long, arduous voyage, Klondike headed for a small platform that ran alongside the end of the line. Earlier, he had spread the word that he wanted to say a few words on arrival.

Now, he stood atop the small stone embankment and waited for all the talent and roustabouts to gather round.

Lacey, Heavy, Plum and Addison stood just beside him on the platform as the train's passengers all gathered before them by the sports centre.

Klondike surveyed the sea of faces before him. The talent all seemed to group together at the front, with the roustabouts at the back and sides. The usual set-up. His people looked tired, weary and confused.

The boss held his arms out. "Alright, folks. Thank you for coming over to hear me out. I appreciate it. It's been a helluva train ride." He looked out at the football field beyond. Huge posters advertising the circus were hung everywhere, filling noticeboards, walls and the gates to the field. They seemed to sparkle in the moonlight. He tried to smile.

"You all know by now what happened out there on the train. Well, I'm still struggling to come to terms with it myself. Another attack, yes. This time a fatality. Another crazy incident. Another moment of madness on this unbelievable season. But, folks, and this is very important, I want to stress that this…this was the last attack. The final chapter. I know it is hard to believe that so many people would want to hurt us…would want to hurt the show. That a man would want to kill me, right there in my office. But…" he tried to sound uplifting. He felt weak and doubtful. "But it's over. It's all over, folks. Please believe me. The most important thing for all of us right now is Saturday night out there on the football field. Another capacity crowd. Another sell-out. Another spectacular on our road to Washington. This is our destiny…this is our triumph. And, dammit it all to hell, we will succeed."

Holding his fist aloft, he had expected a rousing cheer and cries of elation. He should have known better. The sea of faces stared back at him, many in bemusement.

"So, what, chief…that lion man is just being wrapped up and sent to the morgue, and we are expected to just carry on with the next show?"

It was Tip Enqvist. Stood at the front, arms folded, he looked wired. Aggressive. Klondike frowned. The stunt rider seemed to enjoy confrontation.

"Well, Tip," he said slowly. "What else would you have us do? Let a madman finish the circus for good? You want us all to pack up and stop just because of a crazed killer?"

Enqvist snarled up at him. "We are a circus, damn it. People are being attacked, killed now, and you're taking on mobsters in New York. Does this all sound normal to you, Kal?"

Klondike looked down at him coolly. "No, it doesn't, Tip. But these people, all together, have been trying to break us. Trying to stop us performing. And we've shaken them off at every turn. We owe it to ourselves, as well as the fans, to keep going."

"I think what Mr Klondike is trying to say..." Lacey chimed in, moving slowly alongside Klondike. "Is that the circus fans, our beloved customers, have spent the year waiting to see us in their locality. We cannot ever let them down. That would be a betrayal." She eyed Enqvist shrewdly. "Think of all the children in their Daredevils replica outfits. All waiting to see you and your boys. All across the Eastern states. You are their heroes. And you want to let them down because of...because of bandits?"

For the hundredth time in the past two years, Klondike thanked the heavens that Lacey Tanner had come into his life.

Enqvist shifted slightly. Everyone in the group stared at him.

"A man died," he mumbled, still looking angry. "That's all I'm saying."

Klondike squinted down at him. "I'm well aware of that. He meant to kill me."

An uneasy silence settled over the group. Klondike looked at the faces. Suzi, stood by Olsen at the front, had tears in her eyes.

Others seemed distant, almost afraid.

"Listen," he bellowed, "everything's going to be alright. We've just got to keep going, keep giving it our all and...and, I..."

"We are the heroes!" Lacey suddenly cried, addressing the gathering like a political leader. "Our lives are not mapped out and lived like other mortals. We are beloved. You are beloved...by thousands of fans across the country. It is our job to be the heroes. To inspire and give the people the joy and excitement they get from attending the circus. That is our mandate. Granted, it is not a normal life. But, hell, none of us signed up for a regular lifestyle. We signed up for a circus life. For adventure. For risks. And, well, when you're the best damn circus in the world, risks are part and parcel of your life."

This seemed to go down well with the majority. There were still no cheers and whoops. But everyone seemed to nod and murmur a response in the affirmative. Klondike nodded at Lacey, who smiled her own delicious smile.

Corky was the next to speak up. "It's alright, Kal. We're just all a little shaken up by all this."

Shapiro, stood in front of everyone, nodded. "Who wouldn't be?" He looked up at Klondike. An unspoken understanding seemed to pass between them. "Nothing affects a performance, Chairman. Nothing! I speak for everyone, methinks, when I say we will all be fine and ready to go come Saturday."

Klondike pumped his fist. "That's the spirit."

Penny Fortune took a step forward. "Won't all this publicity affect the crowds? The fire, all the trouble on the road, and now this? A man killed falling off the train?"

A curious, dry laugh emanated from Lacey. "Darling girl. There is an old saying in showbusiness. No publicity is bad publicity. All of these horrors will only attract more interest in what we are doing."

Klondike looked at his publicist. She was suddenly back to her old self. Just like that. It was extraordinary.

Olsen spoke next. "Well, it has certainly been a season unlike any other. I guess all we can do is make sure we end it right. On a high!"

"Damn straight, kid," Heavy roared, joining Klondike and Lacey at the front of the platform. "We can do it! Starting in three days right here in St Louis!"

Everyone murmured their approval at this. It seemed an ideal point to end the meeting.

Klondike held up a hand and offered his thanks to everyone for attending as the crowd dispersed, with the team slowly heading back to the train just yards away.

As everyone lurched wearily towards the comfort of the Barrowman Express, Klondike leapt off the platform and subtly motioned for Shapiro, Olsen and Enqvist to hang around. The three performers looked at him, glared at each other, and loitered by the platform.

Klondike positioned himself between them.

"Alright guys," he said quietly, "we're in the home straight for this season now. I need you three to lead by example and keep it professional. Remember, you guys are top billed for Washington. The spotlight is about to get brighter than ever."

Shapiro rolled his head back, as if amused. "The spotlight on me is always red-hot, chairman. Gino Shapiro can handle it."

Enqvist looked around, still angry. "Don't worry about me and my boys, Kal. We know too well how important that show is."

Klondike turned to Olsen. The kid looked like a high school student, dressed in a sky blue anorak and jeans. He looked up and smiled. "Why, I can't wait for Washington, Mr Klondike. It will surely be our finest hour."

Klondike grinned. "That's the spirit, kid." He studied the youngster. "Jesus. Nothing ever phases you does it?"

Olsen looked back to the train, where people were still climbing back onboard. "I've seen the worst, Mr Klondike. All this, everything, the circus…this is a dream."

Enqvist laughed bitterly. "You're full of garbage, kid." He glared at Klondike. "Was there anything else?"

Klondike frowned at him. "No. That was all."

With that, the stunt rider stormed off down the pathway. Shapiro watched him for a moment, then said a solitary farewell to Klondike and headed for his stateroom.

Olsen hovered awkwardly by the platform. Klondike stood beside him. "Think we'll ever get you three around a table again?" he asked.

Olsen shrugged. "We're all very different, I guess. All with a different point of view."

"And all at the top of the bill. My three aces."

The two stood there in the night for several moments, admiring the train before them.

"Did you mean it, what you said earlier," Olsen whispered. "That it's all over now? All this violence?"

Klondike looked at him. "Hell yeah."

"I sure am sorry you've had to put up with all this, Mr Klondike. I wish none of it had ever happened."

"Listen Roddy," Klondike breathed. "You just keep on doing what you've been doing under my big top. All the way up to Washington. People love you. Kids, women, working men, the elderly. And that's a hell of an accomplishment. Leave the behind the scenes stuff to me and my team. We'll deliver you to the people."

"You and Miss Lacey…"

Klondike smirked slightly. "That's right."

"You both mean the world to me, Mr Klondike. You know that."

He took a deep breath. "And we care about you a great deal, son. We love having you in our troupe. Hell, we're all like a family."

Olsen slowly began to move away. He half-turned as he walked into the night.

"That's something I always wanted as a kid."

Chapter Twenty-Seven

Kal Klondike's carefully chosen words turned out to be quite prophetic.

As the circus train slowly headed East, the big top continued to play out to capacity crowds. And, indeed, there was little incident. Certainly not like before.

The Barrowman Express rolled relentlessly on, from city to city, as Klondike's Circus continued its cross-country route.

Indianapolis, Cincinnati, Cleveland, Buffalo, Boston, Philadelphia and then on to Pittsburgh.

The troupe was greeted at each stop by the obligatory gathering of fans. The youngsters were still there, dressed as their heroes. Local dignitaries fell over themselves to meet the performers.

And each show was a smash.

Then, before they knew it, they were heading to Washington. Just two days after the New York show at the Fairfax Centre, the train was heading south again for the extra date in this season's diary. Superstars and Stripes. The big one.

Despite all the trouble along the way, the many obstacles overcome, Klondike's Circus had defied the odds and made it to Washington.

And waiting for them would be a sight, a spectacular, the likes of which none of them had ever dreamed.

WASHINGTON GRIPPED BY CIRCUS FEVER!
By Jim Ballinger, Washington Sentinel

The nation's capital is all set to celebrate this year's Independence Day with a red, white and blue bash straight out of wonderland.

Superstars and Stripes is a circus spectacular, and an historic night for all in question.

For this show brings together a 'supercard' of talent gleaned from three different circus promotions.

Klondike's Circus, Wurley's Circus and Chico's Circus have all joined forces to create this one-off special, with performers from all three shows set to appear.

Superstars and Stripes is the brainchild of Las Vegas casino owner Claude Hershey, with the event to be broadcast live on ATV.

Mr Hershey said: "This is a completely unique, one-off circus spectacular. As the United States celebrates our Independence Day, we have put together a stunning line-up of entertainers for a special, purely patriotic showpiece. I can guarantee no one will be disappointed."

The superstars on show are some of the biggest names in the circus world today.

From Klondike's, there will be trapeze sensation Gino Shapiro, ventriloquist Roddy Olsen, motorcycle stunt crew The Daredevils and beloved clown Corky.

From Chico's, we have legendary clown troupe the Chiquettes, the all-female acrobatic troupe The Hightops and monkey trainer Sam Lentini.

And from Wurley's, there is cowboy Duke Anderson, knife throwers the Kershwin Brothers, trapeze flyers the Van Horn Family and strongman Hans Erlinger.

And, as a special surprise, ringmaster for the night is TV's own Lloyd Masters.

It is a breath-taking line-up and, with tickets selling out weeks ago, a lively atmosphere is guaranteed.

Now, where's my candy floss…

The tent itself was as much of a spectacle as anything that would proceed within it.

Made up of hundreds of large American flags, all seemingly sewn together at great care, it was as patriotic a sight as anyone could remember ever seeing.

Superstars and Stripes was to take place inside this mammoth red, white and blue big top, erected within Washington Polo Grounds.

Now, the men and women of Klondike's Circus wandered around the great behemoth, enthralled by the spectacle before them.

The sawdust beneath their feet felt like fur, and looked like gold filings.

Everything looked pristine, beyond perfect.

Klondike waded over to the tent's edge and delicately felt the fabric. "Man alive, they sewed all these old glories together," he said in awe.

Heavy and Richie were with him. "What a great idea," said Heavy.

"Makes me feel patriotic," Plum put in.

They turned at the sound of a thunderous laugh.

There he was. Claude Hershey. Grinning like a jester as he approached, the million dollar casino king in a tanned suit. He shook hands with the three men warmly.

"Hell, you made it Kal. Heavy. Richie. Can't tell you how glad I am to see you and your boys."

"It's a great pleasure to be here, Claude," said Klondike, still gaping at the tent. "This is spectacular. Look at this place. You really pulled out all the stops here."

"But of course." Hershey looked like a proud farmer whose crops had met a record yield. He ran a hand through the air. "It was put together by my uncle's textile factory in Newark. Hell of a job they did out there."

Addison and Lacey joined them.

"Hey Daryl, good to see ya," Hershey boomed. "And Lacey. You look more beautiful each time we meet." He gallantly kissed her hand.

"A pleasure, Mr Hershey," she gushed.

"Are we all set, Claude?" Addison asked nervously.

"Absolutely. Chico's and Wurley's got in yesterday."

Klondike cocked his head. "Where is Zack Wurley? I've got to thank the hell out of him."

Hershey chuckled even more. "Why Kal, he's right there." Everyone turned to where he pointed.

An elderly but lithe and fit-looking man dressed in a waistcoat and plaid shirt approached.

Klondike wanted to bearhug him but instead offered his hand.

"Zack Wurley. Been a long time, old friend. I don't know how the hell to thank you, man. Your tent saved my circus. We all owe you. In hearts and diamonds."

Wurley waved a hand through the air. "Forget about it, Kal. As soon as I heard you were heading here, to be a part of this, I would've done anything to help. Hell, this is a historic coming together for my guys. Sharing a big top with the great Klondike's Circus. We are honoured."

Klondike nodded. "The feeling is mutual, old buddy."

"How long has it been, Kal? Six years?"

"Almost seven. The Salt Lake Jamboree. Remember that?"

The older man grinned, shaking his head. "I remember meeting you. And being impressed by your plans."

"Well," Hershey thundered, manoeuvring himself into the middle of the gathering. "What a moment this is. Two of the greatest circus men in America today here together. Under my...yes, that's right, for one night only, MY big top."

He laughed some more. A newsboy appeared out of nowhere and asked for a picture. They all posed in the centre of the arena. The flash went off and the boy scrammed, yelling his thanks.

Klondike looked around. All of his performers were conducting a tour of the tent. All splintered off in their usual small groups.

He watched as the Rocking Robins dance troupe chatted to scores of admiring male workers attending to last minute jobs.

Addison approached him from behind and spoke into his ear.

"You know Kal. It is almost like destiny. Fate. Look at all you've had to put up with this season. You all got through it. And now this...this spectacular for July 4. It's like a movie, in many ways."

Klondike nodded. "A movie..." he whispered. "Every movie has its heroes and villains. But usually there aren't any loose ends left hanging by the time the end credits roll. This...this is different."

Addison looked at him blankly. "What does that mean?"

Absently, Klondike walked away from them all. "It's funny. I don't even know myself."

Then, he was gone.

He caught a cab into the city centre. All the way to the grand and opulent Colosseum Hotel, just off Capitol Hill and the political district.

Like a man possessed by some otherworldly spirit, he strode straight into the lobby.

Ignoring reception completely, he jumped into the elevator and rode to the top floor, which housed six grandiose penthouse suites.

Still showing little emotion, he paced down the plush carpeting and stopped outside a room door that was marked with the Roman numeral IV.

With a deep breath, he banged on the oak surface.

Ten seconds passed. Then it opened swiftly.

An elder man dressed in a burgundy smoking jacket and holding an ornate pipe stood there calmly. He smiled.

"There you are Kalvin. What kept you?"

"Hello Eric."

The two men stared at each other for several moments. Some unspoken truism seemed to pass between them.

Finally, Ribbeck spoke. "Come on in."

Klondike entered. He had been in this suite many times. Just not for some years. It was Ribbeck's Washington base, essentially.

Whenever they had played DC, he would house himself at the Colosseum to conduct his personal business.

The floors were covered in Persian rugs and the tables and cabinets were marble topped. A leather couch sat at the end of the main room, next to a grand piano.

"What can I get you?" Ribbeck said as he followed. He paused at a huge mahogany bar. "I have everything here."

"Scotch."

Ribbeck poured two then carried them over into the lounging area. Klondike remained standing as he accepted his glass. He looked out of the huge floor to ceiling window at Capitol Hill outside. "Always living like a king," he muttered, eyeing the suite as he sipped his whiskey, seemingly in disgust.

"That is allowed when you get to the top." Ribbeck toked at his great pipe. "But of course you wouldn't know about that, Kal. You were once on that path but...well, alas."

Klondike sneered at him. "I still am on that path. Just a different route. The honest one."

Ribbeck sighed in disappointment. "Kal, my days of verbal sparring with you are nearing an end. I'm too tired, dammit. Why don't we just skip the usual name calling and hogwash and just get to the point. You knew I would be here. Now, say your piece. Then, my boy, I will say mine."

Klondike eyed his great rival with disdain. Every time they met, he seemed to have aged significantly. The skin more craggy. The eyes more hollow.

Finally, he spoke. "I know about you and Paul Agostino."

Ribbeck's eyes seemed to inflame. "Agostino! That no good, two-bit yahoo! Why, I tried to help him break into the circus business. I was his advisor and executive consultant. The yellow yard dog! He screwed me over. Gleaned all the knowledge and tricks he could outta me. Then, he calls me to tell me I ain't needed no more! What the hell! I was helping him launch his own troupe."

"You were helping him destroy my one!"

Ribbeck did not hesitate. "That's not true, son. We were studying your circus as an example of how a circus starts up. From scratch, and the like."

Klondike shook his head wildly. "Don't you 'son' me, Eric." He paced the suite like a caged animal. "That son of a bitch attacked us. He burnt our tent down. Dammit all to hell, he could have killed hundreds of innocent people! Do you understand?"

Ribbeck remained impassive, toying with his pipe. "I heard about the tent…"

"Oh, you did, did you?"

"The investigation is still ongoing. You can't pin it on him yet." He seemed to choose his next words carefully. "I saw he was bad news, Kal. I saw he was mob. A gangster. A psychopath, in many ways. That's why our partnership never got off the ground. I was glad he pulled the plug, in all honestly."

Klondike was incredulous. "You expect me to believe any of this?"

"I don't give a damn what you believe! I got people coming to me all the time asking for help. Everybody wants a damn piece of me. That jasper was just another one. He disrespected me…and he disrespected the circus trade."

Klondike stood still, staring at his old mentor. He wondered if he had ever truly understood the old man.

"I asked you two years ago, Eric. And I ask you again now. Why do you do it?"

Ribbeck threw the whiskey down his throat. He gargled slightly. "What's that, sonny?"

"All of this. The skulduggery. The schemes. The endless games. Trying to nail me." He seemed to calm down. "You must be pushing 70. You're wealthy beyond most men's dreams. A king. Yet you play this never-ending game, with me and so many others. Mixing with gangsters. Crazy people. I…I just don't get it."

Ribbeck actually nodded. He slowly dropped into a leather armchair, sinking into it like a pebble in quicksand. Crossing his legs, he lit a match and put it to his pipe. "Why, indeed," he mumbled absently. He stared at the awesome view outside, beyond them.

When he spoke next, his voice had a lost, faraway tone. "You remember when you first came to me, Kal? All those years ago. On that bench, down by the Hudson…"

Klondike shook his head in awe. All the great successes the man had experienced over the past 50 years. And he still remembered that one small meeting. "I'll never forget it."

Ribbeck smiled. "You said you'd do anything to join my troupe. Said you were the trick shot champion down at Coney Island. Ha! You wanted to join Ribbeck's World Circus because it was the best. Known throughout the country. The biggest, and the best. At that time, we'd only just started touring nationwide. But we were well on our way, for sure. And then…" his shining green eyes blazed as he glared across the room at Klondike.

"And then you came along. Kal Klondike. The most natural talent I had ever seen. And even more than that, the greatest circus mind in the business. You rose and rose through my organisation. Talent manager. Chief scout. Executive vice president. My top man. And then, then…. then you…" he let the sentence die.

"Then I saw the truth," Klondike said quietly. "The bribes. The pay-offs. The mistresses. The absolute corruption. From top to bottom."

Ribbeck snorted angrily as he shook his head. "Your betrayal had a greater effect than you will ever understand, Kal. And to think…you became my competitor. Starting out with nothing. You, Corky and Gino. The show, the franchise, that you created." He snorted again. "It is frightening."

Klondike arched an eyebrow. "Frightening?"

"How you do these things. So easily. Everything you touch. It always succeeds."

"So, that's why you do it? Because I frighten you?"

Ribbeck sat very still, pipe hanging in the corner of his mouth. Poised there in the vintage smoking jacket, he suddenly looked 100 years old. A dinosaur, clinging on to his old ways and traditions. One who had survived vast modernisations and technological advances since he had first erected a circus tent all those years ago.

"You are a formidable opponent, Kal," he mused at last. "That is why I go to these, ah, extreme lengths to try to nullify your draw."

"You know there's a thin line between what you do and what some outlaws do?"

"The line may be thin. But it's not invisible."

Klondike stared at him across the plush suite. "All the many troubles I've had this season. All the troublemakers. Agostino. Vesnick. That madman Rance. All of it…" he slowly pointed at Ribbeck. "It was you, Eric. You orchestrated this. All of it. Didn't you? I know it! It was all you."

Ribbeck shot up, nostrils flaring. "You're way out of line, my boy! You can't come in here making those allegations. And, besides, you haven't a crumb of evidence. Nothing!"

"Ever the master manipulator," Klondike shot back, smiling. "You ensured there was none. You were always good at covering your tracks, Eric."

The older man raged: "I don't know what makes you think you can throw around this talk! They say you killed that lion man. You're a killer, Kal!"

Klondike glared at him. "Oh my god. Did you know? Did you know about that psychopath? That he meant to kill me?"

Ribbeck's weathered features remained cool. But, inside, his mind worked frantically. "We crossed paths. Agostino, he, er, was planning to hire him as a consultant for the new circus outfit. That was, until we realised he was irreversibly insane."

"No, no, no…" Klondike seemed to pull at his hair, locked in despair and angst. "A madman like that trying to bring me down…it was just another plus for you and your cesspit of a business." He eyed him squarely. "You knew."

The old man waved a hand angrily though the air. He appeared to be making a grand effort to keep his cool. Unexpectedly, he wandered over to Klondike, grabbed at his glass, ambled back to the bar and poured them both a hefty refill.

As he handed Klondike back his Scotch, his tone became more official. "Listen, enough of this cow punching. Are we gunna talk business today, or what?"

Klondike stared at him in shock. "Business? What in hell do you want to discuss?"

The atmosphere had cooled considerably now.

Ribbeck wandered around the suite, hugging his pipe and his glass close to him. "I'm in the process of creating the greatest circus show on earth. Ever! We will tour the world, and play the biggest stages in America. It will be a new show, a grand spectacular. But…we need new stars. Big names. As with everything I do, we need the best." Klondike looked back at him doubtfully.

The older man continued. "You've thwarted my every attempt to buy out the contracts of Gino and Roddy. For two god damn years now. Well, now I'm upping the ante, son. Upping it into the highest echelons."

"For Chrissakes, Eric," Klondike cried. "Those contracts aren't for sale. How many times must I tell you?"

"Half a million dollars!"

Ribbeck blurted the figure out, like an actor screaming a confession in a play. He shook slightly, squinting as he addressed his great rival. "I will pay you half a million for the services of Gino and Roddy. Sign them over to me, son, and you'll be rich. Hell, you can retire to Palm Springs. Forget about all this racing around the country on a train, putting up tents at each town. This offer will make you, Kal. It's everything you've ever worked for. All you have to do is sign them over."

Klondike was incredulous. "Are you outta your mind?" He crossed to the window, feeling weak. "Half a million! For two performers. You could run a show of top guys for that. Jesus, how much have you got hidden away?"

"Enough." Ribbeck watched him eagerly, wetting his lips. "Come on, Kal. You know I'm not going to stop as far as those two are concerned. They belong with me, dammit!"

Klondike shook his head. "They wouldn't sign for you. Gino would never come back to your show, after everything that happened. And Roddy? His loyalty is to me and Miss Lacey."

Ribbeck took another step closer. "That's why my offer is to you, my boy. If you sign them over, they will have to join. Or else find a contract elsewhere. But nobody will offer even half of what I'll pay them. Ha! They'll have no choice but to join me."

Klondike actually chuckled. "You just think if you throw enough money at something, it will bend to your will."

"You're god damn right!"

"No." Klondike uttered the word with great finality. He downed the contents of his glass and slammed it down onto a marbled tabletop. "My answer is no, Eric. No to your offer, and no to all that you stand for."

Ribbeck seemed to wince, as if he had been punched in the solar plexus. "You're saying no to half a million dollars! You crazy jasper! I'm offering you a life, a future. Everything you ever dreamed of."

Klondike walked across the suite, heading to the exit. "Everything I dreamed of…" he mused majestically. "All of my dreams…I'm living them now, Eric. All my life, all I ever wanted was my own circus. With such wonderful talent. Nothing, in my mind at least, can ever top that."

He reached the door and turned back to face his old foe one last time.

"You don't turn down a half a million!" Ribbeck raged.

"I'll see you around, Eric."

With that, he walked out, gently closing the door behind him. Ribbeck stared at the shut door for a long while. Then he looked at his glass, back at the door, and then above, to the heavens.

"Son of a bitch."

The interview room in the New York State Penitentiary felt cold and damp.

Paul Agostino, dressed in his grey correctional jumpsuit, was sat at a table, looking down at notes and interview manuscripts prepared by his attorney.

He was rapidly losing faith. In everything. Himself. His lawyer. His future.

"Come on, man," he snarled. "We can mend this. Do like I said before. You gotta lean on these people. Speak to DiGeorgio uptown. He'll understand."

The lawyer, Patrick Sweeney, was a youthful figure with thick red hair. He looked more like a college professor in his crisp blue suit and tweed scarf. He sighed.

"Like I keep trying to tell you, Mr Agostino. There is nothing anyone can do. You simply have to plead guilty. Take the plea! It's the only way you'll be out and still young enough to dance at your club again."

Agostino angrily screwed up some of the notepaper. "This don't happen to guys like me. I told you. Lean on the prosecutor. The judge. That damn police captain from outta town."

Sweeney was getting tired of it all. "Listen, Mr Agostino. You could arrange to have every judge in the state killed. Threaten every lawyer with instant death. For Chrissakes, none of it matters. Don't you understand? They have a confession on tape. They have you explaining what you did. You even name yourself. You implicate yourself in every possible way. This is the surest sure thing any of these guys have ever seen."

"Dammit!" Agostino stood up and pushed most of the papers on to the floor.

Sweeney watched him. He found it surreal how Paul Agostino looked weak and vulnerable now, simply being dressed in the prison outfit. And placed in this environment.

"We'll get you a good sentence."

Agostino shook his head. "The woman. Valance. Still nothing on her, huh?"

Another sigh. "I would've told you if anything had come up. It's like she never existed. The contact trail ran cold. Your guy Felix never actually met the guy that put her on to him. Just knew him by reputation. Why the hell didn't anyone run a check on her? For Chrissakes! No one in Vegas has ever heard of her."

Agostino stared into nothingness. "Why, for sure." He recalled the meeting in his penthouse. "She was good, whoever she was. Too god damn good."

Sweeney frowned. "You ask me, I still say this Captain Richards recruited her. He has a whole task force dedicated to taking down gangs. Probably has a team of undercover tricksters from all warps of life. All dancing to his tune."

"It was Richards all right," Agostino hissed. "He has made an enemy for life. Mark my words."

"And now he has a star witness in this Vesnick fellow."

Again, Agostino winced, looking sick all over. "Vesnick! That good for nothing rat. He will be lucky to make it to court, that one. I have a contract on his head."

Again, Sweeney sighed. It was all growing tiresome to him. "Like I said, Mr Agostino, he has been put up in a safehouse until the trial. There's nothing you can do. Nothing anyone can do."

Agostino shook his head in astonishment. Slowly, silently, he paced over to the window. There were no bars on this one. He stared out at the grassy knoll beyond. Somehow, he remained calm now.

"Why did you do it, Paul?" The lawyer's disbelieving voice floated across the small room. "This whole circus business. What was the point of it all?"

Agostino placed a hand on the glass. He squinted into the distance. A bunch of kids were all pushing each other around in a playing field beyond the prison walls. He could just make them out.

He turned and faced his attorney. For the first time in many years, he felt lost. He was out of answers.

And he just couldn't answer that last question.

Chapter Twenty-Eight

"And now, ladies and gentlemen, please give a big hand for one of the most astonishing acts in circus today. They are acrobats. They are dancers. They are a sensation. They are…The Hightops!" Lloyd Masters completed the introduction and held his arm aloft.

The TV quiz show host was dressed in a shiny tuxedo, and was relishing his role as ringmaster, a large mic in one hand.

As the applause grew, the Hightops emerged from the entry flap. A team of 12 young women, all dressed in jazzy gold leotards.

The Superstars and Stripes big top was a cacophony of noise and wonder, as spectators cheered and screamed at the astonishing array of talent assembled for the one-off spectacular.

The acrobats raced into the middle of the sawdust and began creating a human dome, balancing on top of each other in a sea of arms and legs.

Due to the nature of this show, the flap was a hive of activity, with each of the three circus company's officials all gathered around directing affairs.

Klondike stood in the far corner, proudly clutching his cane. He studied the Hightops dancers in awe. They were all climbing upon each other like a swarm of ants, now forming a human tower.

He turned to Heavy, slightly behind him. "Just look at that. All those girls coming together, as one. Like parts of one big machine."

Heavy was equally amazed. On a break from his usual ringmaster role, he was dressed in blazer and slacks. "Incredible. Maybe we should put an offer in to Wurley."

"What, poach some of his talent after all the help he has given us?" Klondike shook his head. "Wouldn't be right."

He looked out at the grandstands enveloping the immaculate arena floor. Hershey had been right. This felt like a spectacle above anything they had ever experienced. Looking out at the cheering patrons, he idly wondered whereabouts Ribbeck was seated.

The voice of Lloyd Masters brought him back. "And now, ladies and gentlemen, the Highcats will perform…the human wheel."

Klondike turned and poked his head out of the flap. An enclosed tunnel had been erected leading to the trailers. Tip Enqvist and the Daredevils were right there, sat on their motorbikes, ready to enter the action. For this show, they had all bought new stars and stripes-styled jumpsuits, and looked like comic book superheroes.

"Well boys," Klondike mused. "You'll never have a better chance to be superstars than out there. Right now. The crowd are hot. The cameras are rolling. Millions are probably watching at home, enjoying their fourth of July."

Enqvist flashed a rare grin. "This is why we came here. To America. For nights like this."

Then, he looked at Klondike wistfully. "Listen, Kal. We've all been a little tense this time around. I, we, the boys, we all want you to know we are grateful for this platform. This night."

Klondike nodded. "Forget it. Just get out there and do what you do best."

He moved back inside as the Hightops finished their routine and jogged back outside.

"And now…" Masters' finely crafted voice drowned out the cheers. "Please give a warm July 4th welcome to one of the sensations of the circus world today. Performing one of the most spectacular stunts ever seen on the planet, prepare to be amazed by the superstar stunt riding team known as…The Daredevils!"

The riders burst through the flap and on to the sawdust, revving their engines to the delight of the fans.

As Klondike and Heavy joined in the applause, they were suddenly joined by Steve Irving, who had wandered down from the TV studio box above the entranceway.

"Steve, you old son of a gun," Klondike said. "How is the ATV presentation going?"

Irving nodded as he watched the motorbike crew. "All fine, Kal. I'm doing the opening and closing segments from the box so, well, I'm lucky enough to be free to watch everything."

"That's a blessing," Heavy said, slapping a hand on the diminutive comedian's back.

"I want to thank you, Steve," said Klondike solemnly, "for getting ATV involved in this. All the work you've done out here. You're getting my guys a whole load of national exposure. For us, it's priceless."

"No, thank you, Kal," said Irving smoothly. His lips seemed to be permanently curled at the corners, as if he was constantly trying not to burst into laughter. "This show is a winner for us at the station. And it's another big plus for me. Just like Circus of the Stars two years ago. It's a hit I've helped deliver. More acclaim for the executives. They love me for it. And…I love you!"

Ever the joker, he stood on tiptoes and grabbed Klondike's face, kissing him on the cheek.

"Hey, get out of here!" Klondike said, laughing as he wiped his face. Irving chuckled. "Come on. It's time for the Sphere of Death. I can't wait."

"This will give your viewers something to remember," Heavy drawled, inching towards the edge of the sawdust, enraptured as always.

"Say," said Irving, glancing around. "Where's that broad you've got doing all the publicity? Lacey? I haven't seen her yet."

Klondike thought for a moment. "I dunno." He looked back, beyond the flap. "Probably doing some last-minute promotional work. Somewhere…"

At that moment, Lacey was making her way through the event trailers behind the big top.

Dressed in a bright yellow skirt suit, she cut her usual glamorous, business-like figure as she paced around in her high heels.

Pausing outside one trailer, she hopped up the metal steps and rapped on the door, before entering coolly.

Roddy Olsen was all dressed up in his trademark silver waistcoat and purple pants. He turned in shock as Lacey burst in.

"Miss Lacey…" he looked at her, in a kind of awe. "Wow. You look beautiful."

She smiled easily. "Thank you, Roddy. But, more to the point, so do you. Now, are you ready for the big one?"

He looked at her. "Well, I am now."

Lacey threw him a mystical gaze. "And what is that supposed to mean, champ?"

He chuckled. "Now I have seen my good luck charm, my muse. Now, I'm ready for anything."

She nodded absently. Their eyes locked. She found herself looking him over. The shining blond locks, sky blue eyes and golden tan.

Every inch the star.

"You were made for television, Roddy."

He nodded shyly, picking up his big suitcase and shuffling around the dresser. "This is another fantastic opportunity you and Kal have given me. A show like this. Live on ATV."

Lacey fiddled with her hair. "How are you feeling?"

Olsen looked up at her awkwardly. At that moment, he could have passed for a 16-year-old high school kid. All innocence and confusion. He took a deep breath. Real deep. "Like I'm in love."

She tensed all over, suddenly in great pain. The skin around her mouth tightened. "Oh, Roddy! Please. Don't say it. You're about to go on. You need to concentrate."

"I'm sorry," he said quickly. "I just can't play these games any more. What is the use? I feel it."

Lacey was more flustered than she could imagine. "Yes, yes, I know. I feel it too, ok? But it's wrong. It's immoral. It's just not right. I'm your manager. Your press secretary."

Olsen looked downwards. He shrugged. "I know that too." Delicately, she took his arm. "Roddy, listen. You have one of the biggest, most vibrant audiences of your life out there. All waiting for you. This is your moment. And…I want to share it with you. That's why I came over. To escort you to the flap."

"I'm sorry, Lacey. Really, I am."

She guided him towards the trailer door. "Don't ever say that, Roddy. Don't be ashamed of how you feel. Our bond…what we have, it's crucial to your success. Now, let's do this!"

She pushed open the door and hopped out.

They walked across the polo field turf towards the fantastical Superstars and Stripes big top. Keeping to the fenced pathway for circus staff, they reached the small tunnel that led into the domain.

Gino Shapiro and Penny Fortune were already there, doing some stretches and minor muscular exercises. Both looked immaculate in their fireball jumpsuits.

"Well, well," Shapiro said as they approached. He leant against the fencing and chuckled. "You two make a lovely couple, you know that."

Lacey gave a look of mock concern. "Now, Gino. Talk like that will get you in my bad books."

He gazed at her with a strange, predatory look. "Well, I was really addressing only you, madam publicist. You look like an angel from the heavens."

Penny rolled her eyes. "Gino, you really need to work on these awful lines."

Shapiro and Olsen seemed to square up to each other as they stood outside the tunnel. As the two main draws for the show, they were performing last. Shapiro's trapeze routine would be the final act.

"What a moment this must be for you, dollmaker," Shapiro said playfully. "Your nation's capital. Thousands of fans here for the fourth of July. A live TV audience. A super show. All in this magnificent tent." He eyed Olsen's gleaming, rhinestone-encrusted waistcoat. "You've come a long way from the Fresno Fair, eh?"

Olsen shook his head. "So, it all comes down to this, Gino. You and me. Closing the show. The greatest show of them all."

"That's right," Shapiro spat out. "This is the big one, amigo. All these wonderful acts the three big circuses have recruited. And now we come to the grand finale. The pressure, the expectation..." he rolled his head around, as if inhaling a favourite aroma. "I live for it."

Lacey looked at him as if he were mad. "OK, boys. I think that's enough bravado for now. Let's all just take a moment and concentrate on our act."

They all paused as the crowd erupted inside the tent, just a few yards away. Lloyd Masters' voice on the mic boomed across the polo grounds.

"There you have it, ladies and gentleman. The fastest gun in the wild west, king of the cowboys Duke Anderson."

As the electrifying applause bled out of the tent, the four all stared at the great wall of sewn-together American flags before them.

Then, instinctively, Shapiro turned and locked eyes on Olsen. Olsen stared back. They nodded in unison. Shapiro spoke in a low tone.

"It's showtime."

"So here we are, Rusty. Independence Day. Makes you proud to be an American, doesn't it?"

"When am I going to get my independence from you, Roddy? Your hand is getting mighty uncomfortable."

The crowd laughed jubilantly. All eyes in the Superstars and Stripes tent were on the stool in the centre of the arena, where Olsen sat with Rusty Fox.

For this show, the youngster went through most of his recognised repertoire of material. He had an extended set and made the most of it.

He started with the usual banter with Rusty. Then came the introduction of Napoleon, with the three of them singing Rock Island Line to the usual cheers.

With this being July 4th, the character of Napoleon proved particularly popular and Olsen exploited this factor. There were plenty of jokes about the old-timer's experiences in the US Army. The back and forth arguing and patter between Rusty and Napoleon drew cheers and whoops.

Olsen had decided on a change of routine for this outing. Something special for the super show.

"Ladies and gentlemen," he began, gently putting Rusty and Napoleon on a pre-placed bench. "In honour of Independence Day, I would like to sing a very special song for you all tonight. It's in honour of our veterans, like Napoleon, and all our servicemen and women around the world and at home. We are all honoured by you, and in your debt. The song is called…America The Beautiful."

With that, the sound of soft piano music grew over the tannoy. The audience applauded in approval. Olsen bowed to an American flag flying on a pole next to the flap, and held a microphone before him. Then, he began singing the patriotic classic. His voice sounded as beautiful as that of an accomplished tenor. And he moved like a veteran of the Grand Ole Opry, punching his fist with each line.

Just as he reached the opening chorus, belting out the lyrics with gusto, he was somehow drowned out by another voice.

"Hold it! Hold it! What the hell are you doing, son? I sing the big numbers, around here. Remember?"

Olsen stopped singing and looked around in shock. The whole arena went quiet, many fans looking confused by the sudden interruption.

"Who is that?" Olsen roared into the mic, still looking around in alarm.

"You know damn well who it is! Me! The greatest crooner in America today. I just got in from Vegas, man. Now…help me down!"

Olsen looked upwards, towards the ceiling, and smiled. "Ladies and gentlemen, there he is! The king of the Las Vegas Strip, Tony Tan!" Every head in the tent darted upwards, and every pair of eyes widened at the sight before them.

The Tony Tan puppet was being lowered from the ceiling to the sawdust by an abseil rope, slowly descending to join Olsen. Despite being suspended far above, he was still talking and moving as if being operated by the ventriloquist. And Olsen was somehow projecting his voice to sound like it was coming from above.

No one could believe it. Tony was dressed in a stars and stripes-themed suit and bow-tie, in a patriotic version of his usual tuxedo. As he came down from above, he landed perfectly upon Olsen's outstretched arm, like a pet falcon, and suddenly he was alive with his master.

The applause was deafening, with looks of disbelief and awe dotted around the stands on faces young and old.

Then, the music stirred again, and Tony and Olsen began singing together, one line at a time.

And, for the rousing finale of the tune, both man and puppet somehow sung together, with Olsen creating an effect where it sounded as though they were holding notes in unison.

As America The Beautiful finished, both held their arms aloft, cherishing the applause.

Then, a beaming Olsen picked up Rusty and Napoleon as well and, his arms overloaded, held all three puppets before him and produced a bow for all four of them.

The applause was thunderous, with many faces still looking up high to the tent ceiling, trying to find where the abseil rope was attached. At the flap, Klondike and Heavy applauded mightily too.

"I knew they'd lap this up," Heavy cried. "July 4th. Washington. Something like that. The place is going crazy."

"Yeah," Klondike said airily, as if in a daze. "I think having Tony Tan come down from the roof stunned them all. Look! Everyone is still trying to figure it out."

He laughed out loud at the spectacle. Then, his eyes fell on Lacey. She had wandered into the flap area, and was clapping happily at the rear.

Klondike cocked his head. "Incredible, huh Lacey?"

She looked almost shy. "Always, Kal. Always. With that one."

They both looked up and around at the thousands of cheering fans. It was like being in a colosseum in days of old. Everyone seemed to be calling out in joy.

With a grin, Klondike looked alongside them. Charles 'Chico' Adams and Zack Wurley and their various associates were also clapping heartily at the act.

Wurley stepped over to him. "Now I can see what all the fuss is about with that kid."

Klondike smiled. "We've still got Gino to come."

The older man seemed smitten. "What a show. I'm so happy. To be part of all this. Thank you for agreeing to it, Kal."

"It was a sincere pleasure."

He turned and looked at the flap entrance. Shapiro and Penny were stood there, poised, like panthers in a hunt.

He winked at Shapiro. The Mexican/Italian showman made that same, unusual smelling the air gesture, signalling he was in his element.

It was time.

"And now…"

Lloyd Masters practically screamed into his microphone, trying to drown out the raucous crowd. He read the introduction from a small cue card.

"Ladies and gentlemen, prepare yourselves for the first wonder of the circus world…the most incredible act in America today…an extraordinary showcase of trapeze! On first ring, the queen of the skies…an angel from high above…the beautiful Penny Fortune! And, on centre ring, the world's greatest flyer. Cheer him, love him, never forget him. Superstars and Stripes is proud to present the worldwide sensation…the debonair king of the air…Gino Shapiro!"

Shapiro and Penny felt as if the eyes of the world were upon them as they charged into the arena and pulled themselves up their support ropes. It felt like they were contained within four walls made entirely of screaming humanity.

The duo performed their standard moves for several minutes, taking it in turns to perform a double and then a triple loop Shapiro produced a classic standing twirl, hurled up high by Penny before dropping to centre ring again.

Back and forth across the top of the tent he flew, before taking a brief rest on a support on one side. Then, Penny performed several solo pieces, vaulting through the air, from ring to ring.

Shapiro then entertained the crowd with a few seldom-seen special tricks— a frog jump, shooting star and a 'bomb', where he crouches into a ball, arms and legs tucked in, before extending again to grab the centre ring.

Then came the high wire showpiece. Only, this time, the set-up looked very different. The two platforms were suspended from the ceiling, 100 feet in the air, at opposite ends of the tent, and about 40 feet apart. The wire seemed thicker, and had extra material underneath it. Not that anybody noticed.

Shapiro climbed his support rope all the way to the summit, moving nimby onto the support rigging attached to the tent's ceiling.

He slowly manoeuvred himself to the platform nearest to him, as the entire audience stared upwards in shock, every single neck arching back.

The flyer deftly dropped himself onto the metal platform, then rubbed the customary wire chalk into his daps.

Penny had quietly descended her rope, and now joined Klondike and the others by the flap. They all stared at the delicate set-up high above.

Then, he began. Arms outstretched, Shapiro began his walk, one foot falling in front of the next like a robot. Methodical as ever, in his zone. From the flap far below, he resembled a tiny orange-clad fly, walking on air.

When Shapiro got halfway across, he suddenly stopped. Confusion reigned on the faces of all watching.

Shapiro turned to his left, so that his toes were now facing outwards, away from the wire. He stood very still.

Everyone held a collective breath. Below him was a straight drop to the sawdust. Still, he stood motionless. At the flap, Lacey closed her eyes. Subconsciously, she grabbed Klondike's hand and squeezed hard. He squeezed right back. This was it. The ultimate finale.

Then, it happened.

Shapiro bent his knees and then executed a perfect backward somersault, turning head over heels in mid-air. As he came down feet first, he let his body fall behind the wire. As his hands passed the underneath of the thick plastic cord, he grabbed at a small leather handle that he had been standing over.

Grasping the strap firmly, he let himself fall. And as he plummeted, pulling the handle, an enormous banner fell with him, extending as he went down.

The huge sheet quickly bled out in the centre of the big top, revealing a giant, glorious Stars and Stripes flag, the biggest anyone had ever seen.

It extended to its full length in seconds, pulled to the bottom of the arena by the flying Gino Shapiro, who descended gracefully to the ground with a grin almost as resplendent as the flag he bore.

The slow unravelling made for a comfortable landing, and he let go of the strap when he was eight feet from the ground.

The enormous American flag now dominated the big top.

Its unveiling was met with wild, frenzied cheers from all around. The ovation felt like a seismic entity, as if an earthquake had rocked the polo grounds.

It seemed the perfect final touch to a show filled with magic and wonder.

Shapiro merely stood there, glancing up at the sheet of fabric that stretched high above. He performed his usual gallant bow and blew kisses to the fans, many of whom were screaming his name.

"Have you ever seen anything like it, folks?" The booming voice of Lloyd Masters again filled the speakers. The TV host was striding across to Shapiro. And the flag. "This is Superstars and Stripes. And there is your Stars and Stripes, circus-style! The greatest symbol of patriotism and heroism you'll ever see." He reached Shapiro and put an arm around him. "And now, ladies and gentleman, let's hear it for the debonair king of the air—Gino Shapiro!"

As the next round of applause rang out, Shapiro pointed at the great flag and pumped his fist.

"And now, ladies and gentlemen, please show your appreciation for all of tonight's stars. Three circuses, one show…and a galaxy of talent. The superstars of the super show!"

For this one-off extravaganza, all the performers from the three touring companies would come out to receive the final ovation, with everyone lining up under the bottom of the flag.

As Masters reeled off their names one by one, every act that had performed trotted out of the tunnel and made their way to the centre, beneath the stars and stripes.

A small wooden stage was brought over and Shapiro immediately placed himself upon it, standing above all the other talent and clapping enthusiastically as the acts slowly gathered around.

The applause was endless as the performers all came together. The Hightops all cartwheeled and somersaulted over. All of the clowns were led over by Corky, making balloon animals and producing bouquets of flowers from their costumes.

The cowboy Duke Anderson rode across on his golden palomino. Strongman Hans Erlinger carried several of the acrobats on his immense shoulders. Monkey trainer Sam Lentini walked across with a chimpanzee balanced on his head.

The Daredevils then all rode into the arena, performing several laps of the floor before cruising over to the centre.

The next to appear was Roddy Olsen. He had a white towel around his neck as he jogged onto the sawdust, waving to the fans all around.

The youngster joined the throng of stars in the middle of the floor, all gathered around the mini-stage just below the immense flag.

Olsen was greeted like a saviour, with everyone shaking his hand and slapping him on the back. Slowly, he found himself propelled towards the freshly erected stage. Everyone seemed to push him along.

He touched the wood, and looked up. There was Shapiro, glaring down at him. But, in a surprise move, the trapeze flyer reached down and pulled him up.

They both stood there on the platform. Shapiro and Olsen.

Then, Shapiro shocked all who knew him. He clasped Olsen's wrist and whispered into his ear.

"You deserve this, kid."

With that, he raised Olsen's arm triumphantly into the air. He held it high, aloft, for several moments. Then he stepped back, behind Olsen, and joined the applause.

In many ways, it was the most extraordinary moment of young Olsen's life. For Gino Shapiro to make such a gesture, after all their history. He was flabbergasted, and merely stared at the flyer in stunned silence. Shapiro subtly motioned to the cheering thousands all around them.

Olsen smiled and finally offered a bow. It was the sweetest of moments. One he would never, ever forget.

At the flap, Klondike watched on proudly. "How about that?" he whispered, almost to himself.

Lacey and Heavy both hugged him, at the same time. The others gathered by the entrance all smiled happily at the scene.

"I never thought I'd see it," Heavy was blabbering excitedly. "And here, now! On this stage, the biggest one of all."

Lacey held them both, like a proud aunt embracing her favourite nephews. "What a wonderful, beautiful moment. I think I'm going to cry!"

Lloyd Masters was now in the middle of the hubbub, pulling himself frantically onto the wooden stage.

"There you have it, folks," he cried. "You've seen it, and you'll never forget it. Superstars and Stripes!" He stood between Olsen and Shapiro. "Now, goodnight everybody. And god bless America!"

The steady stream of applause slowly died down, and within 60 seconds the spectators were moving towards the exits. All still stared at the all-consuming flag planted in the middle of the tent. As the large group of performers began milling back to the flap, Olsen looked at Shapiro on the small platform.

"Gino…" he gasped. "I can't believe you just did that. I, well, I am speechless."

Shapiro looked stern. There was little warmth or joy. He rubbed at his shoulder. "You did good, kid."

Olsen was in shock. "Thank you, Gino. For that gesture."

He huffed slightly. "Sometimes…you've got to act for the greater good."

They both jumped down from the platform, and followed in the wake of the others in a slow procession to the exit.

They walked side by side, several yards behind the rest. Then, a jubilant Penny was on them, hugging both wildly and then walking between them, an arm around each.

As they neared the flap, they were all there. Klondike, Lacey and Heavy greeted them at the edge of the floor, all clapping cheerfully. Richie Plum and Daryl Addison were stood just behind, also applauding.

Tip Enqvist and his Daredevils were dismounting their bikes in the tunnel entrance, and even they looked up and clapped their hands. Corky then stepped forward and handed both a giant bouquet of roses. It was a beautiful scene, and one that would remain in hearts and minds for ever.

All of the troupe hugged each other and laughed out loud in pure delight. Suzi Dando suddenly appeared and ran into Olsen's arms. Everyone slowly seemed to turn towards Klondike.

The circus boss took off his hat and ran a hand through his hair. Then he spoke.

"The eyes of the nation were on us tonight, folks. Klondike's Circus. For this incredible, spectacular showpiece. And we did what we always do. We excelled. We thrived. In the show of shows. This night will never be forgotten by all these people out here, in this glorious tent."

He looked at Shapiro. "And, thanks to that grandest of grand finales from you two…our show will be in the hearts and souls of the circus-going public for a long, long time to come."

Old Zack Wurley had stayed loitering around the flap, enjoying the scenes. "Here's to you, Kal Klondike," he suddenly cried. "America's greatest living showman today!"

A mighty cheer went up from the group.

Klondike held up a hand in thanks. "I'll never forget this night. Thank you all so much. Everyone. All the guys out back. Everyone who didn't perform tonight. Every last roustabout out on the trail. We are nothing without you!" His heart thumping madly, he raised his hands aloft. "This is the circus, folks. This is what it's all about, nights like this. I love it, and I will never leave it. I'll forever have sawdust in my shoes…and sawdust in my heart."

The applause simply never died.

All of the performers, staff and management cheered together. Everyone seemed to look at one another as they all stood, awestruck, at the flap.

They truly were all superstars. And, on this night, they had earned their stripes.

Chapter Twenty-Nine

A gentle breeze cast a refreshing wave of vitality over the grey, foreboding scene.

The cemetery was quiet and deserted, and still as a crypt. Aside from the faint hum of motor engines far in the distance, there was hardly any sound at all.

The headstones were all granite and decrepit. Many had stood untouched for decades. Row upon row of old, forgotten graves. Their inhabitants some of society's less fortunate. Children of a lesser god.

To many mourners and visitors, the Cole View Cemetery in Bellchester, New York, felt like the end of the world.

Kal Klondike strode down a gravel pathway that split the grave plots. He was dressed uncharacteristically in a black suit, with no fedora hat. Nestled in his right arm was a large bouquet of luscious carnations.

He looked around earnestly as he walked, then slowed. Squinting into the afternoon haze, he made his way down a side clearing.

Then, he stopped.

With a sorrowful, pained expression he stood before a small, discoloured headstone, hidden among the hundreds of others. With a bow, he gently placed the flowers atop the weed-covered, mudded burial patch. Then he stood for a long time, reading again and again the simple epitaph.

CATHERINE HART

JUNE 1919-AUGUST 1956

A BELOVED DAUGHTER AND FRIEND

That was it.

Idly, he wondered how many people had attended the funeral. Who was there from the old neighbourhood? Who represented the Cobras? Was there anybody?

He shook his head with regret. It was all too damn tragic. And now she rested here, in this lonely, godforsaken place.

Klondike stood for several minutes, very still. Then, he made to leave. Before he did, he stared at the gravestone one last time, right at the name chiselled into the stone. He finally let out a whisper.

"I'm sorry."

Klondike walked sadly back through the cemetery site and into the parking lot that sat alongside.

Lost in his thoughts, he kept his head down until he approached his rental car, one of four vehicles in the whole lot. He looked up. Then, he froze.

Lacey Tanner was there, leaning against the car bonnet, dressed in black slacks and a cardigan. A queer look of understanding was fixed into her features as she watched him approach.

He stopped next to the car in dismay, and seemed to deflate. "How did you know?"

She stood to her full height. "I'm sorry, Kalvin. It's just…well, I was worried about you. The way you left after the party last night. You vanished from the train so early as well, they told me. Then the rental car. The secrecy. I…"

He nodded vaguely. "So you followed me."

"I didn't mean to! It wasn't spying or anything like that. You were just acting so damn odd. I had to, Kal. Someone has to care about you."

Klondike looked back at the cemetery, then down at the gravel beneath them. "It's alright, Lacey. That's no bad thing, I guess."

She moved slowly towards him, her face a mask of deep concern. Then she asked, "Who was she?"

He glared at her. "Who's saying it was a she?"

Lacey looked at him knowingly. "I'm saying it." She softened slightly. "Because I know it. I feel it, Kal. Every time we talked about New York, the old neighbourhood, Agostino…why, you had this haunted look about you. I saw it every time. I knew there was more to it. And, well, it figures that a woman was involved somewhere down the line."

Klondike nodded quietly. "Always the smart one, lady."

"Women's intuition. Or something like it."

Klondike let out a long, uncomfortable breath. He glanced about flatly, and didn't look at her when he finally spoke.

"Her name was Catherine Hart," he said weakly. "I guess you could say she was my first love. Back in Hell's Kitchen, when I was a kid. She worked at the

311

Shaker Maker, everyone's favourite hangout back then. She was small, pretty, but also intelligent. Full of wisdom. I'd never met anyone like her."

He stood there, lost in his memories. Lacey stood obediently, completely silent. Finally, he continued.

"I asked her out several times. She would never come. She worked in that joint, and looked after her sick uncle, who had raised her. There was no time for romance. For fun. She was dedicated to raising money, to get the care for the old man. It was…it was a desperate situation." The last line was said in a bitter tone.

Lacey's eyes enlarged with a hint of fear. "What…what happened, Kal?" she whispered gently.

Klondike's face seemed to implode. "Paul Agostino. That's what happened. She went to work for him. He exploited her. Made her work in his clubs. It was a cruel life. A cruel, hard life. And it ended…it ended at a young age. So god damn young. A beautiful, bright, caring woman. Destroyed like that."

Lacey had a column of questions forming in her mind like a checklist. But she remained cool. "And you feel guilty, Kal?"

He shook his head sadly, fists clenched. "I'd forgotten all about her. Years and years before. I had left the Kitchen. I had the war, then the circus, then all this. The old neighbourhood was the last thing on my mind. It was a damn cesspit! But there was Cath. She was there all the time. And I had forgotten all about her."

He sat, defeated, on the car's trunk. Lacey joined him and placed an arm gently around his hulking frame.

"It's alright, tiger," she said quietly. "This poor girl was hardly your responsibility. We can't go through life worrying about all the 'what ifs' that inevitably crop up. Nagging at our minds and souls. Life was never meant to be easy. We should all remember that."

She looked him over, her violet eyes soft and attentive. "I can see that you loved her."

"Hell, back then I was crazy about her. But I had forgotten all about her, Lacey, I really had. I could've helped her. Given her a job, a life, anything…"

They both sat very still on the trunk. It was a truly desolate place, this, devoid of life or motion.

Lacey chose her words carefully. "You may not have been able to help Cath. But you have helped many other women like her, Kal. By ensuring Paul Agostino goes to prison. By putting him away, you have saved god knows how many people from falling into his evil clutches." She stood. "And that is something to be very proud of. We will never know how many have been saved. You could say that the best way of honouring the memory of Cath Hart was to nail Agostino."

He shook his head. "Hell, we couldn't have done it without you, Lacey. You nailed him!"

She tried to smile. "Well, yet again, it was a fine collaboration. Between you and me, tiger."

Klondike tried to grin, and shake off his misery. "Yeah. Well, between us we seem to have that knack."

"We sure do, boss man."

He stood now, loosening his tie. He made for the driver's door, but her hand gently stopped him. "I'll drive. You just make the decision."

He stared at her blankly. "What decision?"

She rolled her eyes playfully. "Come on, Kalvin. It's the end of the season. Time for our annual date! I've been on tenterhooks for weeks, wondering where you might be taking me this time." Lacey opened the door and leant on the top. "So, Romeo, where to?"

Klondike finally got into the spirit, smiling widely. He paced around to the passenger side. "Alright. Well, the United Wrestling Alliance has a show tonight at Madison Square Garden. If we can beat the traffic, we might…"

"Like I said," Lacey interrupted, with a coy gesture, "where to?"

Klondike nodded in understanding. "There's that new John Wayne picture out now. I know a great theatre in Brooklyn that…"

"Incredible!" Lacey cried in mock astonishment. "We spend months and months together, rolling across the country on that train, day in and day out. Yet, somehow, you don't know anything about me. Or, I might add, how to show a girl a good time."

Klondike laughed out loud, and took on a lighter, gentlemanly tone. "I know all about you, Lacey. And I have something in mind."

He flopped into the passenger seat, closing the door.

Intrigued, she followed suit and slid behind the wheel. She gaped at him. "Well, dear boy?"

Klondike reached into his inside breast pocket and produced two small blue pieces of card.

"Ballroom Days!" he announced. "Tonight, at the West Fort Playhouse, Broadway. Stall seats, front and centre."

Lacey's eyes looked like they might pop. "The show I worked on back in San Francisco!" she gasped. "My big break! You remembered! After all this time."

He laughed. "I wanted to see what all the fuss was about."

"It's a magnificent show!" she gushed. Then, she turned and looked at him tenderly. "Oh, Kalvin. Thank you! Now that…that is a treat. A true treat. Worthy of our end of season celebration."

He nodded. "Well, it's three o' clock now. If we get a move on, we can make dinner at Brigante's for six, and be at the show for the curtain roll."

She laughed excitedly, like a child heading for a county fair. "Now you're talking," she gasped, turning the keys in the ignition and looking around as the engine started. "I take it all back, my dear Kalvin. You are the perfect gentleman…and you know me all too well."

The car pulled out of its parking space, rumbled across the gravelled lot and turned out of the exit, on to the highway.

Klondike settled into his seat and eyed Lacey as she concentrated on the road. "I'm happy to know you, Lacey. And I'm glad you came out here…to meet me today." He took one look back, then focused on the way ahead. "Now, let's put all the madness and stress of this god almighty, up and down season behind us. And enjoy a night out."

She was beyond delighted. "I'll drink to that. As soon as we hit town. Now let's get moving!" She put her foot down, and the car roared off down the highway.

Soon, the giant, dominating skyscrapers and tower blocks of New York City came into view on the far horizon.

But this time, they appeared bright and welcoming, offering hope and freedom.

An ideal path into the future.

Epilogue

A lone figure stood on a balcony adjoined to a plush apartment block, watching the sun go down as he nursed a martini.

There was nothing like dusk in San Francisco, he thought idly. As the golden sun slowly nestled behind the ocean, falling from view and leaving its bright, red-gold illuminations to settle across the bay, it felt like heaven.

He could see it all from high up here. Fisherman's Wharf. Nob Hill. The Marina. Even Alcatraz. It was a breath-taking view, and he was proud to call it his own.

Dr Howard Thornton was lost in thought, clutching his drink as he admired the many significant sights before him.

"How about some more champagne, darling?"

The husky female voice awoke him from his reverie. He smiled happily at himself. Life was good right now.

Without turning from the view, he called back into the bedroom behind him. "What do you think of my place?"

"I think it's the most beautiful, powerful suite I've ever seen. Let alone slept in."

He grinned, savouring her words. "I've never had a woman like you up here before."

A dry laugh emanated from indoors. "You were saving yourself for me."

Thornton shook his head. He was lost in his own inner delights and fantasies. "I fell for you from day one. The first moment I laid eyes on you." He hesitated, sipping his drink. Still, he studied the Bay before him. "I…I could see what had happened to you. What had really happened. And I knew I could help. Help in every way possible."

This time there was a pause before the woman answered, "I know that I owe you a lot, Howard. And, believe me, I am very willing to repay you. Every way I can."

Thornton began pacing on the balcony, looking at the patio doors that led into the bedroom. It was hazy within.

"What happened between us…" he said vaguely. "You never would have gotten out…out of Wrangways. If it wasn't for me. It was my influence, the trust I have with the board. They listen to everything I say. It's just, well…it's just never been like this before."

"Doctors fall for patients all the time."

"Yeah, just not like this." He wandered slowly to the big glass doors, and leant on one. "I…I had to get you out. Out of that terrible place."

Her voice was warm and airy. "And, again, let me show you how much I appreciate it."

Finally, he moved inside the room. There she was. Lying in bed, the sheets around her chest, as she propped herself up on two giant pillows. She was smoking a cigarette, a glass of champagne close by on a nightstand. And she looked at him as if he was a god. A look of pure admiration and lust. A look he had never experienced before.

Then he said her name.

"Jenny Cross."

She smiled beautifully. "At your service, Howard."

Thornton shook his head in awe. "How does it feel to be free?"

Jenny took a long toke on her cigarette, and released the smoke in a swirling cloud that hung over the large bed.

"Delicious. I can practically taste it."

He sat on the end of the bed and studied her curiously. Despite his wonder and amazement at having Jenny in his life, doubts and worries nagged at his mind. He could not help it, he was a psychiatrist. He knew he had become deluded, maddened with power and desire. Yet, he could not help himself. He had never known this feeling.

"What are you going to do, Jenny? Now that you are out? Now that you have your life back?"

And then a strange, twisted look filled her beautiful features. The eyes seemed to darken, the skin paled and her dazzling smile went south. She suddenly looked evil, no longer the innocent angel.

"Oh, I don't know," she uttered dryly. "Lots of things. In time. But first, there are some people I must go and see. Some old friends I have to catch up with."

She seemed almost hypnotised as she stared, trance-like, at a fixed object somewhere beyond them. A twisted smile formed on her lips.

"Dear, old friends."